THE STOLEN BOYS

A gripping crime thriller filled with a huge twist

JOY ELLIS

Published 2018 by Joffe Books, London.

www.joffebooks.com

ISBN- 978-1-78931-042-9

This one is for Luke. Thank you so much for introducing me to the strange and exciting world of the 'drop day' and weird and very expensive streetwear!

Also to Ivan and Jackie, for all your help and support over the years. What a great family to know!

NOTE ON STREETWEAR

It may seem to stretch the reader's credulity to suggest that sports clothing and streetwear could sell for thousands of pounds. However, in fact, brands like Supreme attract dedicated fans who will queue overnight and some of the items do end up selling for very high prices. And for our American readers, trainers are what British people often call sneakers. Ironically, the term has crossed back over the Atlantic and is sometimes used by British youths. Please note "resell" is used by aficionados to describe resale sites for these items.

CHAPTER ONE

Late one night, two young men sat opposite each other, faces pale in the half light of the café, empty but for them. Elbows on the table, faces cupped in their hands, heads close together, they kept their voices low.

'What's the risk?' Tommy said.

'Minimal, I promise you.' Dean's conspiratorial smile was very white, the perfect teeth gleaming. 'I've been doing this stuff right here in Saltern-le-Fen for over a year now, and no shit, Tommy, it'll be the easiest money you'll ever make.'

The first boy wasn't so sure. He'd been caught out before, sold a whole spiel of lies. He stared at Dean, trying to work him out. Dean had been two years above him at school, the kind of boy everyone wanted to be friends with but was scared of too. Dean was wild, unpredictable and clever. Always in trouble but getting away with it every time. Tommy knew that Dean's father was well-off and wondered if money talked when it came to rescuing his offspring from bother.

'Honest, Tommy, you're made for this game, and I can get you in — if you want it. There's plenty of perks if you do the job well. I'm telling you, this could be your big break.' Dean pushed his chair back. 'I'll get us another coffee, and you think it over, okay?'

Tommy watched Dean saunter up to the counter and order two more Americanos. He was still charismatic. Tall and well-built, unlike Tommy, who was small for his age and scrawny. Dressed in urban, sports-inspired streetwear, Dean was clean cut, everything minimal. Tommy, on the other hand, was now a skinny nineteen-year-old, his low-cut hipster jeans barely staying up. Dean's hair was blond, Tommy's was almost jet black. Most importantly, Dean was loaded and Tommy was on his beam end.

He stared at the table. Shrugged. What did he have to lose? His parents were screaming their way towards a divorce, his brother had joined the army, and his sister had moved in with her boyfriend, an apparently charming man who was privately frying his brains with cocaine. When the rift between his parents finally came, Tommy knew that his father would go back to Scotland, and his mother, well, his mother spent a lot of time with a "close friend," who wouldn't want a teenager in his home. So Tommy couldn't even be sure of having a roof over his head. He'd lost his job — through no fault of his own for once. Things looked grim.

By the time Dean set down the coffee cups, Tommy knew what he would say. He was terrified of going to prison. He had a rather "cute" face and looked much younger than nineteen. Tommy had heard the stories about what happened to newbie inmates that looked pretty. Still, he'd do it.

Dean flashed those teeth in a white grin. 'So, you've come to a decision, our Tommy.'

'Low risk, you say?'

'Uh-huh.'

'So, what do I have to do?'

'Just shake my hand, Tom-boy. You've made a wise decision there. Now you sit back and wait till you hear from me, okay? Just be ready to move at short notice. Can you do that?'

'No sweat. I've nothing else to do right now.'

Dean handed him a mobile phone and a charger. 'Take this. Keep it safe and switched on at all times. Never use it to ring anyone other than the number that's already in it — me. The only calls you'll get on it are from me. Understood?'

Tommy nodded, and pushed the phone deep into his pocket.

'And this is to tide you over until you start earning. Keep it to yourself, and don't go mad and have people looking at you and wondering. I'm sure I don't need to tell you that, I know you're no fool, Tom-boy.'

If Tommy was surprised, he didn't show it. He didn't count the money but stuffed it into his pocket with the phone.

Dean drained his coffee. 'Now, you keep a low profile and I'll set the wheels in motion with my boss.' He held out his hand once again. 'You won't regret this.'

Tommy gripped the hand across the table. What the hell had he just signed up for?

* * *

Some thirty minutes later, on the other side of town, Dean stood before an old banker's desk, almost hopping with excitement, looking across at the man in the chair opposite him.

'What kind of boy is he?' Darke asked.

'A boy in crisis,' Dean replied.

'Excellent. And what else?'

'Shrewd, can think on his feet, but he lacks direction. He's struggling with a disintegrating home life.' Dean said.

Darke nodded. 'Malleable?'

'Absolutely, with the right handling.'

'And you want him, do you?'

3

'He trusts me,' Dean laughed, 'up to a point. But the main thing is, he has huge potential.'

'So, not a foot soldier?'

'Definitely not. He's no street kid. He comes from a nice home — well, it was before the parents fell out. You need to see him. He's perfect for what we want. Elite material, I know it,' Dean said eagerly.

Darke stared down at a leather-bound notebook on the desk in front of him. 'Okay, give me his details.'

Dean rattled off Tommy's name, address and date of birth. He had done his research, he knew a lot more than that about Tommy Peel. But for now that information would stay with him.

Darke scribbled in the notebook. 'Anyone else?'

'Just one. But he'll be more suited to Trez's unit. He's feral — a dangerous, greedy lad.'

Darke raised his eyebrows. 'I'm assuming he does have *something* that'll make him useful to us?'

'He's fast, ruthless and not very bright. Unless I'm wrong, he'll see Trez as his hero and follow him into hell if need be.'

'The best kind of foot soldier, then? But is he malleable?'

'Too much so, I should think. Trez'd have him eating out of his hand in no time at all.'

'Okay, I'll tell Trez to check him out tomorrow, and then we'll make a decision on him.'

'And Tommy?' Dean asked.

'He's all yours. Usual stipulations — a short trial period and watch him closely. Any reservations, you pay him off.' The man stared at him coldly. 'Whatever way's the most appropriate. Understood?'

Dean nodded, but failed to meet those ice-cold eyes. He loved and hated this man, idolised and feared him.

'Don't forget, Dean, don't get too close. That boy's expendable.'

'Aren't they all?'

CHAPTER TWO

It was an hour before their shift was due to start, and DI Rowan Jackman and DS Marie Evans were alone in his office. Jackman wanted to talk to her privately before the others got in.

'How's the leg?' he asked.

Marie shrugged. 'Well, I passed the fitness test, that's the main thing, but it still aches, and it doesn't like the cold mornings. I'm actually considering buying a lighter motorbike this time, not my usual kind of big beast. With this leg as it is, I'm not sure I'll be able to handle a heavy bike for quite a while. Still,' she smiled at him sadly, 'I keep reminding myself it could have been worse. Much worse.'

Jackman knew exactly what she meant. They had both been injured on duty some months before, but both had survived and come through pretty well intact, so they had a lot to be grateful for. They were still haunted by the fact that the killer they'd been chasing had got away. Now, although things seemed to have returned to something like normality, Jackman knew that each member of the team was waiting for Alistair Ashcroft to return and launch a new reign of terror.

They sat opposite each other at Jackman's leather top desk and sipped coffee.

Jackman looked at her over the top of his mug. 'Apart from the influx of illegal steroids into the area, and a few rather odd break-ins, we're not exactly run off our feet, are we?'

'Do I sense a new job hanging in the air?'

Jackman smiled at her. 'You know me too well.' His smile faded. 'Look, I know they launched a major manhunt to track down Ashcroft after he took off, and it came to nothing, but—'

'It's time to start again?' Marie became equally serious.

'Yes, it is. Okay, it's an ongoing investigation and another team's still looking into it, but the super has given us the go-ahead to make some enquiries ourselves. This time we'll be very thorough indeed. One area at a time, until we are happy there's nothing more to glean, then we move on to another path.'

'And where do we start, boss?'

'We need to find out exactly where he went after the crash. He was hurt, wasn't he? So where did he go?'

Marie's face darkened. 'Hurt badly, I think.'

Jackman knew Marie's thoughts had gone back in time to the moment before Alistair had kicked her into unconsciousness.

'His arm was all but useless. Definitely broken. And there was blood on his face, although I don't know where that came from,' she said.

'Well, that's our starting point. We hit every medical facility in the area and we look for a badly broken arm presenting on the same date as he disappeared, and also several days afterwards, just in case he lay low somewhere before having to seek help.' He took in her dubious expression, 'I know it was all done at the time, but we could get lucky. We might find someone who wasn't on duty for the last enquiry, or maybe just get lucky, end of.

We need to pick up a scent and run with it. Someone must have seen him or helped him.'

'Do we liaise with the other team, sir?' asked Marie.

'Absolutely. We'll use every bit of intel they have, but we won't let it colour our judgement. We'll look at it from our own perspective, re-interview everyone concerned, basically we'll be starting again, but using their database as a platform.'

'Well, no one knows Alistair Ashcroft as well as us, so maybe we are better placed to do this, even though . . .'

Jackman didn't need her to complete the sentence.

Ashcroft had decimated Jackman's own family, terrified the team, and his legacy plagued their every waking moment and troubled their nights. For all their brave talk about catching him, their assertions that justice would prevail, they all knew that until he really was located and locked up, he would continue to taint their lives.

It was Jackman's job to lift their spirits, fire them up and inspire them to keep going, but in the wee small hours, he was as tormented as any of them. Even more so, because apart from the personal heartbreak that Ashcroft had caused, Jackman blamed himself for the killer's escape.

'I have to catch him, Marie. I have to.'

'I know, sir.' Marie gave him a brave smile, and he was relieved to see that it held a touch of her old resilience. 'He got away once. He won't do it again. This time round, we'll get the bastard.'

* * *

Rain started to lash down on Cassel Hill Fen, and the horizon disappeared into a grey miasma.

Daisy Cotterill had lived on the fen for sixty-four years — all her life. The rest of her family swore she had a "nervous disposition," whatever that meant. She didn't tell them that her "condition" disappeared overnight, after her husband Barry dropped dead while shovelling the coal.

Just like her father, Barry had an acid tongue and a quick temper. She had never loved him. She didn't know what loving someone actually meant. She was pretty sure her mother had never loved her father. Mum always said that she respected Dad because he was her husband, but Daisy thought it had more to do with fear.

She had only married Barry Cotterill because in this backwater of a rural wasteland, that's what women did. The women of Cassel Hill grew up, married and had children. No other life was possible. She and Barry had produced two boys. She didn't like either of them much, but Terence was by far the worst. He had been a spiteful child and had grown into a cruel and hateful young man. Just after Barry died, Daisy caught him kicking Sheba, her German Shepherd dog, and she threw him out. Now he lived with people more suited to him, in a secure unit somewhere up north. A year later, Sidney had left home, to try to make a life for himself in the city. Evidently there were more takers for drugs on the streets of London.

Now she and Sheba were alone on the fen, and Daisy had never been so contented. The two of them would walk for miles, following the sea-bank and watching the birds out over the marshes and the Wash. Her home was small and she needed very little. Luckily Barry had taken out a life insurance policy without telling her. He'd never been that thoughtful when he was alive. So, with the savings that she had squirrelled away from her days working on the fields, and a meagre inheritance from her mother, Daisy and Sheba managed quite well.

From the moment she had found herself alone in her tiny cottage on Cassel Hill, she had never once felt afraid. Until a few nights ago.

Sheba had stood at the door, refusing to go out for her night time pee, a low growl rumbling in her throat. Daisy had had to practically lift her over the step to get her into the garden, where she'd stood stock still, staring into the darkness and growling.

Daisy had seen and heard nothing, but the dog's odd behaviour had sent her hurrying inside, where she locked and bolted the door.

The next night Sheba was still edgy, but better, and Daisy chanced a walk to the sea-bank. She suspected poachers, but if so, they would probably be some of her relatives and she wasn't unduly worried. Then, after she had climbed the steep sided bank to be rewarded with a view across the marshes to the black waters of the Wash, she had seen the lights. Tiny pinpoints in the darkness, then answering ones from somewhere else. They flashed, remained constant, before disappearing. Later, there had been stronger beams, moving this way and that.

Daisy was a country girl with little schooling but strangely, she wasn't superstitious. She didn't believe in the jack-o'-Lantern, or the corpse candles that supposedly hovered over the marsh. The dead didn't scare her, it was the living she was wary of. And there was definitely some hanky-panky taking place out on the marsh.

Daisy and her dog hurried home. She pulled the curtains tightly closed and checked the doors and windows twice. They turned in early and snuggled together in her big old double bed.

This morning the rain had started before dawn, and it was still drenching everything. She had planned on taking a flask and her binoculars and setting out early to walk the three-mile length of the Cassel Hill to the Tanner's Fen stretch of the sea-bank. Maybe she'd see something that would explain the strange lights. She wondered, not for the first time, why her village was named Cassel Hill, when the terrain was flat as a witch's tit. Still, it made it difficult to hide things. If something was going on close to the river or the marsh, Daisy would probably see it. She was an observant woman, some might say nosey. She preferred curious.

Daisy stared out of the window into low cloud and driving rain. 'Maybe not today, huh, Sheba?' She looked to where Sheba normally sat on the mat gazing longingly at the back door, eagerly awaiting her walk. But the mat was empty.

She looked around and saw the German Shepherd curled up in her bed, eyes tight shut.

'Well, that's a first, my lady! Is this weather too much even for you?'

By way of an answer, Sheba nestled deeper into her blankets and emitted a long sigh.

Daisy put the kettle on the stove. 'I think you've got the right idea, girl.'

Whatever was going on out there, it could wait until later.

* * *

When Jackman and Marie went back into the CID room, they found PC Gary Pritchard engrossed in a report on some recent incidents involving the theft of designer clothing.

'Good morning, Gary. You look particularly perplexed today, even more so than usual!' Marie placed a coffee on his desk and went to her own station, where she logged into her computer.

He looked up at both of them and shook his head. 'Morning, sir. Morning, Sarge. I was just wondering where these kids' brains are. This boy reckons he paid £750 for a hoodie! And look at it! I wouldn't know the difference between that,' he stabbed his finger at the photograph, 'and something from Matalan!'

'Ah, well, you're not a connoisseur of fashion, and you're not nineteen either,' Jackman said.

'Thank heavens,' muttered Gary, the puzzled expression still firmly in place.

'You can leave that to Max and Charlie, it's far more up their street.' Jackman pulled a spare chair up to Gary's desk and told him about their intention to find Alistair

Ashcroft, starting from scratch. 'Marie is going to liaise with the team that are already working the case and put them in the picture, but in the meantime, Superintendent Crooke needs us to tie up as many loose ends as we can before everyone pitches in, okay? So, you and I need to make some headway with this influx of illegal steroids and where they are coming from. They worry me far more than a few items of overpriced clothing.'

'True. So where do we start, sir?' Gary asked.

'I think I need a bit of background on what we are dealing with. I'm not very well up on anabolic steroids.'

Gary spoke like he was reading from a document, 'Class C drug, now illegal to import or export using postal, courier or freight services. Can only be sold by pharmacists with a doctor's prescription. Sporting organisations have banned certain steroids and test regularly for them. Possession with intent to supply can lead to a term of up to fourteen years in prison. What else is there to know?'

'Lots. What they are. Where they are produced. What market are they targeting? Who is buying them? And most of all, how are they getting into Saltern-le-Fen?' Jackman said.

Gary closed his report on the clothes. 'Ready when you are, boss.'

'Right, first stop will be the FMO. He can fill us in on the medical side.'

'Then maybe that big fitness club out near the airfield?' Gary volunteered. 'One of the trainers can give us the lowdown on what effects they produce, and who might be likely to purchase them.'

'Excellent. You go tell Max and Charlie that they've just joined the "fashion police," and I'll find out where the FMO is. We need to get some answers as quickly as we can, Gary, because I don't want Marie spending too long working on her own. Finding Alistair Ashcroft is a job for all of us, as a team.'

'Understood, sir.'

Gary hurried off to find DC Max Cohen and DC Charlie Button. Giving a brief wave to Marie, Jackman went to locate the medical officer. He'd give the drug problem some immediate attention, but no way was he going to spend too much time on it. If he couldn't get some answers pretty fast, he'd hand the case over to someone else. He had bigger and substantially more deadly fish to fry.

CHAPTER THREE

Shut in the toilet with the bolt drawn, Tommy counted his money. He'd counted it the night before, as soon as he got home, but for some reason, it hadn't sunk in. It was almost as if he didn't dare believe that the meeting in the café had been real. He had fingered the small package over and over, but each time stuffed it back in his trouser pocket and left it there.

This morning he knew it was real. Dean had handed over a cool three hundred quid, just as a retainer! He counted it again and shook his head in disbelief. Part of him was terrified of what he was going to have to do to earn this kind of cash, but a bigger part tingled with excitement.

From downstairs came the sound of china breaking. There hadn't been much left of the Royal Worcester dinner service anyway, now he guessed there'd be no plates at all. He wondered if it was significant that the set had once been a treasured wedding present.

His parents had gone beyond reconciliation. Tommy was sure they really hated each other now. It would be best for everyone if they just split up and went their separate

13

ways. Then he would be well and truly in the shit. No way was he going with either of them!

He stared at the money and a small smile spread across his face. Maybe it wouldn't be the disaster he had dreaded after all. He had a get out of jail free card now. If he did whatever it was that Dean wanted and got paid for it, his parents could just bugger off. He wouldn't need them anymore.

He dreamed of a flat somewhere in town, where no one was throwing crockery or competing in a who-can-shout-loudest contest. But now it was within his reach. He rolled the money up tightly and thrust it into one of the deep zip-up pockets of his cargo pants. He would do as Dean had instructed and not throw it around. Not for the reason Dean had given, but because he would need every penny to find somewhere to live and to keep himself fed.

He stood up. He flushed the toilet to avert suspicion, not that his warring parents would notice, and hurried to his room. He had to plan what to take with him and what could be ditched. He was making a new start and didn't want to be hampered by stuff from his past that he didn't need. It wasn't as if it had been a very happy past, was it? So sod his mother, sod his father and sod his stupid brother and sister. From now on, Tommy was going it alone. He couldn't wait.

* * *

Jackman was back in the CID room, having heard enough about steroids to last him a lifetime. The bottom line was that there was a huge market for them. He hadn't realised. When people talked about drug smuggling, they were usually referring to heroin and cocaine, but steroids were fast becoming very big business. It seemed that they had a "distribution centre" right here in Saltern-le-Fen. The problem was that no one seemed to know exactly where the stuff was coming from. If nothing else, he could now pronounce the street names for steroids or roids —

gym candy, pumpers and juice — like an expert. He still found "Arnolds" mildly amusing.

DC Max Cohen came over. "Sir? Charlie and I've been checking out this designer gear and the thefts related to it, and we think this particular caper is a great deal more complex than we thought.'

Jackman flopped onto a spare chair and leaned back. 'Okay, educate me on the word from the streets. But, please, do it so that a man of my limited knowledge of modern fashion can at least vaguely comprehend what you're saying.' Jackman's style was country casual. Smart, but a long way from being trendy.

Max sat down opposite Jackman. 'Well, I don't know if you understand anything about the way this modern branded clothing game works, but it's become almost a cult thing. The streetwear fetches a fortune, guv.' He pulled out his iPhone and opened the browser. 'There are a few really iconic brands. The biggest ones release limited editions of certain items of clothing, just a minimal number of units of one design, worldwide. It's all released on the same day, at the same time, eleven in the morning. It's called a "drop day." It's a weird setup. The stores have bouncers on the door, no mobile phones allowed, you can't buy more than one of the same product, and the kids — all males by the way — queue for twenty-four hours, then what they want is sold out minutes after the doors open.' He grinned. 'And you can buy online too. Sometimes you have only a few seconds to make a bid, before someone cart-jacks you and you lose out.'

It was worse than the steroids game. 'This is for real?' Jackman said.

'Look, sir. It'll give you an idea of what I'm talking about.' He held up his iPhone and played a video.

Jackman stared in amazement at a seemingly never-ending queue of young men, all wearing what he thought were strange, odd-looking jackets, hoodies and sweatshirts. 'Where is this?'

'London, sir. My neck of the woods. Kids come in from everywhere, just to spend twenty-four hours standing in a queue, and maybe getting nothing at the end of it. But that's okay. You do it again another day, and you might get lucky. It's worth a try. Guys pay other kids to queue for them, then sell the stuff on at triple the price.'

'But how does this affect us and our thefts?' Jackman was truly puzzled.

Max was patient. 'It's the resell value, sir. There's collectors. Some of the rarer pieces, they call them "grails," as in "highly coveted," fetch a bleedin' fortune. For some reason, there's a whole bunch of kids right here in Saltern that are into buying and selling. I heard about a kid who paid fifteen hundred for an ultra-rare T-shirt, and I spoke to one guy who was quite willing to pay seven and a half for a secondhand puffer or trucker jacket, if it was a hype grail. If it was a leather one, he'd go to fifteen grand.'

'Utter madness.' Jackman shook his head. Paying a thousand pounds for a Burberry cashmere wool pea coat or reefer jacket was one thing, but £7500 for a secondhand cotton trucker jacket was something else entirely. 'Where do they get the money to start off with?'

'Buy one cheaper item, sell it for double. Buy another, more expensive item, sell it for triple. Simple.' Max rubbed his hands together. 'Money, just for sticking something up eBay or Instagram.'

'I see. Someone has cottoned on to the resell value of these items and is helping themselves rather than spending twenty-four hours in a queue?'

'Looks that way. There's some pretty unhappy guys out there, I can tell you.'

'Well, you and Charlie stick with it, Max, while Gary and I pursue the influx of steroids into the area. Robbie'll be back from leave tomorrow, so he can help Marie. Just shout if you need a hand with anything, okay?'

About to turn away, Max paused. 'Is the Sarge okay, sir? Only she looked a bit troubled, then she went off out without saying anything.'

Astute kid. Jackman told Max of their plans to trace Alistair Ashcroft.

Max's expression turned grim. 'About time, if you'll forgive me for saying so, sir. *We* need to be the ones going after that murdering psycho, not some other team who never met the shit! Sorry, sir, but you know what I mean.'

'So get a handle on those thefts, and then you're free to help Marie.'

Max straightened his back. 'You got it, guv.'

* * *

The rain eased, and Daisy's curiosity got the better of her. She had to find out more about those mysterious lights on the marsh. She donned her waterproof jacket and boots and called to Sheba. This time the dog was ready for her exercise and bounded excitedly around her legs.

'Okay, girl! Give me a minute.' Daisy checked that she had plenty of bags for dog waste, and picked up her pocket digital camera. She used it mainly for photographing the numerous waders and water fowl that visited these marshes. This time she wanted it for a very different purpose. She needed to prove that something bad was taking place out on the estuary, and if she discovered what it was, she'd go straight to the police.

They began their muddy walk, Daisy speculating on what might be going on. Last night she had called her cousin Jude, knowing that he and his boys poached in that area. But he had told her that no one had been out that way for a while.

Her other thought was lamping. She hated the thought of this, but it did go on. She stood and waited while Sheba sniffed feverishly at a dock leaf, and they walked on.

It wasn't illegal to use lights to mesmerise rabbits and foxes, then either shoot or set dogs on them. It used to be classed as pest control but in her eyes, it was a totally vile way to hunt. Often just one man, a gun and his mutt would go out at night and catch rabbits this way. More recently she had seen the mayhem caused by idiots in 4x4s careering through the countryside with high-powered spotlights attached to their vehicles, trashing fields and smashing gates while they poached hares and deer. People had died. A beam of light glinting off someone's gun could easily be mistaken for fox eyes. Add some trigger-happy shooter into the equation, and you have a dead friend. Daisy shivered. Her own nephew had been injured in that way, accidentally shot by his own brother. That was the end of lamping in their family.

When she reached the top of the sea-bank, Daisy paused. The vista always took her breath away. There, spread out as if just for her, the river, the marsh, the fields and the sky. So much sky!

So, if it wasn't lamping or poaching, that left one thing — smuggling. She bent down and ruffled Sheba's ears. 'And if that's the case, lass, I'm staying put at night with me doors locked tight, and you can cross your legs till dawn.'

Sheba looked up at Daisy adoringly. Apparently this was fine with her.

Half an hour later, Daisy slackened her pace. It was hard to say, but she thought she was probably roughly in the vicinity of where she had seen the lights. She noticed a small inlet from the wide tidal river. The banks of the small watercourse were thick with wet mud that glistened like potter's clay ready for the wheel. She stared at the river. This was where she had spotted the lights. The tide was fairly low, and the inlet would have been navigable with a rowing boat or maybe even a very small motor boat.

Daisy had never strayed off the path before, but today she ventured down. She wanted to see where the inlet led.

Sheba following, she slithered carefully down the grassy bank onto a narrow path at the edge of the waterway. The dog suddenly ran on ahead of her, and then stopped and whined, pawing at the ground. Daisy paused at her side.

In front of her was a small wooden slatted area set into the bank, a tiny jetty, just big enough for one fisherman and his rod to sit and wait for a catch.

Behind it, on the other side of the grassy track, Daisy found an opening into a field.

Sheba was still digging happily at one of the wooden slats. Daisy moved her aside and saw cigarette butts and what looked like a half-eaten sandwich underneath the narrow planks. For some reason, she felt certain no fisherman had waited on the bank. Someone else had been here. 'Not for you, my girl. Heaven knows who was eating that! You might catch something! Come away!'

Reluctantly, the dog left her treasure, flopped down on the path and stared back longingly. Daisy turned her attention to the field. Even after the rain, it was clear that a vehicle had been parked there recently. Tyre tracks were etched deep into the muddy path.

Daisy took out her camera and carefully photographed the tracks. Then she took a shot of the cigarette butts and the discarded food. Might be nothing, just a fisherman, but then again . . .

She looked across the field. It was ploughed and ready for planting, but there was no crop to tend, and absolutely no reason to drive around the perimeter of the field to that remote, insignificant spot.

She grimaced. 'Unless you were doing something you shouldn't be. What do you think, Sheba?'

The dog stood up, shook herself, then turned and made her way back to where they had come down.

'You're right, we've seen all we are going to see here. Though I'm not exactly sure what we *have* seen.'

With a sigh, Daisy pushed the camera back into her pocket and followed her dog.

Just after three thirty in the afternoon, Max put down the phone and almost ran to his boss's office.

'Sir! Uniform have just reported a youth in the car park at the back of the cinema. He's been badly injured.'

'Is this a CID matter, Max? It sounds like something uniform normally handle themselves.'

'I asked them to let me know if they get any calls to anything connected with the streetwear thefts. The thing is, this kid seems to have been mugged, not for his wallet or his smartphone, but for his trainers.'

Jackman bit his lip. 'Off you go then. Check it out.'

Max grabbed his jacket and hurried downstairs. It wasn't worth taking a car. The cinema was only five minutes away, and he was pretty fit. He could run there in no time.

As he arrived, the young man was being loaded into the back of an ambulance. He didn't look good.

'What happened?' he asked Sharon Baines, a WPC.

'Took a blow to the head, then the muggers, two of them, pulled off his trainers and legged it. Didn't touch any of his other belongings, just the fancy footwear. He's in a bad way, Max. They are talking fractured skull and maybe an internal bleed. All for a pair of trainers?' Sharon raised a disbelieving eyebrow.

'Do we know what kind of trainers they were?'

'A witness gave chase for a few hundred yards, then gave up, he reckoned they were bright lime green with a purple logo.'

Max made a mental note. He didn't know too much about this particular brand of streetwear, but all the clothing that seemed to be fetching silly money had a purple logo.

He watched the ambulance pull away and turned to leave. There, standing close to the rear entrance of the cinema, was one of the young men he and Charlie had spoken with about the sought-after clothing. Giving him a rueful grin, Max went across. 'Hi, Josh. I hope that guy isn't a mate of yours?'

For a moment the lad didn't answer. 'His name is Denzi Church, and yeah, he's a mate.'

'Did you see what happened?'

'No, but I can guess. The idiot was walking the back streets of town in some very rare sneakers. It doesn't take too many brain cells to fathom out what happened.'

'What brand?' asked Max.

'The same one I was telling you about, Hybird X. The one with the purple diamond logo.' Josh kicked at a bit of gravel and watched it skitter across the concrete.

'What's the value of these sneakers then?'

Josh shrugged. 'Resell? A limited grail? £1500, maybe more.'

'For someone's secondhand shoes?' Max exhaled. 'And cave a guy's skull in to get them?'

'There's some rich kids out there, y'know. Their daddies buy them Hybird X so they can look cool and streetwise, and they turn their kids into walking targets! A kid can walk past you in H-X streetwear, and you know he's toting seven-and-a-half, maybe eight grand's worth of clothing on his back! If you was a thief, what would you take? The gear, or some smartphone that will be out of date in a month?' Josh sniffed. 'No brainer, huh?'

'Yeah, I'm beginning to see the bigger picture.' Max shook his head. 'So, say I find out you're a collector and I break into your home, what kind of money would we be talking if I sold it on?'

'I'm no collector, get that straight, but I know a guy who is, and I'd guess at £200,000 of stuff all in one room.'

'Jeez!' Max exclaimed.

'You wanted to see the bigger picture, my man, and that's it!'

The rain was back with a vengeance, and Max drew his jacket tighter around him. 'Thanks, Josh. I'd better get to the hospital and see how your mate is.'

Josh looked at him bleakly. 'It won't end here, you know. There's a cell round here now that's after grails. No kid wearing Hybird X will be safe anymore.'

Max nodded. 'Thanks for the heads-up, and if I were you, mate, I'd stick to cheaper brands.'

Josh pointed to his hoodie. 'Factory outlet store, fifteen quid. I wanna stay healthy!'

* * *

Max hitched a lift in a squad car to the hospital. When he entered the busy A&E department, he saw a gaggle of people waiting outside the resus room. All was far from well regarding young Denzi. A stunned looking man had his arms around a woman, whose whole body was racked with sobs.

Max's heart sank. He went to find someone in charge.

A few moments later, he faced a sombre emergency consultant.

'The boy died.' He ran a hand across his face. 'We had no chance of saving him.'

Max was aghast. 'My God! How hard did they hit him? And with what? A witness said it was a single blow.'

'Not hard at all, Officer. The boy had a congenital bone disease and his skull was fragile. Any normal kid would have suffered a concussion, but Denis Church was not a normal kid.'

Max exhaled. 'The law states that the attacker is liable for all consequences resulting from his actions, even if the blow wasn't intended to be severe.'

The doctor nodded. 'I know. It's the eggshell rule, isn't it? I'd say someone is looking at a charge of manslaughter, wouldn't you?'

Or worse, thought Max. This was a deliberate attack on a defenceless kid. Who knew what someone might make of it? 'I'm afraid we'll need to bag and tag all of his clothes and possessions for forensics, sir. I'll organise police officers to do that immediately.'

'His mother and father are here, Detective. They'll be wanting to see him.'

'Of course, but I have to ask that they don't touch him. If there is any evidence on him that will lead us to whoever did this, we need to find it as quickly as possible and we can't afford for them to contaminate him.'

'I understand. I'll go and explain that to them now.'

The doctor moved off to tackle his unenviable task. Max found two uniformed officers who had not been involved in bringing the boy in, and told them to collect Denzi's things and log everything carefully. Then he rang his boss. He'd had a premonition that this apparently minor bit of thieving was worse than it appeared. Well, he'd been right. Now they'd be hunting for a murderer.

CHAPTER FOUR

'Dead? And all for a pair of trainers?' Jackman said.

Jackman was pole-axed. He gathered himself together, he had to get the ball rolling straight away. Max had said there was a witness, so they had a starting point. And CCTV, that must have caught something. Even if it didn't get the incident itself, they might pick up the assailants as they made off with the kid's shoes. He strode out to the CID room and called out for Gary.

'Put a hold on the steroids, Gary. We need to help find this boy's attackers, okay? Uniform are already on the ground, and Max is looking after the hospital side of things. We'd better get a CCTV search started.'

Gary started getting people together, leaving Jackman to report to Superintendent Ruth Crooke.

As he was leaving the room, Charlie Button called to him. 'Sir! I've just taken a call from a woman who lives out on the fen at Cassel Hill. Reckons she's seen weird lights on the marsh at night.'

Jackman groaned. 'Oh no, not more superstitious stuff from the rural folk. Can you deal with it, Charlie?'

'She's not some over-imaginative carrot-cruncher, boss, she's talking about people out on the river in the dead of night, where they shouldn't be. She says she's taken photographs of some tyre tracks.'

The possibilities suddenly became apparent to Jackman. 'Smugglers? We haven't had smugglers on this stretch for donkey's years! It's so shallow here, not the easiest water route to navigate with all those sandbanks. You need to use the tides, and there is only one main navigable channel for larger boats—'

'But not for small craft,' said Charlie. 'And at high tide, very small craft can even make it into some of the creeks.'

'I guess a local could do it.' Jackman wondered if this might be the solution to one of his problems. He had heard that there was a clandestine laboratory producing illegal steroids from veterinary drugs, close to the coast in Holland. And where better to ferry the drugs to, than straight across the North Sea and into the Wash?

'Just because no one has used this route for ages, it doesn't mean to say that smugglers can't use it now,' added Charlie.

'How many times has your woman seen these lights?'

'Just the once, but she thinks it's happened more often than that, because her dog has been acting strangely at night. Very unsettled, apparently.'

Jackman tensed. He'd grown up with dogs and knew exactly how quickly they picked up on strangers. 'What do we know about her, Charlie?'

'Widow. Lives alone with a big German Shepherd dog. No near neighbours. Her name is Daisy Cotterill.'

'Ring her, Charlie, then go and see her, and tell her to be very careful. She's not to go nosing around those areas again, especially the place where she saw the lights. She doesn't want to draw attention to herself. Not a good idea if she lives alone.'

Charlie stood up. 'On my way, sir.'

'And, Charlie? Don't frighten her, okay?'

'Don't worry, boss, I've got this. I just hope her dog is friendly!' Charlie grinned rather warily and closed the door.

* * *

Superintendent Ruth Crooke looked stressed, but then she often did. She was a narrow-lipped, thin-faced woman who rarely smiled. For the most part, she seemed not to like anyone much. Jackman and Marie were probably the only exceptions, having seen her softer side, and in turn, she treated them in an almost friendly manner.

'Rowan, come in and sit down.'

Ruth was also the only person, besides his mother, to call him by his first name.

'We have a dead youth, ma'am. Two thugs mugged him for a pair of trainers, and he died in hospital.'

Her thin lips tightened further. 'For *what?*'

Jackman explained.

'And do you think this is going to be a real problem for us?'

'I do. If what Max has discovered is true, we have some vulnerable youngsters walking the streets thinking they are cool and trendy, and providing ready quarry for some pretty ruthless thieves.' Jackman was still finding it hard to understand this strange new culture, but he saw the potential for serious trouble on the streets of Saltern-le-Fen.

Ruth shook her head. 'We need to get on top of this before we have a fashion riot on our hands. We don't want every other greedy little tea-leaf in town jumping on the bandwagon to get themselves some easy money.'

'Max and Charlie are working it at present, Gary and I will pitch in, and Robbie Melton is back tomorrow. We'll hit it hard, Ruth, don't worry.'

'And, Marie?'

'I'll leave her liaising with the other team over the Ashcroft case. I think it's important to get everything set up so that we can move on it as soon as we're free.'

Ruth Crooke gave him a rare, but sad smile. 'Rowan? Do you think you should have sent Marie, of all people, to set this up? After all, Alistair Ashcroft nearly killed her.'

'Ma'am, I can think of no one better. Marie is totally committed to getting that psychopath locked up where he belongs.'

'And you? Are you honestly up to this, after what he did?'

Jackman steeled himself. Hadn't he asked the same question of himself over and over in the past few months? 'I am, Ruth. I'm ready.'

She stared at him. Jackman guessed that she was trying to assess the truth of his reply.

'Okay, then naturally I'll support you all I can. Just tell me what you need and I'll do my best to get it.' The smile vanished. '*After* you've defused this stupid clothes war.'

Jackman stood up. 'I'll go and get on.' He paused. 'Thank you, Ruth. I appreciate your backing. Marie said the same thing — we *will* get him this time.'

'Until we do, no one here will ever really relax, and that's a fact. When that man disappeared, it was as if someone stole the spirit out of this station.' She narrowed her eyes. 'And I want it back.'

Jackman wanted to say that they would do it, no matter what, that they would die trying if it came to it. But he kept silent.

'But sit down for a moment, Rowan. There's another matter I need to talk to you about.'

He sat. He didn't like the look in her eyes.

'Have you ever heard of an officer called Vic Blackwell?'

He frowned. 'Yes, Detective Sergeant. Not particularly well liked as I recall. Looks out for one of the rural patches, doesn't he?'

'Saltby Eaudyke, and we are closing it. He is to be relocated.'

Jackman knew what was coming.

'The thing is, he'll be offered several options, and one is to return here and work as a pool detective in CID.'

'Sorry, but why should that be a problem?'

Ruth sighed. 'The reason he was shunted out to the boondocks was because he developed a profound dislike for DS Marie Evans. His mouth got the better of him one day, and he went too far. He was lucky to keep his rank, but he was removed from this station under a cloud.'

'Marie? But she's never said anything about this!'

'It was long ago, Rowan, before your time. And none of us ever knew what was behind it. Marie chose to let it go, so we didn't see fit to cross-examine her over it. Now, with all these closures, and along with the fact that we've had no trouble from Blackwell since, it's been decided to offer him the chance to relocate to another force or division or return to Saltern.'

'And, Marie? Does she know about this?'

'Not yet. I thought I'd find out what Blackwell decides before I even mention it.'

'What about Blackwell?'

'He's coming here tomorrow morning to be formally notified about the closure. At this point, Rowan, no one knows about it, other than you.'

'And if Marie objects? What happens then?'

'Let's just see what the man decides, shall we? And I promise, if Marie is uncomfortable about it, or he shows no remorse for what happened, he's out, okay?'

'Should I talk to her about it, Ruth?' Jackman had always thought that he and Marie had no secrets, but now he was hearing this. He felt confused and a little bit hurt.

'Wait until I've spoken to Blackwell, please.' She gave him a cool smile. 'And don't get all miffed with her either. I get the feeling it was a very private matter that she wanted buried. It might be painful, so no digging, okay?'

He nodded. Ruth was right of course, but he still felt somehow wounded at the fact that Marie had never talked to him about it.

He went back to his office and closed the door. He sat staring at his desk, trying to work out what could have happened between Marie and Blackwell. He thought he knew everything about Marie Evans, including how she had never felt attracted to anyone after her husband's tragic death. So, where did Blackwell fit in?

One thing he knew for sure, Marie didn't lie. He and she were close, they had been through hell and high water together, and he loved her, though not in the romantic sense. He admired and respected her as a brave and honest police officer, and above all, he liked her. He had trusted her with all his deepest worries and problems, shared his doubts. He had told her about his relationship with Laura Archer, the force psychologist, which was not going as he had hoped. And Marie had been open too, or so he thought. So why this secret?

He stood up abruptly. He was being a total idiot. As cockney Max would say, a right big girl's blouse! He had a murder, plus the worrying prospect of more attacks. Bad steroids were flooding the streets. It was time to get a grip and start behaving like a detective inspector.

Gary stuck his head around the door. 'Boss? CCTV isn't clear enough, I'm afraid. The cameras picked up the two attackers, but their hoodies obscured their faces, and after they ran from the car park, they split up and disappeared down the lanes where there's no coverage.'

'Thought that might be the case. Damn it!'

'The witness might give us more of a description. Max rang and said he's asked the guy who chased them to come in and give us a statement as soon as he can. Until then, or maybe if uniform find someone else who saw them run away, we're pretty well stymied.'

'Has a description of the stolen trainers been circulated?' Jackman said.

'Yep. If someone tries to flog them round here, there'll be a knock on their door bright and early in the morning.'

'I'm thinking they'll move them out of the area. Get someone to keep a careful track on the internet sites and online market places. They could just turn up there if, as Max says, that's the way to sell them.'

'Will do, sir.' Gary looked around. 'Ah, the sarge is back. She looks bushed. I'll just go grab her a coffee.'

'Good idea, Gary.'

'One for you, sir?'

'Please, and bring them both to my office, if you would. Tell Marie I'll see her here.'

Gary hurried off, while Jackman decided not to even think about the mysterious Vic Blackwell. He'd concentrate entirely on what Marie had managed to find out about the Ashcroft investigation. Though it was going to be difficult.

Gary had been right. When she entered his office, she looked drained.

'That bad?' Jackman asked gently.

'Worse.' She sank down onto a chair and shook her head. 'Talking it over with Ralph's team in Fenchester brought it all back.' She puffed out her cheeks and exhaled. 'They've worked damned hard to find him, sir. Pretty well no stone left unturned. They're as frustrated as hell. He's just vanished.'

'We know that. It's why we have to start again. He's out there somewhere, Marie, and at some point one of us will ask the right question of the right person, and we'll get that lead we need. I'm certain of it.'

'Me too, I guess. It was just daunting, seeing all the work they've put in. Boxes full of interview statements and reports, and now we have to go over them all again.'

'The reality of police work,' Jackman said. 'But, as soon as we can get a handle on these muggings, the whole team will be with you.'

She picked up her coffee. 'Any news there?'

'Not yet, but Charlie is out seeing a woman who suspects dark deeds going on after nightfall on the river and the marsh at Cassel Hill.'

Marie made the connection immediately. 'The steroids?'

'Maybe. It's certainly possible. I'm going to be very interested to see what Charlie comes back with.' He looked at the clock. 'Time to go home. Why don't you get straight off? Get an early night.'

To his surprise, Marie agreed. 'Gary tells me he's got a steak and ale pie that is far too big for just him, so I've kindly offered to help him out. Then I'm going home and I'll crash until the alarm wakes me up.'

Gary lived in the same village as Marie, and being an avid cook, often "over-cooked" in order to make sure that Marie ate well. Jackman had noticed that Marie never said no.

'Excellent. He's one of the good ones, our Gary.'

'Salt of the earth, sir.'

He looked at her. 'Are you still okay with the Ashcroft case?'

She nodded without hesitation. 'Absolutely. Now I've got over the first hurdle, it'll be down to work and business as usual.' She drained her beaker and looked him full in the eyes. 'If anything, I'm even more determined that this time, he's ours.'

'I'm here, Marie. You know that, don't you? Always. Don't take on too much alone and if anything bothers you or upsets you, just come to me, okay?'

She raised her eyebrows, and then smiled. 'Of course. Who else would I go to?'

* * *

After all the recent rain, the narrow pathway along the side of the cemetery was slick with mud. The boy negotiating the puddles was chilled to the bone. Dressed in a thin hooded sweatshirt and shabby jeans with ragged bottoms, the only decent thing he wore was a pair of new trainers.

He slipped silently through the back gate and into the graveyard, then made his way to a small Gothic-style chapel. The old building, now long defunct, was starting to collapse, and he climbed inside through a damaged window frame.

It smelt horribly of damp and decay, but the boy was used to it. He came here regularly. Sometimes when the weather was better, he slept there at night. Over a period of time he had brought some old sacking, some curtains and a discarded duvet cover, rescued from bins and a skip. He covered up the windows and chanced using a small torch, nicked from Wilko along with a handful of batteries, to provide some light without drawing attention to himself.

One other person knew about the old chapel. Alice. She was his only friend, the only person he trusted. She would sometimes meet him there and they would talk for hours. There were times when she was the only person he spoke to all day long. He suspected it was the same for her. Neither of them had anyone to care about them, and neither of their families bothered if they were out all night or didn't come home. Alice had told him an elderly neighbour would watch from behind a grubby curtain and wave to her when she went past. It was the only friendly face she ever saw. Mossy wasn't sure which of them was the loneliest, the forgotten old woman, or the neglected teenager.

He called himself Mossy. It wasn't his real name, he just liked moss. He liked the way it covered the gravestones in the cemetery, adding a bright green splash of colour to the dreary grey stones. He liked the way it grew on dead things too, like rocks and old fallen trees, giving them the semblance of life. Moss appeared to live with no help from anything other than the damp air around it. Much like him. And Alice.

A month or two ago he'd managed to steal enough money to buy her a cheap mobile phone. It was only a supermarket value model but it meant he could keep in touch with her. He had called her and asked her to meet him tonight. He hoped she could make it, because he had some news for her.

He sat waiting in the darkness and went over what had happened in his mind. He touched his pocket and felt the small roll of notes. Still there. Some guy had actually handed him money without him doing a thing! He didn't trust the jammy git. He wouldn't trust anyone with teeth that white! The guy'd told him not to spend the money, to keep cool and lie low until he heard from him. His laugh resounded in the empty chapel. As if! That rich git didn't need to worry about spending money, he had cool clothes and expensive shoes. He didn't have to wear sneakers that had the uppers tied to the soles with string. So Mossy'd gone straight to Shoe Zone and spent twenty quid on some black lace-up trainers. Sod the rich git!

He stood up and stretched. Maybe Alice's father had gone on another bender and locked her in her room. He'd done it in the past, before he trashed the house. Didn't look that different afterwards, it was a shit-hole to start with.

Mossy sighed. That's what he wanted to talk to Alice about. If the "tooth fairy" had been telling the truth about working some heist, he could earn some serious money, then he could get Alice away from what for lack of a better word she called "home." He was sixteen years old, and his one aim in life was to get them both as far away from Saltern as possible.

Everyone thought he was stupid, and he let them. But Mossy was no idiot. He had plans. If he did manage to get in with the tooth fairy's gang, he might just be able to realise them. He checked the time on his phone. He'd give her another hour, then text her. If something was wrong, he'd just have to wait until she could get away.

Mossy shivered with cold and pulled his hoodie round his face. This was no way to live, it wasn't a life. He wanted some of what the tooth fairy had, and one way or another, he was determined to get it.

* * *

Saltby Eaudyke had the smallest police station on the fens. It was little more than a prefabricated box containing a cramped office, a store-room and a tiny kitchenette and toilet. It had one marked police car and an unmarked vehicle for backup. Manned by two officers, it was only open for a few hours a day, yet it was responsible for policing a huge area of remote farms and cottages. It was known as the "privy of the fens," partly because the building had all the charm of a public convenience, and because of its location in the muddiest, most remote spot in the wetlands.

DS Vic Blackwell stacked a pile of coloured folders against the wall and slumped onto the rickety office chair. Absentmindedly, he reached for the stained coffee mug that sat on the stained surface of his chipboard desk. He glanced at his watch. Nearly midnight. He drained the cooling coffee and exhaled loudly. He had no idea why he was sitting there, instead of sleeping in his own bed, or another's for that matter.

The fact was, he just couldn't rest. He couldn't sleep. He hated his miserable rented two-up, two-down cottage in the village, hated this horrible station, hated this bleak stretch of cheerless fenland. He hated being stuck out here in the boggy backwater. Okay, it had been his own fault. Well, partly. One other person should take most of the blame. DS Marie-bloody-Evans.

He still wondered at the way things could change so radically and so fast. One minute he had been on a fast track to the top, then, in the blink of an eye, he was policing hundreds of acres of cabbage fields. He supposed he'd been lucky to hold onto his detective sergeant's position, he could easily have been demoted back to the ranks. Not that his position meant much out here.

The superintendent herself had summoned him to present himself at the Saltern-le-Fen station tomorrow. It could only mean more shit. He hated it at the main station almost as much as he loathed this crappy little beat in the bog villages. He resented the looks he got from the young probationer bobbies, who all knew about his fall from grace, even if they didn't know the reason for it. Other than Evans, few did. Which was just how it could stay.

One day he'd find something else, something worth doing. Then he'd say adieu to the web-feet and this watery landscape and bugger off to a better life. Yeah, one day. After he got his payback.

CHAPTER FIVE

Max stared at the purple diamond logo and wondered how one small piece of corporate artwork could cause such an uproar in the streetwear fashion world. He looked closer. It was a simple thing, just a horizontal, elongated diamond shape with a small stylised white bird at the top, and the name Hybird X in black underneath. Nothing fancy, but in regal purple, black and white, it looked impressive.

Max had sat up for hours the night before searching the internet for every bit of information he could find about Hybird and its followers. It was just as big as Josh had told him. Clothing was changing hands for an extraordinary amount of money, especially the "grails," the rare, limited editions. Like most young men, Max loved his clothes, but this was just bizarre. He also started to get a feel for the shadowy underworld beneath the hype and the adverts for the "drop day" sites. It had a ruthlessness about it that just didn't tie in with brightly coloured cargo pants and hooded pullovers.

He sat back in his chair and stretched. He had been first in and the office was empty. Investigating this was addictive. He grinned sheepishly when he recalled finding himself looking at one of the "special offers," a smart black sweatshirt, understated, with a black on black version of the logo across the chest. He had coveted the thing! For a moment he forgot that he and Rosie, his wife, were saving every penny. With a new baby on the way, he should be looking for prams and strollers rather than overpriced sweatshirts.

He stood up and walked out into the corridor. The coffee machine stood next to the lifts. After several attempts, and a swift thump on the side of the machine, he received his drink.

'Make that two, mate. White, two sugars, please.'

He looked up and a smile spread across his face. 'Robbie! I'd forgotten you were back today. You're very welcome too. We're up to our necks again.'

'I've only been off a week! What are we working on now?' Robbie said.

'Drugs case. There's illegal steroids coming in from somewhere, and we had a death yesterday.' Max told Robbie about Denis Church dying for the sake of a pair of trainers, and he showed him the logo.

'Hybird X!' Rob said. 'That stuff is so cool! Have you seen it?'

'Rob? I didn't have you down as being into that kind of streetwear. Please don't tell me you queue for hours to buy a two hundred quid pair of boxer shorts!'

Robbie laughed. 'No way! But they do have some very nice stuff hidden amongst the more, er, *trendy* street gear.'

Max thought about the black sweatshirt. 'So, what do you know about this set up?'

Robbie slung his jacket over the back of his chair. 'I know it has a kind of cult following, and I've seen what some of the grails fetch, especially if you try to sell them abroad. Funny money doesn't come close! I mean, I know there are other even bigger brands out there collaborate with mainstream fashion houses, and their stuff is priced in the thousands too. This one, Hybird X, copied their marketing formula and just seems to have gone viral.'

'And now kids are getting killed because of it,' Max added.

'I suppose that was the real reason for the boy being mugged, and not just a cover for something else?'

'We can't see any other motive. I'm dead certain it was the Hybirds that were the target.'

'And you think this is the start of something? Someone stealing branded goods to sell on the collectors' market?'

Max pulled a face. 'Talking to some of the buyers of this Hybird gear, I got the feeling it's been going on for a while, but the kids don't come to us and report it.'

'Have you heard about the 1:1s?' Robbie said. 'That's "one to ones."'

Max shook his head. 'What are they?'

'They're fakes, mate. Replicas of the grails. There's a huge market for them too. I think they come out of places like China and Thailand. There are guys out there who make big money verifying genuine items and identifying the 1:1s. They're so good that even the "experts" can be fooled. Sometimes it comes down to counting individual threads.'

Max frowned. 'How come you know so much about this streetwear stuff? I'm not being rude, but you're older than me.'

'I found it out when I was trawling through some urban blogger's site. It really fascinated me. I looked further, and got onto some really intense sites for this streetwear community.' He grinned sheepishly. 'Comes from being a nosey detective. You always want to know more, don't you?'

'Very true, my man!'

'So, how's lovely Rosie doing?' Robbie asked.

Max puffed up with pride. 'Bloomin', Rob! Just bloomin'! You should see her — well, why don't you? Come round after work, she'd love to see you.'

'I'll do that. Not long to go now, is it?'

'Six weeks.' Max grinned from ear to ear. 'Me, a dad! I can't believe it!'

Robbie laughed. 'That baby will be spoilt rotten!'

'No way, chum! No spoilt brats in my house! I've seen, and arrested, too many results of crap parenting.'

'Good for you.' Robbie squeezed his friend's shoulder. 'I reckon you'll learn fast. Nappy changes, night time feeds, no sleep, burping, vomit . . .'

'Bring it on.'

'Bring it *up,* you mean.'

Jackman came in through the door. His expression immediately ended their laughter.

'Morning, boss.' Max looked at him apprehensively. 'You okay?'

After a pause, Jackman said, 'Good to have you back, Robbie. In answer to your question, Max, I'm not quite sure. I'll tell you later.'

'Can Rob help me, sir?' Max asked. 'He knows more about this Hybird stuff than I do.'

'Absolutely. I want this sorted before someone else gets hurt.'

Jackman went to his office.

'Not like the boss,' murmured Max. 'Something's eating him.'

'Then we'd better do as he says and get this sorted.' Robbie sat down and switched on his computer. 'Okay, Big Daddy, bring me up to speed.'

* * *

Mossy hurried down a cobbled alleyway to a tiny square. It had a sad bit of garden in the middle of it, little more than a single tree, some ragged grass, a bench and a litter bin. But this morning, Mossy smiled at the sight.

Alice was sitting on the seat, waiting for him. As always, she caused something to stir inside him, a sense of hope, reminding him that there were some good things in this shitty world.

Did he love her? Mossy had no idea what love was. There had certainly been no love in his life so far. His parents showed no evidence of it.

'Sorry about last night.' Her voice was low, almost a whisper.

She looked tired. Mossy noticed that her face was puffy. He thought she'd been crying, then he looked closer. 'He hit you!'

'As good as. He pushed me so hard I knocked my head on the edge of the door.' She sounded matter of fact.

Alice's father was getting worse. He and her mother neglected her because of the drink, but they didn't usually hurt her physically, unless you counted not providing food.

Mossy was determined now. He would do whatever was asked of him, and do it well. He would take their money, and more, if there was any way of acquiring it. He had to get Alice away. And quickly. Mossy had seen how fast neglect could turn to serious abuse. He'd bought the sodding T-shirt, hadn't he?

He sat down beside her and let out a long sigh. 'Listen. I think things are going to change for both of us. I just need you to hang on a little bit longer, then we'll go away.'

Alice took his hand and squeezed it. 'You're so sweet sometimes, Mossy. I know you want to cheer me up, but don't say things we both know won't happen.'

'Ah, but this time it will.' He took the small roll of money from his pocket, split it in two and gave her half. 'Get some food. Go to the charity shop and get a warm jacket, but don't wear it around the house if your parents are there. We can't let them think you're thieving, or that someone is helping you.'

Alice stared at the notes. 'I can't take this! Where did you get it anyway? Please don't say you stole it!'

Mossy gave her a rueful grin. 'Alice, how could you think such a thing?'

Alice tried to hide a smile.

'Hell, Alice! How else are we going to survive? But this time, no, I really didn't steal it.'

He told her exactly what had happened. 'Whatever I have to do, it'll be worth it. All *you* have to do is decide where you want to go. I mean, London? Birmingham, maybe? Or somewhere quieter, like the seaside? The country? Wherever you want, we'll go, okay?'

Her grip on his hand tightened. 'You mean it, don't you?'

'Alice, I really do.'

His new phone rang.

This was it. 'Yeah?'

He listened to the curt instructions.

'I'll be there.' He hung up and turned to Alice. 'Get your head around where you want to go. We're on our way!'

* * *

'So, you were impressed with Daisy, were you?' Marie asked.

Charlie Button grinned. 'And her dog. I got homemade ginger biscuits with my tea, Sarge.'

'Well, that's nice. But did you find anything vaguely connected to the case?'

'Oh sorry, yes.' Charlie took out his notebook. 'I think Daisy sees herself as a bit of an amateur sleuth, Sarge, but the boss told me to tactfully tell her not to get involved.' His smile faded. 'Even with that great big dog, she's very vulnerable out there.'

Busy gathering up her things ready to head back to Fenchester, Marie only half listened. Her thoughts were with the team there. A little more time with them and she should have gathered sufficient info and enough names to get their own inquiry started.

'Daisy located the place where she believed the lights were,' Charlie was saying, 'down by the river, and she even worked out a kind of possible scenario from what she saw. And I think she's spot on. She believes the first lights she saw were much further out, a signal from a boat. Then there was an answering flash from the river bank, and another a little further down, at the inlet. The final stronger lights were vehicle headlights moving away from the river.' He looked up from his notes. 'Then she finds the inlet, finds indications of recent use of a small landing stage, and tyre tracks in the neighbouring field, *and* she photographs the evidence. Pretty smart, huh?'

Marie raised an eyebrow. 'Get her to apply to CID.'

'She went one step further and checked the tide times. She saw the lights at a time when high tide allowed a short window of opportunity for access to the inlet. Any lower and it would have been just a trickle across the mud.' Charlie closed his notebook. 'I checked with the man who farms that area, and he said he hadn't worked that particular field for a week or more. So, Daisy's tyre tracks weren't from any legitimate access.'

Marie closed her briefcase and pulled on her jacket. 'Nice work, Charlie. That should cheer Jackman up.'

The boss had looked unusually sombre this morning, but she had chosen to ask no questions. She needed to keep her head in a good place in order to deal with the Alistair Ashcroft case. She'd wait until she got back to see what was troubling him. 'I'm off. My mobile's on if you need me. See you later, Charlie.'

She missed her motorcycle, but right now the car was more comfortable until she could recover more mobility in her injured leg. Nevertheless, she dreamed of the day when a brand new model arrived and she could ride again. Recently she'd been scouring the spec sheets and had found a rather snazzy sport roadster that could just fit the bill. In any case, it was something to look forward to, and who knew, she might get back to full fitness, and could once more take to the road on a big fast bike.

But right now she had to shelve her daydreams and get down to the harsh reality of finding a ruthless missing killer. It was a sobering thought for anyone to start the day with.

Marie unlocked her little SUV and eased herself in. Somehow she had to put the things Alistair Ashcroft had done behind her. No way did she want her old fears and memories creeping into this new investigation and contaminating them.

She put the car into gear and pulled out of the police station, her face set. Easier said than done.

* * *

The shopping centre, if you could call it that, just ten or so shops in a covered precinct, was busy. Dean and Trez stood in the doorway to a card shop and stared across to the entrance of a small alfresco café, where a scruffy kid stood fidgeting, obviously ill at ease.

'That him?' Trez asked.

'That's him. Calls himself Mossy. Real name's Richard Willoughby. Sixteen years old, and feral.'

Trez looked at the youth through narrowed eyes. 'He does look desperate. I could definitely use that. And after yesterday's shambles, I now have a vacancy.'

'I'm sure you could use him, once you've hobbled him.'

'I'll enjoy that immensely, Dean.'

Trez was tall, well-muscled, maybe in his forties, Dean wasn't sure. He had a shaved head, and his deep-set dark eyes viewed the world with suspicion. His name was pronounced 'Tray,' and he made sure that everyone knew it. He was a hard man, perfectly suited to the job he did. Darke valued him, so that was fine by Dean. However, Dean didn't much enjoy his company, and he decided to make his escape. 'Over to you, Trez. I'll be interested to hear what you think of him.'

'You must rate him, or we wouldn't be standing here.'

'You know his kind better than me, but yes, I think you could work him pretty well.' He flashed a white grin. 'Have fun.' He stood back and watched Trez make his way to the café.

A few moments later they were both gone.

Dean walked back to the car park. 'Job done. Now it's my turn. Time to see how Tommy feels about a little initiation ceremony today.' Dean pulled out his phone, keyed in Tommy's name and waited for an answer.

Only two rings! Good boy. Eager, and ready to play.

* * *

Jackman stared at the CCTV footage, hoping to spot something about the two muggers that might assist with an identification, but the hazy pictures of young Denis's attackers were useless.

He was annoyed that they'd drawn a blank so early in the investigation. A boy was dead, and they had no idea who his attackers were. Their best hope was on the streets. Keeping their ears open, listening to gossip and trying to convince the snouts to cough up something useful.

His desk phone rang. 'Jackman.'

'Ah, good morning. Well, some might say so, but I, on the other hand, have had nothing but a string of disasters!'

'Ah, Professor Wilkinson. I'm assuming you rang me for a reason? Other than listing your morning's catastrophes.' It was the Home Office pathologist. Jackman rolled his eyes.

'Damn! And I so thought you'd be my agony aunt for the day, I've got such a lot to share! Oh well, if you insist on sticking to business, it's bad news regarding your mugging victim I'm afraid, poor soul.'

'Nothing on him?' Jackman asked.

'Nothing of use. In fact, there seemed to be very little contact at all. One blow and he went down, then they grabbed his shoes and were off. It must have taken seconds.'

'And we can't trace the attackers through the street cameras either.'

'Oh dear. Maybe I'm not the only one to be having a bad day then. Better get on, sorry not to have more helpful news. Bye-bye.'

Jackman was left staring at the receiver. He replaced it slowly in its cradle and wondered what to do next. He looked up and saw a vaguely familiar face walking past his door. Jackman tensed. The visitor was familiar all right, and unwelcome. 'Vic Blackwell,' he muttered. 'Crunch time in the super's office. Thank God Marie has left already.'

He hardly dared consider what the man's choice would be. He prayed that Blackwell wouldn't want to work here. For Marie's sake.

CHAPTER SIX

Tommy stood staring at his reflection. The mirror showed him someone else entirely.

Expecting a briefing in some grimy basement, followed by a heist or thieving spree, he had instead been escorted into an upmarket unisex hair salon where he was given a totally new look. Dean and the stylist had discussed at length exactly what kind of cut would suit Tommy, and now he was sporting a cool tapered style, full on top and close cut at the neck.

Dean was nodding in satisfaction. 'Stage One. Most acceptable, Thomas. What do you think?'

'I love it, Dean.' And he did, but he was worried that it was about to eat up a large chunk of his nest egg. Even here in the fens, a restyle like this did not come cheap.

'Okay, good. You go wait in the car while I settle up here,' Dean said.

Tommy heaved a sigh of relief and hurried out of the salon, more perplexed than ever. What was his role in Dean's scam to be? Still, if nothing else, he was now sporting the best haircut he'd ever had, and it felt amazing.

A few minutes later, Dean returned. 'Sorted. Now, Thomas, my man, what size are you?'

Tommy shrugged. 'Small for most things. Why?'

'Good. Small is good, it's very good.'

Tommy frowned, not understanding, and Dean laughed. 'They don't produce so many small sizes, so they're worth far more. Don't fret. It'll all become clear as we go along. Sit back and enjoy the ride.' Then his tone became serious. 'Tell me, would your parents object if you left home?'

'I doubt they'd even notice,' said Tommy bitterly. 'They're too busy tearing each other apart.'

'Are you sure you're not a pawn in their game? They're not going to fight over you? They don't use you as a tool to get one over on the other?'

'They let my sister go and live with her druggy boyfriend, so they won't care too much about me.' It was a fact. It would probably be a huge relief to them if he did go. He stared at Dean. What exactly was he saying?

'Then tonight, you go home and tell your parents you've got a new job, and it's live in. Tell them you're going to be working long hours and won't be seeing too much of them.'

'What sort of job? What shall I tell them it is?' asked Tommy.

'What are your interests? Skills?'

Tommy shrugged. 'Mostly unskilled work, manual stuff, but I'm pretty good with my hands. I've picked up quite a bit working with a property care company. I'm good with technology too. My IT teacher said I had a natural flair.'

'Okay then. Say you've got a position in a hotel, general maintenance and all-round assistant. Accommodation provided, and a chance to work your way up the ladder. Keep it simple. Tell them no private calls during your trial period. They can text you if they need you, okay?'

Tommy nodded. He felt torn. Half of him was thrilled at the prospect of escape, the other half was afraid. What Dean had said seemed fine, but where was he really going?

* * *

As Tommy was driven away in an expensive, top of the range SUV, Mossy was not faring quite so well.

He was in the grimy basement that Tommy had been expecting, sitting on a hard uncomfortable chair.

Facing him sat a guy of about his own age. Only this other youth was tied with nylon rope, his head slumped forward so that Mossy wasn't sure if he was even conscious. He'd been beaten, Mossy could see traces of dried blood on his clothes. He wondered if this was a set up produced for his benefit, so as to watch his reactions.

He'd already had a kind of interview with Trez, and had formed the conclusion that the man was a psycho, not someone to piss off. He'd managed to maintain his usual persona, that of a wild street kid with a gullible streak. Meanwhile all his thoughts were with Alice Delaney, their future, their escape.

Trez stood behind him, his hands heavy on Mossy's shoulders. 'This is CJ. His job is yours, if you think you can handle it. You'll need to do a better job than he did.'

Mossy said nothing. He didn't think an answer was expected of him.

'CJ made a big mistake. He's caused a problem that's not just annoying, but could cost us time and a lot of money. The worst thing is, his cock-up reflects badly on me. That's unacceptable. Wouldn't you agree, Mossy?'

Mossy nodded slowly. 'I guess so.'

'Our organisation is a well-oiled machine. It functions smoothly, as long as all the parts, even the small ones, do exactly what's expected of them. Faulty material is discarded, as it should be, and replaced with new. Understand?'

Mossy understood only too well, but was still not sure whether this was a weird show, staged to scare him. Again, he nodded. 'Yeah, I get it.'

Trez abruptly released his grip, walked across to the other youth, and hit him across the face with the back of his hand. The boy gave a low groan.

Mossy finally knew. This was no stage play. This was for real.

He'd seen violence before, and he'd been on the receiving end more times than he could count. It was nothing new to him, but there was a coldness about Trez that frightened him.

Mossy understood anger. He understood passion and fear, he even recognised madness, resulting from drugs or drink or bad genes, but he had never encountered such deliberate callousness before.

Trez stood and stared backwards and forwards, from CJ to Mossy. He looked thoughtfully around the large, smelly basement room. Suddenly he walked over to a table and picked something up. 'Know what this is, Mossy?'

Mossy did. It was a soft cosh. Stupid name for it because it was a hard metal baton, wrapped in crepe bandaging. It inflicted the same injuries, but they were more inclined to be internal, rather than the visible damage an iron bar would leave on the skin. It was quieter too.

Sure, Mossy had seen them, but never in action. His stomach tightened. So much was at stake. He had to be strong. He told himself that this was going to happen anyway, with or without him as witness. He must forget that this was a kid, just like him, and concentrate on what Trez had said — just a malfunctioning part needing to be replaced.

Mossy looked up at Trez blankly. 'Of course I know what it is.'

Trez seemed to stare at him forever. Then, to Mossy's horror, he dropped the cosh into his lap and jerked his head to the prisoner, slumped in his chair. 'Then show me how you use it.'

* * *

Superintendent Ruth Crooke fully intended to make sure that DS Marie Evans did not have to endure working with Blackwell. She didn't know what had happened between them but was astute enough to know that it had been serious, and she didn't want conflict in her CID room. However, for some reason her chief had decided that because of his previously unblemished career, Blackwell should be given another chance. He had done his time in Saltby Eaudyke. DC Rosie McElderry, now Rosie Cohen, was on maternity leave, and they had recently lost two pool detectives. Ruth had no choice but to comply. But she wouldn't make it easy for him.

That was why she had chosen not to warn Marie. She hoped that she could persuade him to move to pastures new, and if Marie did see him here, she would assume it was just a standard briefing about local police matters in Saltby Eaudyke.

When he finally knocked, she wondered how the next quarter of an hour would go. You couldn't second guess DS Vic Blackwell, even if you'd known him for years.

'You wanted to see me, ma'am?' DS Vic Blackwell sat down without being asked to, and stared at her.

'Please, *do* make yourself comfortable.' She thought the sarcasm would be lost on him but from his sly smile, she realised it wasn't.

She drew in a long breath. 'You know all about the cutbacks and the closures in our force, DS Blackwell. Well, I'm sorry to say that the office at Saltby Eaudyke is next in line. You are asked to notify the local residents and make all the necessary arrangements, prepare and box up all records and relevant items for collection.'

Vic's face remained expressionless, but Ruth could imagine the confusion going on in his head.

'How soon?'

'Effective immediately. A team will arrive in three days to clear the station out.'

Vic chewed on the inside of his cheek.

'So, it's time for us to talk, Vic. About your future.'

'Assuming I still have one?'

Ruth stared at the detective sergeant. It was hard to believe that, years ago, Vic had been the golden boy of Saltern-le-Fen, and the officer considered most likely to succeed. He had been well-liked and very efficient. He'd also had courage, which had earned him a commendation after only two years in uniform. Vic had put himself between a knife-wielding drug addict and his intended victim and managed to disarm the man. Apparently nothing could stop his meteoric rise to the top, but something had.

Although Ruth never knew the full details, she did know about the incident that had set off Vic's decline. After ten years of marriage, his wife had been killed in an RTC. And for some obscure reason, Vic appeared to blame Marie Evans. He channelled all his hurt and rage into doing his best to ruin Marie's career. Marie had completely denied any knowledge about what had happened, but Vic remained antagonistic. Then one day he took it too far, and within twenty-four hours found himself policing a rural backwater with no chance of promotion. He was very lucky to hold onto his stripes. If he had not had such a glowing record until that point, he would have been kicked out.

'We have two choices, Blackwell, but the final decision will have to be yours. Initially you were to be offered a DS post at Fenchester, but they have had a bit of a shake-up there too, and the post has been rescinded.'

Ruth wondered how Vic could remain so impassive for so long. Shrewd as she was, for once in her life she had no clue what the man in front of her was thinking.

'So, it comes down to this. The chief has said that you can be reinstated back here in Saltern-le-Fen, working in CID, or,' she paused, 'if you wished to consider a change of scenery, you could apply to another force and relocate to a fresh start somewhere else. Naturally you'll need a bit of time to think it through, to consider your options.'

'No need, ma'am. I accept the post in CID here.'

Ruth was taken aback by the speed of his reply. 'You don't have to give me your decision immediately, you know. I really do suggest you take some time to think it through thoroughly.'

'Honestly, I want to come back here.'

This was not what Ruth Crooke wanted to hear, but unless she could persuade him onto a different course, her hands were tied. She narrowed her eyes and stared at him. 'If that is the case, I have to make some stipulations, Blackwell, and I need your assurance that you will honour what I ask of you.'

Vic Blackwell sat up straighter. 'Superintendent, I know exactly what you're going to say, and I will comply. It was my own fault, what happened all those years ago, and I'm just grateful to be given another chance. I won't let you down.'

Ruth drew in a breath. Vic was saying all the right things. He even looked contrite, but none of it rang true. She cursed silently. She would have to go along with it now. An offer had been made, and he'd accepted. 'Okay, bottom line. Can you work in the same office as Marie Evans?'

'If it means coming back, ma'am, I will act professionally, I promise you.'

'If there is any trouble, Blackwell, even the slightest whiff of it, I'll see to it that you never work here again. Do I make myself clear?'

'Perfectly, ma'am.' Vic Blackwell looked at her solemnly, his eyes wide and clear. 'Thank you for this,

Super. I appreciate it.' He stood up. 'If that's all, I'll get straight back and start sorting things out.'

'Okay, I'll get some boxes sent over later this afternoon, and could you ask PC Jordan to report here as soon as his shift starts? I need to talk to him too.'

Vic nodded. 'Yes, ma'am.'

His hand was on the doorknob when Ruth said, 'I never knew the whole story, Blackwell, and I don't want to. The bit I was privy to made no sense whatsoever. Just remember the trouble your actions caused. What I said, I meant. There'll be no more warnings.'

With his back to her, Blackwell said, 'Understood, Super.'

Ruth stared at the closed door, full of misgiving. She'd been shocked at the speed with which Blackwell had made his decision. More than that, she didn't like him, didn't trust him for a minute. It was the worst basis on which to make a new start. Now they had to break the news to Marie.

* * *

Mossy stared down at the cosh, his mind in turmoil. There'd been plenty of times he'd kicked seven bells out of other guys in a street fight. He'd even given his own uncle a pasting. But it was always for a reason. He'd never deliberately and cold-bloodedly hurt someone who couldn't even try to defend themselves.

The youth groaned. Mossy gritted his teeth and tried to block out the sound. He had to remember his goal, to get Alice to somewhere safe, and give them both a chance at a new life. If he didn't act, then Alice's father would get legless one night and kill her, end of.

Mossy heaved in a deep breath and stood up.

He struck his own hand a couple of times, testing the weight of the cosh. He walked towards the other chair, trying not to look at CJ directly. Alice would never forgive him for this. So she must never know.

He steeled himself and drew back his right arm. He gripped the cosh so tightly that his knuckles were white. With a grunt, he brought the weapon down . . .

Before he could strike a blow, a big hand caught hold of his, and brought him up short. He released the cosh. Mossy looked up at Trez, his mouth slightly open.

'It's okay, lad. I needed to test your commitment. I wouldn't let you do a thing like that.' He put the cosh back on the table. 'Come with me.'

Mossy paused at the door and looked back at CJ. 'What about him?'

'He'll be fine. He's learned his lesson. One of the others'll be here soon to sort him out. Now it's time I told you a bit about me and the way we do things around here.'

Mossy loped along after Trez's imposing bulk. After about ten minutes, Trez stopped outside a newsagent's. 'Come on in.'

Ignoring the bored looking woman behind the counter, Trez went through a door at the back of the shop into a narrow hall with a steep flight of stairs at one end.

The place had an odd smell that reminded Mossy of the graveyard chapel. Damp, he guessed.

Trez unlocked a door into a big open room with a high ceiling. Mossy assumed the two other doors off it led to the bathroom and kitchen. He saw a double bed, neatly made, and wardrobes and storage units with their doors open. All the clothes were pressed and hung in order — T-shirts, shirts, jeans, utility pants, jackets. The other side of the room was given over to a treadmill, an exercise mat and a whole series of weights. Besides the bed, a small sofa, a table and two chairs were the only other furniture.

'Ex-military?' Mossy chanced.

'Old habits die hard. And it's a good one to cultivate, tidiness.' Trez looked down at Mossy. 'You could do worse than to copy it.'

'If I had somewhere worth looking after, maybe I would.' He thought about where he usually slept, the box room, under a pile of crusty old blankets on a filthy mattress.

'Well, while you're here, you'll abide by my rules.'

Here? Mossy looked at the double bed and shivered. He'd done a lot of things for money, but not that. No, he wouldn't!

'There's a small room next to this. It's yours until you've finished training. But while you're under my roof, you look after yourself and your room, understood?'

Relief flooded Mossy. 'Sure.'

'Then start by getting cleaned up. You stink.'

Mossy'd been dirty for so long he didn't even notice the smell.

'Jump to it.' Trez opened the bathroom door and pointed at the shower. 'Yours are the grey towels. Do *not* touch the white ones. Your toiletries are in that plastic basket next to the cubicle. Do not be tempted to use any of the other stuff, alright? Fresh clothes over there. If they don't fit, improvise.' He pointed to a neat pile of garments on a small stool. 'In future, you will shower every evening when we come in, then you may wash again at exactly 0700 hours in the morning. You have fifteen minutes of ablution time, and that includes cleaning the shower. Then back to your room. Got it?'

Mossy nodded. 'Does this mean, I'm in?'

'It means nothing. It means you have one week of my special training. After that, I decide if you're in or not.'

CHAPTER SEVEN

'He's accepted the post here?' Jackman's voice rose.

'Against my advice. There was nothing I could do about it.' Ruth said through gritted teeth. 'But I did paint a clear picture of what would happen should there be even a hint of animosity towards Marie.'

'Shall I tell her, Ruth, or will you?' Jackman asked.

'You are closer to her, but I suggest we both talk to her. Bring her up to my office when she returns this afternoon.' Ruth frowned. 'Part of me wants to believe he's sorry for what happened, but an even bigger part thinks he's about as trustworthy as a hungry cobra.'

'When is all this going to happen?' Jackman asked.

'The satellite station is officially closed as from now. He and PC Jordan are packing it up. He should be here in four days' time, if all goes according to plan.'

'That soon?' Jackman heaved a sigh. 'Marie won't even have time to get her head around it.'

'If I had the slightest opportunity to block him, I would, but sadly, I don't. I'm just praying that Marie is made of stern stuff and will weather this.'

'If we knew what the problem was, it would help.' Jackman started pacing the office.

'I believe that she'll tell you now. She can't keep it locked away.'

'I hope so, I really do.'

Jackman was starting to wonder how to handle this man. The fact that he was a sergeant didn't help either. Jackman's team were close, and he could foresee trouble if Blackwell made even the slightest derogatory comment about Marie. Max in particular didn't mince his words, and Robbie was fiercely protective of her. He could see them closing ranks around her, if the need arose. He would himself if he felt it was called for, but it didn't make for peace and harmony in the workplace.

He cared about Marie and was not going to see her hurt any more than she had been already. Life had dealt her some pretty wicked blows, and DS Vic Blackwell wasn't going to hand out any more, not on his watch. Not while he had a breath in his body.

'I can see that you're thinking along the same lines as me, Rowan.' Ruth interrupted his deliberations. 'But we have to give him a chance. One only.'

'Why do I get the feeling that one chance will be one too many?'

'Well, let's not get too worried until we've talked to Marie. She might just shed some light on it all. You never know, maybe it's not such a problem anymore. It happened a long time ago.'

Jackman nodded, but he wasn't convinced. If it was no big deal, Marie would have told him about it years ago. He dreaded having to be the one to tell her what was happening.

* * *

In the large airy lounge, Tommy stood and looked around him in awe. Dean was only a few years older than him, and he owned all this? The flat was in a quiet side-street a short distance from the town centre. The building had once been a warehouse, but had been renovated to form half a dozen luxury apartments. The flat was modern, all monochrome and shades of grey, with steel and marble used to stunning effect. Tommy's parents weren't poor, but he'd never been inside a flat like this.

'This'll be your home for the next week or so. Stop gawping and take a look around.' Dean lounged elegantly against the doorframe, clearly enjoying Tommy's confusion.

'I'm staying here?'

Dean laughed. 'Come on, I'll show you your room. Just don't get too comfy, this is short stay only. Then, after we decide if you're going to make the grade, we'll sort out something permanent for you.' He waved an arm around. 'Not like this, of course, but it won't be a slum either.'

Tommy noted the word "we," and wondered who it referred to.

Twice the size of the one at home, his room was decorated in blues and greys. Very masculine. It had a fitted wardrobe, a tallboy and a chest of drawers. He'd never had a double bed before. *And* there was a TV and a computer!

Tommy liked it. A lot.

'Right. A quick tour of the place, and then we'll get down to work. A brief introduction to the business, and after that you have some studying to do.' Dean opened a door. 'En-suite. This is yours. You'll find everything you need in the bathroom cupboards. You saw the lounge. Kitchen and dining area speak for themselves. The master bedroom is mine and strictly out of bounds. I do "entertain," if you catch my drift, and I like my privacy.'

Tommy nodded vigorously.

'Now, we'll work all afternoon, and later we'll go out to eat. There are some people I want you to meet.'

'I don't have a change of clothes. Should I go home and get something?'

'You've got plenty of clothes, Tom. Look.' Dean threw back the doors of the wardrobe.

Tommy gasped. The rails and shelves were packed with clothes: jeans, chinos, shirts, jackets, T-shirts, sweaters, hoodies and even two suits. All of it the latest in menswear fashion.

Tommy sat on the edge of the bed. 'Dean, I just don't get it. I don't get *any* of this.'

For a moment he thought he might cry. He was overwhelmed by it all. It felt like he'd wandered out of his shitty home into a bizarre dream world. 'I thought this was a scam, a heist, something illegal. But so far, all I've got is a load of cash, a trendy haircut and a room full of designer wear. What the hell is going on?'

'Cool it, Tom. I did tell you there were perks to this job, didn't I? You might not own all this,' Dean pointed to the clothes, 'but they're yours to wear for as long as you're working for us. Now, relax. I said I'd tell you about the setup, so come into the lounge and I'll explain.'

Tom followed Dean out of "his" room and sat, rather awkwardly, in a large leather recliner.

'Wait there.' Dean went out of the room and came back carrying several pieces of clothing over his arm. He laid them out on the floor in front of Tommy. 'Know what these are?'

Tommy looked at the streetwear. Everything bore the purple diamond logo. Every guy his age was familiar with that particular label. He whispered the name almost reverently. 'Wow! Hybird X.'

'And what do you know about it?'

'As much as anyone who likes streetwear, I guess. One thing I do know is that the stuff is way out of my league.'

Dean picked up a hoodie and chucked it over. 'Try it on.'

Tommy didn't need asking twice. He pulled it on and zipped it part way up. It was black and purple, with some crazy, multicoloured lightning strikes across it. He felt like a million dollars. He'd seen this stuff on rich kids and on websites, but he'd never had a chance to actually wear it. 'This is so cool.'

'Okay, hands in pockets. Throw a moody pose.'

Tommy did as he was told.

'That's good,' said Dean thoughtfully. 'But you're going to be so much better. Okay, that one is yours, for keeps, but for now you only wear it when I tell you. Got it?'

Tommy nodded dumbly. A Hybird X hoodie! That would cost hundreds of pounds. Then he remembered one of his dad's favourite sayings, no such thing as a free lunch. Exactly what was he going to have to do to earn it? He grew fearful. 'Dean, I really need to know what you want from me.'

'You, my friend, are going to be what the boss refers to as a "spotter." You'll be mixing freely and easily with some very well-off people, and you'll get to know a lot about them. You'll also learn about street culture. You'll hang out in some seriously trendy places, and while you do, Tommy-boy, you'll be listening and remembering what you hear.'

'Listening for what?'

'You're going to spot targets, Tommy. Guys who're toting serious money in the clothes they wear. You are especially listening for talk about collectors, Hybird X ones. You'll memorise addresses, get to know these guys' habits and where they go, and then,' Dean smiled benignly, 'all you have to do is report to me and move on to the next venue.'

Tommy was starting to understand. He was to find the marks, and someone else would relieve them of their valuable streetwear.

'The best thing, Tommy, is that *we* don't get our hands dirty. You will never know, or have anything to do with, the crew that does the dirty work. No one'll be able to pin a thing on you. Do your job well, and you'll make good money.' Dean picked up another piece of clothing, this time a multicoloured puffer jacket. 'See this? It's Hybird, right?'

'Yeah . . .' Tommy frowned. 'Well, it's got the logo, but is there something wrong with it?'

Dean grinned broadly. 'You're going to be good at this. Just looking at it, you sense it's a fake, don't you?'

'I'm not sure.' Tommy reached out and touched it. 'It doesn't look the right kind of material for these jackets. I've only seen them on websites, but this one, well . . .'

'You're spot on. Now, you'll be spending this week getting up to speed on everything Hybird X, okay? You have a computer in your room, and there's the real thing hanging in a cupboard in the spare room. That, and learning how to talk the talk, getting to know all the trendy places to hang out.'

'Dean, there are no trendy places in Saltern-le-Fen. This area is crap for young guys. We all dream of getting away to a big city, somewhere with a night-life. Places for kids like us.'

'You won't be staying local all the time. There are clubs and bars and restaurants springing up in the bigger towns around here, and London is just an hour and a half away by train. But don't forget, there are some very rich farmers and businessmen in this area, and they have sons, so these are the guys you'll be mixing with to start with. Maybe it's boredom, I don't know, but there are one hell of a lot of kids sitting in their bedrooms waiting for the new gear to drop, doing all they can to bag a little piece of Hybird X for themselves. It's big and it's global, Tom, believe me.'

'Maybe it's because you can do the whole thing online,' Tommy said. 'Buy and sell. Even if you're stuck in this backwater, you can get a piece of the action, just by going online.'

'I guess so. But the main thing is, this area is ripe for the picking.' Dean stood up. 'Right. Now, I want you to go and change into something that you think looks really cool, okay? But incorporate the hoodie. Then come back out here.'

Tommy chose tonal shades. He found some black skinny jeans, a purple T-shirt and some black sneakers with grey and purple flashes. With his new haircut, he thought he'd never looked so cool before. He went back to the lounge. 'Will this do?'

Dean stared at him for what felt like hours. 'Come with me.'

He followed Dean into the bedroom he used for storing the streetwear. A long mirror hung on the far wall. Dean pushed Tommy in front of it. 'What do you see?'

Tommy hardly recognised himself. He'd always been told he was good-looking, but had never taken any notice. He thought he looked far too pretty. His face was effeminate, almost girlish, and he'd spent years trying to make himself look tough. Now, with the new hairstyle, and the expensive clothes, he suddenly saw a different kind of guy, like the ones that stared back at you from the pages of the male fashion magazines.

'I've a feeling you're seeing what I'm seeing. I tell you, with a few tips on grooming and an aftershave that smells of money, you'll shine, Tommy-boy!' Dean clapped him on the shoulder, 'Time to start work. You are going to learn everything there is to know about Hybird X, and maybe a few other hot brands too, just to make your cover sound authentic. And then we're going to get you a new history. I'm guessing you aren't well-known in the circles I've been talking about?'

Tommy sniffed. 'To tell the truth, I've got very few mates. My closest friends have moved away, and since my parents started fighting, I stopped bringing anyone home. I've mixed with a few guys from where I used to work, but they're a pretty rough lot.'

'And that's where you learned a few bad habits, was it? Thieving and the like?'

Tommy nodded. 'I had a few close calls, but I never got nicked.'

'I know.' Dean smiled darkly. 'I know a lot about you, Thomas. So, right now, we're going to change your life — literally — and we're going to start with a call to your mother. Sound excited, alright? Say you've got a new job out of town, and you won't be home tonight. You're staying over at the hotel to get an idea of how it all works. You'll be back home tomorrow to collect some things. Be vague about details. Be nice. Be happy. And above all, be convincing.' Dean laughed. 'It'll be good practice for your new career — Tommy the liar and con artist!'

At that, a vulpine glint appeared in Dean's pale eyes. It would have frightened Tommy, if he'd looked up. But Tommy didn't look up.

* * *

Marie strode into the CID room, her step a whole lot lighter than the previous afternoon.

All in all, it had been a pretty good day. She knew the Fenchester detectives better now. She felt relaxed with them and spoke more candidly about how much Alistair Ashcroft had damaged them and made them suffer. Marie provided some details that the Fenchester team were unaware of, which they appreciated. So, when she left Fenchester that afternoon, she came away with a wealth of information and contacts that would help them when they themselves took up the investigation.

She also came away with the impression that they were all very glad of help from Saltern. For once, there was no animosity towards another team moving in on their case. They were frustrated and angry at having made so little headway and they positively welcomed Saltern's assistance.

Marie hung her jacket over the back of her chair and looked around. Nobody there. Jackman's door was closed, which was unusual.

She set down her bundle of files on her desk and looked towards Jackman's office.

He was not himself right now. He hadn't been the same since Alistair Ashcroft got away, and Marie knew that despite his repeated denials, Jackman still blamed himself for it.

Initially there had been a lot of brave words spoken. They were going to rally together, hunt Ashcroft down and throw him behind bars. Now it seemed that enthusiasm for the crusade had waned. As their physical wounds healed, a kind of ennui descended upon them. They were no longer the vibrant and enthusiastic team they had been before Ashcroft.

Marie stared at the closed door and thought about her friend. At the time of the Ashcroft case, Jackman had embarked on a relationship with Laura Archer, the force psychologist, a person Marie liked a lot. She'd been sad when things didn't work out for them. They should have been a terrific couple — they complemented each other perfectly. In her opinion they still did, and she suspected that Laura felt the same. But Jackman's guilt and dedication to his work had ruined it. He'd never really opened up to Marie about it. He'd told her a lot, but never what was really in his heart.

Marie stood up. Maybe it was down to her to ask? She and Jackman were close, they always had been, and she didn't like to see him so serious, so subdued. Okay, why not now? It was quiet, most people were out, and the others were preparing to go off shift, so what better time to beard the lion!

Jackman looked worse than he had this morning, and Marie felt a stab of real concern for him. 'Bad day?' She smiled and flopped down into a chair, deciding to keep it light until she knew what was worrying him.

'Ah, Marie, you're back.' Before he could say more, his desk phone rang. With a curse, he picked it up and his face dropped. 'Oh, I see, well, yes, of course I will, ma'am. Can't be helped. We'll speak tomorrow.'

'Know what, Jackman? You look like you lost a pound and found a penny.' She gave him a worried smile. 'Is it Laura? Do you want to talk about it? You know it won't go any further.'

Jackman emitted a short bark of laughter 'Me? No, Marie, it's nothing to do with Laura. In fact, it's not about me at all. It's about you.'

Marie stared at him. 'Me? Why? What have I done?'

'Nothing. It's not something you've done, but it is something that concerns you.' He went to the door and closed it. 'Ruth Crooke had something urgent that she needed to talk to you about, but she's had to go make a statement to the press about the search for Denis Church's killer, and it can't wait.' He returned to his chair. 'So now it's down to me.'

Marie was puzzled, worried, and from the look on Jackman's face, so was he.

'There's no easy way to put this, so I'm just going to say it as it is. Then maybe we can talk it through?'

'You're scaring me, Jackman.'

'Sorry, but I'm completely in the dark about all this. I have no idea how important it is to you, but DS Vic Blackwell has been reinstated to CID. Here in Saltern.'

Marie froze. The breath left her body as if she'd been sucker punched. She knew it showed when she saw Jackman's shocked expression.

He stood up again. 'I'll go and get you a drink. A cup of tea?'

Marie nodded. All she could hear was the name, Vic Blackwell.

Left alone in the room, she tried desperately to gather her thoughts. She had been under the impression that Blackwell would never again set foot in the station while

Marie worked there. Now he was being re-instated! It was unthinkable! She rocked in her chair, trying to make sense of what she'd just heard. But there was no sense to it. No sense at all.

Jackman returned and placed a mug of tea on the desk in front of her. He squeezed her shoulder gently, 'I realise this is a shock. Are you okay?'

'Shock! I'll say it is.' She wrapped her hands around the mug as if trying to gain some strength from its warmth. 'I don't believe it! Oh, what a mess!'

Jackman stood by her side, his hand still on her shoulder. 'Can you tell me about it? I'm here for you, Marie. You know that. Always. I have no idea why you haven't mentioned it before, if it's this serious.'

Marie could have laughed. She had gone to his office intending to get him to pour his heart out to her, and it turned out to be the other way around.

She sighed, looked up at him. He was a lovely man. Suddenly she understood that he was hurt because she had never shared this with him. They had been through so much together. He knew her entire life story. This was probably the one thing she'd never told him about. 'There's not much to tell, really, even though it's haunted me for years. You might not believe this, Jackman, but it's a mystery that even I know very little about.'

He returned to his seat and leaned forward across the desk. 'Then tell me what you do know.'

She had just had to find the courage to walk back into the Alistair Ashcroft case. Now she was going to need to plumb new depths to summon even more strength to tackle Vic Blackwell.

She exhaled. 'We were crewmates for a while, when we were in uniform. Vic was a powerhouse back then, full of all the right values and scared of nothing. Everyone thought he had an unstoppable career. We made a good team, and we got on well.' She sipped her tea. 'His wife was called Tania, and we'd often go out as a foursome, Vic and Tania, and Bill and me. We were good mates for years, until my Bill died. We kind of drifted apart after that. Both Vic and I were with other crewmates by then, and we were both studying for CID, but I still used to go for a coffee or a glass of wine with Tania every so often, just to catch up, you know?'

Jackman nodded. He was a good listener.

'Then I noticed a difference in Tania, and it worried me. Something was wrong, but she never said what it was. We stayed in touch for years, and I did wonder if something wasn't right with their marriage. I tried hard to get her to open up, but she wouldn't. She never did.' Marie stared into her tea. 'Not long before you joined us, she died in a car crash late one night. She was the only person involved, no one else, and I always wondered where she was going and what happened? Tania hated driving at night. She had poor night vision, and rarely got behind the wheel in the dark.'

'What did you suspect?'

'I had no idea at all, I swear, Jackman. All I could think was that they'd had a row and that she was running away from Vic, although that was just conjecture.' She took a drink of tea. 'She remained loyal to the bitter end. But then Vic started to flood me with questions — what had Tania said to me about where she was going — and in the end it became unbearable. Then it escalated, and he got it into his head that I knew something, though I didn't. I still don't. But he believed I had something to do with what happened.'

'And he never saw sense? He continued to think you were involved in some way?'

'He swore I *was* involved. Then he started to make allegations and accusations. Some were very nasty indeed. They were damaging and could have put my job in jeopardy.' She looked up at him miserably. 'So, one day I flipped and reported him. Next thing, he was policing the cabbage fields. He's never forgiven me.' She paused.

'Jackman, I never spoke about it because when he was finally gone and the whole thing became yesterday's news, I buried it. I was ashamed of the things he said and what he accused me of. If I'm honest, even after all he'd done to me, I felt guilty about derailing his career. He would have gone to the top, I know he would. But I brought that dream crashing down.'

'Yes, but hell, Marie! Not without reason!' Jackman exploded. 'You can't just go accusing people of things. You have to pay the price.'

'And now they are bringing him back.' Marie felt sick.

'Ruth's hands were tied. She doesn't want him here and she's told him as much. One wrong move, and he's history.'

'Where's he going to work? Not on our team, surely?' Fear flooded through her.

'No, as a pool detective, general duties.' He pulled a face. 'He says he'll toe the line if he can get back here and into CID again.'

'He would, wouldn't he?'

'Ruth says we have to give him one chance.'

'Do we?' Marie finished her tea. 'When is he due here?'

'Three or four days. Saltby Eaudyke is being cleared out as from today.'

'Oh great. Just great.' She looked at him. 'You do know that I might not be able to handle this, sir? I might have to ask for a transfer.'

'Like hell you will! No way is he going to break up my team! I'll keep you apart as best I can. You'll never have to work with him, I'll see to that.' He ran his hand through his hair. 'Look, please, Marie, just hang on for a while and see what happens, then we'll re-evaluate. Ruth is on our side, so if there's so much as a whisper of discontent, he'll be out, I promise.'

Marie wanted to scream. They didn't know Vic like she did. His presence here in CID seemed like a death knell. Her life with the team would be over. It was the beginning of the end.

* * *

As Marie left the office, Jackman stared after her, horrified. So much for Ruth's idea that the whole thing would have faded with time. Marie was reeling. Jackman cursed himself for not telling her in a more sensitive way. He could only guess at the things Blackwell had conjured up out of his grief-stricken mind to throw at Marie. Now was not the time to ask her, but he would, when he felt she was ready to talk about it.

The problem right now was how to tackle the situation? He would tell Ruth, as soon as possible. Just maybe there would be some way to at least delay Blackwell's arrival in CID. Possibly the thought of losing such a valuable and dedicated detective as Marie would sway the balance in favour of getting the man shipped out to another station.

Before he could think further, his phone rang. He picked it up.

'Inspector, I've just had a call from PC Stoner. He's reported finding a body.'

Jackman drew in a breath. 'Where? Do we have an identity?'

'No identification on him, sir, but he's an IC1 male, probably in his late teens. He's been found in amongst some dump bins at the back of the parade of shops in Mayflower Lane.'

His heart sank. Another boy killed for his taste in streetwear? 'Anything missing? Like his trainers, Sergeant?'

The desk sergeant grunted. 'Not this time, sir. I know what you're thinking, but this is no rich kid, and his clothes are far from collectible. Will you attend?'

'On our way.' Jackman hung up. All the others were still out. He hated having to ask Marie to go with him, but maybe it would give her something else to think about for a while. He followed her out into the main office. 'Sorry to say this, but we have another dead teenager. Are you up to coming with me?'

Marie nodded. 'Of course. I'm shocked, but I'm not incapacitated.'

'I never thought you were.' Jackman grinned at her sheepishly. 'Oh, Marie, I'm really sorry I didn't put it better. I had no idea it was such a serious and sensitive issue. I made a complete pig's ear of it, didn't I?'

She threw back a rueful smile. 'You wouldn't have had to if I'd told you about it in the first place, so it's my fault, not yours.'

'Friends?'

'Always. Now let's go see what sad discovery uniform has made.'

He knew she was putting on a brave face, but she would, wouldn't she? He'd have expected nothing less from brave Marie Evans.

* * *

Mossy had never worked so hard. Trez had said it was a boot camp, and he hadn't been lying. He still didn't know what kind of job he'd be doing in the setup, but it was clear he would need to be fit, fast and streetwise. Trez told him he needed to monitor his physical stamina, so as to know exactly what he was capable of. So he'd been put through his paces. Then the mental stuff began. Trez wanted to see how he would react in a series of different situations to gauge his mental stamina. At every stage, Trez had made notes.

Now Mossy was sitting in front of a computer screen watching an interactive map of Saltern-le-Fen. Trez would give him the location of an incident, and Mossy had to show him the route that he would take to get away from it, to avoid being captured. Mossy found this part pretty easy. He already knew the whereabouts of every camera and every danger spot in this town, and several others close by.

This was his patch. Every rat run and hidey-hole belonged to him.

He gave Trez a surreptitious glance, and saw the satisfied smile. He reckoned he'd passed this test, even if he hadn't got full marks in some of the others.

Mossy wanted to do well, he *needed* to. He kept seeing Alice's bruised face, and each time he felt the rage building inside him. Whatever it took, he'd do it, just to get her away from her drunken father.

Trez was shutting down the computer. Mossy wondered what was coming next.

'Food.'

Mossy looked at him suspiciously. Trez hadn't meant they were having a bite to eat. Was it another test?

'It's in my best interests to keep you fit, so we need to work out a diet that'll suit you.'

Mossy didn't answer. The word "diet" wasn't in his vocabulary. Food was just something you grabbed when it was available, and dreamed about when it wasn't.

'Okay, kid. I need to calculate your BMI. No doubt you've lived on crap for most of your young life, so I have to get you eating properly. Get over there and stand on the scales.'

Mossy did as he was told. He had no clue what a BMI was, and he didn't care. Trez seemed to have it all in hand, and it looked as though for the first time in his life, he was going to have proper meals. Bonus!

'How tall are you? Around five foot six?'

'I guess.' Mossy looked down. He'd never really taken too much notice of his body. Now he was wearing a clean black T-shirt, black joggers with a white stripe down the sides, and a pair of trainers that were streets ahead of his Shoe Zone ones. He even had fresh underwear and socks! The clothes weren't expensive, but they were the best he'd ever had, and they were new too, not from some charity shop or a Sally Bash handout.

Trez was staring at him. 'Bit of a culture shock, isn't it?'

For a moment there had almost been compassion in the hard man's expression. Mossy experienced a sense of belonging.

He didn't answer. It *was* a culture shock. It was a weird, crazy dream, as if someone had picked him out of one world and dumped him in another. A strange one. He didn't know the language, the lay of the land, or anything else about this other country.

Trez cuffed his arm. 'It's okay, kid. I think you've earned a rest and a meal. Go chill out in your room for a bit while I get you something to eat. I'll shout when it's ready.'

'Thanks, Trez.' Mossy wanted to say more, but he didn't know how. So he just went to his room.

He lay on his bed and stared at the ceiling, wondering where Alice was now. He'd texted her earlier, but he had a feeling that before long, Trez would find his phone and confiscate it. Phones were off limits here. He fished it out from under his mattress and saw he had a message: *Take care. I'm scared of what you might be asked to do. A. xx'*

No more scared than I am, Alice, he whispered. But scared or not, he'd bloody well do it.

CHAPTER EIGHT

The body was hard to make out amid the black refuse sacks and other discarded items. Jackman's first impression was that whoever had killed this young man had simply put him out with the rest of the rubbish. Already he loathed this killer. Years of seeing the worst things people were capable of hadn't made it any easier to bear yet another callous act.

Marie must have been thinking the same thing, if the expression on her face was anything to go by.

'Bastards,' she whispered.

Jackman had the sudden urge to rush in and push all the garbage to one side, take the boy in his arms and pull him away from that stinking mess. But he stood at a distance and stared. Forensics would take care of him, and until they showed up, he would have to remain where he was. In situ, they called it, don't contaminate the evidence. Jackman saw it as a final degradation.

'Funny, isn't it?' Marie said quietly. 'We've seen the results of what a twisted mind can do, the tortured bodies and horrific injuries, but every now and again it's something very simple that really gets to you.' She looked at the dead lad. 'It's the casual indifference, the insensitivity.'

Telepathy. There were times when Jackman thought that he and Marie truly had it. They came from such different upbringings, they'd had such different lives, yet they still managed to think in exactly the same way. 'Nicely put, Evans.' No, he was not going to lose this. He couldn't. He didn't care what the top brass said about second chances, Ruth Crooke was going to have to find a way to get rid of Vic Blackwell. He couldn't stand by and let one man break up a team that worked so well together, that had loyalty to each other way beyond the call of duty. First thing tomorrow, he would be in the super's office and tell her exactly how it was. And no bleedin' messing, as Max would say.

'Rory's here.'

Jackman saw the familiar figure get out of his ancient Citroen Dolly, and was relieved. Now the lad would be properly taken care of. Professor Rory Wilkinson was the best, so very soon they would know exactly what had happened to the unfortunate young man. However, it would be down to them to find out *why*. That was the difficult part.

Rory must have read their serious expressions, because he refrained from greeting them with his usual black humour. He went straight to the dead boy and very gently examined him. After a while he looked up. 'I'm puzzled. A rare occurrence, I know, but nonetheless, I admit I'm a tad confused.'

Jackman raised an eyebrow. 'How so?'

'From the information I was given, the location of the body and his apparent age, I assumed he'd got into a fight and had maybe been stabbed, or he could have been mugged and left for dead.'

'And what has changed your mind?' asked Marie.

'This young person has been badly beaten, but not recently. There are signs of bruising around his wrists. I need to do a thorough examination as soon as possible, but it's my belief that he's been held somewhere, died, and then brought here and dumped.'

'Held? As in prisoner?' Jackman didn't like where this was going.

'I'll tell you for sure tomorrow morning, but this young man is setting off alarm bells. There's something about him that doesn't quite add up.' He looked at them. 'And don't ask me what I'm rambling on about, dear hearts, because I haven't a clue. It's like when someone has put a wrong piece in your jigsaw puzzle and thrown the whole picture out.' He gave a mock frown. 'Damn! Now you know about my *penchant* for jigsaws. I blame my great aunt Joanna, but that's another story.' He sniffed, became serious again. 'This young enigma is number one on my list for the morning.' He looked down at the ragged bundle that had once been a teenage boy. 'He's not been here long, Jackman. I suspect he died earlier this morning. Time of death should be fairly accurate, and you'll know, as soon as I do.' He beckoned to his two scene-of-crime officers. 'Now, perhaps, you'll allow my cherubs to get on with their unpleasant, but necessary task?'

There was little more to do here. Uniform were talking to all the shop owners and checking the back lane for any security cameras. And it was getting late.

For a moment Jackman watched Rory and his SOCOs start work. He turned to Marie. 'Unless you're dining at Gary's Café again, would you like to join me for supper? I hate to sound exactly like Gary, but Mrs Maynard threatened me with one of her amazing chillis, and there's generally enough there to feed the five thousand.'

For a moment he thought she would say no, but then she nodded. 'I'd love to. Since this horrible thing with Vic Blackwell has shone a spotlight on my past, I'd quite like to talk to you about it, if you don't mind? Kind of share the anguish?'

'I'd be happy to share, in fact I'd be grateful. I need to know everything, then if I'm called on to make a judgement, it'll be an informed one.' He smiled at her. 'And of course, I'm just plain nosey.'

As they walked back to the car, Jackman felt they had regained something.

That closeness, the camaraderie that had been missing for a while had returned, and it brought him renewed energy. Perhaps something good would come out of this dreadful situation.

* * *

They sat talking until almost eleven. Afterwards, Marie felt as if a dark cloud had lifted. She still didn't know if she was going to be able to work in the same station as Blackwell, but she was certain that she had Jackman well and truly in her corner. Now he knew some of the terrible things Blackwell had accused her of, and could understand her reluctance to be anywhere near him. And the icing on the cake was that, finally, Jackman had unburdened himself about his split with Laura Archer.

'I'm not sure that two professionals, both of whom are so embroiled in their careers, can ever find the space or time to really make things work,' Jackman had said.

He'd looked almost bedevilled, torn between work and a meaningful relationship.

'The stupid thing is, if it had just been a casual thing, I reckon we could have easily fitted it in around our weird working hours, but it wasn't. We really felt something for each other . . .' he'd tailed off, but Marie understood.

'If things were different, I think we could have been so happy together, but . . .' Again, he ended in silence.

'There would never be enough time to devote to a partner, not in the way that you would want to, or that they deserved,' Marie finished.

'And Laura has all these amazing ideas. She has papers she wants to write, lectures she needs to attend and to give. She's on the verge of an incredible career. She couldn't give that up to be a copper's wife, even if she wanted to. We talked about ways to keep the status quo and both work, but we realised very early on that the compromises were too great.' He had sighed. 'We called it a day before the hurt became too damaging.'

Marie guessed they were both still hurting. No matter how brief their relationship had been, it had been real, and you don't heal quickly from the real thing.

Marie drove out of Cartoft village and headed for home, still naturally anxious about what the future would bring, but at least she didn't feel so alone. She felt oddly peaceful. There were no more secrets left to dredge up from her past.

* * *

Vic woke to the smell of stale beer and unwashed clothes. He took a deep breath and tried to gather his muddled thoughts into some semblance of order. Where the hell was he? And who was this woman lying next to him with her mouth open and her make-up smudged?

A sliver of grey light seeped through a gap in the ill-fitting curtains and the room came into focus. He looked around slowly. The last thing he wanted was to wake her. He needed to be well away when that happened. They were lying on a mattress on top of a wooden pallet. The bed linen, such as it was, was creased and it reeked.

He cursed himself and his uncontrollable needs. Then he thought about Marie Evans, and cursed her even more vehemently.

Carefully, he slid off the makeshift bed and crawled towards his discarded clothes. With a hammer crashing away at the inside of his temples, he picked out his socks and underpants from a dingy brassiere and some cheap nylon underwear. As he slipped an arm into his T-shirt, she shifted, turned, and gave a soft moan. He froze, and did not move again until he was sure she was still asleep. He stood upright, and was forced to grip his head with both hands until the thundering passed, then eased himself into his jeans. He checked the pockets, making sure his wallet, warrant card and keys were still where they should be, and made his way to the door.

The hinge creaked and he prepared to run, but a glance back showed her figure, still motionless, curled into a foetal position, filthy sheets pulled tightly around her thin body. Deeply asleep. For a moment, before he tiptoed down the dark staircase, he looked at the sleeping girl and wondered how old she was. Not that it mattered, they were all slags, and he was ninety-nine percent certain she wouldn't remember a thing about last night.

His features twisted into a sneer. He hadn't left the pub with her and no one had seen them together. He wasn't on his own patch, and she was a newcomer to the area. He was much more careful these days. He had to be. He knew that if he made another mistake, Superintendent Ruth Crooke would be there waiting, and no way would he give her the satisfaction of taking him down.

He let himself out into the empty alleyway and, still thinking of the thin-lipped superintendent, spat onto the dirty concrete path. The headache was getting worse, and he thanked heaven that no one other than Sean Jordan would be at the station to see him. Over a period of time, Jordan had seen hundreds of his hangovers, and no longer even bothered to mention them.

His car was still parked in the market square. Most of the residents of this small town left their own vehicles there overnight, so no one would have noticed it. He slumped gratefully behind the wheel, and thought again about the girl.

He wasn't sure how long he'd be able to keep up his little games. This was a tight-knit community, and he had to pick his women very carefully. Even in Fenchester, none of the whores wanted his money anymore. He dreamed of a big, urban metropolis, London maybe, or Newcastle. Some anonymous place, where his particular cravings could be satisfied easily. The engine spluttered into life and he pulled out of the parking space, recalling his one and only trip to Holland. Now there was a country that knew how to cater for a man like him.

He drove out of the town and picked up the main road towards the coast. How he hated this flat, cabbage-stinking county! But he mustn't give up, because things were finally going his way at last. He had been presented with a golden opportunity to finally settle his old score, for good this time. If he was clever, he could be on his way out of this miserable fen to the bright lights of the city in no time at all. The thought of all that concrete, metal, glass and all-night bars lifted his spirits, and he sped across mile after mile of neatly planted fields, able at last to envision the whole thing coming to an end.

CHAPTER NINE

Daisy had woken long before dawn. She had seen nothing untoward on the marsh since reporting her findings to the police, but for some reason she felt certain that something was amiss. This left her unsettled and anxious.

So, at five thirty a.m., she and Sheba were walking the sea-bank, their feet soaked from the long, wet grass. She had been told not to go to the spot where she had taken the photographs, but she was just taking a walk, wasn't she? With her dog? Nothing out of the ordinary in that, surely?

As she approached the inlet, she saw a 4x4 in the farmer's field, close to where the landing stage was situated. She slowed down, pretending to be staring out over the river and the marsh, but keeping an eye on the vehicle.

She wanted to get closer but was afraid of drawing attention to herself. She should just turn back now and retrace their footsteps. She called Sheba and made a fuss of her when she came bounding back. Keep it normal, Daisy.

Turning to go home, she hesitated. As the weak dawn sunshine broke through the clouds, there was a glint of something inside the windshield of the vehicle. Two bright points reflected in the light. Binoculars? She was being observed.

An icy shiver slid down her spine. Time to get out of here. It was a lonely, remote spot. Trying hard not to panic and break into a run, Daisy Cotterill called Sheba to her side and headed for home.

* * *

The man called Darke sat alone in the office. He was not normally an early riser, but sometimes it was good to get one step ahead of the rest of the world. And that was where he liked to be, ahead.

His small empire had been running smoothly for months, then there had been that damned fatality, and he wasn't best pleased. Arranged disappearances were fine. Carefully planned and perfectly executed, they were all part of the operation, but something as stupid as that was unforgivable. He grunted. Now there was another possible fly in the ointment. He hoped it wasn't the start of more problems for them. He had built in a series of fail-safes, but he didn't want to have to take his foot off the gas when things were just gaining momentum. No, for now, they would keep moving, as fast as possible. Dean was on a high with his new "find," anxious to push the kid in at the deep end. He believed the guy was a natural, and was desperate to prove it.

Unbeknown to Dean, Darke had taken a sneaky look at the young man, and was excited too. They had never recruited someone with looks like that before. If he was as amenable to learning as Dean thought, then they were onto a winner.

Darke shifted in his chair. If things didn't work out as planned, he had another very special use for that beautiful boy. And if all else failed, he knew people who would pay big money for looks like that. It would be a shame to lose him, but he hated waste, and that young man was a very desirable commodity indeed.

He sighed and dragged his mind away from the young Adonis. He glanced at his watch. First, he had something to attend to. He opened a drawer and removed a set of heavy keys. It was a bit earlier than usual, but no matter. They would hardly be complaining, would they?

* * *

Vic Blackwell was bleary, sick and bad-tempered after his night out, but after breakfast, a couple of ibuprofen and a sachet of rehydration crystals, he started to feel human again. Well, as human as he ever felt these days.

He knew he couldn't go on like this, especially if he was reinstated back into Saltern CID, but he didn't seem able to control himself. If he was honest, he didn't want to control these urges. Losing himself with a woman who knew exactly what he wanted was probably the only satisfaction he ever got. To him, sex was an anaesthetic. It deadened the pain.

For now, his appetite was sated. As soon as the headache subsided, he'd function properly again. The terrible thing was, it wouldn't last. It never did. Before long he would have to go looking for another woman willing to dole out his next fix.

He knocked back a glass of sweet fruit juice and his head started to clear.

It was still early. Today he intended to make a big effort to get the privy of the fens into some sort of order. The packing boxes had all arrived, and it shouldn't take long to fill them. Anything important was always sent direct to HQ anyway, so he didn't have a mountain of reports and files to deal with. His plan was to send PC Jordan out to tell the locals that they were to be left to their own devices.

Vic gave a grunt of amusement. They probably wouldn't give a damn! The place was hardly Gotham City! The locals rarely contacted the police for anything. Very little happened here, and if it did, they had their own ways of sorting things out, and it rarely involved going to the police. There were one or two professional complainers, but weren't there always? They were the ones he foisted off on Jordan to deal with. Sean Jordan had an easygoing nature and even if he wasn't the brightest cop in the academy, he was good with people.

So, today he would be industrious and toe Ruth Crooke's line. When the axe finally fell on Saltby Eaudyke and the shutters came down for the last time, he'd be ready and eager to move back to the CID department again. The place that Marie Evans had seen him removed from and sent to this shit-hole! Well, she and all the rest of the brownnoses there would see a very different Vic Blackwell from the one who left. Until it was time to remove the mask. Then Marie would see the real him, and she wouldn't like what she saw. He'd make sure of that.

* * *

The CID room was packed for the morning meeting. Jackman was always astounded at the speed with which news travelled around a police station. Everyone knew about Vic Blackwell's imminent return, and although no one appeared to know the reason for his fall from grace, gossip was rife.

Marie was very quiet. He now understood why, so he jumped in immediately. 'Okay, everyone. Calm down. There's no point in me informing you that DS Blackwell's joining us after Saltby Eaudyke is closed, as you all know already, *but*,' he emphasised the word, 'whatever happened years ago, I want left strictly in the past, understand? We need to move on now, so no trying to rake up old history, and no tittle-tattle guesswork as to what occurred. Forget it, okay? He'll be in the CID pool to start with, and I want you all to work with him as you would any other officer. Now, before I fill you in on last night's murder, Robbie? Max? What have you got for us on the Hybird X front?'

Max stood up. 'We've discovered that it's far bigger and more widespread than we realised, boss.' He glanced down at some notes he'd made. 'We've contacted Fenchester, Greenborough and all the surrounding areas, and they've all reported similar thefts. Greenborough had one specific theft from a house in the town where over £100,000 worth of grail items were stolen. They knew nothing about this particular brand being collected, so they're pretty grateful for our input.'

'Any leads?'

'Nothing yet, sir,' added Robbie, 'although we are trying to cultivate a couple of local guys who are smalltime collectors. They mix with quite a few "names" in the Hybird world, so they could be of help.'

'The death of Denis Church has made a few of these lads really twitchy, boss, so we are leaning quite heavily on these two dudes. One, a kid named Josh Baker, is our go-to man for background on Hybird X.' Max grinned at Rob. 'Apart from our own in-house H-X expert, of course.'

'Keep on it.' Jackman turned to Gary. 'Anything more about Denis Church's attackers?'

Gary looked thoughtful. 'Nothing concrete, but there's word on the street about two missing boys.'

'Missing? From where?'

'They're more or less street kids. Rumour has it that they come from really poor families out in one of the backwater villages. When they did a runner from home, no one reported it because it was just a mouth less to feed.'

'So, who is missing them?'

'Jim Cousins, for one.'

'The chap who runs the shelter in Bridle Street? Are they two of his kids?'

'Not exactly. He said he tried to get them into the hostel, but although they accepted a meal, they never stayed there. He said they were due to come back and collect some handout clothes that he'd acquired for them, but they never showed.'

'Not unusual with that kind of kid, surely?' said Marie.

'True, but some of the other street dwellers think they were up to something, and after the attack on Denis, they disappeared.' Gary shrugged. 'They're odds-on favourites for being the attackers.'

'Names?' Jackman asked hopefully.

'Only street names. I've tried to check them out and run into a brick wall.' Gary frowned. 'Their tags are Biz and Jaz, and apart from that, I know sweet Fanny Adams about them. Other than the fact that they fit the height and ages of the two muggers seen on the CCTV.'

'And now they are probably miles away.' Jackman groaned.

'I've got a few more people to speak to, and Jim has offered to make a few discreet inquiries for me. Those kids he looks out for trust him, so maybe he'll have more luck.'

'What about talking to Artie down at the Saltern Baptist Church? He's always taking food and hot drinks out on the streets at night,' Marie suggested. 'He sometimes gets vulnerable kids off the streets and into safe places. He's worth a try.'

Gary nodded. 'Definitely, and maybe Laurie Stephens. I know he normally just coaches deprived kids in footie and other sports but he's been known to take in the odd waif and stray.'

Jackman nodded. 'You stick with that, Gary, and post their descriptions out to all forces as persons wanted on suspicion of unlawful killing.'

'Wilco, sir.'

Jackman told them about the dead teenager in the rubbish. 'Forensics will be contacting me this morning regarding how he died, so I'll update you all at the four o'clock meeting, okay?'

'Could he be one of the two muggers, sir?' asked Charlie Button.

'Possibly. We'll know a bit more about him after we've spoken with Rory.'

'Only I was thinking, if one is dead, then we might find that we have another body soon.'

Jackman smiled to himself. Good old Charlie. Trust him to think of that grim possibility. 'Let's hope not, Charlie. They could be on their toes and trying to get as far away from here as possible.' He straightened up. 'Right, everyone, you've got plenty to do. Back here at four, okay?'

Chairs scraped the floor, and the sound of quiet conversation filled the room as the officers moved out to start another day.

'I still keep seeing that poor kid lying in all that rubbish.' Marie looked upset and angry.

'Me too. I don't like what we might be dealing with here, Marie. Such total disregard for a human being is sickening.' They went to his office. 'Ruth wants to speak to both of us this morning, but she has some kind of meeting going on at present. I'm trying to keep well away. Too much gold braid in one room makes me giddy.'

'I know what you mean.' Marie smiled half-heartedly. Jackman could see that her thoughts were on Vic Blackwell and his imminent arrival.

'Let's get out of here,' he said suddenly. 'How about a visit to Rory? That'll be good for a laugh.'

Her smile became more like her usual one. 'It comes to something when a trip to the morgue is the only thing that'll cheer us up!'

'Any port in a storm, eh? Come on.'

* * *

Dean decided to allow Tommy a lie-in. They'd been out until two in the morning, and by the time they left the venue, Dean knew he'd found a golden boy. He'd transformed into a beautiful butterfly.

Tommy had been accepted by the people Dean wanted to impress, and he'd stuck to his newly adopted fictitious persona as if he'd been given months to get used to it. What's more, he'd been careful. He'd been friendly and polite, but hadn't overdone it. He'd stuck to what they'd rehearsed, and didn't get carried away adding window dressing, which could have tripped him up.

Dean went into the kitchen and started preparing breakfast — fresh fruit, fat-free Greek yoghurt and manuka honey. He had the feeling it had been a long time since Tommy had been treated to breakfast in bed. Well, he deserved spoiling after his performance last night.

With proper coaching, Tommy would be absolutely perfect. Dean recalled that he'd been brilliant in the plays at school. He didn't drink too much either, as one or two of the others had done, and he kept his cool, seemed relaxed and at ease. Dean had procured some pretty successful boys in the past, but Tommy was going to be his number one.

A few moments later, he knocked on Tommy's door and went in. 'Breakfast is served, sir. But don't get used to it. It's just a treat, okay?'

Tommy eased himself up and rubbed his eyes. 'What time is it?'

'Half nine, and time to shine.' He set down the tray on Tommy's bed and watched his face light up.

'Hey! This is really kind of you, Dean. Thank you.'

Dean perched on the end of the bed. 'You did well last night, kid.'

'Really? I was shit scared. I'm not usually good with strangers.'

'You were a star, bro, a real star. They loved you and I'm reckoning you'll be getting invites from all over soon.'

'And all I have to do is wear something Hybird, and be nice? Stick to my background story, and remember everything they tell me?'

'That's all.'

Tommy began to eat. Between bites he said, 'And no one gets hurt?'

'No way. It's purely about theft, acquiring the grails and any Hybird X streetwear. Then it's all sold on, but even that's done by others. No link to you or me, and no trouble. So don't worry, Tom-boy.'

Dean was a good liar. Though, to be fair, that was what they hoped would happen. In a perfect world, the tea-leaves would get in, nick the merchandise and get out, job done. Trez's crew had different methods of course, but even they wouldn't want to actually kill someone, like that kid with the trainers. Still, that had nothing to do with Tommy. 'I forgot to ask, how did your parents take the news that you're leaving home?'

Tommy shrugged. 'Like I expected. I got a half-hearted, "Good for you," from my father, then Mum took the phone. She did sound a bit pleased for me, but, you know,' he swallowed some food, 'they never even asked me where I was going.'

Dean felt sorry for Tommy, but relief soon overcame any compassion. They wouldn't be nosing around trying to find the boy.

'I said I'd collect a few things today, but Mum said they won't be there.' He stared at his breakfast, 'For all they knew, it could have been the last time they ever saw me, but never mind. They had more important things to do.'

'Chin up, Tom,' said Dean softly. 'You've got a new life now. You wait till the day you go home to visit, with money in your pocket and shiny new leather on your feet. Who'll be laughing then?'

'I won't have a home to go to, Dean. From what I overheard, Dad's already arranged to stay with his brother in Dumfries, and I know my mum will be off with her "friend."'

'It'll take a while to sell the house, and divorces don't happen in the blink of an eye. You'll see them again, Tom, and you'll be in a much better place than them, I can guarantee that.'

This seemed to cheer Tommy up, and he got on with his breakfast. 'So what's next?'

'Do you remember a guy last night called Aidan?'

'Tall guy, dark hair, wore a super skinny blazer and cream trousers with a very expensive T-shirt.'

Dean grinned broadly. 'Oh, you are getting into the whole clothes thing, aren't you? You've got a good memory too. Anyway, his favourite hangouts are the Lemon Tree in Fenchester and the Ginger Sheep here in Saltern. So you and I are going to drop in tonight for a cocktail or two.'

'Cool. They're the trendiest bars in the area, aren't they?'

'By far. And Aidan has some pretty well-off mates, one of whom I happen to know is getting interested in Hybird X collectibles. He's pretty new on the scene and I want you to get buddy-buddy with him, okay? Don't try to get too much from him this time around, just chat. Make him believe you're a friendly guy with a shared interest.'

Tommy nodded. 'Got it.'

'And to draw him in, you'll be wearing a rare grail jacket. Try to behave as if it was just any old number from your wardrobe. Don't start acting like a diva because you have a couple of thousand quids' worth hanging off your skinny shoulders.'

'And I get paid for this?' With a shake of his head, Tommy plunged a spoon into his bowl. 'I still can't believe it.'

'Well, it's a fact. Bring us the goods, and you'll get paid very well.' Dean stood up. 'There's coffee in the kitchen when you're finished. Then it's back to studying. A new site for resell Hybirds has just sprung up. I want you to memorise what's available and how much they fetch.'

'You got it. And thanks for breakfast, Dean, I appreciate it.'

'I know you do, Tom.' Dean looked long and hard at his temporary lodger. 'You're very welcome.'

* * *

Mossy didn't like the breakfast cereal. It was like bird food, and the yoghurt stuff on top of it tasted weird. The eggs were good though, even if the bread they were on tasted like the birdseed in the cereal. But he didn't complain. He was in this now, for Alice's sake, so if he was told to eat shit, that's what he'd do.

Already this morning, he'd been out running, Trez timing him with a stop watch. He was fast, he knew, and although Trez was feeding him garbage, it seemed to be doing him good. He was sure he already had more stamina. Win, win, he thought. He'd managed a very short text chat with Alice, but it had left him feeling even more anxious. She sounded really down, and nothing he said seemed to lift her spirits. Mossy wondered if she'd be able to hang on until he started earning some proper money. If she couldn't, he'd find a way to relieve these guys of some of their cash, and do a runner. He didn't want that, but if she needed him, he'd be there.

He finished his meal and washed the dishes as he'd been instructed to do. He dried the crockery and put it away, and wiped down the drainer. All per instructions. Mossy was going to be the perfect student . . . until he was ready to clean these guys out and do a runner. Then Alice and him could find a better life somewhere.

* * *

Rory was delighted to receive his unexpected visitors. 'I get *so few* willing callers.' He swept a hand across his brow like a tormented Lady Macbeth and sighed loudly.

Then he grinned. 'So, come in, come in, and make yourselves at home.'

Marie winced. At home? This was the morgue!

'Coffee?' Rory asked.

Marie looked dubiously at the autopsy tables, the big steel sinks, all awaiting the next corpse. Perhaps not.

Rory laughed. 'In my office.'

Marie smiled sheepishly. 'White, one sugar, please.'

They seated themselves around Rory's desk. He took out a folder and opened it. As ever, his glasses had slid down his beaky nose, and he shoved them up. 'This boy still bothers me. He's a mass of contradictions. He was beaten to death, no question about that. I believe he died about six hours prior to his discovery. There is residue on his clothes that would indicate that he'd been moved from his place of execution, put in a car boot, and driven to the rubbish dump. I've found fibres that are consistent with the kind of material used in the utility areas of certain vehicles, mainly Fords. One of my minions is in the lab narrowing that down as we speak. He should find a make and model if he's diligent, and he will be.'

Jackman nodded. 'That's brilliant. It'll help a lot if we find a suspect.' He sipped his drink. 'But what is so puzzling about this kid, Rory?'

Rory scratched his neck. 'Well, he's dressed in kind of low-end clothes, new, but cheap. He's clean and well-nourished, but there are indications that that wasn't always the case.'

'Poor family who managed to get it together?' asked Marie.

Rory looked distracted. 'No, I don't believe so. He shows all the signs of serious early malnutrition, but get this, his last meal was fillet steak with porcini mushrooms, and salad with avocado and watercress and a vinaigrette dressing! And his shoes. They're reasonable trainers, probably from an outlet store, and they fit him properly. They weren't passed down from a sibling or picked up in a charity shop. But his feet are stunted. His bone quality and general health is poor, but clearly improved over recent months.'

'Adopted? Fostered into a really good home?' Jackman surmised.

'I'd agree, if it wasn't for the fact that not all of his injuries were inflicted in that final beating. He showed indications of constant physical abuse over a long period of time. Not life-threatening stuff, but there's scarring and small deformities, such as old healed fracture lines in his fingers.'

'Then maybe fostered into a really *bad* home,' Jackman added.

Rory shrugged. 'The more I look, the more confused I get.'

'How about dental records?' asked Marie.

'Mmm, I've circulated his X-rays and all the details I have, but I don't hold out much hope. I'd say he's had little or no professional treatment probably since his early school days. He'd been brushing his teeth recently, but the malnutrition had done a lot of damage.'

'Can we get a photograph of his face that'd be decent enough to use for ID purposes?'

'Naturally, I can work my usual wonders. And most of the damage was to the body — the chest and the abdomen — so his face is pretty well intact. I'll clean him up nicely and make him presentable, then Ella can get a good shot for you. She'll be in any time now, so we'll do it ASAP. Then you can start asking questions.'

Jackman stood up. 'Thanks, Rory. At least the bit about the fibres from a car is good news.'

'I'll send my prelim report over to you by lunch time, so long as the good people of the fens don't decide to snuff it *en masse* before noon.' He looked at them, eyes wide. 'My workload seems to double every day! It's just *so* fortunate that I'm such an *a-may-zing* pathologist, isn't it? No one else would cope, I'm certain, dear hearts!'

'We both agree with that.' Jackman stuck out his hand. 'Thanks again, Rory.'

On the way back from Rory's lab in Greenborough, they talked about the dead teenager. Marie was beginning to feel as confused as Rory. 'We really need an ID before we can do anything, don't we?'

'Yes,' said Jackman thoughtfully. 'It's that last meal that bothers me. Even if he was taken into foster care with someone who wasn't doing a proper job, they wouldn't give their ward a fillet steak with a very special salad and dressing, would they? Most lads of that age would prefer a burger anyway.'

'I don't even know what porcini mushrooms are! Bottom line, abused kids don't get posh steak dinners.' Marie shook her head. 'Doesn't make sense, but . . .' She stopped.

'Yes? *But* what?'

'I just had a déjà vu moment. But it's gone again.'

'About the kid's Michelin star meal?'

'I guess.'

But it wouldn't resurface. Best to let it ride until it surfaced of its own accord. Nevertheless, all the way back to Saltern-le-Fen, she was bothered by that fleeting moment. She was sure it was important. It could even be vital.

CHAPTER TEN

At around two p.m., Trez drove Mossy to an old deserted factory unit on a small industrial estate just off the main road through town. He unlocked a pair of big sliding doors and they went inside. It was a prefabricated metal construction, in dire need of repair. Whatever machinery once operated there was long gone, leaving nothing but debris, old shelving units and junk.

Mossy was suspicious. Why had Trez brought him here?

'Don't look so twitchy, kid. Trust me.'

Yeah, right! thought Mossy. *Like I'd trust a man-eating tiger in a locked room.*

Trez strode across the dusty floor, his footstep echoing. 'Come on.'

There was another door at the back. Trez produced a second key and unlocked it.

Mossy hesitantly followed him in, and stopped in amazement. The big anteroom was laid out like a gym. Ranged around a large central floor mat were punchbags, weights, a treadmill, an exercise bike and various other pieces of equipment.

Trez grinned. 'We've spurred off an electricity supply from next door.' He glanced at his watch. 'The others should be here any minute.'

'Others?'

'Your sparring partners. Today, you're going to learn a few tricks of the trade. Some of my more experienced crew members are going to show you the ropes.'

Doubtfully, Mossy shrugged. 'Cool.'

A few moments later, two guys arrived, both wearing the same black hoodies, T-shirts and joggers as he was. They looked slightly older than him, but didn't seem particularly intimidating. Pretty lightweight, in fact, like him. Wiry, and built for speed.

'Mossy, meet Gordi and Zane,' Trez said.

The three of them nodded at one other.

Trez addressed the newcomers. 'Mossy here is light on his feet and fast out of the blocks, but so far, he's got no idea of what we are all about. I'd like you guys to show him. Okay?'

Gordi and Zane nodded.

'We're street thieves, Mossy. Muggers. We rob people.'

Trez looked at him intently. Mossy remained impassive. Sure they were thieves. What else? 'And?' he asked tonelessly.

'What makes us different is the type of things we steal. We are very discerning. You will only take exactly what you're told to take, and nothing else. If you help yourself to any little extras, you'll get the same treatment that CJ did, and you'll be no use to us anymore. Is that completely understood?'

'Understood,' Mossy replied. *Maybe.*

'There's a new market out there, and it's a very lucrative one. You won't have come across it before, due to your background, but if you toe the line, it'll make you a good living. Got it?'

Now Mossy was interested. He'd been thinking of money, credit cards, iPhones, jewellery or even drugs. 'But what *are* we stealing?'

'Clothing and footwear.'

What? He had to be kidding! How could a few rags make money for all this crew and their boss — whoever *that* was.

Trez and the others were smiling at his puzzled expression. Trez turned to the two boys. 'Show him, lads.'

Gordi gave a shrill whistle, and from the back of the room another kid appeared. This one, however, wasn't wearing their uniform black T-shirt and joggers. He was dressed in fancy streetwear. His hooded down jacket was a work of art, it had a mass of bright jungle foliage printed onto a black background. He also had some camo cargo pants in black and grey, and some of the weirdest trainers Mossy had ever seen.

'Go!' Trez said.

As the boy reached the floor mat, Gordi and Zane sprinted forward. The next few seconds was a blur. In the blink of an eye, the new boy was lying prone on the floor, and his trendy clothing was heading out the door.

'Impressive!' Mossy meant it. He'd seen ace pickpockets at work, and had even tried dipping himself, but this was a whole new ballgame.

'Come back, lads!' Trez helped up the third boy. 'You okay, Bubble?'

'Fine.' The third kid brushed himself down.

'The art is not to do any damage.'

'To the mark?' asked Mossy.

They all laughed.

'To the clothing, muppet!' said Zane. 'That jacket's worth two grand. The pants maybe five hundred quid and the sneakers as much as the jacket. So,' he pointed to the clothes lying in a heap on the floor, 'you're looking at close to five grand in one hit. It needs to be undamaged, though.'

'Jeezuss!' Mossy gasped. 'That's impossible! No one spends that kind of money on a bleedin' puffa jacket!'

'Wrong, sunshine. They spend a whole lot more.' The boy called Bubble brushed at his T-shirt. 'But we don't get to practise on the grails.'

'Grails?' Mossy was lost.

'Really expensive gear,' Trez said. 'Now, shut up, sit down and listen.'

They all sat on the floor mat.

Trez explained to Mossy that there were ways of taking down your mark, of removing his clothing quickly and effectively without tearing or ripping. If the mark resisted, there were also ways to knock him out without causing major trauma. Mossy'd guessed that Trez was ex-Army, and he was right, but the solider had later turned mercenary, and knew all there was to know about guerrilla tactics.

Mossy listened carefully — in fact, he was mesmerised. He was learning new life skills.

'For the rest of today, you'll work with my crew. They'll show you exactly how they disabled Bubble and removed his gear so quickly. Then they'll show you how to do it. Once you've mastered that, you'll go out on the street and see my boys in action. Then it'll be your turn.'

'But how'll I know who is wearing this mega expensive stuff? It looks pretty crap to me. How am I going to recognise it?'

'You'll be shown. You don't have to think, just act. You're told who your mark is and where he'll be, and what to take off him. And that is that. As I said before, no extras. No nicking his watch, no half-inching his wallet. If you do, it's sudden death for you.'

Mossy had a feeling Trez wasn't using that expression lightly. He was still not sure what Trez had meant about CJ being "looked after." It had sounded innocent enough then. Now he was not so sure.

Trez stood up. 'I'll leave you boys to it. I have to go see the boss. I'll pick you up later, Mossy. Enjoy the rest of your day. Listen and learn.'

After he had gone, Mossy chanced asking who the boss was.

Gordi looked uncomfortable. 'We're Darke's boys. That's all you need to know. Just try not to do anything that takes you into his office, okay? Stick to what Trez tells you, and be a good boy.'

Mossy wanted to know more, but no one was talking. He usually went his own way, taking orders from no one, but given the circumstances, he decided he'd better do as his new crew suggested. He'd seen their faces when the name Darke was mentioned. They were terrified.

* * *

Charlie Button put down the telephone receiver and hastened to Jackman's office.

'Just had a call from Daisy, sir, the lady out on the marsh.'

Jackman and Marie looked up.

'She says she's had another scare, sir. She was walking her dog up on the top of the sea-bank and she saw a 4x4 in that farmer's field, the one close to where she found all the "evidence."' He put this in air quotes. 'What bothered her most was that someone in the front of the vehicle was watching her through binoculars. She saw the lenses in the sunlight.'

'Damn!' grumbled Jackman. 'I thought you warned her away from that area. What was the silly woman thinking?'

'She admits she was wrong to go there, but, well, she just wanted to help.'

'And put herself right in the firing line of some ruthless smugglers! Great!'

'Apparently not, sir,' Charlie said patiently. 'That's why she phoned. It's all been a terrible mistake on her part. She says she's sorry, she just wanted you to know.'

'Mistake?' Marie asked. 'How come?'

'A few minutes ago there was a knock on her door. When she looked out, she saw two bird watchers, complete with all the kit — cameras, tripods, bird identification books, the lot. She spoke to them, and they asked if she'd seen any other birders on the marsh, or maybe she'd seen this rare bird they were looking for.' He glanced at his notebook. 'A white-billed diver?'

Jackman and Marie looked blank.

'Only seen twice in the last twenty-one years, they said. Anyway, after chatting to them for a while, she realised that the people she'd seen were twitchers, not smugglers. Hence the binoculars trained on the sea-bank, and the discarded sandwich and so on.'

'And the lights?' asked Marie, still not entirely convinced.

'They admitted that some avid enthusiasts will drive out, meet up and wait all night somewhere, to catch a sighting around dawn.' Charlie pulled a face. 'She gave these two a cup of tea and after a long chat with them, she realised she'd sent us on a wild goose chase.'

'Almost literally!' Jackman sighed. 'It's possible, I suppose. Sometimes you can hardly move at sites like Frampton Marsh, when a rare migrant has been spotted. These people are obsessed with finding and listing as many birds as possible.'

'Daisy said they'll travel thousands of miles to see a rare bird.'

'But I thought just one mention of a sighting brought them out in droves, and don't they use GPS to find exact locations?' Jackman looked sceptical.

'That's what these two guys told Daisy, but they also said it's extremely competitive, and it's quite usual for someone to keep a possible sighting secret until they've been the first to confirm it. Anyway, they were going to go to the spot by the inlet and see what they thought. They said they'd drop in again on their way back later today.' Charlie closed his notebook. 'Daisy said she was sorry. She thinks seeing the lights spooked her, and her imagination took over.'

'Okay, let's hope she's right.' Jackman didn't look completely convinced. 'But, Charlie? Give her another ring, maybe tomorrow, just to check on her, okay?'

'I was going to anyway, sir. I rather liked her, and she's in one heck of a remote spot out there. Especially living alone.' He paused at the door. 'Sorry, that's rather blown our steroid smuggling route out of the water, hasn't it?'

'Maybe, maybe not. Anyway, Charlie, you pitch in with Gary, if you would, and help out with the hunt for Denis Church's attackers.'

'Wilco, sir.'

Charlie left the office, promising himself to keep an eye on Daisy Cotterill. If the boss was uneasy about her, he should be too, even if Daisy had sounded totally convinced by her visitors. Maybe it was all a bit pat, a bit contrived?

Charlie stopped and heavily underlined the name "Daisy" in his notebook.

* * *

After Charlie left, Marie and Jackman sat quietly for a few minutes. They didn't need to say what they were thinking. Neither had bought the story about the twitchers. In fact, it had reinforced their belief that something untoward was afoot down on the marsh.

'I'm thinking about putting men out there at the next very high tide,' Jackman eventually said.

Marie nodded. 'Absolutely. Although it will be difficult for them to conceal themselves on that stretch.'

'I've thought of that. There's a spur off the sea-bank a little way after the inlet, where there's a drainage pump and an access path for the waterways maintenance guys to get down to it. If we get out there early enough, we can set up an obbo site, and just wait.'

'Can I make a suggestion, sir?'

'Of course.'

'Why not leave it until the *second* very high tide? If they're doing what we think they are, let them get away with another drugs drop. That way they'll be thinking Daisy has been completely taken in, and that we've taken her word for it.'

'Good thinking. It might also take the heat off Daisy. I'm assuming they've thrown her a lifeline with this bird-watching story. But I don't think their generous spirit will last long if anyone starts nosing around again.'

Marie looked worried. 'She's a bit of a wild card, isn't she? Unpredictable. That could be dangerous.'

There was another short silence. 'Do you fancy a nice healthy walk, Marie?' Jackman said. 'Just you and the fresh fenland air? Exercise for your leg muscles?'

She smiled. 'Like somewhere along the sea-bank, maybe?'

'What a good idea!' His expression turned serious. 'Talk to her, Marie. Make sure that this time she really does stay away from that area. Tell her that we buy her story, so that she doesn't get spooked all over again, but say that as a matter of procedure, we need to clarify everything, and we don't want her drawing attention to the area again.'

'Don't worry. I'll tell her to walk her dog in the other direction.'

'Good. And don't look like a copper. Wear hiking boots, be a rambler for a bit.'

'When shall I go? I've already got boots and my fleece jacket in the back of the car.'

He glanced out of the long casement window, the one Marie had always loved.

'Weather's fine. No rain. Ruth has had to cry off our meeting yet again, so why not now?'

She stood up. 'See you later then, sir.'

Twenty minutes later, Marie was parking in a grassy area from which a path led to the sea-bank, about five minutes' walk to Daisy's cottage. She locked the car and followed the path between the fields until she came to the wide wooden steps that led to the top of the sea-bank. When she got to the top of the sea defence, a chilly wind hit her. She zipped up her jacket and shivered. It was often like this, even in summer. In front of her, on the other side of the bank, was a wide stretch of bleak, boggy marsh, and then the pewter grey band of the tidal river. Miles ahead lay the horizon and the silver waters of the Wash, but today the low cloud met the water, and it was impossible to see where sea ended and sky began.

Marie breathed in the cold, salty air, happy to be out of the office, back in a place that she loved.

She began to walk, looking and listening all the time. It was a wild stretch, with many wonderful birds, some local residents, like the elegant avocets, the lapwings and redshanks, and some visitors, like the flocks of greylag geese. There were rarities too. The twitcher story might actually be true, there were always stories of some sighting in one of the nature reserves. But this particular one had been far too convenient.

Marie walked on for a few minutes. Gradually, thoughts of Vic Blackwell rose to the surface and spoiled her cheerful mood. Since she had been told of his return, he had begun to haunt her waking moments, her every footstep, along with her other constant and unwelcome companion, Alistair Ashcroft.

If she didn't love her job so much, and Jackman, she'd walk away from all this anguish. If she were miles away and no longer a police officer, Ashcroft and Blackwell would have no interest in her. But being where she was, and what she was, they were always there.

Ashcroft had not been heard of since he ran off, leaving her drifting into unconsciousness on a fen lane. Some people would be pleased with this conclusion. Ashcroft had disappeared for good. End of story. Marie knew better. He had sworn to come back, and she knew he would. He was biding his time. He had told them once before that he was a patient man, and he had proved it. Now, as far as she was concerned, he was doing it again. The worst thing was that if his plan was to keep them in a constant state of apprehension and high alert, it was working.

Not a day went by without her, or any of her team for that matter, thinking about him, and wondering, will it be today?

And for all his apparent contrition, Blackwell hated her. Marie had seen how hate festered and distorted formerly healthy minds. He wasn't sorry. Like Ashcroft, he'd have an agenda, and she would feature prominently in it.

She shivered, but it had nothing to do with the chill wind. In these parts they called it a snide wind. Marie quickened her pace. She could see Daisy's cottage in the distance. She just needed to go down the next set of steps, and then along the lane. She could see a car around the back of the property, and hear a dog barking, so Daisy must be in.

Marie pushed Ashcroft and Blackwell back into their box and slammed the lid. She began to work out what she would say to Daisy Cotterill.

* * *

Trez sat on the opposite side of Darke's desk and stared at him. He had just been asked a question, and wasn't sure how to answer it. Darke had asked what he thought of his new recruit.

After a moment, Trez said, 'I can't read him. He's the first one I've had that I can't see through to the real him.

He's either the best kid I've ever had, or the most devious little bastard we've ever recruited. The jury is out.'

'Would you like me to assess him for you?' Darke said.

'Not yet, Darke. It's early days, and he does have the makings of a perfect little thief. I'll give him a bit more time.'

'I suggest you throw in a short, sharp shock, something that might make him rethink any devious thoughts he might have.'

'Maybe. If I start getting warning signals.'

'Be careful, Trez. I sense you rather admire the little scumbag. That will never do. He's just a cog in the machine, and you'll do well to remember it. I expect that kind of silly behaviour from dear Dean, not from you.' Darke narrowed his eyes. 'Don't start showing a softer side, Trez. That is not something I require from you.'

'I'm not soft,' growled Trez. 'And you fucking know that. Who does your dirty work for you? Your *dirtiest* work.'

'Ooh dear, I've hit a nerve.'

Trez stood up. He was best out of there before he landed one on Darke. That would never do. His lucrative livelihood would dry up in an instant. He'd already pushed the barrier by swearing at the slimeball. 'If that's all, I'll get back to the boys.'

Darke nodded. He looked down at his notebook.

* * *

Trez went to collect his new recruit from the factory. Mossy looked exhausted and excited. His "tutors" said he did well, he'd picked up the knack faster than most. Trez was pleased. Darke had put him in a foul mood, and he was anxious not to take it out on his charge.

They drove back to Trez's flat in silence. Inside, he made Mossy sit on the floor mat and wait while he dealt with some messages on his laptop.

When he was finished, he went into the kitchen and made them both a tuna sandwich. Mossy ate his, sitting on the mat, while Trez perched on a chair and watched him. He wanted to believe in this one, but he had serious doubts. There was a side to him he wasn't showing anyone, certainly not Trez.

Trez stood up and took their plates to the kitchen, reached into a cupboard where he kept cleaning materials, and brought out Mossy's old clothes.

He marched into the main room and threw them down on the mat next to Mossy. 'Put them on. You're going home.'

Mossy looked at them, shocked, then up at Trez.

'No! No, Trez, please! I've been good! I've done everything you told me, everything! You can't send me home.'

'I can do anything I want. And right now I want you to put those filthy clothes on. Get it?'

'Please, Trez? Please?'

'Put the clothes on.' His voice was hard and cold. He watched the lad slowly take off his black tee and joggers, and pull on the stinking rags that he'd arrived in.

'Good. Now. Go home, Mossy.'

Trez could see that the kid was fighting back tears. 'And I want you back here by eight sharp, okay?'

Mossy's face was a picture of confusion. 'Back? But, Trez?'

'I need them to see you, you idiot! Your family. The people at home and on your street. We don't want someone deciding you've gone missing, do we? They might start asking questions. And you can hardly go home looking tidy and clean, can you? Show your face, then get back here, okay?'

'Yes! Yes! I will.'

With the biggest grin on his face, Mossy folded up his new clothes and took them to his room.

As the front door closed behind him, Trez went to the fridge and poured himself a beer. The kid hadn't been acting. The tears were real. He wanted to stay. Mossy had earned himself a stay of execution, and no way was Trez going to let Darke anywhere near him!

CHAPTER ELEVEN

Marie arrived back at the station to find Max and Robbie hurrying towards one of the fleet cars.

'Burglary, Sarge! Looks like a Hybird X job,' Robbie said.

'Anyone hurt?' she called back.

'Scared out of his wits, but not seriously injured,' Robbie shouted. 'Sounds like thousands of pounds worth of gear stolen. See you when we've taken a look.'

Marie watched the car speed out of the station. It still seemed strange for CID to be getting hyped up over the theft of a few bits of clothing, but this was much more than mere random muggings. Someone had hit on a very clever idea and was making big business out of it.

Walking up the stairs — good exercise for the leg — she realised what a cunning ruse it really was. If you stole antiques or jewellery or collectibles, you'd have to move the stuff on, source particular markets for it. You'd have to know the fences or handlers, and be very, very careful about whose hands those items finished up in. The Hybird market was guaranteed, dead simple. The collectors were only the click of a mouse button away, anywhere in the world, all scrambling for what you had to offer. The buyers would go to any lengths to get your highly sought-after items. It was a huge seller's market. Easy!

When she reached the office, only Gary and Charlie remained.

'I hear you've been to see my two marsh-dwelling friends,' said Charlie. 'Is she okay?'

'She's fine, and I didn't say anything to scare her, I promise.' Marie grinned. 'You're getting quite protective of our Daisy, aren't you, Charlie?'

The young detective threw up his hands. 'Guilty as charged, Sarge. I just hate to see good people not being able to go about their lives in peace, because of some load of dross roaming the countryside.'

'That's why we're here, lad!' Gary laughed. 'We're the dross-removal squad.'

'So, there's been another Hybird hit, has there? Where?' Marie flopped into her chair with a groan. Her leg was telling her that she'd just done a sea-bank walk on an uneven surface, and climbed a flight of stairs.

'Posh drum out near Leedyke End apparently. Six-bedroom new-build in acres of ground. Owner's in the food industry. He told uniform he has three teenage kids, and the two boys are well into Hybird X streetwear.' Gary pulled a face. 'Well, they were. The intruders went in when one of the sons was actually in his room. They overpowered him and tied him up, then they ransacked the whole house.'

'Is the kid okay?'

'Apparently. Shocked and distraught more than anything. Max and Rob'll get the finer details.'

Hybird X. Marie kept thinking it should be Hy*brid*, then Max had told her it was written that way for dumb kids who couldn't spell *hybrid*. Plus the fact that they wanted a logo with a bird on it, because the founding company manager's name was Keiron Bird.

She looked around the office thoughtfully. It wasn't the most thrilling case they'd ever worked, although it was certainly quirky, but for once she was relieved. After the high-octane, roller-coaster of an investigation involving Alistair Ashcroft, she welcomed something that didn't threaten the lives of everyone around her.

These guys, her team, along with their nearest and dearest, were precious to her. She never wanted to be in another situation where she was looking over her own shoulder while watching everyone else's back at the same time. She massaged her leg gently. Right now, she was happy that her team were pursuing a bunch of thieves, and not some psycho killer. Yes, there had been deaths, two of them, but one was unintentional, and the second was most likely related to a criminal gang, not a ruthless predator that had everyone she loved in his sights.

I'm still here, Marie . . . The voice reverberated inside her skull.

* * *

Robbie was making a list of all the stolen goods. Luckily, the boys had pictures of everything, either in selfies, or from the sites they purchased the clothing from. Now the shock had worn off, the elder of the two teens, Lee, was incandescent with rage at losing his precious Hybird X wardrobe.

Max finally calmed him down sufficiently for him to give an approximate description of his attackers, but this was more or less useless. Three of them, all in black — Ts, hoodies and tracksuit bottoms. Dark silk scarves across the lower part of their faces making ID impossible, and none of them spoke, so there were no names, no accents to help narrow the field.

'Would you say this was an organised raid?' asked Max.

'Absolutely it was!' Lee exclaimed. 'They knew exactly what they were after. They must have known Mum and

Dad were away on a mini-break and I was alone in the house. They worked like some swat team. Room after room checked and stripped of anything Hybird. They must have been in and out in less than ten minutes.' He snorted. 'Not bad for ten minutes' work, eh? One hundred and fifty grand of Hybird stuff, all gone.'

'Has anyone been showing any extra interest in your H-X collection recently?' Robbie asked.

'Other guys always show interest. It's cool and it's beyond most people's reach.' Lee was merely being honest. His dad had money. Not his fault.

'No one asked to come and see your streetwear, maybe someone you didn't know well?' asked Max.

'Not that I can think of.' He looked at Max hopefully. 'Do you think you'll be able to get my stuff back? Will you catch them? Some of those things were limited edition grails. I'll *never* be able to replace them.'

Robbie felt sorry for the kid. He had no hope of seeing any of it again.

Max was diplomatic. 'We'll do our best, Lee. We could get lucky, but I have to tell you that if they were as professional as you say they were, there's a very good chance they'll already have a resale plan. Don't get your hopes up.'

Lee groaned. 'My parents spent a small fortune on that stuff, and we — my brother Tim and me — we've really looked after it.'

'Then let's hope your parents insured it,' said Rob. 'I know what you're saying about the limited editions though. I can tell you're passionate about Hybird, so I guess you guys are just going to have to start again.'

Lee shook his head. 'I don't think so. Those thieves scared the hell out of me. They could have killed me. Thank God, my sister came home when she did and found me, and called the police. If she'd been half an hour earlier she could have walked in on them, and God knows what might have happened to her.' He hung his head. 'My father's going to go mad when he gets here. He's going to kill me.'

'Not literally, I hope,' said Robbie.

Lee didn't look too sure about that.

'We can wait with you until they get here, if you like,' Max offered. 'Break the ice a bit? And I'm sure they'll realise it's not your fault. Robbery is a very serious offence. They'll probably just be pleased to know you aren't hurt.'

'Thanks, mate, but you don't know my dad. Mind you, it's Tim who'll be really gutted. He had a collector's leather trucker jacket with purple flames down the arms. It was his pride and joy, and the first thing those bastards took.'

Robbie frowned at Max. 'First? As in they knew where to find it?'

Lee frowned too. 'Yeah. Come to think about it, they did! Tim and I share a dressing room, and they went straight to the tallboy.'

'Can you show us?' asked Max. 'We shouldn't actually go in the room, because forensics will be taking prints and that, but can you point out where they went?'

They followed Lee up a wide flight of stairs and across a landing to a room with two triple wardrobes, two chests of drawers and a tallboy.

The boy pointed from the doorway. 'Tim has the rail on the left, and I have the shelves on the right. The jacket hung there, with a couple of other coats, not in the wardrobe.'

Rob looked at Max. 'Chance?'

'No way. If I was looking for clothing, I'd head for the wardrobes first, wouldn't you?'

'I would.'

Back downstairs, they assured Lee they'd do their best to find the thieves and returned to their vehicle, leaving Lee with a uniformed officer and the unenviable task of explaining to his parents what had happened to their expensive clothes.

They sat in the car and looked at each other.

'This is no little gang of toerags after a quick buck, is it?' Robbie said. 'It's a carefully planned operation.'

'This is proper organised crime, mate. So who's behind it?'

Robbie finally broke the silence. 'I'm thinking—'

'What I'm thinking?' Max gave him a quick sidelong glance. 'Infiltrate? We get inside?'

'Uh-huh. Just trying to fathom a way of doing it. We could pose as collectors or online shoppers, and try to find them that way, or we could send out a decoy. That would be best, I think. What do you reckon?'

'You're thinking that someone is eyeballing kids in Hybird gear,' Max said, 'then checking out their addresses, maybe even talking their way inside their homes to check out what they have, hitting their drum when the time is right, and stealing the gear?'

Robbie smiled. 'Exactly, so if an undercover cop was to go out wearing something a bit tasty, he might attract the attention of one of the gang members.'

'We grab that gang member and put the squeeze on him. Cushty!' Max started the car. 'Let's go talk to the boss.'

* * *

Instead of going straight home, Mossy sent a text to Alice, asking her to meet him in their little square. She texted him back immediately, saying she was on her way.

'I've been worried sick about you, Mossy.' She stared at him. 'But you look different.'

'I'm wearing my old clothes, so my parents don't get suspicious, but I guess three meals and two showers a day have made a difference.'

'So they're treating you well? Whoever these people are?'

'Yeah, it's good, Alice. I've got new clothes and a real bed to sleep in, with pillows and a duvet!'

Hearing Alice's laugh, Mossy was satisfied that what he was doing would be worth it, even turning street thief.

'Look, there's every chance I might not be able to call for a while. We aren't supposed to have mobiles and mine could get taken off me, but I'll contact you when I can, okay? And as soon as I get some money, I'll find a way to get some of it to you.' He looked at her. At least there were no more bruises. 'I miss you, Alice.'

'I miss you too. But, Mossy, please don't take any chances. I know you'll see me when you can, so don't worry about me, I'm fine. See this coat? I bought it in the Heart Foundation shop like you told me, so I'm warm now. And I still have plenty of money for food.'

Now he noticed the coat she was wearing. It was a padded, lined walking jacket in deep turquoise, waterproof and cosy. He stared at it with pride. He'd done that. He'd provided for her.

Mossy was suddenly overwhelmed. He'd stolen before, done all manner of things, but nothing felt like this. Giving something to someone you care about is far more powerful than stealing and getting away with it.

'I have to go, Alice. I have to see my scummy parents and let a few locals see my ugly face.' He shrugged. 'Though I'd rather just stay here with you.'

She squeezed his hand tighter. Sounding amused, she said, 'Then mess your hair up a bit first. You look far too clean! And, Mossy? Be careful. Promise?'

He covered his hair with his dirty hoodie. 'I will. You too.'

Then he did it, at last. Mossy leaned over and kissed her cheek. Just a peck, it was probably the most meaningful thing he'd ever done.

Mossy hurried away across the little square. He didn't notice a figure watching him from the shadows of a shop doorway. He didn't notice that person's gaze resting on Alice. When she stood up to leave, the figure emerged from the shadows and followed her.

* * *

'Have you guys thought this through properly?' Jackman twirled his pen through his fingers. 'For starters, I don't think Ruth Crooke's budget will run to buying limited edition streetwear, especially if there's a chance it'll get nicked.' He looked from Max to Rob. 'And who were you thinking of sending out as bait?'

Robbie raised his hand. 'Me, sir. I know a fair bit about Hybird X.'

'And he doesn't look his age, does he, boss? He could pass for ten years younger than he is,' Max added.

'True,' Jackman said. 'But what about the clothing?'

'I'm prepared to buy a couple of items, sir. Then, when it's all over, I'll sell them again.' Robbie grinned. 'Might even make a profit.'

Jackman considered the idea carefully. It had its merits. It might even work. Robbie came from a wealthy family, so if anyone could pull it off, he could. And as he said, he knew more about this streetwear cult than any of the rest of them.

'If they follow me home, you know what my pad is like, sir. At least I'll look the part, even if I don't have a room stocked out with Hybird X.'

Jackman recalled Robbie's luxury apartment. If they were to go ahead with the plan, he was certainly the right man for the job.

'Give me till tomorrow to think it through, Robbie. I'll run it past the super. On the face of it, I think it's a good idea. Well done, lads. Now, get off home.'

They were just leaving when Marie arrived. 'The super wants to see us both before we finish up tonight.'

'At last. I've got something to tell her too.' He told Marie about Max and Robbie's idea.

'A bit risky, but I think it could work, don't you?' Marie sat down, still nursing her aching leg. 'What do you think?'

'If Ruth gives us the go-ahead, I'm happy to run with it. Although I can't let Rob pay for the clothing.'

'Well, I'm pretty sure Ruth won't have the funds, so who will?'

'Me. Let's just hope all the talk of the resell value is true.' He stood up. 'Shall we go upstairs?' He peered at her anxiously. 'Your leg playing up?'

'Walked further than I meant to along the sea-bank, that's all. A hot bath and a few painkillers and I'll be fine, honest.'

'Are you sure? Only if—'

Marie stopped him mid-sentence. 'Yes, I'm sure, Mother.'

Jackman held up his hands. 'Okay. But just tell me if you're struggling, understand? We'll take the *lift* upstairs, and go visit Grandmother.'

* * *

They had barely sat down when Ruth Crooke began. 'Marie, I'm truly sorry about Blackwell. I've only just found out why we have this ridiculous situation on our hands.'

Marie couldn't wait to hear this one.

'It appears there was a similar thing going on at Fenchester some while ago, but the officer in question wasn't given any options and was shipped out. He protested, and it turned into a complete fiasco. Lawyers, the police federation, the press, you name it.'

Like everyone else, Marie had heard about it, but not in any detail.

'The upshot of it is, the chief constable doesn't want the same thing happening with Blackwell. They had to give him the option of returning here and, sadly, and against my advice, he accepted.' She sighed. 'I didn't mean to leave it to Rowan to tell you about this, believe me, but the two recent deaths took precedence, I'm afraid. However, I want you to know, that my eyes won't leave Blackwell. As far as I'm concerned, all his promises to be the model detective are a crock of shit. One tiny misdemeanour, and he's history.'

It was reassuring to know that the super was behind her, but Marie knew Vic Blackwell was devious. If he wanted to, he could play a part very well, and easily conceal his real intentions. While they remained under the same roof, Marie would never be able to relax or let her guard down for a moment. And she still wasn't sure whether she wanted to live her life like that.

But for now, there was nothing she could do. She thanked Ruth for her support and they moved on to Robbie Melton's suggestion that he hit the streets as a cool Hybird X fanatic.

Ruth's lips almost disappeared. 'I would sanction that proposal, but, if what you say is true about these clothes, can you see their faces when I ask for a couple of thousand pounds for a jacket and a T-shirt? Get real, Detectives.'

Jackman laughed. 'Don't fret, Ruth. We'll source the material, one way or another. Your budget will stay paying for toilet paper and printer ink.'

'If you can do that, then by all means send your man out on the streets. We've caught many a crook with an undercover officer, and Robbie isn't as well-known here as some of the others.'

'Thank you, Ruth. We'll sort it first thing tomorrow. Er, can I ask, do we have a date yet for Blackwell's arrival?'

'The day after tomorrow, unless there are any holdups at the Saltby end.'

'Can I ask a favour?' Jackman said.

'You can try.'

'Could he and some of the other pool guys take over the steroids investigation? It'd free me up for this streetwear scam and the two deaths.'

'Good idea. In fact, a very good idea. Pass what you have over to DI Jenny Deane, and then let her delegate it to Blackwell. That'll cut your team out of the loop and he won't need to ask you any questions.'

'My thoughts exactly. I'll do it first thing,' Jackman said.

'Well, good luck with your undercover operation, and make sure to keep me up to speed.' She turned to Marie, 'And I want regular reports from you. I want to know whether our prodigal son is stepping out of line in any shape or form.'

'Yes, ma'am.'

Marie realised that she had just one more day to enjoy being in the CID room with the people she loved and cared about. After that, everything would change.

* * *

PC Kevin Stoner was on the late shift. They were still searching for the ID of the dead boy he had found in the rubbish, and he readily took part. Having found him, he felt a kind of personal responsibility toward the lad, secretly hoping that he'd be the one to make a breakthrough. He read through his list of people to call on, and noticed the name Jim Cousins. That was the place to start.

Jim was an ex-con turned good Samaritan, and something of an enigma. There were many stories about him, and Kevin was never quite sure which of these were true. What he did know was that Jim owned a very big house on Bridle Street, a massive property whose origins were murky. Jim had turned most of it into a refuge for kids who needed a meal and a bed for the night. Some stayed for longer. He had managed to find jobs for some of these youngsters and, for a small contribution, allowed them to stay until they found their feet. He also looked out for kids on probation. Jim now had a couple of volunteers who helped with the cooking and the cleaning. He was stocky, and fairly well-built with short greying hair. The kids he looked out for seemed to like and respect him.

'This is the second time I've had you guys here this week. The first time was about my missing boys, Biz and Jaz. Now what can I do for you?'

Kevin handed him the forensic photograph.

Jim stared at it and shuddered. 'Post-mortem?'

'We need to know who he is, Jim. This is all we have. His dabs aren't on the system and he obviously hadn't seen a dentist in many years, so we've nothing else.'

'Missing Persons? Tried them?'

'If no one reported him missing, they won't have a record.'

Jim looked at it again. 'He's not a kid I recognise, Kev. But can I take a copy? There's some people I could ask, and I'll see if any of my "flock" recognise him.' He paused. 'I'm not keen on showing them dead people, but sometimes it serves as a wake-up call, a warning of what can happen when you're out on the streets.'

'It's not too awful. I've seen worse.' Kevin grimaced. 'But, yes, take some copies by all means.'

Jim slid the picture into his scanner. 'Do you know anything at all about him?'

'I wish we did. From what the PM tells us he had a bad start in life, but was pretty well fed lately, so maybe things were starting to turn around for the poor guy.'

'But too late. Sad.' Jim handed back the original photo. 'I'll do what I can, Kev. I'll ring you if I come up with anything.'

Kevin thanked him. 'I'm going to try Laurie Stephens next. He might have come across him.'

'Well, he's not at home. He's in hospital. He bust his ankle playing footers with some of his kids, and apparently they found a blood disorder, so they've kept him in.'

'Which hospital?'

'Greenborough General, I think. I'd ring first though, just to check.'

'Thanks, Jim.' Before he could say any more, something kicked off in one of the day rooms.

'Gotta go. World War Three just broke out — probably over a doughnut or a packet of Ginger Nuts. See you soon.'

'Want a hand?'

Jim laughed. 'No way! You go do the important stuff. I've got this covered!'

Takes all sorts, thought Kevin. *I wouldn't want to deal with problem kids all day every day.* It didn't occur to him that some people would hate to do his job.

CHAPTER TWELVE

As the afternoon faded into evening and the sky took on its hues of pink, apricot and grey, Vic Blackwell packed the last box of files, and looked around the privy. He ought to be exhausted, but instead he felt more energetic than he had in years. He grinned maliciously. Marie Evans certainly wouldn't be feeling this way.

He threw a couple of dirty mugs into the small sink. They could wait till tomorrow. He sat down and looked around. There was nothing here to miss. Soon, his dingy cottage would be up for rent, though he didn't know who'd want it, stuck out here in cabbage country. In a small park just outside Saltern, he'd found a static caravan with a short rental agreement. It was perfect for a temporary address, until the time came to move on permanently.

Tired though he was from all the packing, the old craving began to surface. Vic groaned. Maybe it was the excitement about the move, but this was happening too often for comfort. He hunted through his pockets and found a slip of paper. He'd found a new girl who was apparently not averse to taking on demanding customers as long as the price was right. The problem was she was located in Skegness, miles away.

He closed his eyes and wished things were different. More than anything, he wished Tania would come back, but his wonderful Tania was rotting in Saltern cemetery.

He picked up the phone, and made his call. He locked up. He needed a shower badly, and wanted to make a good impression on "Big Rita." If he could control his desires, just hold back and not scare her off, she might prove a regular solace. He knew this was an illness, an addiction, and he also knew that he wouldn't be able to cope in CID without some occasional relief.

* * *

'Glad I caught you,' Rory said.

'Rory. Have you got something more for us?' Jackman smiled into the receiver.

'I have, and it's not pleasant. Our deceased friend, who we've decided to call Harry, as he has a scar on his forehead, was not only restrained, he'd been drugged. I, in my eternal wisdom, decided to run a tox screen on him, and I've found an opiate in his system.'

'Something to keep him quiet,' whispered Jackman.

'Exactly. I'm still checking for the exact drug, but it was certainly administered as a sedative.'

Jackman's mind started to imagine terrible scenarios. 'Had he been sexually abused, Rory?'

'He was a sexually active young man, but no, no sign of abuse. Which is something of a blessing, I suppose. Anyway, better get on. I have your PM report to do before I can go home to my beloved spouse. Au revoir.'

Jackman smiled. He liked Rory. Despite his camp humour, Rory cared deeply for the luckless people he worked on, and he did his utmost to get those bodies to tell him everything they possibly could. Rory was a detective too, a forensic one.

He looked up. Out in the CID room, Marie was pulling her coat on. He glanced at the clock. Another day had sped by, and he was no closer to finding Denis Church's attackers or knowing who their other dead teenager was.

He beckoned to Marie. 'Our young John Doe had opiates in his system. He was doped and kept tied up before he was killed.'

Marie frowned. 'Correction. Doped, tied up, *fed fillet steak,* and then killed.'

She was right. But what for? 'Who *is* he? All our enquiries so far have come back negative, and Kevin Stoner says that even Jim Cousins didn't recognise the photo. He was our best bet.'

'What about Laurie, the football coach?'

'Kevin says he's in Greenborough hospital, but one of DI Galena's team, DC Cat Cullen, called in and had a word with him for us. Laurie didn't know him either. Kevin has yet to get hold of Artie Ball, the guy from the Baptist church who goes out with his mobile soup kitchen. I'm beginning to think the killer is from out of our area.'

'Then why dump him here? I think it has to be a local. Whoever put him there knows this area well. Mayflower Lane has a lot of rubbish from the shops along that parade, and it was the night before the waste collection lorries were due. That was not just a random dump, sir. They'd thought about it.'

'You could be right, Marie. I just wish we had a name for him. It always bothers me when we have an unidentified dead youngster. Someone, somewhere, must be missing him.'

'We should give him a name, until we know what his real one is.'

Jackman raised his eyebrows. 'Rory's beaten us to it. He's named him Harry, after a certain young magician, as he has a scar on his forehead.'

Marie nodded. 'Fair enough. At least it humanises him. So, Harry it is.' She stood up. 'I'm off home now. Are you getting away soon?'

'Shortly. Oh, and you didn't miss anything at the four o'clock meeting, by the way. There was nothing of significance.'

'Better luck tomorrow — let's hope.'

'Ruth is giving a media conference first thing in the morning about Harry, and his picture is being released to the national press. Someone *has* to recognise him.' He glanced towards the open door. 'Have the others left yet?'

'Gary and Charlie have just gone, and Max and Robbie have gone to try and get their hands on some Hybird X gear.' She smiled. 'They're like a couple of kids.'

'In that case, they'll be needing some serious money.'

'Rob told me to tell you that he'd sort that side of it for now. Between you and me, Robbie has quite a bit of money. He told me he has a Premier account that allows him to take out a grand a day in cash.'

'I still don't want him laying out his own money for an official police investigation, even if this one is somewhat unorthodox.' Jackman closed down his computer. 'I'll talk to him in the morning.'

'Okay, but I get the feeling he wants to buy this streetwear, and then try to sell it later. He's well into this Hybird stuff. And now get home, Jackman. You look tired out.'

'I will. Actually I'm going over to my mother's after work, to have dinner with the family. I try to go every couple of weeks, mostly to see Ryan and Miles. They grow up so quickly.'

He loved his nephews. Since the Alistair Ashcroft case, which had affected his whole family, he had tried to be there for them, and the rest of the family too.

'How are they?' Marie asked.

'Remarkable. Children have incredible resilience. They are doing really well. Oh, and my mother said to tell you that as soon as your leg is strong again, she wants to see you at the stables for your first riding lesson.'

'Tell her I can't wait, and I mean that.'

'I've got money on you being a natural, Marie. Don't prove me wrong.'

Marie laughed. 'No promises! A motorbike is one thing, a living and breathing beast is something else!'

* * *

Tommy walked into the lounge and stood in front of Dean. 'Will this do?'

Dean looked up from the leather chair he was lounging in. 'Oh, yes, my man! Yes, indeed.'

He shifted in his chair. Tommy was the hottest property he'd ever recruited. He knew that he'd lose him if he ever tried anything on with him, but that didn't stop him wanting to. Dean was bisexual, and had many different types of partner, but Tommy was his ideal.

'I wasn't sure about the colour.'

'Perfect, Tom. You've got a good eye. That outfit is spot on for the Lemon Tree.'

'Ready when you are, then.'

Dean felt wistful. It would be so nice to be simply going out with Tommy, without all this other stuff. He sighed. 'Too early, mate. We need to give it another hour. We should be fashionably late, make an entrance. So you'll have plenty of time to practise your chat-up line.'

'You make me sound like a tart!'

Dean grinned. 'Nah, just a conman.'

Tommy pulled a face. 'A bit better, I suppose.'

'I suggest you go ring your mum. Keep her sweet.'

Tommy's face fell. 'I'm kind of looking forward to not having to phone her at all.'

'One day, if that's what you want. But for now, we don't want her getting suspicious. Phase them out gradually. Go tell 'em you love your new job and are determined to make a go of it, okay?'

'If I must.' Tommy turned to go back to his room.

'Yes, Tom, you must. Play by the rules, and you'll have your own place before you know it.'

Dean watched him go. He wasn't looking forward one bit to Tommy leaving his flat. But for now, he had to focus not only on teaching the kid how to be a charmer, but most of all, on keeping him away from Darke.

Dean needed Tommy to be squeaky clean, so that the boss never had cause to "interview" him. Darke had secrets. Darke *was* dark. *Oh, very funny, Dean.*

He'd believed Darke trusted him, but now he wasn't so sure. His job was to recruit and coach the "spotters," while Trez trained up the "takers." There were now six active cells, each with three young men, who worked from intelligence provided by Dean's spotters. He counted the names on his fingers. He had five "live" spotters covering a wide area. They all worked independently, and reported directly to him via email and text. They had no communication with each other, and had no idea who the takers were. From the moment the stolen goods were delivered to Darke's depot, another group took over, the distributors. From that point on, Dean had no idea what happened. Though he did know that, through this operation, Darke raked in hundreds of thousands of pounds.

What didn't make sense to Dean was the huge amount of money being used to "pay off" guys that were no longer required. Darke seemed happy to discharge some of his boys with mega payouts on condition they disappeared from the fens and made new lives elsewhere.

Dean was very sharp with figures, and as far as he could see, the numbers didn't add up. There was either a separate income coming from another source, or . . . What? He had his suspicions. Darke was a powerful man with many facets to him, and Dean knew him better than most, but even he didn't know exactly what Darke was capable of.

Whatever Darke might be capable of, Tommy mustn't be the one to find out. The safest thing was to get him trained up and out on his own. It meant losing him, but it would get him as far away from Darke as possible.

* * *

Initially reluctant to help, Josh Baker now seemed to understand the gravity of the situation in Saltern-le-Fen. 'Okay. I told you I wasn't a collector, and I'm not, but I do have a couple of grails.' He stared at the floor, then up at the two detectives. 'I keep seeing Denzi being loaded into that ambulance, and then finding out I'll never see him again. It scares the shit out of me at night. It's changed my perspective.'

'I'll buy them from you, Josh.' Rob hoped the kid wouldn't sense an easy buck and up the price. 'There's an outside chance they could get nicked if things don't go according to plan.'

'Take them. I don't want them.' Josh looked Rob up and down. 'How old are you anyway?'

'Not saying, chum.'

Josh cracked a smile. 'Well, whatever, you look the part and I guess they'll fit.' He left the room and returned a few moments later carrying a denim jacket with the Hybird logo repeated down one sleeve, and some weirdly decorated track joggers.

'Wow!' Max exclaimed. 'These are limited editions, aren't they?'

'Never seen them on any of the resell sites since I got them. I picked them up at the start of the craze, so they weren't the end of the world, cost-wise. Now? I'm not sure. It seems somehow immoral to sell them. Some kid could buy them, wear them, and die for them.'

'Even so, I'll pay you,' Rob said, 'even if it's just what they cost you, and no vulnerable kid will ever own them. The only place they're going is on a police officer's back. They could be instrumental in finding Denis's killer.'

Josh handed them over to Rob. 'Then take them. Do what you need to do. Maybe you'll come see me when this is all over?'

'That's a promise, mate.' Max held out his hand.

Josh grasped it. 'Find the little shites who killed my mate, please.'

'We'll get them alright.' Thanks to Josh, Robbie was pretty sure they would.

'A word. When you wear these, dress them down with plain Ts. Decent trainers, but not really expensive ones. Don't do the overkill. It looks cooler that way, more natural, if you get what I'm saying. That way, you'll draw the right kind of attention and you won't look like a clothes horse.'

Robbie nodded eagerly. 'Got it. We really appreciate your help, Josh. Be seeing you.'

Robbie didn't say so, but he *had* seen something similar on the websites. He left the room aware of carrying six thousand pounds' worth of denim over his arm. And the pants were worth a fortune too, but the jacket was the prize. He looked at Max excitedly. 'We got lucky, my friend, laying our hands on something like this.'

Max looked grim. 'And it took a boy's death to make it happen.'

Rob exhaled. 'Then we'd better make this count.'

* * *

Jackman's phone rang in his pocket. His family's faces took on looks of resignation. They were getting used to his hurried apologies, the swift exits after some summons to come to work.

'Sorry to interrupt what is no doubt either a sumptuous meal, or some delightful *après manger* entertainment.'

Jackman relaxed. At least this call wouldn't drag him away from his family. 'Actually, Rory, my nephews were just thrashing the hell out of me in a car chase. These video games are quite addictive.'

'Then my call is fortuitous. It'll save you from an ignominious defeat. Now, this might be nothing, but I just thought I should pass it on. I was checking through your tox report on dear Harry, when I saw another report come in. It's unrelated, and refers to a recent sudden death I've been dealing with. A young, previously very fit man, dropped dead while running on a treadmill at Saltern Fitness Centre in Pump Lane.' He chuckled. 'Fitting address for people pumping iron — but that's by the by.'

Jackman had been there only recently, talking with the fitness trainers. He wondered where this was going.

'Our hapless young body-builder, one Trevor Maitland, had openly admitted taking steroids to build up his muscle mass, so I wasn't surprised to find them in abundance in his system, but . . .' One of Rory's dramatic pauses ensued. Jackman waited. '*But* I was very surprised to find that they were *veterinary* steroids, probably brought in from abroad, and clearly produced in a UGL.'

'"U" what?'

'Underground lab, dear boy. In the body-building culture, the sources of steroids are either UGL or Pharma, rather like a big brewery versus a homebrew kit. The smaller, private labs aren't illegal, if they are licensed. Some are good, but some aren't, and the user has to be very careful.'

'But *animal* steroids?'

'Oddly enough, they're frequently used by their rippling-muscled advocates, but they haven't been properly tested on humans for use by athletes, which leaves them open to all sorts of tampering. Basically, the one Mr Maitland took was something called MD, or Methandriol Dipropionate, but it was combined with other chemical substances from different steroids. Now, this is the norm, and lots of men swear by them, so it's not something you'd normally be involved with — and here comes another "but."'

'Get on with it, Rory. My nephews are waiting to finally wipe me out.'

'If I must. Well, there was nothing suspicious about Trevor's death. He had an underlying cardiac abnormality and irregularities of the electrical impulses that upset the natural rhythm of the heart. The reason I called you is that Trevor Maitland was definitely taking illegal steroids, something you're investigating, I seem to remember.'

Jackman smiled. 'And you have just provided a perfect lead to the source. Find where Trevor was buying his steroids, and trace it back. Boom!'

Rory sighed modestly. 'Yet another triumph. What would you do without me? I'll send you all the details of the unlucky young man tomorrow. Now, go and suffer your defeat at the hands of your young ruffians! Nighty night.'

The call ended. A proper lead at last, just when he was about to hand the whole thing over to DI Jenny Deane. Excellent. It would give her a head start, and hopefully keep Vic Blackwell busy and out of Marie's hair.

He looked at the two expectant faces behind him.

'Okay, guys. Ready when you are. Let's get this humiliation over with, shall we?'

CHAPTER THIRTEEN

Darke had been working since six that morning, and now it was almost nine at night. It wasn't easy juggling so many enterprises, but it was certainly lucrative and it had countless fringe benefits. It was those added pleasures that he was thinking about right now. Surely, hard work deserved some compensation, didn't it?

He opened one of his ubiquitous notebooks and skimmed down the entries. It was a concise list of his paid "staff." He read each name in turn, picturing the face that went with it, scribbling a few notes in the margin. After some thought, he underlined one name, and crossed out two others. There was no room for weak links in his setup. The great thing about his personnel was that they were all expendable, but he hated waste, so he always found suitable alternative uses for those that fell short of his expectations. He made a few more notes and closed the book with a satisfied sigh. A few people were about to get a well-deserved shock. Another good thing about his enterprise was that only he held all the cards. He alone knew exactly what was going to happen next.

Now, he decided he could switch off and allow himself a little "me time," as his sister, Christine, used to call it.

The thought made him smile. They had been so close. She had taught him everything about life. Their parents had had little time for them. They were always out, either working or socialising. His father insisted this was purely networking, he was a powerful man and new business contacts were useful to him. His wife was a butterfly. Her task was to flit delicately around the social gatherings being delightful and pretty, and attracting other powerful men that might be useful to him. But unfortunately the butterfly became too fond of the nectar, and before Darke even reached his teens, his mother had become an alcoholic.

So, Christine had more or less brought him up. She could have hated him, some girls would. Few girls would want a little brother dogging their every move. But Christine never minded. She let him share everything. Darke recalled that "me time." He would sit on the edge of the bath and watch her pamper herself with expensive lotions and shampoos, and shave her beautiful legs so they shone like water-splashed silk. Christine was never shy, and nothing embarrassed her. If he had a question, no matter what it was, she would do her best to answer it. When he asked her how babies were made, she sat him down and explained sexual intercourse in a way that left him itching to grow up as soon as possible, so he could try it for himself.

He sighed. She was the most beautiful person he'd ever known, and he desperately wished she was still here. He wished she would hold him again, and listen to him ramble on, but she was gone. One evening he had returned from a trip to the pictures with a school friend and found her mutilated body lying in her bedroom. It seemed she had used his absence to entertain a young man. Christine had always been adventurous, but her "partner" had taken things too far. Christine had been asphyxiated, and had apparently swallowed her own tongue. The girl that he adored, once so exquisitely beautiful, had been reduced to something from a graphic horror comic. The man was never identified, and at thirteen, Darke was left alone.

He opened a drawer and took out a shot glass and a half bottle of brandy. He poured a toast. 'To you, Christine.' He drank deeply, and topped up the glass.

It hadn't taken him long to find out that Christine's adventurousness where sex was concerned ran in the family. His tastes were exotic, verging on the bizarre. He finished his drink and stood up. He placed the bottle back in the drawer and took out his set of keys. He liked the feel of them, heavy in his hands. Darke smiled in anticipation. This was not to be hurried. He took a deep breath and made his way out of his office. Time to have some fun.

* * *

Vic Blackwell drove home from Skegness beginning to think that the fates must be feeling kind towards him for once, because something else was now going his way.

He had arrived at Big Rita's and found her having a glass of Prosecco with her new neighbour, a woman who went by the name of Vee. To his surprise, Vee didn't make her excuses and disappear when he arrived, but instead she stayed, and took part.

It felt like the best value he'd ever got for his money. Big Rita might be new to the area, but she was far from new to the game, and she had some moves that surprised even him. And Vee! Vee was not actually a tom at all. She was recently divorced, lonely, and confessed to having a voracious sexual appetite, which had always been a problem for her.

Vic motored down the A52 towards Saltern laughing into the night. Vee's sexual appetite certainly wasn't a problem for him! He had splashed the cash with no qualms at all, and had even managed to charm the two of them into inviting him back.

To top it all, if Big Rita was booked, Vee was very happy to go solo and, as she put it, "slip him in at short notice."

What a bonus! He was finding it difficult to concentrate on driving. All he could think about were those two very capable women, and what they'd done to him. He shivered with delight.

* * *

Tommy had an amazing evening. It was clear, even to him, that he was good at this game. By the end of the evening he'd be able to give Dean not only the address of the newbie collector, but a concise list of the gear he already had, and the name of a contact reseller. He had invited the new guy to meet up for a drink later in the week, if he felt like it. Just to discuss new drops and the chances of getting hold of something special. He played it casual, and it worked like a dream.

Then he circulated, and obtained several nuggets of information that he believed might be of use to Dean.

Dean had spent the evening with Aidan and a couple of his friends, chatting and drinking. Every time Tommy looked at the group, he got the impression that they were enjoying Dean's company. He was that kind of guy. He could hold an audience. He had always been that way, even at school. Tommy couldn't help noticing that he was also getting more than his fair share of admiring glances. These clothes were a magnet for Hybird lovers and he felt good in them, they gave him confidence. He held back, and did exactly as Dean had said. This was his passport to a better life, and he wanted to succeed at it. It no longer even bothered him that what he was doing was criminal. He saw nothing of that side of the operation, so it was easy to forget about it.

Dean ordered a taxi, and Tommy was surprised to find another teenager with them. He accompanied them all the way home.

In the apartment, Dean sent the young man to the main bedroom, took Tommy aside and asked eagerly, 'How was it?'

'Good, very good.' He looked at the retreating figure entering Dean's bedroom. 'Who's he?'

'Mind your own business, Tom. He's just a distraction, okay? I did tell you I liked to entertain.'

Tommy felt strangely hurt. Suddenly, all he had done that evening seemed unimportant.

Dean was smiling at him. 'Come on, Tommy. It's nothing serious, just an itch I need to scratch occasionally. You write down everything you've found out, and we'll go over it in the morning, all right?' He squeezed Tommy's shoulder, and whispered, 'I was watching you tonight. You were brilliant.'

Tommy went to his room, undressed and put his clothes away. Then he did as requested and listed everything he could remember. He padded to the kitchen and took a bottle of water from the fridge. On his way back, he paused in the corridor that led to the master bedroom. He couldn't help hearing the moans and gasps, and his reaction confused and puzzled him.

Was he jealous? How could he be? He was straight. He liked girls. So why the possessiveness toward Dean?

Tommy shook his head. This was crap! It was late, he'd been drinking, that's all. He told himself to forget it. If he knew Dean, they'd be off out somewhere else the next night, and he needed his sleep. He got into bed, but couldn't help listening to the sounds coming from Dean's room.

* * *

Mossy couldn't sleep either. He couldn't switch off. Soon, he'd be on the streets, robbing other kids of their precious clothes, and evading cameras and witnesses. After that, he'd be joining a team of guys for the actual break-ins, which was where the big money was to be made.

Mossy had no intention of playing by the rules when that time came. He'd been an opportunist all his short life, and he wasn't about to give up now. If there were valuable "extras" lying around, he knew he was quick enough to liberate them without his fellow thieves seeing a thing. It was what he did. Otherwise he'd have starved by now.

Only Alice had stopped him turning really bad. He certainly wouldn't be doing this if he thought there was any other way to get her away from her drunken father. Maybe he'd tell her one day. Guilt stole over him. Well, maybe he wouldn't.

* * *

Three in the morning. Daisy Cotterill was in her kitchen, making a cup of tea. She hadn't slept a wink. Sheba had been restless too, and Daisy wasn't sure if this was because of her own tension, or something else.

The wind was blowing in from the Wash, carrying noises from several miles away. At around one a.m., she'd been sure she heard the sound of a motor boat. Not a powerful one, but the gentle chugging of a small craft. No one made their way up this stretch of the river at night.

She sat at the kitchen table and sipped her tea. Winds of a certain strength and direction could cause sounds to travel over very long distances. Even out here, if a south easterly wind was blowing, you could sometimes hear the hum of the traffic on the main A road into Saltern, seven miles away. Daisy was perfectly aware that everything seemed worse or more sinister at night, but it was starting to worry her that the police had taken the trouble to follow up her simple phone call with a visit. She'd have thought they'd be far too busy. The detective sergeant had been really nice, and hadn't worried her at all at the time, but at three in the morning, little doubts turned into huge concerns.

Had she been deceived by those birders? They had seemed so knowledgeable, so convincing. They had called back as they said they would, but were very downbeat, certain the report had been false. Anyway, they said, that particular bird never visited that location. They had left, shrugging their shoulders and thanking her for her help.

And now she was hearing boats on the river.

'Should I tell the police, Sheba?' She lent down and gently tousled the dog's fur. But Sheba had no answer for her. Daisy sighed. She should try to get some sleep, maybe things would look different in the morning. But wait! She'd heard the engine at just after one am. She stood up, went to the kitchen drawer where she kept various odds and ends and found the tide timetable. She knew them approximately, but she wanted the exact time for this morning's date.

High tide was at a quarter past one! The perfect time for access to the inlet. So she was not imagining things. There were smugglers on the marsh.

CHAPTER FOURTEEN

Jackman was up and in the shower by five thirty a.m. He enjoyed having a slow start to the day for once. He would often get an urgent call and have to hit the ground running, so it was nice to be able to take his time and prepare himself for the day ahead.

And what would that bring?

His soapy hand touched the puckered skin of the bullet wound, and his thoughts turned to the man who had shot him — Alistair Ashcroft. If Marie hadn't landed that kick with her motorcycle boot, he probably wouldn't be here at all.

Now they were once again prevented from getting back into the hunt. It was frustrating, but the cases they were working took precedence. The Church family were up in arms that the police couldn't seem to find their boy's attackers, and Jackman didn't blame them. Then they had the other dead boy to try to identify, and Harry was proving a real problem.

He had to prioritise their workload.

Max and Robbie were racing ahead with the Hybird X thefts, so he would leave that to them. He smiled grimly to himself. He was glad they were working on that case. It was a straightforward crime. Having noticed an opening for a new kind of market, some clever villains had seized the opportunity and while it lasted, they were milking it for all it was worth. It was what Jackman considered an "understandable" crime, all about making serious amounts of money very quickly. Even Denis Church's death had been unintentional, so Max and Robbie were hardly likely to run into some dangerous madman like Ashcroft.

That was all he wanted, to keep the team safe. That, and to get the old spirit back. He finished showering and stared at himself in the mirror. Not good. They had all been damaged by Ashcroft, and if there was to be a resurgence of energy and resolve, it would have to come from him. But how did you instil enthusiasm in others when you felt — and looked — like shit yourself? This was now compounded by the fact that Marie's old nemesis, Vic Blackwell, would soon be putting in an unwelcome appearance.

Sometimes he wondered if the only way they would ever recover their old spirit would be if Ashcroft crawled out from whatever stone he was hiding under and threatened them again. And if he did, would they all rally and rise up fighting? In truth, he wasn't sure if they had the strength to confront another reign of terror.

Never in his life had Jackman felt this bad. Maybe he was suffering from a form of depression. The only person he had confided in was his mother. She had assured him that wasn't the case. It was perfectly understandable, given what he and those dearest to him had suffered, and his split from Laura. "Whatever do you expect, Rowan darling? If anyone has been through the mill in the last six months, it's you! Don't be so hard on yourself, just give it time."

She was probably right, but how long was he supposed to give it? He shook himself, dressed and went downstairs to make breakfast. Okay. Max and Robbie on

Hybird X. Gary, Charlie, he and Marie would stick with Harry and the hunt for Denis's killers.

Eating his toast, he wondered about a possible connection between the two investigations. He didn't think that was the case. It had been suggested that Harry could have been one of the muggers that attacked Denis. To him, the kid just didn't fit the bill, but he couldn't say why. Anyhow, it wouldn't be his first line of enquiry.

Maybe Rory would save the day, as he had so many times in the past, and produce something that could help them ID the dead boy. If they were really lucky, maybe young PC Kevin Stoner would get one of Saltern's street people to help them with info on the two muggers. *Someone* knew who they were and what had happened to them. Someone always did. It was just a question of finding them and getting them to talk. Well, if anyone could, it would be Kevin. He was probably the most tolerated cop on the streets. Some of the old lags actually liked and trusted him. Jackman wasn't surprised. Kevin Stoner was a kind young man, a copper who really wanted to help. Maybe some of his father had rubbed off on him. Kevin didn't say much about his parents at the station, but Jackman knew that his father, Michael Stoner, was the county diocesan bishop. On more than one occasion, Jackman had suggested that Kevin apply for CID, but the young copper had said he needed more time on the ground, and Jackman respected him for that.

Jackman gathered his things together and opened the door to a chilly morning. Come what may, today he was going to make some headway. Today, he was going to tackle everything with renewed vigour. Today, he was going to make a difference.

He strode over to his car and looked up at the dark sky. No rending of the clouds or flash of brilliant light confirmed his decision. Instead, the heavens bestowed a thin, watery dawn that crept slowly through the departing night clouds. It would have to do, he supposed.

Daily orders were dispensed with quickly — there was little to say — but when it was over, Max and Robbie almost danced into his office.

'You should see him, sir!' Max was alight with anticipation. 'We went back to my place last night, 'cause Rosie wanted to see Robbie, and he tried on the gear we got from Josh. It was awesome! We dressed him just as Josh told us to, and he really looks the part.'

'So what next?' asked Jackman.

'Tonight, boss. Josh has given us the name of a place where he's likely to meet some pretty trendy guys.'

'We'll use this as a trial run, sir,' added Robbie, 'just to see what I'm dealing with. I won't stay long, just have a quick drink and do a recce. Then, tomorrow, I'll start socialising.'

'Josh has given us the name of a kid who'll help us if we need a bit of support. He'll kind of "vouch" for Robbie, you know? Say he's seen him around before and he's an okay guy.'

'Are you going too?' Jackman asked Max.

'Not as such. I'm going to be in a car a little way down the road, with my camera. Thought it might be useful to get some of the punters' faces. And next time, Robbie'll wear a wire, and I can listen in to any interesting conversations.'

Jackman smiled. 'You guys seem to have this well in hand, so I'll let you get on with it.'

'Thanks, boss.' Max and Robbie turned to leave.

'Oh, Robbie?' Jackman stopped them. 'Have you paid for these Hybird clothes?'

'No, sir. We're settling up with Josh after the event. After seeing what happened to Denis Church, he doesn't want to make anything on them, but I'll see he's not out of pocket.'

'I'll pay. Just tell me how much, when the time comes.'

'No need, sir.' Robbie grinned. 'I might keep the jacket, it's my size and I hate to say it, but I actually like it!'

'Not so sure about the jungle print joggers though, mate,' said Max dubiously. 'Bit OTT for my taste.'

'Me too, I guess, but they're prime bait for our Hybird fanciers. We could reel in a nice tasty fish with those joggers.'

As the two detectives left the room, PC Kevin Stoner came hurrying in.

'Have you got a moment, sir?' The young constable looked anxious.

Jackman indicated the chair opposite him. 'Of course. What's troubling you?'

'I thought you should know that we've just had two more burglaries reported. Apparently they took place last night, and both involve this type of streetwear clothing, sir. One man thinks he's lost around twenty grand's worth of jackets.' Kevin pulled a face. 'Can't see what all the fuss is about. I wouldn't be seen dead in any of them, they're really bizarre, all bright colours and stupid logos.'

Jackman sensed that Kevin's anxious face wasn't to do with the burglaries. 'And?'

'Another kid mugged for his hoodie, sir, early this morning. He's not badly hurt but he's terrified.'

'This is escalating, isn't it?'

'It has to be some well-organised group, sir. Both burglaries took place at the same time, but at opposite ends of the town.'

'Two teams working in unison?'

'Looks that way. They used the same method of entry, and the same MO. In both cases, they worked with split second precision — in and out in minutes, nothing else touched or taken.'

'And the boy who was mugged, Kevin? Could he identify his attackers?' Jackman had little faith in the answer.

'Black joggers, black hoodies. All over him in seconds, then away. He barely knew what had hit him.'

'And *did* they hit him?' Jackman was thinking of Denis Church.

'No, sir. Just used the element of surprise. They immobilised him, threw him to the floor, and ripped off his hoodie. Over in a flash.' He gave Jackman a resigned look. 'And of course, it took place in a spot not covered by CCTV.'

'Thank you, Kevin. I'll pass this on to Max and Robbie. It's their baby at present.'

'Shall I tell them, sir? On my way out?' He paused. 'I was going to offer to help them out from street level, if they need anything. That okay?'

Jackman nodded. 'Excellent idea.' He stood up. Time to let DI Jenny Deane know what Rory had said about the illegal steroid user, Trevor Maitland.

Jenny welcomed him in and closed her office door. 'Just so you know, the super has filled me in on the DS Evans, DS Blackwell problem.' She sat down. 'I'll do my very best to keep him so bloody busy that he doesn't know what day of the week it is, let alone even think about harassing Marie.'

'I'd appreciate that, I really would. We really don't need this on top of everything else that's happened these last few months.'

Jenny looked at him. 'Do you know Blackwell?'

He shook his head. 'Not well. Our paths have never really crossed.'

'Well, I do.' Her small mouth tightened.

She met Jackman's eyes. Jenny very different from Marie. She had cropped blonde hair, was tiny, wiry as a marathon runner, and a powerhouse of energy. He could never decide what age she was, she looked anywhere between twenty-five and forty, but he wasn't good at guessing ages. 'Would it be rude of me to ask how?'

'Not at all. I worked with him for a few months a long way back, and then again just before he was shipped out to the nether regions.' She frowned. 'He started off as a great guy, and a very good cop, but he changed, and I didn't like what he turned into.' She shuffled some files around on her desk. 'I'm praying he's changed again, or at least isn't the bitter, spiteful person I last had the misfortune to work with.'

'The super can't read him. Apparently he's saying all the right things, but warning bells are ringing.'

'I'll keep you posted about what I think.'

Jackman smiled. 'Please do. Now, I've got something for you regarding the steroids. It might keep your problem detective busy for a while.' He told her about the veterinary drugs and Trevor Maitland's death.

'Oh, sweet! A lead.' Jenny beamed at him. 'Guess who's going to be chasing that up tomorrow.'

Jackman stood up. 'Better get back. I need to make some headway with finding Denis Church's attackers. His poor parents are at their wits' end. Plus I have an unidentified dead boy, and not a single lead to who he is or where he came from.' He threw up his hands. 'Why the hell has no one come and asked where their son is?'

'There's more than 570 missing person incidents logged every day in this country, plus all those that are unreported, so it's not exactly surprising.' Jenny shrugged. 'I'm not being callous, it's just a fact.'

'And on that depressing note, I'll leave you.' Jackman made up his mind that Harry was not going to become a statistic in some unsolved missing persons case. 'And good luck with Blackwell.'

'Let's hope I don't need it.'

Jackman made his way back down the corridor feeling sorry for Jenny. She had inherited a very nasty problem indeed.

* * *

'PC Stoner?' came the voice over the phone.

Kevin recognised the voice immediately. 'Jim Cousins! What can I do for you?'

'I've got Artie here. You know, the guy from the Baptist church who tries to feed half the street kids with his travelling soup kitchen? Well, I showed him the photo and he might have something for you on your dead boy.'

Kevin had pulled on his jacket and was halfway out of the station before the call ended. This could be what he was looking for.

In ten minutes he was outside Jim's home for waifs and strays. As always, he was amazed at the size of the house. This time he'd ask Jim how he came to own such a property, but first there were more important things to talk about.

Artie was a scruffy man, hair too long, heavy stubble, craggy weathered skin. His clothes looked little better than those worn by some of his street kids. Kevin wondered if he did this deliberately, to try to make the kids feel at ease with him. In any case, he had a kind face and twinkling dark eyes, and if it wasn't for him, a lot of street people would be sleeping on an empty stomach.

'About six weeks ago, I was up near the old war memorial close to the entrance to Marlborough Park, and there were some new faces in the queue for a hot drink. One was a kid with a really pronounced Geordie accent.' Artie scratched his chin. 'I could be wrong, PC Stoner, but I think it was the kid you're trying to identify. He wasn't wearing the clothes that were in the description — he was pretty dirty — but I'm sure it's that lad who was killed.'

'Did you speak to him, Artie?' asked Kevin.

'I tried, but he wasn't in the mood to chat. Just told me he had only recently arrived in Saltern, thanked me for the drink and melted away.'

'Do you think you could give me the exact date of when you saw him? It could be important.'

Artie muttered as if to himself. 'Let's think. Wednesdays I cover the High Street, and I'm in the alleys on Thursdays, so . . .' He looked up. 'So the park entrance would be a Friday, six weeks back. You'll need to check the actual date on a calendar.'

Kevin reminded himself to do so.

'And another thing, none of my regulars saw him after that night. He'd told a couple of them he was planning on staying for a while before heading back up north again. Then he disappeared.'

'Not unheard of,' added Jim. 'These kids move off at a moment's notice if the fancy takes them.' He turned to Kevin. 'And I don't suppose you've any news on Biz and Jaz, my missing boys?'

Kevin shook his head. 'Sorry, mate. Nothing at all.'

'There's no news on them from the streets either, although word has it they are still the odds-on favourites for being the muggers who attacked that lad for his sneakers.' Jim looked unconvinced. 'I didn't get that impression myself, though. I thought they just seemed scared, wary.' He grinned. 'They're a volatile bunch, these runaways, most of them are damaged in one way or another. We can't blame them for not trusting us, can we?' He looked at Artie.

'Amen to that. Poor souls.' For a moment Artie looked sad, and then the smile was back. 'Still, we can't give up on them. Which reminds me, I need to get back and beg, borrow or steal some more food for tonight's round.' His smile widened. 'Forget I said *steal*, won't you, Officer?'

Kevin grinned back. He took a five pound note from his pocket and held it out. 'It's not much, but I guess every little helps.'

Taking it, Artie slapped Kevin's shoulder affectionately. 'You'd be surprised what I can do with that fiver, son. It'll make quite a difference to tonight's offerings.'

'Thanks for your help, Artie. Er, can I ask one more favour? I know you saw the photo, but would you be up to seeing the boy's body? If you could tell us whether or not he was definitely that Geordie lad, it might give us a clue as to where he came from.'

Artie nodded grimly. 'If you think it would help, of course. How about later today?'

'Shall I pick you up at the Baptist church at around two?'

'I'll be there.'

Kevin and Jim watched the big man leave.

'He's a saint,' murmured Jim. 'Every night, all weathers, high days and holidays, finding the homeless and getting hot drinks and food to them.'

'You don't do so badly yourself, Jim,' Kevin said. 'I don't know many people who'd be willing to open their home to a bunch of runaways, dropouts and jailbirds.'

'Correction. A bunch of lost souls.' Jim stared up at the big house. 'I was a jailbird once myself. I also felt I needed to do something to earn my inheritance.' He nodded toward the house.

Kevin tried not to smile. It looked as though he was going to get his answer without even having to ask the question.

'My uncle was Jacob Cousins,' Jim said. 'Does that name ring a bell?'

Kevin's eyes widened. '*The* Jacob Cousins? The Fenchester bank robber?'

'*Alleged* bank robber. He was acquitted on insufficient evidence, remember?'

'But he did it, didn't he?' Kevin said.

Jim grinned broadly. 'Oh yes. Without a doubt, though he never admitted it. And he already owned this house, long before the robbery — in case you thought it was the product of his ill-gotten gains.'

'Never crossed my mind,' said Kevin, though it had.

'Uncle Jacob was a shrewd businessman. He saw opportunities and chanced his arm, and he made a packet. He put it all into property. At one point, you know, he owned this whole row.' Jim pointed to the four houses in the row of big Georgian terraces.

'And he left you this place?'

'Jacob took a shine to me, back when I was a little kid. I think he liked the fact that I was a bad boy like him. He was the only one who visited me when I was in prison. He was like a dad to me, far more than my real father — the loser. I was really sad when he died in his early fifties.'

'And you inherited.'

'Everything. There was only the one house left, and some money. I was going to sell it and split the proceeds with my family but, you know, they were so piggin' hateful to me when I was a kid, I thought, no, I'm going to do some good with this place, and sod the relatives.'

'Jim!' A youth ran down the steps, 'Can you come? Ragga is kicking off. He's saying someone's been through his stuff.'

'Ragga doesn't *have* stuff! Even his clothes are from my donations cupboard.'

'He reckons he had a gold watch.'

'Heaven preserve us!' He raised his eyebrows. 'As if! Better go and sort this, Kev.'

Kevin smiled. 'No problem. Oh, by the way, do you get any complaints from the neighbours about the noise?'

'Haven't got any. This house is an end of terrace, and next door is empty. The old guy died intestate, so they tell me. It's been empty for months. The next house after that is split into flats, and there's some families living there with kids, but they're good as gold. There's a miserable old sod in the far terrace property that has a rant every so often, but other than him, we're sweet.'

A howl went up from inside the house.

'Think you'd better go before Ragga wrecks the joint.' Kevin raised a hand in farewell. It was time to check in and report what Artie'd said about the dead boy.

* * *

Marie put down the phone and thought for a moment, nibbling a fingernail. Daisy Cotterill had heard activity on the river at night, but this time she had sensibly stayed put behind locked doors. It all added to their growing suspicions about a smuggling operation. She scribbled down what Daisy had told her and went to find Jackman. His idea of getting some men down there at high tide under cover of darkness was seeming more and more like the thing to do.

'It'll be up to DI Jenny Deane now, as I've passed over this investigation to her, but I'm sure she'll be out there like a shot.' Jackman looked pleased at the thought. 'And she can take a certain new CID member with her. She says she's going to work his butt off, and I'm sure she will.'

Marie was trying not to think about Vic Blackwell, so she said, 'I suggest you pass on Daisy's details to her. And tell her not to underestimate our Daisy. She's no fanciful cop chaser, but a sensible woman with a good brain and an eagle eye.'

Jackman smiled. 'Ah, I see Charlie Button's got another member in his Daisy Cotterill fan club. You like her as much as he does!'

'Can't help it. And Charlie's right, her homemade ginger biscuits really are to die for.'

'Maybe I should go myself next time.' Jackman's smile faded. 'I've just heard that, apart from the two robberies that took place last night in the neighbouring towns, there were another three, scattered through the local villages. Max has alerted everyone in the Fenland Constabulary to let us know about any of these types of crime. We need to try and find a pattern.'

'Good. Has there been any reaction from the public to the photograph of Harry?'

'I've got Gary on that. He says nothing has come up that seems even remotely likely. I'm afraid our Harry's staying anonymous for a bit longer.'

'That steak dinner still bugs me,' Marie grumbled. 'And that feeling of déjà vu I had never surfaced again either. It's really annoying.'

'So is the fact that we've had to shelve Alistair Ashcroft, just when you'd got all that information together,' Jackman said.

'At least it's all here and ready to go when this clothing thing is tied up,' Marie said. 'We need a clear run at getting it off the ground, with as few distractions as possible.'

'You're right, but it's still irritating.' Before he could say anything further, Jackman's phone rang. 'Hello, Kevin. Yes, right. Really? Excellent! Would you like one of us to come with you after lunch? Perfect, and well done.' He replaced the receiver. 'Kevin's got a lead on Harry. It's not a name, but if Artie Ball does recognise the dead boy, it'll place him in Saltern on a specific date, and it might lead us to where he comes from.'

'It's a start, so that's good. Am I on morgue duty?'

'No. He said he'll handle it and report back. You and I have got to go and see Mr and Mrs Church with an update on the search for their son's attackers.'

Marie puffed out her cheeks. 'Oh shit! Sorry, didn't mean to say that, sir.'

Jackman stood up. 'Don't worry, I echo your sentiments entirely. But it has to be done.'

Marie thought that for once, the morgue would have been the better option.

* * *

Trez had gone out after breakfast, telling Mossy to wait for him, leaving him alone in the flat. Today he was supposed to watch Gordi's crew in action on the street, and he guessed that Trez's absence had something to do with that. Mossy felt edgy, and he wasn't sure why. He ought to be feeling great, especially as he had managed to see Alice. He had dared to kiss her, and she hadn't pulled away! He wanted to kiss her properly, spend time with her, go places and have fun, like normal people did. Well, he could have all that, if he could just make some real money. So far, he hadn't once stepped out of line. He aimed to be the perfect apprentice and make Trez believe in him. That way he could get out to work earlier, and earn that much needed cash, plus maybe a few perks on the side. His only secret was his cheap mobile phone, still safely hidden away in his mattress. The worst thing was having to leave it charging at night. Once, Trez had come into his room to check on him, and Mossy was afraid he'd do it again when his phone was on charge.

Mossy needed to be doing something, so he climbed onto Trez's exercise bike and started to pedal. Maybe it was because Trez had told him to go home. He had honestly believed he was being thrown out, and his dreams of taking Alice away had crashed and burned. He pedalled faster, thinking about Alice. He'd been so proud when she showed him her new coat. He, Mossy, had done that. He'd provided for her. For the first time he'd felt good about himself, and understood that there was more to life than thieving and lying. As soon as all this was over, Mossy intended to change his ways.

Trez finally came through the door to find his apprentice not lounging in front of daytime TV, but working out on the bike. To Mossy's delight, Trez smiled at him.

CHAPTER FIFTEEN

PC Kevin Stoner had accompanied Artie Ball to the tiny viewing room in the morgue where Harry's body lay.

Artie stood and looked down at the body for a long time. 'It's him, I was pretty sure from the photo, but actually seeing him, I know now.' He looked at Kevin, his eyes full of sadness. 'May I say a prayer for him? Would anyone mind?'

'Of course they wouldn't. Go ahead.'

Kevin stayed with him. After all, he was used to prayers at home. The familiar words brought some small comfort.

'Amen.' Artie looked up.

'Amen,' Kevin added. 'Thank you, Artie. At least we now know something about the lad. Our colleagues in the Newcastle area can give us a hand.'

'I lived in Gateshead for quite a while, so I know proper Tyneside Geordie when I hear it. I just wished I'd connected more with the lad,' Artie said sadly.

'You've done well to recall him at all after six weeks.'

'I know all their faces, Kevin. Never forget a single one.'

Kevin sensed a deep sadness driving Artie Ball out onto the streets at night with sustenance for the homeless and the runaways. But this wasn't the time to ask.

Artie was quiet and thoughtful on the drive back, then he said, 'I see a lot you know, traipsing the streets at night and working with these youngsters.'

'Me too,' said Kevin. 'Only people are inclined to run away from me.'

'I'm sure.' Artie chuckled. 'But I was going to say that I have a suspicion something is going on at the moment, something unusual. I sense an undercurrent among the homeless kids, especially the slightly older ones. I can't put my finger on it, and no one is talking, but it's there alright.'

'Isn't it because of those deaths? The mugging, and then that boy's body dumped in the rubbish?'

'Probably that's part of it, but there's something else,' Artie said. 'They whisper about it, but the words don't reach my ears.'

'Then keep listening, Artie, and please ring me if you hear anything definite.'

'Don't you worry, I'll be on the phone like greased lightning.'

Kevin stopped to let Artie out. 'Keep those eyes and ears open, Artie.'

'I will, and you find out who that young Geordie was and what happened to him, okay?'

Kevin nodded.

* * *

Dean got up late, wishing he had done things differently last night. Sure, he fancied the guy he'd brought home, but his heart wasn't in it. In the end, he'd ordered the kid a taxi and, at around two a.m., had almost pushed him out of the door.

He'd been too aware of Tommy just down the hall. Tommy himself had seemed a bit nettled by his entertaining someone else. What was that all about?

Tommy was straight, he knew, so why had their visitor put his nose out of joint?

Dean sighed. Tommy was different to the other youngsters he had groomed. It confused him, and he had no idea how to deal with it. He knew Tommy needed the money to escape from his parents. He was going to be an ace player and bring in plenty of work for the takers. He was a natural, with the added bonus of having a remarkable memory. The downside was that Tommy was naïve and trusting, and this game was not as harmless as Dean had made out. He had lied to Tommy when he said no one got hurt.

He could hear Tommy moving around in his room. What would he be wearing today? Tommy was obviously overwhelmed by his new wardrobe, and Dean saw how much he enjoyed picking out gems from the extensive collection of streetwear. Tommy had flair. The trouble was, he looked good, almost too good, and Dean knew he wasn't the only one casting an eye over Tommy Peel. He'd seen Darke on several occasions, staring at his new protégé from the shadows. It made Dean uneasy.

Dean opened the curtains, and stared back at the tangled bedclothes. With a grunt, he tugged the whole lot off and threw it onto the floor. He wanted to forget last night. He'd made a mistake, acting the way he had, and now he regretted it. He took fresh linen from a cupboard and began to make the bed.

He'd make it up to Tommy. He'd be especially attentive and show him he was really pleased with his work yesterday evening. He had to keep Tommy away from Darke. Dean remembered how much he'd admired Darke at the beginning, even the ruthless treatment he meted out to his underlings. Now he hated and feared the man.

The previous day, an angry Darke had waved a flyer in front of his face. It was a mugshot of a young man. "D'you know him?" Darke had shouted. Dean shook his head. He'd never seen that face before. Darke thrust the paper closer. Dean had asked him what the problem was, but Darke merely glowered at him. Dean now knew that the face belonged to a dead boy, found in Mayflower Lane. He wondered what that boy had to do with Darke.

Recalling this incident, it suddenly came to him. He didn't want Tommy to be one of Darke's boys at all. He would just have to find another way to help Tommy escape from his disintegrating home and earn some money.

Dean himself did it for the kicks. He had money enough. It was his way of rebelling against a controlling father. If his job with Darke fell through, he could go and work in the family business, which would please his dad no end. He even liked the rough street kids, all attitude and posture. After his privileged and protected childhood, he found these boys exotic. Tommy, on the other hand, had no other option. Then, when he'd had a taste of what it had to offer, he grew really keen. It had been he, Dean, who'd sold Tommy the dream. Now he wanted to take it away from him.

It wouldn't be easy.

* * *

After a gruelling hour with Denis Church's parents, Jackman and Marie were back at the station. All she had wanted was to be able to tell those grieving parents that they'd found the attackers. It wouldn't bring him back, but at least they'd have justice for their son. But she and Jackman could only offer promises, and in her heart of hearts, Marie wondered if they would ever find those two hooded killers. Indeed, one of them might already be dead.

'Excuse me, Sarge. Have you got a couple of minutes?'

Charlie Button brought her out of her reverie. 'Sure, Charlie. What's the problem?'

'Not a problem, exactly. Come with me.'

Charlie led her out to the car park, where he opened up the boot of his car and pointed inside.

Marie saw a large and very comfortable looking dog bed, along with a neatly folded pile of fleece blankets and colourful towels.

'My dad has just lost his old setter, Sarge. Said he couldn't bear to look at the empty bed any longer, so I thought . . .'

A smile spread across Marie's face. 'So you thought, "I bet Sheba would like that." Didn't you?'

'Well, Daisy doesn't have much money, does she? And Dad spent a packet on keeping his old girl warm and comfortable, so,' Charlie shrugged, 'what do you think?'

'I think you are a right big softie! It's a lovely thought, Charlie, and it's also an excellent reason to pop out to the marsh and make sure she doesn't get any more silly ideas in her head about turning detective.'

'My thoughts precisely, Sarge. Do you think I could shoot off now? It's lunchtime, and I haven't got anything to do at the moment. I won't be long.'

'You go. I'll square it with Jackman, don't worry. He's as worried about Daisy as we are.' With a twinkle in her eye, she gave him a look. 'And no drinking tea and eating ginger biscuits all afternoon. We have work to do, besides being boy scouts!'

Marie watched him go, and then went to tell Jackman what Charlie was up to. Jackman was just putting the receiver down.

'Another mugging — in broad daylight. This time it was a pair of Hybird X cargo pants and a matching baseball cap.' He shook his head. 'I think it's time we made the public aware of what's happening, try to deter kids from going out in this stuff.'

'That won't work,' said Marie. 'In fact it could egg them on. You know what kids are like. It'll be all, "Too chicken to wear your Hybirds, are yer?" You know how it goes.'

Jackman frowned. 'I guess you're right. And I suppose that if we give the stuff too much publicity, it could drive the resell market even higher. Sod it! It's a Catch 22, isn't it?'

'Who's dealing with it?'

'Max has gone out to see what uniform have got. Robbie's keeping a low profile until after his late night sortie. Doesn't want someone to spot him on the street and blow his cover.'

'Sensible.' After telling him about Charlie, Marie said, 'I'd better liaise with Newcastle about our dead Geordie kid. I've already sent them the photograph. It's a start, but it's still a long shot. There's a lot of people in Tyne and Wear.'

'Ah, but don't forget what Kevin said. Harry mentioned hanging around for a while before heading back up north.'

'Let's hope you're right.' Marie knew that if a missing person remained missing for too long, the odds on identifying them weren't good. Right now, they needed a bit of luck. It was long overdue.

* * *

Charlie didn't fancy walking too far carrying a big dog bed and a pile of bedding, so he drove round the winding lanes to a narrow track that brought him out at the back of Daisy's cottage. It was pretty overgrown — most likely only Daisy and the postman ever used it.

As he approached the back of her garden, he was surprised to see Sheba running towards him.

He stopped the car and got out. 'Hey, Sheba! What are you doing out on your own?'

The dog ran up to him, panting. He knelt down and saw that one side of Sheba's coat was matted with fresh blood. He managed to get hold of her and check to see how badly she was hurt, but he could find no injury.

Charlie's heart sank. What should he do? His first instinct was to rush into the cottage. He controlled the impulse and, as calmly as possible, put the dog safely into his car. What next? Oh yes, radio for backup. He pulled out his phone and told the station what he had found. He knew what he should do now — wait for assistance. "But, Daisy . . ." Charlie said aloud. She could be lying injured and bleeding. So Charlie hastened through the back gate and into the vegetable garden.

From here he could see a big black 4x4 parked up on the sea-bank, in a part of the bank where only waterways workers or the farmer who owned the fields were allowed access. Visitors were supposed to park in one of the car parks and proceed on foot, or chance the winding, narrow back lanes. This didn't look good. Charlie took a deep breath, wishing that backup was not so far away. It would take at least fifteen minutes for them to get out here.

Bending to keep from being seen out of the windows, Charlie made his way towards the old cottage. He had no idea how many people had arrived in that vehicle. He would need to assess the situation carefully before rushing in.

He inched slowly along the wall to where he saw a window slightly ajar. He stopped and listened.

There were movements coming from inside. They sounded as if whoever was inside was in another part of the cottage. Charlie listened for a few moments, and then chanced a look. The window gave into a small neat dining room. Empty. Charlie listened. He heard voices, and guessed that whoever was speaking was in the kitchen. He thought of the blood on Sheba's coat.

The window was set low, and, like the rest of the cottage, it was old. With the utmost care, Charlie eased it fully open, praying it wouldn't squeak. To his relief, it swung back silently. He pulled himself up and over the sill, and slid down into the room.

Charlie crept towards the door and listened. This time he was able to make out the words.

'Your miserable mutt has run off and deserted you, so I suggest you do as you're told, and stop being so stupid. Put the fucking knife down!'

What was going on in there? Whatever it was, Daisy obviously wasn't lying there unconscious. If these people weren't in full control of the situation, possibly he could catch them off guard. But first he needed to see what he'd be dealing with.

The dining room led into a small hallway. The lounge was directly opposite, with the kitchen to his right. He tiptoed past the dining table and chairs, and peered through the partially open door. He could make out the back of one man, but there had to be at least two of them.

Another man joined in, speaking calmly.

'Come on, lady. You don't stand a chance if we rush you. Surely you can see that? Put the knife down, and no one will get any more hurt than they are already. We only want to talk.'

'Then rush me. Go on! Do it!' Daisy said.

One of them had been hurt, then. That'd even up the odds. And Charlie had the advantage of surprise. He just had to get the timing right.

Suddenly he heard a scrabbling and a crash behind him, and the German Shepherd dog launched itself over the dining table, and brushed past him into the kitchen. Dammit! Charlie recalled his partly open driver's window. He had no option but to follow her.

In the tiny kitchen, Charlie found himself grappling with a man a good foot taller and a great deal stronger than he was. Sheba had taken down the injured man, and was standing over him, growling, with Daisy screaming at her not to bite him again.

Charlie's opponent lifted him off his feet and threw him against a wall. The air was forced from his lungs and he gasped in pain. He slid to the floor. The room faded in a fog, a confusion of shouting and noises in his ears. As he struggled to his feet, he saw the big man haul up his friend and push him out through the back door. Daisy, still holding the knife, her face scarlet, was holding Sheba back.

Charlie started to give chase, but a searing pain in his chest made him grab hold of the door frame. He guessed at a broken rib. Soon, the roar of a car engine told him he was too late anyway. The 4x4 was already careering along the top of the bank and heading along one of the farm tracks.

'Sorry,' he whispered. 'Sorry, Daisy.'

Daisy and Sheba were at his side. 'Sorry? You saved the day! You and this wild beast of mine. I couldn't understand why she left me, but she must have heard you and gone for help.' Daisy helped him back inside and sat him down. 'We need to get you an ambulance.'

'I've just cracked a rib, I think. I'll be fine.'

'Don't be a hero. You need checking over.'

Before he could stop her, she had found her phone and dialled 999.

'The police are already on their way, Daisy. Don't worry about an ambulance.'

'Rubbish. I saw how hard you hit the wall, and I think you caught the edge of the draining board too.'

Maybe she was right. The pain was pretty bad when he breathed in. 'What happened, Daisy?'

She cleared her throat. 'Er, I think I may have been a little bit stupid.'

'You went out again, didn't you?'

'Something like that.'

'Something *very* like that!'

Daisy nodded. 'But my girl does need her walks.'

'Okay, tell me the story.' He leaned on the table and put an arm against his damaged rib.

'I went back to where I found the evidence last time. When I heard that motor boat on the river, I knew I'd been fooled by those so-called bird watchers, so I wondered if I could find where the boat came in.'

'And did you?'

'I never found out,' she said with some irritation. 'Before I could even look, this big black Volvo thing came hurtling across the fields and chased me up onto the sea-bank. I was terrified!'

'You didn't run all the way back here, did you?'

'No, they got hold of me and bundled me into the car. Poor Sheba was left behind.'

'They brought you back here?' Charlie asked.

'They pushed me in through the door, but I managed to grab a knife from the knife block on the work surface. Then Sheba came bursting in and bit the shorter man.'

'I'm surprised they didn't kill her.'

'I called her off. She came to me, and then she jumped up and ran out. Now I know why.'

Charlie was beginning to feel sick. Breathing in was getting really uncomfortable. He really wasn't feeling good at all. Perhaps Daisy had been right about the ambulance. Then he heard a welcome sound. Two-tones, echoing across the fens.

CHAPTER SIXTEEN

They were to be debriefed. Trez summoned Mossy and Gordi's crew to meet him at the old deserted factory unit. Earlier, from the window of a café on the first floor of a half-empty department store, Mossy had observed the crew liberate a bagful of Hybird gear.

'You guys were amazing,' said Mossy, meaning it.

Gordi shrugged. 'It went well, I guess.'

'So where's the stuff now?' Mossy asked.

'Oh, it's a long way off by now,' Trez said flatly. 'It had already been transferred to a waiting moped before you and I finished that bloody awful coffee.' He looked at Mossy. 'As I said, it's a well-oiled machine, everything planned to the millisecond. You're right, these guys *are* good.'

'When do I get a chance?' Mossy asked eagerly.

'Not yet. You need practice, and we need to work out who you'll be teaming up with. That's why you're here now. I want you to do some test runs with each of them, Zak, Gordi and Bubbles, one by one. You'll find you work better with one of them, and that's who you'll go out with. Got it?'

Mossy was disappointed, he'd expected to be underway immediately. He hid his impatience. 'Sure, Trez, whatever you say.'

As they went through the motions, he found that he and Zak synchronised perfectly. Mossy had found his new partner.

Zak was skinny with a tanned complexion. He had enormous, long-lashed brown eyes. And the guy was smart. He didn't say much, but that was fine with Mossy. They were working partners, not bosom buddies. Mossy knew that if he were to be really good at this, he needed a perfect teammate, and Zak fitted the bill. Even Trez said he was pleased, but Mossy sensed that something was troubling his tutor. Trez was smiling, but his eyes said something else.

'Okay, lads. Now we show Mossy what it feels like.' He handed Mossy a jacket and some joggers. 'Swap your joggers for these, and put the jacket on over your T-shirt. And try not to duff the clothes up too much, there's about two grand's worth of gear there.'

This seemed nuts to Mossy. What he could do with two thousand pounds! He thought of Alice, perfectly warm in her charity shop anorak, and grew angry. The arseholes who wore this stuff deserved to get it nicked! One sodding jacket meant two months' rent on a flat for him and Alice. The idiots had it coming.

'Right. Now you just stroll over to the exercise mat,' Trez instructed.

Mossy knew what to expect, but even so, it came as a shock. Without knowing quite how it happened, he was on the deck, arms and legs being wrenched this way and that. The jacket and joggers were gone in what seemed like seconds. Mossy's pride was wounded, he'd thought he wouldn't be an easy target.

Mossy wondered how he'd feel if he were a rich kid, and his precious Hybirds had been taken. Most likely he'd be worrying about what to tell Mummy and Daddy. Well, tough!

'That's enough for today, I think.' Trez gathered up the clothing and handed it to Bubbles. 'And nicely done earlier, Gordi. Neat and efficient.'

'Thanks, Trez.' Gordi gave a kind of bow, and he and the others left the hall.

Mossy looked at Trez. The big man showed no signs of moving.

'Jump on the treadmill for a bit. I need to talk to you.'

Mossy went to the walking machine and turned it on. After a while, Trez came up and stood beside him. 'We have a problem. Well, you do.'

Mossy took a deep breath. Now what was coming? 'Me?'

'You do remember everything I told you about rules, don't you?'

'Yes, Trez, of course.'

'Well, it seems you've broken one of them.' Trez sighed. 'The thing is, those rules are there for a reason. We are very, very careful. If just one person steps out of line, it could jeopardise the whole thing.'

The phone! He'd found the phone. Mossy tried to think of an excuse.

'I'm assuming it's your girlfriend you're ringing.'

'She's not my girlfriend!' The term "girlfriend" seemed to demean their
relationship somehow. 'Sorry. She's a kid I know. Her dad beats her up, her mother forgets to feed her and she's at rock bottom. I care about her. I try and help her, that's all.'

Trez looked pensive. 'I see.'

'I'm sorry about the phone, honest, but I've only ever phoned her, no one else. I don't see how that could upset anything.'

'I never found your phone.'

Mossy stopped walking and stared at Trez.

'*I* didn't, but Darke knows about it.' He looked hard at Mossy. 'Seems you have a bug in your room. And before you say anything, I never knew anything about that either. I've since swept my flat, there's nothing else, just the one listening device. '

'Darke spies on us? What kind of creep is he?'

'The worst kind, believe you me. But he runs a tight ship, and he clearly didn't trust you. Unfortunately, you proved him right.'

'No, Trez! He's *not* right. I've done everything you've asked. Everything! I'm totally committed to this. A couple of calls to check on a friend, that's all. Surely that hardly counts as being untrustworthy?'

'I understand where you're coming from, kid, but Darke won't. He expects complete obedience. He called me earlier, and he wants you taught a lesson. And what he had in mind for you wasn't good. Not good at all.'

Now what? He was doing really great, then this.

Trez looked at him long and hard. 'Darke knows where Alice lives.'

Mossy swallowed. How did Trez know Alice's name? He'd never mentioned it.

'The way he looks at it is this — if Alice wasn't around, you wouldn't be distracted from your work.'

'Not around?' Mossy began to tremble. 'Oh, please, Trez! Help me. Darke mustn't hurt Alice! This is my fault, not hers! Let me talk to him.'

Trez gave a hollow laugh. It echoed around the empty room. 'You think you can just go and talk to Darke? Jesus, how naïve are you? No one reasons with Darke.'

'I have to try.'

'You really do care about her, don't you?'

'More than anything.' Mossy's voice shook.

'Do you really mean that?' Trez had an odd look in his eye. 'I mean, *really*?'

Mossy nodded. 'Yes, I mean it.'

He never saw the blow coming.

The punch knocked him clean off the machine. He heard a bone crack, and his whole head erupted in a volcano of pain.

Trez was picking him up from the floor. He set him down carefully, with his back against the wall. Then he left.

Mossy groaned, lost in a turmoil of pain and anguish. Oh, Alice! What had he done? Had he really put her in danger? He looked up and saw that Trez was back, carrying some ice wrapped in a towel, and a wedge of damp kitchen roll.

'You may not believe this, kid, but I may just have saved your neck — along with your Alice's.' Almost gently, Trez patted at the blood and pressed the towels against his nose. 'True, you won't look the same, but it's something you'll get over.'

Mossy still didn't understand. He coughed, and saw blood.

'I'm really sorry I had to do that. Darke wants to see you, and I want to be able to tell him you've learnt a hard lesson, but you're back on side. Do you understand? It'd be no good if I just took you in and said, "Here he is, Darke. I've told him off and he promises to be a good boy." It wouldn't wash, would it? Now we've something to show him.'

'And Alice?' Mossy coughed again. More blood fell onto the paper towel.

'We'll give him your phone, smashed to pieces. You'll tell him she was just some girl you liked to fuck. Tell him she's nothing, okay, and you make him believe that. Don't for one second think of giving him the shit you just told me. Then he might just forget about her. Got it?'

Mossy was starting to comprehend. Trez was on his side.

'Now, we need to get you patched up. I can't take you to the hospital, 'cause it'll go on record. I've got a mate who was an army medic. He takes care of Darke's boys' *problems*. He'll sort that nose out. Then, we pick up your phone from my flat, and we go visiting.' He looked at Mossy's mess of a face. 'I'm really sorry, kid. But if this works, you'll be one of Darke's boys very soon. Then you'll earn some big money, and one day you can run away with your Alice.'

'If she lives that long,' he muttered. 'Between her father and Darke, I'm not too sure about that.'

'I'll do you one favour, to say sorry for what I just did to you. You write her a note, and I'll see she gets it.'

'What should I say?' Mossy spoke as if he had a bad cold.

'Tell her to go stay with a friend or relative, say you're scared for her safety. Tell her to be in the Saltern Indoor Market, Wednesday, two weeks from today, at midday. You'll contact her then. Tell you love her, tell her anything you want, but never try to phone her again — for her sake as well as yours.'

Mossy managed to nod, and Trez helped him to his feet. Pain washed over him in waves.

All for some fucking overpriced clothes.

* * *

Marie stayed with Daisy Cotterill, and Jackman got into the ambulance with Charlie. Suspecting a pneumothorax, the medics put their foot down all the way to the hospital.

Jackman spent the journey alternately worrying himself sick about his young detective, and cursing Daisy for ignoring their warnings. Cursing himself, too, for not keeping a closer eye on a vulnerable woman living alone on the marsh. Though maybe "vulnerable" wasn't quite the right word for Daisy Cotterill. Not many people would have been quick-thinking enough to grab a knife to protect themselves.

Jackman watched Charlie being rushed into the A&E department, and then prepared himself to wait. The doors to the resus room closed behind the medical team. If only he could change places with Charlie! In the course of doing someone a good turn, Charlie Button had been thrust, all unsuspecting, into a life-threatening situation. He didn't deserve this.

'Jackman? What are you doing here?'

He looked up to see Laura Archer looking down at him with a concerned expression. Oh, God, how beautiful she was! A torrent of intense emotion swept over him. He'd told Marie that the two of them had separated before either got too badly hurt. It was a lie. It hurt him just to look at her. 'It's Charlie,' he said. 'Poor bloke waded in and took on someone twice his size.'

'Charlie Button? Oh no. Is he badly hurt?'

'Broken ribs, I think, and he's struggling to breathe.'

Laura sat down next to him, bringing with her a hint of the perfume she always wore. 'They'll help him, don't worry. He'll be fine.'

When she touched his hand, a shiver ran through him.

'I'm glad I saw you.' She paused. 'I was going to ring. I . . . I wondered if we could have a drink, sometime? I'd like to talk to you.'

Those blue eyes of hers. They looked serious. Sad.

He wanted to say no. He couldn't cope with more hurt. Instead, he said, 'Of course. How about this evening? I don't know what time I'll be free, but I could ring you.'

'That's great. I'll see you later then.' She stood up. 'Thank you. And give Charlie my love when you get to see him, won't you?'

'I will.' He watched her go. What had he just done? What did she want to talk about? And why on *earth* had he agreed to meet her? They had called it a day. He was trying hard to forget.

'DI Jackman?' He looked up. A doctor was approaching him. She was smiling.

He stood up. 'How is he? Can I see him?'

'I'm Gina Bentley, one of the emergency medical doctors. Charlie has got a small pneumothorax caused by a broken rib. I've released some of the air around his lung through a needle and the lung is now expanding nicely. He shouldn't need a chest drain, but we're going to keep an eye on him for tonight. He has three broken ribs and he's going to be in a lot of pain.'

'But he's in no danger?'

'As I said, we'll monitor him carefully, but hopefully he'll be fine. You can go in now, if you'd like to?'

Jackman thanked her and followed her swishing ponytail into the resus room.

Charlie looked much better, and he was breathing easily.

'That'll teach you to wait for backup in future, Detective!'

'Sorry, sir.' Charlie looked more like a scruffy schoolboy than ever. 'But I thought she might be injured. I couldn't leave her, not knowing what had happened.'

'It's alright,' Jackman said gently. 'I'd have done the same. How are you feeling?'

'Like I took on King Kong.'

Jackman found a chair and sat beside Charlie's bed. 'Does King Kong have a description, by any chance?'

'Around six foot four, heavily built, shortish salt-and-pepper wavy hair, and he was wearing a black zip-up anorak and indigo jeans. Didn't notice his footwear.' Charlie stopped and took a few breaths. 'The other guy was around my height, fair hair, stocky. Sheba had given his right arm a nasty bite. He had a navy blue bomber jacket on, and sort of dark trousers. That's all I can remember. It was chaos in there. I'm just sorry I couldn't chase after them.'

'That's fine for starters. You can take heart from the fact that if you hadn't turned up when you did, Daisy might be dead.'

'They said they just wanted to talk to her. I heard that much.'

'Yes, but most likely to get her to put the knife down, Charlie, then I doubt they'd have done too much talking.'

'You're probably right, sir.'

Jackman saw he was tiring, and clearly in pain. 'Who can I call for you, Charlie?'

'My dad is on his way, sir. The nurses rang him. You get away, sir, I'm fine now, honestly.'

'No, I'll wait until your father gets here, then I'll ring Marie and get her to pick me up.'

Charlie looked relieved. For all his brave face, shock was beginning to set in. 'I guess Daisy's scuppered DI Deane's plans for an obbo on the marsh. They'll probably move to a different location after this.'

'Maybe, maybe not. They'll probably lie low for a while, but they'll know our resources are limited and, let's face it, we have no real evidence that anything is going on at all, only one old woman's suspicions, and the fact that two men threatened her. Could have been over anything.'

'Don't be too hard on Daisy, sir'

'I could happily throttle her, Charlie Button!'

'Please, boss. I don't want her thinking I got hurt because she didn't listen to what she was told. You should have seen her with that knife! She's a really feisty lady. It was a case of put your money where your mouth is, guys, and bring it on!' Charlie started to laugh, and then thought better of it. 'Oh shit! That hurts.'

'Then don't laugh.'

Charlie took a few breaths. 'Oh, I forgot. My car's still out there.'

'Don't fret. If you give me the keys, we'll get it taken back to the station.'

'In my jacket pocket, wherever that is.'

Jackman felt beneath the bed and found a plastic sack containing Charlie's effects, including the keys.

'And the stuff in the boot is for Daisy. Marie knows about it.' Charlie groaned. 'This pain is awful.'

Just then, a nurse arrived and checked his monitors.

'He's hurting, nurse. Can you up his painkillers?' Jackman asked.

She nodded, and smiled at Charlie. 'The doctor'll be back shortly, and we'll make you more comfortable. And then we'll get you moved to somewhere a bit quieter.'

She closed the door behind her. It was immediately opened by a tall man who looked at Charlie anxiously.

'My dad,' said Charlie. 'Now you get away, sir. You've got more important things to do than babysit me. And please tell the others I'm sorry to let them down when we're so busy, I'll be back as soon as I can.'

'Oh no, you won't!' Jackman said. 'Those ribs won't heal overnight, young man. You're officially stood down until further notice.'

'Glad to hear it.' Charlie's father nodded emphatically. 'He's coming home with me when he's let out of here, and I'll hear no arguments.'

Jackman smiled. 'Perfect.' He shook the proffered hand, told Charlie he'd keep in touch and went out to phone Marie.

Waiting for Marie outside, in the cold, damp afternoon, he thought about Laura Archer.

CHAPTER SEVENTEEN

Kevin Stoner was officially off duty. Finding himself at a loose end, he decided to take a walk around to Jim Cousins's "House of Fun." Now he knew how an ex-con had come to own a big, flashy terraced house. It was a bit of a relief. He was very impressed with the work that Jim, and Artie, were doing for the homeless and the runaways, all the deprived kids of Saltern. He'd really like to help them, if he could. There was something in the way Jim handled his extended family of undesirable youths that Kevin truly admired. How did he manage?

As he neared the house, he saw Jim talking to a skinny, agitated man, wearing an old-fashioned suit and tie, who was gesticulating angrily at him.

Kevin crossed the road and approached them. 'Can I help?'

'Mr Hawkins here tells me he can hear the kids yelling, even when he's got his doors and windows closed. I'm trying to tell him that my boys are all well in order this evening. No fights, no arguments, and no loud music,' Jim said.

'Your house is a disgrace! All those terrible delinquents coming and going at all hours! It's not fair on the peaceable folk who live close by,' the man said.

There was the occasional minor riot, Kevin knew, but in general Jim had them well under control. It was toe the line, or bugger off. Most kids accepted this. It was a small price to pay for a roof over their head, a clean bed and decent food. 'Sir,' he said, 'Mr Cousins does a remarkable job for Saltern. Without him, there'd be a lot more vulnerable kids on the streets and a lot more petty crime. Plus, I don't think people come and go when it's late. There's a curfew in place.'

'Vulnerable! Vermin, more like!'

Kevin's eyes narrowed. Beside him, he sensed Jim grow tense. Maybe the guy had a point about the noise, but Kevin didn't like the way he was putting it over. This Hawkins man sounded almost threatening. Kevin produced his warrant card. 'Okay, sir, my name's PC Kevin Stoner. Perhaps you'd like to take me inside your house and let me hear this unacceptable noise for myself?'

'No, I would not. The least you can do is take my word for it as a law-abiding citizen.'

'I don't disbelieve you, sir, but I can't help you if I don't know exactly what I'm dealing with, can I?' He used his most reasonable tone. 'Come on, Mr Hawkins, two minutes of your time?'

The man seemed to think about this, then he stomped back to his house, leaving the front door open. With a wink at Jim, Kevin followed him inside.

From the outside, Hawkins's house looked delightful, all old world charm. But the interior had been ruined — utterly bastardised. All the original period fittings had either been removed or replaced, leaving a jumble of mismatched furniture and knick-knacks. They went into several of the rooms, but apart from the distant hum of traffic from the main road and a barking dog, Kevin couldn't hear anything.

Mr Hawkins looked decidedly put out. 'Well, he's stopped them, hasn't he? The minute we came inside, he'll have gone and shut them up. This is always happening. It's not fair that I should have to live with this. This was a nice street with decent people in it, till he moved in and started collecting riffraff.'

'That's a bit harsh, sir. He runs a pretty tight ship, all things considered, and he keeps a lot of kids out of trouble and gets them into proper work again. I'm sure they do kick off occasionally, but some of these youngsters have been very badly treated, they deserve a second chance. Can't you find it in your heart to tolerate the odd outburst, and be grateful that someone is trying to help them?'

'Nice sermon. You sound like a bloody bishop, not a policeman.'

Kevin thought of his father, and blanched.

Hawkins marched back to the door and flung it open. 'Thanks for nothing.'

'I'm sorry I can't help you.' He handed the man his card. 'If it happens again, phone me. I'll get here as soon as possible.'

Hawkins said nothing. The door slammed shut behind Kevin with a resounding bang.

Kevin made his way back to Jim's place.

'Maybe it's the phases of the moon, but Hawkins goes on the rampage roughly once a month, and it never coincides with any of my kids having a fliddy. I don't know why he does it.' Jim raised his hands. 'I'd be the first to apologise if any of my lodgers got out of control, but I absolutely don't tolerate bad behaviour. Two strikes, and you're out.'

'I know, and no one has ever called to complain,' Kevin said. 'What do you know about Hawkins? Is he just a professional moaner? He seems pretty vitriolic.'

'No idea. He's lived there all his life. The house was his father's before him. More than that, I can't tell you.

I've never had a civil word out of him, the grumpy old git.' Jim grinned. 'So what can I do for you this time, Kev?'

Kevin told him he was simply there to offer his help, if there was anything he could do.

'That's a really nice gesture, Kev, and don't think I don't appreciate it. You have to understand, though, that a lot of these kids really are messed up, and they haven't had good experiences with the police. I'm not sure how they'd react to a copper being around.'

'I thought of that. I rather hoped I could convince them that we really do have their best interests at heart.'

'*You* do, mate. Sadly, that's not universal.'

Kevin knew that to be true. 'Well, I meant it, so if you think there's anything I can do, let me know.' He gave Jim a gentle cuff on the shoulder. 'Don't want to upset things by adding a cuckoo to the nest.'

'You're a good bloke, Kevin. If I can think of some way around it, you might just have a point. These kids didn't trust me to begin with, but they came round in the end. Maybe we can re-educate them.' He frowned. 'The only reason I baulk at giving it a try right now is that with all this bad stuff going on, what with missing and dead boys, they might think the police have stuck a mole in here.'

Kevin nodded. 'You're right. Bad timing. Still, there's no time limit on the offer. Once this investigation is sewn up, I'll ask you again. Deal?'

Jim stuck out his hand. 'Deal!'

* * *

Tommy and Dean ate an early supper and discussed their plans for the evening. Dean thought it might be a good move to pay a casual call on a couple of the bars where collectors were known to hang out, just to get Tommy used to new places and faces.

Tommy took the plates into the kitchen and stacked them in the dishwasher. His hand brushed the cutlery rack and his finger caught on an upturned paring knife.

'Ouch! Shit!' He drew his hand back, and saw that blood was already streaming down his middle finger.

Dean ran over. 'Hold it up. I'll get a cloth.' He opened a drawer, produced a white tea towel and wrapped it tightly round Tommy's raised finger. 'That'll need stitches.' He bit his lip. 'Oh. I can't take you to the hospital. Darke likes all his people treated, er, privately.' He ruffled Tommy's hair. 'It's okay, don't worry. I'll get the car keys.'

A few minutes later, they drew up outside a small house on the edge of Saltern. 'Let's go see Martin. He's just the guy when you're in a fix.'

Martin Haverstock was a giant of a man, with a weathered face and a shock of wavy grey hair worn slightly long. In his well-worn Six Nations rugby shirt, he didn't give the slightest indication of being a medical man. Tommy wasn't sure about this at all.

'Wait in the lounge, Dean. I'm just finishing up with another wounded soldier.' Martin's voice was deep, with a hint of a Scottish accent. 'Two minutes.'

'Is he for real?' Tommy said.

'Don't be fooled. That man was a frontline field medic, specialising in dealing with trauma in hostile situations.'

'So what's he doing here?'

'Working for Darke. He, er, fell foul of the law at some point.'

Tommy got the message. 'How big is Darke's network, for heaven's sake?'

'Even I don't know.' Dean sounded grim. 'I thought I did, but now I'm not so sure.'

The worried note in Dean's voice wasn't lost on Tommy. For the first time, Dean seemed unsure of himself. What was that all about? Before he could ask him, the "surgery" door opened, and two men stepped out.

'Thanks, Martin, much appreciated. You're a good man in a crisis.' This was the older of the two.

'Ought to be, don't I?'

Dean raised his eyebrows and addressed the speaker. 'Evening, Trez. I see your lad's in the wars as well.'

'Ah, Dean. Got a moment? Outside?' He turned to his companion. 'Sit. I'll be a couple of minutes, that's all.'

Eyes on the floor, the young man with the battered face did as he was told. Dean and the stranger went outside, closing the door behind them.

* * *

Apart from the smiles for the medic, Trez looked almost grey with worry, something Dean had never seen before. Until now, Trez had always been the same, a rock, and a scary one, a steely, solitary man. Dean wondered what had happened. Did it have something to do with that injured boy? One thing was for sure, Dean wouldn't be asking. Trez was Darke's right-hand man, and anything he said would go straight back to Darke. And right now, Dean was planning to remove the best spotter the organisation had ever had.

'We're on our way to see Darke,' Trez said.

The words hung in the air like an impending thunderstorm.

'Bad luck,' said Dean lightly.

'I need to ask you something, but I don't want it going any further. Understand?'

Dean grew wary. This didn't sound like Trez. 'Okay.'

'I know you're not my best buddy, Dean, but you're the only one I think I can talk to. I'm worried about Darke. When we started all this, I knew the game plan, knew the whole strategy, and it was a bloody good one. Now, I'm thinking I'm only seeing part of the picture, and I don't like being held back on.'

'Kept in the *Darke*?' said Dean flippantly. 'Sorry.' He became serious. 'I know what you mean. I feel the same.

He used to confide in me, now he doesn't trust me at all. He watches me and my boys. I've seen him.'

'He's bugged my flat.'

'What? You? Of all people! What's going on?'

'I wish I knew,' Trez said. 'But some of my lads, one crew in particular, think he's got another operation going, maybe two, and he doesn't want one hand knowing what the other is doing.'

'What do you think he's into?' Dean asked. 'Drugs?'

'Maybe. But recently, boys have been disappearing. I'm thinking some kind of trafficking.'

Of course! The boys that had been paid off! Suddenly it all fell into place. Had they been sold? For what? If it were true, this was bad, really bad. Selling boys for the sex trade was sick.

'Looks like you're thinking what I'm thinking,' Trez said sombrely.

Dean's thoughts flew to the beautiful boy sitting waiting for him in Martin's lounge. He knew Darke was watching him. Shit! He'd have to move fast. But how much should he share with Trez? The answer was written all over Trez's face. He was genuinely worried about what was going on.

'He's watching Tommy, Trez, I know it. I'm regretting ever recruiting him. He's a great kid, and I've promised him the earth. Now I want to get him as far away from Darke as possible.'

'I know what you mean,' Trez said glumly. 'I feel the same about that little toerag in there. Sure, the lad's in no danger of being sold for his looks, even less now, but I like him, and I don't want Darke getting his hands on him. Sounds funny coming from me, but he actually has some morals.'

Dean was flabbergasted. 'Sorry to say it, but you've always been so hard on your boys. Why the change of heart?'

Trez kicked at the ground with the toe of his boot. 'You tell me. Maybe it's just things Darke's been saying recently. Like he was going to remove the kid's girlfriend from the area, just so he'd stop trying to contact her. And when he said "remove," I wasn't sure what he meant.' His brow was a mass of furrows. 'She's just a sixteen-year-old kid whose parents treat her badly, that's all. What kind of threat can she be?'

'So what are you going to do?' Dean asked.

'I don't know.' Trez shook his head. 'I've got a lot tied up with Darke, and if things were as they used to be, we wouldn't be having this conversation. But right now, I'm having serious doubts about him.'

'He scares me,' Dean said.

'You want to know a secret, Dean? He scares me too.'

* * *

Mossy was trying hard to pretend he wasn't in pain, but it wasn't working. The medic had said the swelling needed to go down before he could see if his nose needed resetting. He had taped the small cut on the bridge and given him some paracetamol for the pain. He'd checked Mossy's breathing and declared that he'd live. Big deal. He glanced across the room at the other guy and realised he knew him.

'Tommy? Tommy Peel?' Mossy said.

'Mossy! Jesus! What happened to you?'

Mossy had once said that the only person he trusted was Alice. But he'd forgotten about Tommy Peel.

'I haven't seen you for years. Apart from the nose, are you okay?' Tommy asked.

Mossy looked at the bloody towel and realised that if Tommy was here for treatment, then he had to be one of Darke's boys. Tommy. But he was such a good guy . . .

It was seven years ago. Other kids were always ganging up on Mossy, but this time his attackers were vicious. He was on the ground when out of the blue, he heard someone shouting, "Leave him alone and sod off!" Tommy Peel, only three or four years older than Mossy, rushed over and began kicking at them until they gave up and ran away. He helped Mossy to his feet and gave him a handkerchief for his bloody nose.

Then Tommy stayed with him for over half an hour, listening to him until he stopped whimpering. It was the first time anyone had been kind to him, and Mossy had never forgotten. He even kept the handkerchief, until it eventually fell apart.

'Are you working for Darke? Are you a spotter?' Mossy whispered.

Tommy nodded. 'I guess you're a Taker, Mossy.'

'If I survive the apprenticeship.' Mossy tried to laugh and winced in pain. Then he suddenly remembered what Trez had said. They were supposed never to have any connection with the guys who carried out the other side of the business. 'We shouldn't be seen talking, Tom. It's dangerous.'

'I know. But who hurt you?'

'That guy who was with me. My boss, Trez. He says it's for my own good.'

Tommy laughed bitterly. 'How did he come up with that one then?'

'It's complicated. Maybe he's right, I dunno. Tommy, where are you staying? Just in case things get really bad.'

Tommy gave him the address.

'But for fuck's sake, don't just turn up,' Tommy hissed. 'You'd be in worse trouble than ever.'

'Don't worry, I won't. Actually, I *can't*. I'm not a free agent.' He lowered his voice to a whisper. 'Don't tell me you're living with the tooth fairy?'

Tommy smiled at this. 'I am, but he's not so bad, actually. I'm not free to come and go either, well, not yet.' He sat forward. 'So where are *you*?'

'Over the newsagent's in Pond Street. I've got a room in Trez's flat. He's very strict, but he's not all bad.'

'What? After doing that?' Tommy nodded to Mossy's nose. 'You're very generous.'

'As I said, it's complicated.'

Martin came out of his surgery and they stopped talking.

'I'm not sure where Dean is,' Martin said, 'but I'm sure you'll be able to tell me what happened. Come through, and let me see the damage.'

With an almost imperceptible nod to Mossy, Tommy followed Martin inside.

CHAPTER EIGHTEEN

Bright neon lights announced the bar Max and Robbie had chosen for their first excursion into the world of men's streetwear fashion.

'Shall I bring you back a small snifter of something?' Robbie asked.

'Rosie'll hang me out to dry if I go home stinking of booze, but thanks for the thought.' He paused. 'And don't you get tanked up either. You don't have a very good relationship with alcohol, do you? Bit of a lightweight, as I recall.'

'One whiff of a cork and I'm singing rugby songs.' Robbie grinned sheepishly. 'Well, I'm on duty now. Wish me luck!'

'I'll be here waiting for you, taking a few snaps to while away the time.' He nodded to the camera on his lap. 'Message me or ring if you need anything, won't you?'

'Got it.' Straightening his shoulders, Robbie entered the bar.

Max was right. He was no drinker, but he had to keep up appearances. Why go to a bar if you didn't want to drink? This was a very different kind of undercover operation than the ones he was used to. Usually, you tried to blend in and not draw attention to yourself. On this occasion, it was the other way around. Well, he was pretty sure the Hybird X jacket would do the job.

He made his way to the bar and occupied an empty stool. The only drink he did enjoy was a Tom Collins. Trouble was, if made well, they could be pretty powerful. He'd have to pace himself.

Robbie glanced around nonchalantly, and ordered his drink.

While he waited for it, he noticed someone watching him. The stranger gave him a slight nod. This was his contact, the friend of Josh who was prepared to help him integrate. He nodded back, turned to the bartender and paid for his cocktail.

The contact clapped him on the shoulder. 'Hi, Ryan! Glad you could make it. What d'you think so far?'

'Okay, I guess,' Robbie, or "Ryan," said, 'but I haven't tried the drink yet. I'll let you know.'

The young man, Benjamin, who liked to be called Bez, grinned at him. 'Probably pretty crap. There aren't too many connoisseurs in here. But the company's great. Wanna meet some people?'

'Love to, but give us a minute, Bez. I'll just get my bearings.'

'Sure. Come over when you're ready. I'm with a couple of mates over there.' He indicated a table where three fashionably dressed men sat laughing. Bez muttered, 'I've paved the way. Told them you're an okay guy.'

'Thanks,' Robbie murmured, then in a louder voice said, 'Nice to see you, mate.'

Robbie surveyed the room. His jacket was already getting plenty of attention. Josh had provided him with the perfect bait. He drew in a breath. It was going to be a long evening. This was just not his kind of place. He wished he could have brought his girlfriend, Ella, but the clientele here was almost all male. He sipped his drink and grimaced. Bez had been right. It was crap. At least he wouldn't be tempted to drink too much.

* * *

Jackman had only intended to have one drink with Laura, but it was now almost ten thirty and they were still sitting together at a corner table in the lounge of the Saltern Arms.

For once, he wasn't thinking about his latest case, or next day's daily orders. No dead boys crept into his mind. All he was thinking about was Laura Archer and what he still felt for her.

'Bottom line, I suppose, is that I need to know if you're still happy about the decision we came to.' She looked into his eyes. 'And please be brutally honest.'

'I was never happy with it, Laura, and nor were you, but we couldn't see a way through, could we?' He felt caught in her blue gaze.

She looked down. 'The thing is, I'm even more miserable and unsettled than I was before.'

For a brief moment he was afraid. He couldn't be hurt again. Or could he? Did he dare? 'What are you saying, Laura?'

She hadn't looked away. 'I'm saying that I think we made a mistake. We made too much of the potential pitfalls, when what we should have done was seize the moment. I still love you, Jackman, and that's not going to change. I want to try again. Other people with far more demanding careers than we have, manage to make a long-term relationship work. So why can't we?'

Jackman swallowed. It was everything he dreamed of, and the thing he most dreaded.

'Are you really happy? Now you're alone again?' she asked.

He didn't know how to answer. 'I've always been a loner, Laura. I still love you, and I never stopped, but I'm scared that sharing my life and my job with you won't be enough. For you, that is.'

Laura said nothing. Then, 'And what if I'm prepared to take that risk?'

'And if we come to the same point that we did before?' he countered.

'Then at least we'll have tried. If it goes wrong again, I'll walk away and not look back, but at least I'll be able to say I gave it my best shot.' His hand was on the table, and she covered it with hers. 'I'm not talking marriage. I'm just asking you to consider trying again, to see if we can make it work for us.'

Her touch sent a shiver through him. She was right. He wasn't happy. And he did love her. He just wasn't as sure as she was that his work wouldn't get in the way.

'We didn't have the best start, did we? With Alistair Ashcroft threatening everything you loved.' Her hand still rested on his.

'That threat hasn't gone away, Laura. Until we find him, he'll always be hanging over us. What terrifies me is if he does come back, you could be in grave danger.'

'And he could be dead or in another country. Then we'd have wasted our lives living in baseless fear of him. In that case, he'd have won.' Her eyes were fastened on his. 'You can't let him rule your life, my love. If the worst happens, we'll deal with it, or else we could just be happy.'

'And your work? The papers you want to write? The lectures?'

'We'll have to make compromises, I know, but not like before. We were trying to set up a series of rules and regulations. We couldn't live that way.'

'You mean this, don't you?' New hope was rising in him, a new life drawing him on.

Laura nodded.

Jackman took a deep breath. 'Okay then, let's give it six months, as from today. In six months' time we'll come back here, sit in these same seats and talk again. Let's see what happens.' He breathed out. Beautiful Laura had cleared a path. The tunnel that was Jackman's life opened up into daylight. She was right, they needed to try and see for themselves what they were capable of. He thought of the people who had been close to him, and who he'd lost. Yes, life was too short to waste a moment of it.

'Really?' Her eyes shone.

'Really. Now drink up, and let's go home.'

* * *

Robbie flopped into the passenger seat with a loud sigh, and Max drove off. After about half a mile, Max parked the car and switched off the engine. 'Okay, Mister Hybird. Spill the beans.'

'It's too weird for words!'

'Just give it your best shot, Goofy! I need to know that sitting for three hours in a fart-filled car has actually been worthwhile. I mean, I have a lovely wife, a *heavily pregnant* lovely wife, just two miles away!'

Robbie laughed. 'It was worth it alright, mate! I learnt a lot.'

'Well, that's something. Okay. Shoot.'

'There are three main meeting places for guys that are obsessed with Hybird X gear. Thanks to Josh, we hit on one of them tonight.' He touched Max's arm. 'And Bez was brilliant. The fella should join RADA.'

'Good, go on.'

'The whole thing is bizarre. Most of these guys eat, sleep and dream Hybird. It's more like a cult than a fashion trend. And I'm really starting to understand what the thieves have tapped into. It's massive, Max! Someone is making a fortune out of it and I've picked up a few hints about how it works!'

Max stuck up his thumb. 'So our idea is really going to work?'

'Listen up, mate. This next bit sounds like some urban myth, but it's not all rumour. Someone in Saltern-le-Fen is running an organisation that seems like it comes straight out of Charles Dickens. He teaches young lads to thieve, in exchange for shelter and a small wage. And this bit is just rumour, but there's supposed to be a much darker side to it. It seems most of the kids who join this thieves' school disappear after a while.'

'You say the kids disappear? That *is* worrying. Who told you this?'

'A couple of half-cut guys who were very happy to let me buy them drinks. It's not talked about openly, but there's a group of younger collectors who love their Hybirds but are getting savvy to the dangers involved. Then there's another set of guys. These seem to be in a different league altogether. They've clearly got money, and they wear the gear like high fashion clothing. I saw a couple of guys who could have stepped straight off the catwalk.' He shook his head. 'Plus I spent most of the night surrounded by young men who couldn't take their eyes off my jacket. I even had an offer of five grand for it!'

'Bloody hell! I hope you got his number.'

'I was reliably informed that I'd be a mug to accept the offer, as the jacket was a very rare grail and worth double that amount.' Robbie yawned. 'I bet Josh didn't know that much.'

Max looked down at his camera. 'I think I got a picture of your two models going in. I thought they looked too smart to be wearing streetwear, but one had some cracking Hybird gear on his back. Even I liked it.' He flicked through shots he'd taken, then handed the camera to Rob. 'These two?'

'That's them.'

Max stretched. 'So, what next?'

'Report to the boss and see what he thinks. There's still the other two venues to check out, and I suggest we do it pretty soon. Bez says he's willing to play the old mate card again.'

Max thought of Rosie, and sighed. 'The things we do to keep the peace, eh? Another two nights away from the one place I really want to be.'

'I can go alone, mate. I'm not exactly walking into the lion's den. I've got the lie of the land now, and I know what to expect. I can always call for backup if something goes wrong. You stay with Rosie. She needs you more than me.'

'No way are you going off playing the Lone Ranger, chum! Sod that for a game of soldiers.'

'Well, since poor old Charlie Button's out of the game for a while, I guess I'll have to give in . . . wait. Kevin Stoner! He'll take me! Betcher he would! You back off, Max. You have every reason to. I'll ask Kev what he thinks.'

Max was both pleased and disappointed. It was their idea, their baby, and he wanted to see it through. Rosie would understand. After all, she was a copper too. But this was such a special time for them. 'Ask him, but if it's a problem, I'm there, okay? No arguments, and that's final.'

Robbie saluted. 'Received and understood. Now, let's go get a few hours' sleep. I'm knackered.'

CHAPTER NINETEEN

The murder room was packed with officers but unnaturally quiet.

Marie watched Jackman, in order to avoid looking at the new officer — DS Vic Blackwell — but also because Jackman seemed so different.

She looked closer. She wasn't mistaken. She was looking at the old Jackman. His back was straighter, his face alive. Then it dawned on Marie. She drew in a long breath. Laura Archer! It had to be! They were the perfect couple, and if they could just get a handle on how to manage their respective workloads, Marie could see a very satisfactory relationship evolving.

Jackman began the meeting. Yes, even his voice was stronger and more assertive. Marie wondered what the others would make of this sudden transformation. Knowing most of the coppers in the room, they'd probably just think he got lucky the night before.

'Okay. First off, I've spoken to the hospital this morning, and Charlie Button should be allowed home later today, as long as there's no deterioration in his lung function.'

There was a general murmur of relief.

'But he's by no means fit for duty, so he'll be off for a while, and we'll need to pick up anything still on his desk.' He looked up. 'Gary? Will you deal with that please?'

Gary Pritchard nodded. 'Got it, boss.'

'Next, please welcome DS Vic Blackwell to Saltern. He'll be working with DI Jenny Deane on the steroids investigation, as well as other general duties.' He nodded coldly to Blackwell. A few of the newer officers, who knew nothing about Vic Blackwell's past, gave him a smile or a short greeting.

Impassive, and without speaking, Blackwell gave a stiff bow.

'Now, about the steroids. I'll hand over to DI Deane to fill you all in on the progress so far. Then before we get bogged down in the Hybird thefts, she and her team might like to go and press on.' He stood aside for Jenny Deane.

While Jenny was speaking, Marie focused her attention on Jackman. She'd been hoping this would happen for so long. She just prayed that it was going to last this time, even if just for the team. They needed Jackman working at full throttle again. They were lost without his confidence and his sharp mind. His new attitude would give them all a boost, even her. Jackman couldn't make Blackwell go away, but he was clearly trying to cut down any contact between them to a minimum. She couldn't really ask for more than that. She sneaked a glance at Blackwell, and saw him looking intently at his new DI. She fervently hoped they could keep it that way.

Jackman was back again. 'Before we split up, two things. As you all know, we're going to be helping Fenchester with the Alistair Ashcroft investigation. This has been temporarily put on hold until we've tied up our present cases, but, and this is a big but, we are still following Fenchester's progress reports closely. As soon as the Hybird thefts have been sewn up, we'll be launching a major drive to find Alistair Ashcroft, or at least what happened to him. There's been nothing seen or heard of him since he was injured and we were unable to apprehend him. There has to be a trail, and this time around, we are going to find it.'

There was a rumble of talk. Jackman held up his hand.

'Also, the dead boy, the one we're calling Harry. We now know he comes from Newcastle. The boys up there have sent us three possible names of missing youngsters that could fit the bill, and we think we might have a match. They're going to be getting a DNA sample from the mispers people later today, so we should know more by the four o'clock meeting.' He looked around. 'Now for our Hybird stuff so, DI Deane? Would you like to leave us, so you can get on with your investigation?'

Jenny nodded. 'Come on, my team! Let's do some work and get some results, shall we?'

Marie watched them go, and tried to ignore the piercing look that Vic Blackwell turned on her just before he left. For a brief second, all the old venom poured out of him. Then he was gone, and Marie was left wondering if she'd imagined it.

Jackman beckoned for the remaining officers to draw closer. 'We'll kick off with Robbie and Max's late night foray into the Hybird jungle last night. It seems they've done far better than they expected on a first sortie. Max? Rob? Tell us what happened.'

Max stood up, but before he spoke he raised an eyebrow at Marie. His look seemed to say, "Is it me? Or is the boss on something?"

Marie grinned at him, and the two detectives began their story.

'What? Like Fagin in *Oliver Twist*?' Gary looked fascinated. 'Well, why not? Devious criminals have been doing it for years. They used to be called "kidsmen." They'd train kids up as pickpockets and get them to steal in return for food and shelter. And we all know that drug dealers use kids on bikes for distribution.'

'The bit that worried us most, sir,' said Robbie, 'was the talk of them disappearing. I mean, it's not come to our attention on a grand scale, has it?'

'I wonder how many kids we're talking about?' asked Marie.

'Who knows? But a lot of them might not even be missed. There's so many runaways and dysfunctional families that don't give a toss about their youngsters,' added Max. He showed them a clear plastic folder. 'I've printed off some shots of the patrons coming and going at the Ginger Sheep bar, and they do show how many different kinds of guys follow the Hybird trend.'

Marie stared at the pictures. There was a real mix of young men alright, from the downright scruffy to the idle rich, those who really knew how to showcase their clothes.

'Any familiar faces?' asked Jackman.

'No, sir,' Robbie said. 'No one known to us.'

'Did you, at any time, think you were being watched, Robbie? As in someone singling you out?' Jackman asked.

'It was hard to say, boss. My jacket was really attractive to them, more than I thought it would be, but then I didn't know it was such a limited edition. Hence I had a lot of interest paid to me.' He thought for a moment. 'I have to say, I never felt threatened. Not once.'

'So, you plan on going to one of the other venues tonight, is that right?'

'Yes, sir, the Lemon Tree in Fenchester. But I'm thinking of having Kevin Stoner go with me instead of Max. He really should have some time with Rosie, and it's a very late night.'

'I agree,' said Jackman. 'I'll get it okayed with uniform.'

'I'm still up for it, sir, if it's not possible for Stoner to help out,' Max chipped in.

'Speak of the devil,' murmured Gary. 'Here he comes now.'

Marie looked up to see an anxious Kevin Stoner enter the room. 'DI Jackman, sir? There's something here that the desk sergeant thinks you should see.' He handed Jackman a memo.

Jackman read it, and frowned. 'And you think this is connected to our cases?'

'We thought you should be the one to decide that, sir. We just didn't want to give it to someone else, knowing what's going on at the moment.'

'What is it?' asked Marie impatiently.

'Another missing youngster, a sixteen-year-old girl from Old Penny Street.'

'A girl?' Gary said. 'All our enquiries have been to do with boys or young men.'

Jackman pulled a face. 'I don't know. She could be connected in some way. We can't afford to dismiss it out of hand.' He turned to Kevin. 'What do we know?'

'Phone call from a neighbour. Big rumpus at her house the night before last, and she hasn't seen the girl since. Says she always looks out for the poor kid. Could be she's had enough and run away. The neighbour says the parents both drink heavily and fights go on all the time.'

'Then this doesn't sound like our problem, but,' Jackman thought for a moment, 'Gary? Would you and Kevin go and have a word with the neighbour, and see if there's anything we should be worrying about.'

Gary stood up. 'Of course, boss.'

'Oh, and Kevin? What's the girl's name?'

'Alice, sir. Alice Delaney.'

* * *

The buzz of the doorbell roused Tommy from sleep. He felt groggy, even though he hadn't had much to drink the night before. He wasn't sure if he should answer the door, so he left it to Dean.

After a while, he heard a grumbling Dean pad along the corridor and pick up the telecom. 'Who is it?'

Dean sounded well hung over.

He heard a muffled voice, and Dean said, 'You'd better come in.'

Tommy decided to pretend to be asleep. He had a feeling it was trouble of some kind, they never had visitors in the mornings. Better to keep a low profile.

Even so, he was curious.

The person who followed Dean into the lounge wore heavy boots or shoes, and had a deep gravelly voice. He had heard that voice recently, at the medic's place.

It was Mossy's boss, the man who'd broken the kid's nose. What was his name? Ah, that was it, they'd called him Trez. Tommy hoped it was nothing serious. He hadn't been paid anything yet, and he was anxious to start getting some hard cash together.

He slipped out of bed, went to the door and put his ear to it. He could only make out muted whisperings. Tommy hesitated. Should he just walk in? He thought better of it. He hadn't liked the look of Trez. He'd just ask Dean when that Neanderthal had gone.

* * *

Dean pulled his robe tighter around himself. He felt somewhat vulnerable in nothing but his bathrobe. 'Let me get this straight. Darke summoned you, but when you arrived, he wasn't there. Is that right?'

'Exactly. And you know what a stickler he is about time. I took the kid, as instructed, but the place was locked and he never answered the door.'

'Well, that's never happened to me before.'

'Me neither. So I went back this morning, and the same thing. He's gone, Dean, I'm sure of it.'

Dean rubbed at his puffy eyes and tried to concentrate. Gone? Why? The organisation was going full swing, doing better than ever. Why would Darke go anywhere? But Trez was right, he was a stickler for punctuality. He also kept to a strict routine, notes and memos everywhere. 'Phone?'

'No answer. Straight to voicemail.'

Not knowing what else to do, Dean offered Trez a cup of tea or coffee.

'No thanks, I can't stay too long. But there's something I need to know.' He looked awkward.

'Fire away.'

'How well do you know Darke? Like, how did you come to work for him? And do you know where he lives?'

Dean stared down at his hands. 'He picked me up in a club. Not, like, for sex, but he kind of groomed me. Now I know why. I had all the contacts and the knowledge he needed for his scam.'

Trez nodded slowly. 'Bit like me. But it was a dive down by the Greenborough docks where he found me. He asked me to join him as a kind of minder for a gang of thieves he was putting together. At the time I was pretty low and very broke, so I said yes.'

'As to where he lives,' Dean said, 'I have no idea. I always thought that room he uses as an office was attached to his home, but apparently he rents it.'

'I know, and I haven't a clue where he lives. I tried to follow him one day, but then I thought better of it.' Trez nibbled on an already bitten fingernail. 'He's holding a lot of my money. I can't afford to piss him off. We almost came to blows the other day, but I managed to curb my tongue. He owes me big style.'

'Me too. He pays up in the end, but he always holds some back, you know, as a kind of collateral.' Dean was owed a lot more than he was going to let on to Trez. It was only his father's allowance and his own money that enabled him to continue to live the kind of life that he did.

'Do you know where he came from?' asked Trez.

'He hasn't any accent, does he? But it's kind of London, or southern anyway, rather than from up north. He never, ever, talks about himself.'

'Has he ever interfered with any of your boys, Dean? Or you for that matter?'

Dean shook his head. 'No, but they're all frightened of him. They believe he's a pervert. It's what he says and the things he insinuates that gives them the shits.'

'I think he might have done something to one or two of my boys, but they deny it.'

'Embarrassed? Guilty? Scared?'

'All of those, but not scared. I'd say terrified.'

Dean pondered over what Trez had asked him. 'Bottom line, we know sweet fuck all about Darke, not even his real name.'

'And now we don't even know where he is.' Trez took out his phone. 'Give me your private mobile number. I'll contact you the minute I hear anything.'

Dean fetched his cellphone. 'I'll do the same.'

Trez heaved himself up from the low couch. 'There's one more thing, and I'm not happy about this at all. It's CJ and Weed.'

'The two takers who accidentally killed that boy?'

'I gave them a bit of a pasting, especially CJ, exactly as Darke directed. Then a couple of my other lads patched them up and gave them some money and two train tickets, and told them to get the hell out of Saltern, for their own good. They were supposed to travel that evening, but one of my boys saw them going into Darke's office earlier that afternoon, and I know for sure that they never made the train.'

Dean grew cold all over. He had told Tommy that people never got hurt. Now it was time to come clean, tell him that it probably went a lot further than that. 'What do we do, Trez?'

'Leave it with me until later today. I have an idea, but I need to really think it through, alright?'

Dean didn't see him to the door. He was barely able to move. Just what the hell was going on?

* * *

Meg Steeples shook her head sadly. 'That poor little kid. I've been watching her since she was a little mite. It wasn't quite so bad back then, but I could see which way the wind was blowing. The father's drinking habits just got worse and worse.'

Gary glanced at Kevin. They had heard this story so many times before, and had seen the aftermath — a lost childhood and a damaged life. 'We've been next door, Miss Steeples, but there's no answer.'

'Too drunk to hear you knocking. They don't surface till the afternoon, just in time to start again.' She said this matter-of-factly.

'We'll keep trying,' added Kevin. 'Are you really sure you see her every day? No misses?'

'Morning and evening, religiously. We have a kind of unspoken agreement.' She rubbed her cheek with a hand, knobby and twisted with arthritis. 'I don't sleep well, so I sit by the window and wait till I see her come home. She waves, I go to bed.'

'But weren't there times when Alice was poorly, or her parents stopped her going out?' asked Gary gently.

'Come with me.' Slowly, they followed her bent figure up the stairs.

The old woman's bedroom was neat and tidy, and had a homely feel. It was filled with old photos and little knick-knacks, all that was left of this lonely old woman's life.

'These places are little more than cardboard boxes, Officer. They just threw them up.' She laughed, sardonically. 'You see, Alice's bedroom backs onto mine.'

She pointed to one of the walls. Against it stood a small crescent shaped table bearing a glass tumbler. 'You talk to each other?'

'Not talk as such . . .'

She tilted her head, and Gary thought of a blackbird, listening out.

'We've got signals, like. One knock means "I'm here, and I'm safe." Two, means, "I'm sick." *Three* means her father's so drunk she's keeping a low profile. It took a while for me to work that one out, but we did whisper to each other now and then. Not often, in case her parents heard.' She sighed. 'The girl is not there, I know it.'

They all trooped slowly back into the sitting room.

'And you say there was a fight last night?' Gary asked.

'Even worse than usual, and that's saying something. Though come to think of it, I only heard Delaney's voice, not Alice or her mother.'

'Anything else unusual?' asked Kevin, who was making notes.

'There was a stranger watching the house. I told the police officer about it when I phoned. I didn't see him clearly, 'cause it was getting dark, but he was definitely there. A tall, strongly built man. He stood there for maybe fifteen minutes, then he disappeared.'

Gary believed her. But there wasn't enough to go on, nothing that would warrant their intervention. Alice Delaney was sixteen. That made her a minor, but she was old enough to get married, to consent to sexual activity, and a host of other things. Most importantly, she could leave home, with or without her parents' consent. The girl could even apply for a passport or change her name by deed poll! He tactfully put this to Meg Steeples.

'Oh. I know all that, Officer! I'm old, but not daft! But, you see, she would've let me know!' Tears began to form and threatened to spill over. 'You've no idea how special these little signs were to both of us! A single knock on the wall meant neither of us was completely alone. Don't you see? It meant I could sleep for a few hours. It meant Alice knew someone was there for her. Even if I couldn't help her, at least someone cared.'

Gary felt a lump forming in his throat. Sometimes the emptiness of people's lives was almost overwhelming.

'We'll do our best, Miss Steeples,' Gary said quietly. 'I promise.'

* * *

Vic Blackwell had hit the ground running. His new DI clearly took no prisoners, and had thrown him straight in the deep end. By eleven a.m., he was beginning to realise what a cushy life he'd been leading at the satellite station. Yet, and it surprised him, he found himself enjoying it. There must, after all, have been some small part left over of the man he used to be. That first-rate copper who had loved his career.

He was working a real case for once. Bad steroids were changing hands, and money was being made out of poor sods who just wanted to boost their image a bit. Okay, it wasn't a high profile murder enquiry, but it certainly beat petty domestic squabbles and arguments over land boundaries. Another thing was that the hard graft helped him to push away thoughts of Big Rita and her talented neighbour, Vee.

Now he was trudging along the high sea-bank with a rather taciturn detective called Larry, trying to pinpoint a suitable spot for a night observation stakeout. Larry's reticence suited Blackwell just fine, though he was making a concerted effort to be as pleasant as possible to the people he was working with. It was important that they saw him as a reformed character, or if they didn't know any different, just an okay guy.

He looked out across the wide, slow-moving river and thought back to daily orders. For days, he'd been imagining what it would be like to be back in the same workplace as Marie, but he'd been unprepared for the force of the emotions that hit him when he finally walked into that CID room.

She'd aged since he'd been moved out. He could see worry lines where before there had been none, but she was still a strikingly handsome woman. And he had to admit she had carried herself off with considerable dignity, apparently unperturbed by his presence.

He grimaced. Nice bit of acting, Marie, but let's see how you fare as the hours and days pass. He hadn't anticipated the memories of the good times they'd shared as crewmates, and the happy times they'd all had, the four of them, when his beautiful wife Tania was still alive. Blackwell tried to concentrate on the job at hand. He scanned the path for suitable hideouts, but he couldn't stop thinking about Marie Evans. He had followed the Alistair Ashcroft case closely, along with anything else that involved her, and he knew that she and her precious team would be living under Ashcroft's shadow, constantly aware that at any minute he could turn up again. It would wear anyone down. And now he was there too, casting yet another shadow over her well-ordered life.

Perfect! If he never did another thing, it would almost be enough just to know that every night she went to bed dreading the next day, and every morning she woke up to uncertainty. He smiled to himself. *Almost* wasn't enough for Vic Blackwell. Not nearly enough.

CHAPTER TWENTY

'Why are you looking at me like that?' Jackman said.

Marie smiled innocently. 'Like what?'

'You know very well what I mean!'

Jackman was perplexed. He had thought that having seen her nemesis in the same room after all these years, Marie would be either haggard with worry, or incandescent with rage at Blackwell's intrusion. Instead, she looked amused. 'Come on! Cough it up.'

'Hang on, isn't it the other way around? I think it's your turn to explain.' He grinned widely. Then it dawned on him. 'Ah.'

'Ah, indeed.' She returned the smile.

'Am I that transparent? Second thoughts, don't answer that. I clearly am.' He flopped down into his admiral's chair and looked up at her. 'It's just a six-month trial, that's all. We think we didn't give it a fair chance last time.'

'I should say you didn't!' Marie sat opposite him, beaming. 'And you won't need six months, Jackman! Come on. You know already.'

She was right. As soon as they left the pub, he knew they *had* to give it another try. 'I didn't realise it'd be so obvious. Do you think the others know?'

'I should think the whole station knows! You're back to your old self, you're re-energised! It's the best thing ever! Everything would be perfect, if it weren't for . . .' Her smile faded.

'I know.' He felt for her. Everything good in Marie's life would be tarnished by Blackwell's return. All Jackman could do was make it as painless as possible, and keep them as far apart as he was able to. There was a very slight chance that Blackwell was being truthful about wanting to forget the past. Only time would tell, and he was very aware that Marie thought otherwise. That was good enough for him. Marie's instincts were never wrong. 'Jenny Deane will keep him busy, she promised me. Plus, even though we don't work the same shifts as uniform, she's going to try a new rota system with some of her detectives, which will put him working at different hours to you.'

'I appreciate it, but it's going to be like trying to ignore the elephant in the room, even when he's not there.'

'Well, he's going to have to keep his nose very clean indeed. The super meant it when she said that one wrong move, and he'll be out of here like a rocket. And believe me, *everyone* is watching him!'

He saw that his reassurances weren't even touching the sides, her fears were far too deep-rooted.

'Let's not talk about him,' Marie said. 'I'm just thrilled about you and Laura, so I'm focusing on that — and work, of course. So, boss? What do you want me doing today?'

'Pester Newcastle for that DNA result on the missing boy who might be our Harry. We need to know if we have a positive ID, then we can start looking deeper into this "Fagin" theory.'

She nodded. 'When I first heard that, I thought it was one of those urban legends, some story that got established as a fact. Now I'm thinking it's a very real possibility. Someone has to orchestrate this operation, and it's looking like a pretty carefully thought-out one, isn't it?'

'It certainly is. We just need to find proof, hard evidence, and brush aside the gossip.'

'Oh, that's simple then. I wish!' She stood up. 'Right, I'll go phone the Geordies.' She stopped in the doorway, 'And once again, I'm *so* pleased for you. Make it work this time, boss, and that's an order!'

Jackman was still grinning inanely at his closed door.

* * *

It wasn't that Dean didn't believe Trez, but he needed to see for himself that Darke really wasn't there. Maybe he'd returned by now. He left the apartment while Tommy was showering, and drove to Darke's office.

It was a pretty crummy place really. Faded, weathered paintwork on the outer door, and a distinctly seedy hallway. Worn carpet and old-fashioned, scuffed wallpaper. The outer door was always open during working hours because, as Dean now realised, several other people had office space in the old building. At one time it would have been a very grand and desirable residence. Now it just looked forgotten and down at heel.

Today Dean saw it differently. He had always believed that Darke lived there, and maybe rented a few rooms out to small businesses. Now he understood that the one room Darke occupied was all there was to his empire.

He knocked on the door, knowing there'd be no answer. He took his phone from his pocket and rang Darke's office number. From behind the locked door, he heard the muffled ringing of the telephone. After a while the answerphone cut in, and Dean heard Darke's abrupt command to leave a message. He ended the call and walked slowly back to his car.

What was Darke up to?

Dean thought about all the conversations they'd had in that small office.

Darke had always led him to believe that he was a Mister Big, a man with a track record rivalling that of any of the criminal competition. And from the kind of complex scam they were involved in, and the amount of money changing hands, Dean had had no reason to doubt him. Until now. Darke owed Dean somewhere in the region of twenty thousand pounds, and he suspected he owed Trez a very large amount too. Trez had hinted as much. Trez was given money for his little army of takers, from which he handed the kids their cut and made sure they were suitably housed and fed. Dean had never looked too deeply into Trez's side of the business, preferring to concentrate on his own. Now he wondered how it all fitted together. Everything was cloak and dagger with Darke. He told you enough to make you believe that you were in his confidence, but in fact he just fed you insignificant titbits.

Dean sat in his car, pulled down the vanity mirror and stared at his reflection. He looked as anxious as Trez had. What to do next? He supposed he would have to wait and see what Trez came up with. One thing he'd done, was check his apartment for bugs, but thankfully had found nothing.

He drove back home thinking about Trez. He was a strange man and, although Trez had chosen him as his confidante, Dean was still a long way from trusting this former mercenary.

He cursed himself. What a fool he'd been. How could he have been so gullible as to even think that Darke actually valued the work that he did for him? He was just a useful tool. He parked up and slammed the car door behind him. 'Useful tool. Ha!' he muttered aloud.

Tommy was making himself some toast. 'Morning. Or is it afternoon already?'

Without replying, Dean went straight to the kettle and made himself a strong coffee.

'What's wrong, Dean?'

Dean sighed. How to explain to Tommy what was going on? He had no idea where to even start.

'I thought I heard someone here earlier. Wasn't it that man we saw yesterday when I was getting my finger patched up, or was I dreaming?' Tommy said.

'No, no. He had some business stuff to talk about, that's all.' Dean forced a grin.

Tommy was staring at him, looking puzzled. He stared back. Then he decided to take a big chance. Right now he needed a friend, someone to confide his fears to. He picked up his mug and went over to the dining area. 'Come and sit down, and I'll explain.'

Meaning to give Tommy the barest essentials, he suddenly found that he'd told him everything.

'He owes you how much?' Tommy's mouth was open.

'It's happened before. He does pay, but he's crafty. He holds money back to keep you onside.'

'Has he ever fallen off the radar before?'

Dean shook his head. 'Just once. But then he told me he was going to be uncontactable for a couple of days, though he never said where he was going. He's always there, always watching your every move, always on the phone, checking that things are running smoothly.'

'Sounds like Big Brother. So where is he now?' whispered Tommy, as if to himself. 'Maybe he's had an accident? Or he's ill?'

It was possible, he supposed, but Dean was sure Darke was up to something devious. He just couldn't fathom out what it might be.

Tommy looked worried.

'You won't lose out, kid. I promise.' Dean reached across the table and lightly touched Tommy's hand. 'You are brilliant at what you do, so you'll be paid, even if it comes out of my own pocket.'

'I don't want you to do that, Dean. It's not your fault. But I don't want to go back to where I came from either, to that house full of screaming and hate. Maybe we're worrying for nothing. He might have some major family emergency to deal with and just took off.'

'He always gave the impression that he had no family.'

'But he's a crook, Dean, so he lies.'

Dean gave a faint laugh. 'Good point. Anyway, Trez is contacting us later. He says he has a plan, but he wanted time to think it through.'

Tommy frowned. 'Did you know it was him who hit that kid in the medic's place yesterday?'

Dean watched Tommy carefully. How had he managed to get a taker to snitch on Trez so readily? 'I guessed that was the case.'

'And you trust him? Knowing what he's capable of?'

'No way,' Dean said. 'But I need to know what he's thinking. And he's as worried as we are. Darke owes him too, and he needs money far more than me. I suggest we keep to our usual routine until we know what the hell is going on. '

'Okay, but *I suggest* we work out a plan of our own, and we don't share it with that big ape.'

Dean gulped his coffee and winced. He'd made it too strong. Suddenly he was relieved not to be alone in this. Tommy had taken the news of this possible disaster stoically. He hadn't panicked. 'I agree. Council of war?'

Tommy moved his chair closer and rested his elbows on the table. 'Let's do it.'

* * *

Marie replaced her desk phone receiver. 'That's a relief,' she said to anyone who was listening. 'Daisy Cotterill and Sheba are staying with a cousin in Cassel Village. She's given up trying to be a PI!'

'About bloody time!' Jackman stood behind her. 'At least we can stop fretting over what she's going to do next to disrupt the smuggling operation. Pass that on to Jenny Deane, will you?'

'Of course.' Marie stood up.

'No. Pass it on by phone,' Jackman clarified. 'No need to go down to her end in person.'

She understood, and sat back down.

'And while I think of it, I've had an idea.' Jackman perched on the edge of her desk. 'My office is plenty big enough for another desk. Would you like to share office space? I have absolutely no objection and to be honest, it might be convenient for discussing all the things we have to in private.'

Marie's heart went out to her boss. His office was his sanctuary, and he was prepared to give that up so she wouldn't have to be anywhere near Vic Blackwell. 'Bless you, Jackman, but no way!' She smiled at him. 'I'm fine here. The way this big room is designed, I can't even see his desk from here.'

It was true. Saltern-le-Fen police station was a rambling old building, and the CID area must have been some sort of function room in days gone by. It was spacious, and built in an L-shape. DI Deane's detectives' area was around a corner, out of sight, so that the two teams could be working in different rooms.

'I appreciate the thought, really I do, but in a funny kind of way, it would look like I'm hiding from him, and there's no way I'm going to do that.'

Jackman nodded. 'I do understand, but if you change your mind, the offer will still stand.' He straightened up. 'Any news from Newcastle?'

'They said within the hour.'

'It would be so good to get an affirmative on that poor boy,' Jackman said. 'Then he can be returned to his parents. They must be desperate for news about their son.'

Marie nodded. 'Any news, even the worst kind, has to be better than the terrible not knowing. Let's just hope that he isn't one of those lost boys that nobody cares about, huh?'

'Sadly, if he was attached to this alleged-Fagin's gang, there's a strong possibility that will be the case. But let's not jump the gun.'

Jackman went and stood in front of the whiteboard. One whole section was given over to Max's photographs of the Ginger Sheep's clientele. Jackman stared at the pictures, shook his head and returned to his office.

Deep in thought about unwanted and unloved kids, Marie jumped when a young civilian placed a report on her desk.

'Reports about last night's burglaries involving Hybird X, Sarge.'

Marie thanked her and paged through it. Five burglaries in total, goods stolen valued at £150,000. She looked again at the figure. It was astronomical for a bunch of clothes. Then she read that one of the houses was home to a collector of Hybird grails. She let out a long whistle, and took the details to Max and Robbie, who were hard at work on their computers.

'Looks like last night was bonanza pickings, lads. Your Hybird thieves hit the jackpot.' She put the report on Max's desk.

Max looked at it, and passed it to Robbie. 'So while we were in the Ginger Sheep, they were out helping themselves to the goodies, the little bastards!'

'At least we think we have the modus operandi sussed, don't we, Max?' Robbie looked up at Marie. 'And if we are right, and if my choice of clothing is duly noted tonight in the Lemon Tree, my pad could be one of the next ones hit.'

Marie frowned. 'Are you okay with this, Rob? It's a bit risky.'

Robbie grinned. 'I reckon they'll take one look at my apartment and think again. It's like Fort Knox! But the CCTV might show us who's doing the recce.'

'We're thinking that these guys are sort of like cat burglars,' Max said. 'They bust in when you're there, tie you up and nick your gear from right under your nose. We don't think they'd tackle anything with too much security apparatus. They're speed merchants, in and out and gone in minutes.' He waved a sheaf of papers at her. 'We've checked every burglary, and they were all accomplished in no time at all. Rob's gaff would present too many problems, I'm sure.'

Marie wasn't convinced. 'And they might just see that it's a classy, executive apartment, so it could be filled with thousands of pounds' worth of gear. Robbie, have you considered that the other way in would be to accompany you. You might find a knife in your ribs, to encourage you to open the doors for them.' Before Robbie could answer, Marie heard her desk phone ringing. 'Excuse me, Rob, we'll finish this later.'

The caller had a thick Geordie accent. 'We have a match for you.'

Marie gave a mental high five. She began to write down what DC Des Parkins, the Newcastle officer, was telling her.

'He's not one of the mispers that we suspected, DC Evans. He's only just come to our notice, but he's your lad alright. Name's Darryl Townsend, sixteen years old, from the Benton district.'

Marie added the address. 'What's his story?'

'Serial runaway. Has been since he was a bairn. Comes from a very poor family. He usually finishes up at his grandfather's place down near Chester-le Street, but this time no one thought to check with Grandad. He's been missing for exactly the same period of time as you described in your bulletin.'

'Is there someone who could come and identify him, DC Parkins?'

'His father will. One of our lads'll bring him down later today, if that suits?'

'That would be fine, Des. I'll make sure I'm around to meet him, and accompany him to the morgue.'

'Champion! The DNA result will take a couple more days, so Dad's confirmation could be your deciding factor. We do have a photograph taken just before he left school, and there's no doubt that Darryl is your dead lad. I'll email you a copy now.'

As Marie went through a few more details with Des Parkins, she saw the jpeg attachment arrive in her inbox. One look told her that Harry was no more. Their boy's name was Darryl. So, something was finally coming together. They were still no wiser as to who'd killed him, but at least they knew who he was and where he came from, and could move on from there. But the puzzle about his last meal still bothered her. It simply made no sense at all.

Marie thanked DC Parkin, hung up and hurried towards Jackman's office. He'd be relieved to hear this.

He was just putting his phone down. 'That was Gary. He can't see any connection between the missing girl, Alice, and our enquiries, but he and Kevin are still trying to gain entry into the house. They want to see for themselves that the neighbour isn't fretting over nothing. Apparently the kid's parents are in a permanent state of inebriation.'

'What a life! Who could blame her for doing a bunk?'

'*If* she did.' Jackman sounded dubious. 'There are too many odd things happening around here regarding teenagers right now to assume anything.'

'True. Now, I have to tell you — we finally have a name for Harry.'

Jackman's eyes lit up, and then his phone rang again.

Marie watched as his expression turned from delight to shock. 'What? Where?' He listened for a moment and then said, 'Show us attending!' He threw down the receiver.

'I've no idea what this is all about, so don't ask. We just need to get to Cannon Park, fast!'

Without another word, Marie ran from the office and down the stairs, easily catching up with Jackman.

Once they were in the car, he explained. 'It's an incident involving a teenager, over in the park. I know this isn't a CID matter but, because it's a young male, uniform think it might be something for us. Some bystanders there thought he was a drunk or a drug addict, but it's worse than that. He's acting psychotic, and he's got blood on him. It looks like something terrible has happened to him.'

Marie had a vision of the dead boy lying in the rubbish in the alley behind Mayflower Lane. Would they discover a connection?

Soon they were parked up and hurrying towards a small crowd of people gathered in the children's play area of the park. A uniformed officer was trying to hold them back and keep them a safe distance from the distraught teenager, both for their safety and that of the boy.

'Do we know anything about him?' Jackman asked WPC Stacey Smith.

'Not a thing, sir.' She looked anxiously at the young man. 'We need to get him to a place of safety. The easiest way is to arrest him for a breach of the peace, then we can get him all the help he needs. Trouble is, he's too far gone to communicate with us, and if we get too close he starts screaming.' She shivered. 'And believe me, that's enough to turn your blood cold.'

As if on cue, an animal howl rose into the air, reducing the bystanders to a shocked silence.

Marie swallowed hard and stared at the wild-eyed teenager.

It was a surreal scene, and it would haunt her for years to come.

The boy was curled up in a foetal position on a large flat-topped children's roundabout. The brightly painted wheel was gently revolving. His hands were curled inwards like claws, and he was tearing slowly and deliberately at his blood-stained clothing, which was filthy and ragged. His hair was matted, his skin sallow as uncooked batter. His face was sunken, his cheekbones protruded and his bared teeth were yellow and stained.

Marie saw that his exposed skin bore multiple bruising and old scars, red welts and blisters. She had an urge to turn and run away. She couldn't deal with this. It was just too much.

Jackman gave her arm a gentle squeeze. He didn't speak, but he didn't have to. She turned to him and said, 'Call Laura. We need her help.'

Jackman pulled out his phone, and now he was saying, 'She's on her way to the station, and she's asked a crisis team to meet her there.'

Marie wasn't sure how anyone was going to help this poor soul. If he'd been a wild animal, they could have used a dart gun with a powerful sedative. And that was exactly what he was, she thought, a terrified animal, cornered and in pain. At least Saltern police station had an exclusion cell lined with indestructible safety padding. Once they managed to get him there, it would provide a place of safety until the crisis team could take him to a psychiatric unit.

Marie watched the WPC's efforts to try to calm the lad. She had edged a little closer and was speaking softly to him, but he didn't respond. Most likely he couldn't hear her. His eyes registered only terror.

'I cannot begin to think what has happened to him,' whispered Jackman.

Marie merely shook her head.

'The van's here now. Uniform are going to have to restrain him. It won't be pretty. I wouldn't want to be one of the officers who'll have to do it.'

Marie knew the procedure well. She'd done it many times. Force was needed, but you had to be careful not to injure your man.

Four officers were hurrying towards the unfortunate boy. Their task was straightforward, but how to carry it out?

Marie and Jackman watched them pull the lad from the roundabout, place him face down and secure his wrists.

He didn't go easily. He writhed like an eel, screaming all the time. It took one officer for each leg, and two at his shoulders, to ferry him to the open doors of the waiting van. Three of them went in the back with him. Even cuffed, he was desperately trying to hit his head on the floor of the van. It was going to be hard to keep him from injuring himself further.

'Come on,' Jackman said. 'I'm just going to get WPC Smith to organise statements from the people who reported this. Mainly, I want to know where he came from. Then we need to be back at the custody suite before Laura and the crisis team get there.'

Neither spoke during the short drive back. Marie felt sick to her stomach, but puzzled too. As he was ferried past her, she thought there was something familiar about him, even though she couldn't see his face properly. Despite his appalling condition, Marie felt sure she knew him.

The next hour was traumatic for all those involved in trying to help the boy. Finally, Laura emerged into the corridor, ran a hand through her hair and leaned back against the wall with a loud exhalation. The elegant Laura had never looked so fraught.

'Professor Newland is sedating him and he'll be taking him to the psychiatric unit at Greenborough General. They have a bed waiting for him.'

'Has he said anything intelligible?' asked Jackman.

Laura shrugged. 'Very little, I'm afraid. We don't even know his name. The only thing we could make out was the word "dark." He's terrified of the dark.'

'So he's been kept somewhere? Somewhere with no light?' Marie recalled his sallow skin and jailbird pallor.

'He is displaying all the signs of having been held in captivity for some length of time.' Laura dropped her head, almost to her chest. 'In unimaginably horrible conditions.'

Jackman grunted, and then shook his head. 'This is too awful for words, but I can't see how it connects with the burglaries or our Fagin's Den. This is something else altogether, isn't it?'

Marie wasn't so sure. 'But is it? We have a group of well-organised young thieves who on one occasion caused the death of another young man. We have a dead boy, who we now know comes from Newcastle, and a missing teenage girl, all at the same time in the same area — oh, and throw in a possible smuggling operation, so why not add a kidnapper too?'

'Sounds like Saltern isn't a very safe place to be if you're a youngster,' said Laura grimly. Then someone called her name. 'Got to go back in, then I'm following the ambulance to Greenborough.' She turned to Jackman. 'I'll ring you as soon as he's settled and a care plan is drawn up, okay?'

Jackman nodded. 'Go careful, won't you?'

Marie didn't miss their lingering smile. Jackman turned to her and said, 'I have to go and report this to Ruth Crooke, Marie. Hold the fort till I get back.'

After he had left, Marie hung around a while longer, wanting to see the boy again. She still had the feeling that she recognised something about him, and seeing him calmer and sedated might help jog her memory.

Ten minutes later they took him away, strapped to an ambulance trolley. Marie stepped back and let the paramedics wheel him past. This time the sense of recognition was even stronger but, annoyingly, she still couldn't make a connection. Reluctantly, she returned to the CID room.

CHAPTER TWENTY-ONE

Vic Blackwell sat at his new desk. He was poring over the reports on the alleged smuggling route of the boat entering the river at night. It was all perfectly feasible. He knew the area well, and he knew the Cotterills, and the Laceys — Daisy Cotterill's side of the family. They were all toerags, the lot of them. Like so many of the rural families, they ran their lives according to their own rules with little regard for the law. Not villains, just country folk who still poached, set traps and made up their own minds about rights of way and boundaries. Blackwell would have been surprised if they were involved in something more seriously criminal. Then again, having been told that Daisy had gone to stay with a cousin, he was sure he'd seen a curtain move when he walked past her cottage earlier on. He set the thought aside for further investigation if necessary, and moved on.

Yes, a craft could make it into the inlet at high tide. There'd be a limited window of opportunity, but how long did it take to offload a few packages to eagerly waiting receivers? Minutes at the most. Then you could be gone again, beetling back into the Wash, ready to arrange your next collection of drugs. Very neat.

He sat back and scratched his head thoughtfully. For most of the day he had thought only about the investigation. Already he was beginning to feel that old magnetic pull of being the one to make the collar, the officer who made the right connection and got the arrest. He hadn't bargained for this. This whole thing had been just a means to an end. Now the waters were getting muddied, and he didn't like the confusion it caused in his head. He closed his eyes and tried to refocus his mind, but that just made it worse. Earlier, a couple of newbie detectives, who clearly knew nothing of his history, had asked him if he fancied a drink after work! No one had done that for years! He found it oddly unsettling. Part of him actually wanted to go, cried out for that old camaraderie that had been an integral part of his past. But the greater part wanted reparations for a torrid time in his life. That time when Marie Evans had been instrumental in the breakup of his marriage, and then the death of his beautiful Tania. He opened his eyes to a new resolve. That . . . that was all that mattered.

* * *

Mossy swallowed a couple of the painkillers that Trez's medic buddie had given him. His face was agony. Gone was the sharp pain after Trez's fist had smashed into him, to be replaced by a relentless dull pounding that made all thought impossible. Worst of all was that it had all been for nothing. Like his smashed phone. When they got there, the mighty Darke had buggered off. It wasn't the mess Trez had made of his face that upset him, it was the fact that he couldn't make contact with Alice. True to his word, Trez had gone off with a letter Mossy'd written to her, but when he returned he said nothing about how she was, or what she had said on receiving the note. Trez could have stuck it in the nearest waste bin for all he knew.

Mossy lay down on his bed. He sat up again. It hurt his face even more to lie flat. He leant back into his pillows and wondered about Trez, who supposedly cared about him. If he could do this — he lightly touched his bruised cheek — then what was the boss capable of?

He stood up and began to pace the small room.

This wasn't the way to free Alice from her father's clutches. He'd thought he'd been clever, seen the perfect way to make some fast money and run. Now he knew he'd been terribly wrong. He had walked into a lion's den and if he wasn't careful, he wouldn't walk out again.

Trying to ignore the pain, he thought about his situation. So far, he'd done nothing wrong, nothing illegal. That meant he had nothing to fear from the Old Bill. But he had learned some very clever new skills from Zak, Gordi and Bubbles, skills he could use in the future. If only he knew what kind of clothes to steal! He knew nothing about fashion, why would he, coming from where he did? He would need a helper.

A small smile spread across his damaged face. Tommy! The smile faded. Tommy worked for Darke too, and that was bad. Mossy had to get Tommy away from all this. Once, Tommy had come to Mossy's rescue. Now it was time to repay him. Then, if things went his way, they could start making a pretty lucrative business for themselves, just the two of them. Him on the streets doing the thieving, and Tommy telling him who and what to hit, and then being the one to find a home for the goods. Tommy was bright, he could do it with his eyes shut. Simple and sweet.

All he had to do now was get Tommy on side.

But before that, he needed to see Alice. He had to tell her to forget anything Trez might have told her, that he was getting away just as soon as he could, and he'd be taking her with him. They'd be going with nothing, but it didn't matter. Somehow they'd survive. Anything was better than the way they were both living now. And if Tommy played ball, they could live well.

He was ready to leave when he heard a key turning in the front door. He'd have to wait. That was okay. Trez couldn't watch him *all* the time.

* * *

'So what could we be looking at, Rowan?' Ruth asked.

'It's very hazy so far, Ruth. I'm loath to even guess. The facts are that he *is* a drug addict, and some of the older scars indicate self-inflicted wounds. It is also a fact that he was restrained and imprisoned somewhere, but whether that was for his own protection or for some darker reason, we have no idea,' Jackman replied.

'Overall impression of him?'

'He was more than just frightened, he was absolutely terrified.'

Ruth Crooke sighed. 'When will the first report be back with us, from the psych guys?'

'Laura Archer is contacting me as soon as they've had a chance to evaluate the situation. Maybe early evening?'

'Then contact me immediately you know more, Rowan, no matter what time it is. I need to know what the hell we are dealing with here.' She leaned back in her chair and folded her arms. 'Years ago, when I was still in uniform, I found a dead kid in a filthy box room in a big, rambling old house. She'd been imprisoned there by her mother. The woman said they'd tried every kind of professional care, but her daughter had gone beyond help. So she locked her up, saying she would rather have her die in her own home than in a gutter in some back alley. Back then, I didn't know what to say to her, and many years on, I probably still wouldn't . . .' She sat forward again. 'But you have an ID on the John Doe found in Mayflower Lane?'

'Yes. His name is Darryl Townsend. His father is due to arrive any moment to make the formal identification. Marie is trying to trace his movements from when he was last seen in Newcastle, and then after he visited Artie's mobile soup kitchen. It won't be an easy task. He's got previous for running away. He was an old hand at it, apparently, so he'll have known how to cover his tracks.'

'At least you have a name. That will help.' Ruth sat back again. 'And how has Marie's first day with our new officer, Vic Blackwell, gone?'

'Without incident, as they say. I had a quick word with Jenny on the way here, and she says he's been the perfect detective the whole day. She's still wary though, keeps muttering about leopards and spots.'

'I totally agree with her. He's doing exactly as I would if I had a secret agenda. Head down, work hard and lull everybody into a false sense of security.'

'You're right. I have to say Jenny is being great. She couldn't do any more to keep them apart.'

Ruth nodded. 'The saddest thing is that Vic was such a bloody good copper. I sometimes wonder if we, as in the force, let him down after his wife died. I don't think anyone realised how messed up he was. If he'd been given some guidance, maybe this mess could have been avoided.'

'From what I've heard, no one could have guided Vic Blackwell anywhere. He was fixated on Marie, blamed her for everything, and I don't think anyone could have changed his mind.'

'Probably not. It's far too late now anyway.' She gathered up the papers that were spread across her desk. 'I think that's all, but don't forget, let me know what you hear from Laura Archer.'

'Will do, Ruth.' Jackman stood up. 'I'd better get downstairs anyway, and see if Marie needs help at the morgue with Darryl's father. I have no idea what state he'll be in — distraught, relieved, angry? Who knows with a son like that?'

'I'd go with distraught. If you love your kid, you always hope things will change for them, that they'll come good in the end,' She gave him one of her rare smiles, but it was sad, 'even if you know there's not a cat in hell's chance of that happening.'

* * *

'Oh, hi, Trez,' Dean said. This time, Trez had phoned.

'Listen, I don't want to jump the gun, just in case there's a reasonable explanation for Darke's behaviour, so I suggest we keep going as usual for at least a couple more days.'

'I was thinking that myself,' Dean said. 'After all, we don't really need him to be here.'

'We don't, do we? My boys are ready for tonight. The receivers are all lined up, so we'll go ahead as planned,' Trez replied.

'Good. We have a couple of likely targets to check out as well, so Tommy and I'll be working this evening.'

'I've got a boy watching Darke's place in case he returns. I'll contact you if he does.'

'Have you had a chance to think more about a plan, if he really has done a runner?' Dean asked.

'Yeah, I have. But I'd rather talk face to face. What about tomorrow?'

'Sure. Any time after midday. And good luck for tonight.' Dean ended the call.

Tommy was watching from across the room. 'So?'

'Trez reckons business as usual, just in case Darke's playing games with us. He's going to tell us his master plan tomorrow,'

'But we won't tell him ours, huh?' Tommy grinned mischievously.

'No, we certainly won't.' Dean frowned. That grin told him Tommy didn't appreciate the seriousness of their situation. He didn't know Darke, or what he was capable of. Trez too, for that matter. This wasn't some harmless enterprise that they could get away from easily. There were too many things going on that even Dean knew nothing about. Trez had intimated that Darke had more than one racket on the go. One of those could be people smuggling, or selling boys for the sex trade, and Dean wanted no part in that, even by association. Or drugs. Dean liked to be surrounded by beautiful people, not junkies.

'You look well worried,' Tommy observed.

'I have every right to be,' Dean snapped. 'I won't be easy in my mind until we know where Darke is and what he's planning.'

'Sorry, Dean. I *am* scared. I just cover up by acting stupid.'

Dean stared into his eyes. 'Just never, never, underestimate Darke. Tommy, I'm sorry I ever recruited you. If I'd realised how bad he was, I'd never have done it, I really wouldn't.'

'Then let's just pack up right now, and move on. We can find something else. We make a great team, don't we, Dean? We don't need Darke.'

'Maybe he wants us to do just that, in which case I don't think we'd get very far, and I don't fancy your chances if he gets hold of you.'

'I can stand up for myself.'

'I doubt that very much. I'm one hundred percent sure that if Darke had designs on you, you'd stand no fucking chance at all.'

'Thanks for that.' Tommy sounded put out.

'I mean it! He's evil.'

'You used to say you admired him. You said he was good to you.'

'Yeah, well, I was a naïve twat with shit for brains. I was taken in by him. He was the perfect conman and I fell for it, something I've only just come to realise.'

'Then we should run for it, really we should.'

Dean felt like throttling him. 'I want my money. I want *your* money! And I can't just walk out of this place, can I? My father'd kill me! And you never know, we could be making a big mistake in pissing him off. Darke knows we do a bloody good job for him. He's not going to kill the golden goose, is he? We have to know what's going on before we do anything.'

'Okay, okay! I guess Trez was right. Business as usual, but let's try to find out what's happened.'

'And how do you propose to do that, Einstein? Phone the police? Ring the hospitals? We don't even know his real name! Trez's boys are watching his office. What else can we do?'

Tommy shook his head. 'There must be *something*.'

'You think of something sensible, and I'll do it.'

Silence.

* * *

Marie was utterly wrung out.

Darryl's father, Sean, had been inconsolable. He blamed himself entirely for his son's way of life and subsequent death. It appeared that Darryl was adopted. When the boy was seven, Sean and his wife had taken him in to get him away from an abusive situation with an alcoholic family member. Even though he seemed happy, and knew he was safe with them, Darryl couldn't stay in one place for five minutes. He ran off constantly, usually to his grandad, whom he adored.

Marie hadn't been prepared for such an outpouring. In a matter of minutes she knew they were poor, that the teenager loved cheeseburgers, followed the Magpies football club. He swam like a fish. His teachers said he could have done well if he'd not played truant so often.

She tried to reassure Sean that none of it was his fault, but he was having none of it.

By the time he finally left, Marie had had enough. It was too much for one day. The boy in the park had unsettled her, then came the distraught relative, and on top of that the knowledge that at any moment she could bump into Vic Blackwell. It was time to back off, and grab some down time.

In the CID room, she found Max and Robbie with Kevin Stoner, discussing that night's trip to the club in Fenchester. Even their enthusiasm couldn't lift her spirits. She picked up her coat and wished them a successful evening. 'And be very careful, Rob. Watch your back, okay? I don't want them hurting you. They could be really pissed off if they got into your apartment and found no Hybird clothing.'

Rob smiled at her. 'Don't worry, Sarge. We're on top of it.'

On her way to Jackman's office, a civilian handed Marie an envelope. It contained a short note from Rory Wilkinson, telling her that the fibres found on Darryl's clothes, which had been identified as coming from the boot of a car, were sadly a common fabric used on most of the lower range Ford models. The material was also used with several different colours of paintwork, so finding one particular car would be almost impossible.

She took the note with her to Jackman.

'The only time those fibres will become useful evidence is if we have a suspect driving a Ford, then we can compare them with the actual fibres themselves.' Jackman filed the note away. 'But we can't stop every Ford in the surrounding area, that's for sure.' He looked closely at her. 'Marie? Are you alright?'

'I'm bushed. I was going to slope off a few minutes early, if that's okay with you?'

'Of course. You look done in. Seeing that poor kid earlier was enough to knock the stuffing out of anyone, apart from everything else.'

'Before I go, I forgot to ask Kevin how he and Gary got on with that report about a missing girl.'

Jackman's brow creased. 'There's every chance that she's just run away from a terrible home life. Gary said the parents didn't even know she hadn't been home the night before. Can you imagine it? A pretty sixteen-year-old girl, who apparently looks a lot younger, left to fend for herself, and they don't even know if she's in the house or not.'

Marie could imagine it. She'd seen it many times before.

'Gary said her room was really tidy, while the rest of the house was a complete stinking pigsty. He said it made him quite upset to see her neatly made bed, her clothes that were little more than worn-out rags, all neatly hung on hangers. She'd really tried to make the best of what she had.'

'And the old lady next door? What does she think?' Marie asked.

'She swears Alice wouldn't go anywhere without finding a way to tell her first.' His expression darkened. 'And she thinks she saw someone watching the house the day Alice disappeared. That's the only thing that stops me dismissing it.'

Marie yawned. 'I don't think we can ignore anything if it involves teenagers, do you?'

'I'm not going to, believe me.' He pointed to the door. 'Off you go! Get some rest. I'm not even going to phone you after I've spoken to Laura, okay? It can wait till tomorrow.'

Marie nodded. He was right. There was nothing they could do, and if the boy was sedated, there was a good chance that they'd get very little from him for quite some time.

She wished him goodnight and checking for her keys, she made her way out of the station.

She was just about to get into her car, trying to rid herself of that horrible image of the roundabout and the terrified boy when a voice jolted her out of her reverie.

'It's been a long time, hasn't it, Marie?' Vic Blackwell lounged against the wall behind her. 'Pleased to see me?'

Marie swallowed. He looked at her with a kind of triumphant sneer. She didn't answer, trying to work out where the car park CCTV cameras were pointing. There was only one that covered the spot where the staff parked, and she saw that it had been misaligned. In essence, they were standing in a black spot.

'Shame about that.' He had followed her gaze. He shook his head. 'Seems we even have vandals on this hallowed ground.'

'I really don't want to talk to you, Vic. Would you just step aside, please?' Marie felt anger building up inside her, but she managed not to show it.

'Sure. But I just wanted you to know. *You* may have forgotten about what happened with Tania, but I haven't. Not for a single day, not one hour or one second.'

His hard gaze would have scared her if she hadn't felt so angry with him. Suddenly the events of the day, her intense tiredness, and then Vic Blackwell's refusal to grasp the fact that she'd *never* had anything to do with his wife's death, all burst forth. She exploded.

'And what the fuck *do* you think you know about what happened to Tania? You know *nothing,* except what your twisted mind's invented! Tania was my friend, a dear friend, but she never told me a thing about what was going wrong in her life, never. Not once! She was totally loyal to you, you arsehole! The stupid cow loved you! I can't think why. You treated her like shit! Like a possession. You were so wrapped up in your rise to the top that Tania became little more than a pretty accessory to the legendary Vic Blackwell! But though she never told me, I had eyes. I could see it!'

She stepped closer to him. She pulled herself up until she felt as if she was towering over him, though they were the same height. 'All these years, you've had lies festering in your thick head. But take this on board, Vic Blackwell! I had nothing to do with what happened that night. I don't know where Tania was going, or what she had planned. I didn't know then, and I don't know now. All I knew was that she was unhappy. *You* were the reason. What else could it have been?'

'You were having an affair with her! I know you were!'

Marie threw back her head and laughed. 'How could you get it so wrong! Tania was a beautiful woman and a lovely friend, but women aren't my thing, or hers. For God's sake! I don't know where you cooked it up from, but if that's what's been troubling you all these years, well, I'm sorry for you!'

'I found her private diary! I read the entries. The initials M.E. were all over it. M.E., Marie Evans. Phone calls, texts, and meetings, for a good month before it happened. It was you, Marie, you can't deny it!'

Marie frowned. M.E.? The initials meant something. What was it?

Then it fell into place. 'You never knew, did you? Tania was going to a *counsellor*, trying to find a way to make your lives right again. I suggest you check out someone by the name of Michael Everton. Her GP suggested him when she asked him for help. She never said he was a marriage counsellor either, she told me he was a psychologist and she was going to see him privately because she feared she was suffering from depression. She didn't know that I knew Michael, and what his profession was. And I never let on. That was how come I realised your marriage wasn't going as it should.'

'You're lying.' But Blackwell sounded unsure.

'Ask him. Michael Everton still lives in Saltern. Ask him for goodness sake. If you still have that diary, show him. Check the dates.' She stepped back, away from him. She felt drained to the point of collapse. 'All these years, Vic! But now it ends! Come on. For the sake of what we once had when we were crewmates, for all those good times together with Tania and my Bill, do as I ask and talk to Michael. Please? Then for God's sake draw a line. Let it go!'

Vic seemed to deflate as she watched. He looked about him, as if seeking something. Then he murmured,

'No, no, no,' and stumbled off towards his own vehicle. Marie remained standing there as he drove off.

With shaking hands, she got into her car and with difficulty managed to get the key into the ignition. Part of her wanted to run back inside and pour out everything to Jackman. She turned the key. She had to get right way from here. From Vic Blackwell.

Her heart was racing, and by the time she made it onto the main road out of Saltern, she could barely see through her tears. She'd had some pretty shitty days in the past, but this one had to be the worst.

CHAPTER TWENTY-TWO

Laura Archer threw down her coat and let herself drop onto the sofa. 'Why on earth do we do these kinds of jobs?'

Jackman handed her a large glass of wine. 'You're the psychologist. When you find the answer, do tell me.' He sat down beside her. 'I'm heating up one of Mrs Maynard's hotpots. It'll be ready in ten minutes.' He took her hand in his. 'Are you up to telling me what happened at the hospital?'

She took a long drink of her wine and sighed. 'It's not straightforward, I'm afraid.'

'Nothing is these days, is it?' Jackman said.

'We have no idea whether he'll recover. The extent of his mental trauma is extraordinary. From the state of his body, we've assumed he's a drug user, but not long term. He self-harmed in the past, but not for a while. He's been imprisoned, that's for certain, possibly tortured. We suspect he was kept somewhere without natural daylight for maybe six months, or even longer.'

'A prisoner?'

'For sure.'

'Was there anything on him to give us a clue about his identity?'

'Not as such, but he does have some interesting and quite expensive dental work that might help. I'm thinking you could go the old forensic route, using dental records. Oh, and we believe he's local. When he was crying out that he was frightened of the dark, his accent was quite pronounced. He's a yellowbelly alright.'

Jackman nodded. "Yellowbelly" was the local term for someone born and bred in Lincolnshire. 'Any idea of his age?'

'Mmm. The doc thinks he's around twenty. He seems younger because of his emaciated state and his extreme childlike fear.'

That was a surprise. Jackman had reckoned sixteen at the most. 'Sexual abuse?'

'The doctors haven't wanted to risk a full examination, in case part of his trauma stems from exactly that, and they don't want to put him through it yet. Basically, he's been cleaned up and made as comfortable as possible. Oh yes, talking of cleaning up, the blood on him wasn't his own, but there is now a record of it on file, should you need a comparison with someone.' She looked sadly at Jackman. 'It'll be a long, slow haul, and it could lead nowhere.' She drank some more wine. 'But I've seen some remarkable things in my time. Young people who survived terrible ordeals. I'm just hoping that this young man will be one of them. He has a brilliant team working with him, so if anyone can help him through this, they will.' She let out a long sigh. 'What a day! Thank heaven it's over! Now, tell me about this hotpot?'

'Ambrosia! Food of the gods. The perfect thing after a truly crappy day.'

'Then bring it on, because "truly crappy" really sums it up.'

Jackman sat with his arm around Laura. He had rarely felt so comfortable with someone — except Marie of course, but that was a different kind of comfort.

Outside, a security light flashed on, and Laura looked up at him anxiously.

He glanced at his watch, and laughed. 'Archie's on his rounds.' He stood up and led her over to the window. In the shadow of the milltower, a chunky ginger cat was scurrying towards the outbuildings. 'As you can see from his size, he's an excellent mouser. He's also a stickler for routine. Every night at the same time, even in appalling weather, Archie does his rounds.'

'Is he yours?' asked Laura.

'No, he's a farm cat from one of the local farmhouses. I call him Archie because he bears a strong resemblance to an old uncle of mine.' He planted a kiss on her forehead. 'Now, before you waste away for lack of sustenance, hotpot!'

As he dished up their meal an idea came to him. When they'd looked out of the window, the first thing they'd seen was the stark, derelict tower of the Old Mill House, still proud but sadly neglected. He'd been considering the options for over two years, never hitting on the perfect answer. Now he knew what he wanted to do. The ground and first floor were sound and sturdy, only the upper floors were in dire need of either restoration or removal. On a trip to Spalding a while back, he'd seen a beautifully reconstructed mill. Its height had been reduced to the equivalent of a three storey house with attic space, and they'd added an exquisite, traditional "onion-shaped" dome. It had lost none of its character, just a couple of floors of dangerous brickwork and timber.

He opened the cutlery drawer and took out knives and forks, thinking that the mill would make the perfect place for Laura to work in. They could choose a dozen ways to design the interior, but the upshot would be a beautiful spacious office in a quiet location. Whatever happened, he needed to make the tower safe and usable again. He owed that much to the original builders and craftsmen who had constructed it. He was privileged to own it, so he had a duty of care, didn't he?

'You look thoughtful.' Laura was smiling at him from the kitchen doorway.

'I am, but good thoughts this time.'

'Want to share?'

'Oh, I certainly do!'

* * *

'You're grounded tonight. I have to go out, and I'll be back late.' Trez looked distracted, and was clearly in no mood for discussion. However, Mossy decided he needed to put on a show for Trez, the kind he'd expect from him.

'Can't I come with you? I won't get in the way, honest. Please, Trez?'

'I've just said no, haven't I?'

Mossy managed to looked disgruntled, even though having time alone was exactly what he *did* want.

'Two of the teams have got jobs on tonight. One is difficult, and I need to be on hand if I'm needed. I have to be sharp tonight, and I don't need to be wet nursing some snotty-nosed new taker.'

Mossy grunted. If anyone was to blame for the snotty nose, it was Trez.

'Watch some TV, play a game, chill out. Just stay put.' Trez glowered at Mossy. 'And I mean that, don't even think of answering the door to anyone, understand? That's for your own safety as well as my peace of mind. Until we know what's going on with the boss, you lie low.' He paused, looked at Mossy. 'In fact, I'm going to lock you in. It's best all round that way.'

Mossy held back a groan. 'Whatever,' he managed, cursing to himself.

Trez pulled on a long, dark jacket. 'Right. Don't wait up, and if anyone comes to the door, stay shtum. Got it?'

Mossy nodded miserably. 'You don't have to go on about it. I got the message.'

To his surprise, Trez leant forward and ruffled his hair. 'Sorry, kid. I'm kind of twitchy about what Darke is up to, okay? As soon as it's sorted, I'll get you to work and making some proper money, I promise.'

And then he was gone. Mossy heard the key turn in the lock.

Shit! Mossy growled to himself. Still, there was always a Plan B, wasn't there?

An hour later, Mossy was hurrying down a cobbled lane that led to the main road. He had his black hoodie up, his hands pushed deep into his pockets and he looked straight ahead. He didn't want to draw attention to himself, or be recognised. Lucky that Trez's flat was in such an old building, and that he'd been a master escape artist when he was a little kid. The small window in the shower room had been a doddle, and he'd set it up for a swift re-entry.

Now, all that mattered was seeing Alice.

Mossy jogged across to the other side of the town. In fifteen minutes he was on Alice's road. Now the problem of her parents. Would they be there? And if they were, would they be paralytic? He walked slowly past the house, waited for a few moments and walked back. The second time he passed, he saw a shadow at the next-door neighbour's window. He'd once called her a nosey old witch, but Alice had told him off. They looked out for each other, she said, and, apart from Mossy, this neighbour was the only person who cared about her.

Mossy stopped. The shadow lifted the curtain and beckoned to him.

Warily, he approached the door. After a while he heard the click of a walking stick, and laboured breathing, as the old woman released the safety chain and unlocked the door.

'You're taking a bit of a chance, lady. I might not be the innocent, fresh-faced kid you imagine me to be.'

The old woman laughed aloud. The raspy cackle made him jump. 'I'm no fool, me duck! And you're no angel, I know that much.' She stood back. 'Come in.'

He went into a small sitting room stuffed with old-fashioned furniture, knick-knacks and photographs.

'I've seen you before. You're Alice's friend, aren't you?'

Mossy nodded. 'Is she at home? She told me that you watch out for her, and I really need to see her.'

'My name's Meg Steeples. What's yours?'

'Mossy.'

She nodded slowly. 'Then, Mossy, I think you should know that I've reported Alice to the police.'

He stiffened. The fuzz? 'Why?'

'Because I think she's been abducted.'

He drew in a sharp breath. 'Taken by someone? Alice?'

'She's gone, Mossy, and she never let me know. She wouldn't do that. Do you have any other suggestion about where she is?'

A dozen ideas crossed his mind, every one of them bad. Oh God! He'd left it too late! He should have seen this coming. They were getting at him through Alice! Darke! It had to be Darke! And if even Trez was scared of him . . . Mossy's brain went into overdrive. Then he felt a calming hand on his arm.

'I'm sorry, I've upset you, Mossy. But you had to be told. She has so few people that care for her.'

He nodded. 'I know. I have to find her.'

'There was a man watching the house. It was dark, so I couldn't see him properly, but he was tall and strongly built. He stood across the road in the shadows for quite a time.'

Trez? And if it was him, then it meant he really had delivered Mossy's letter. He frowned. Or had he? Did he come for something else, something far more frightening? Mossy closed his eyes. He should've known! It had sounded too good to be true, and now he knew it was.

* * *

Marie fell asleep at once and began to dream about an evil Fagin-type character that looked exactly like Vic Blackwell, revolving slowly on a children's roundabout.

* * *

Robbie and Kevin were just arriving at the Lemon Tree Club in Fenchester. They had decided on a different strategy this time, and both went in together. Kevin, who had chosen to use his middle name of Lee, was the perfect counterfoil to the laid back Robbie. Whereas Robbie always looked casual to the point of couldn't care less, Kevin brushed up rather well, and out of uniform, took great care about what he wore.

'Those cargo pants are going to be the talk of the night, mate,' Kevin murmured as they walked in.

'I feel like a total dork,' muttered Robbie. 'They're monstrous.'

'But very collectible, I'm sure.' Kevin grinned. 'And you do wear them well.'

'Bollocks.'

Kevin laughed as they made their way to the bar. This was a first for him, a bar that was ninety percent male, and probably not one gay boy in sight. Kevin wasn't openly homosexual, although after a rocky coming out he didn't deny it if anyone asked. Those close to him thought nothing of it, and to him it was just a part of his overall make-up. Being a good policeman and a caring human being were much higher on his list of priorities.

He looked around to check there were no familiar faces that might know him as a copper, and tried to sum up the clientele. One glance at Robbie told him he was doing the same.

'Not as relaxed as the place I was at last night. I'm definitely not feeling the love,' said Robbie, as he paid for two massively overpriced drinks.

'Bit cliquey, isn't it?' Groups of guys were talking in small huddles, none appearing to welcome newcomers with open arms.

'I'm hoping our contact, Bez, will be here tonight. He'll break the ice for us.'

'Well, they might not be laying down the red carpet, but those pants of yours are attracting quite a bit of attention. I don't think there's a guy in here who hasn't eyeballed them.'

'Hard not to!'

'Exactly what we want, even if you do feel like a prat.' Kevin glanced down at his designer jeans and was mighty glad it wasn't him wearing those bizarre joggers. He *was* wearing a Hybird X T-shirt though, but just a plain one with a simple logo that Max had managed to pick up on Gumtree for not too much money. It certainly wasn't a collector's item, but it did give him credibility.

'Ah.' Robbie nodded towards the entrance, and lifted a hand in recognition. 'Bez.'

The young man detached himself from his friends, hurried over and clapped Rob on the shoulder. 'Hey! Glad you made it, man!'

'Hi, mate. This is Lee.'

They shook hands. Rob had been right, this lad was Oscar material. He was coming over like a genuine old buddy.

'What can I get you?' asked Robbie.

'I'm okay thanks. My friends will have got me one in. Maybe later?'

'Sure.' Robbie lowered his voice. 'Is it always this welcoming in here?'

'It's posher than the Ginger Sheep, that's for sure, and some of the guys think they're a cut above a dive like that.'

He glanced around. 'It's mostly bored rich kids that come here.'

'They don't seem put off from wearing their Hybird gear, do they?'

Bez frowned. 'I reckon all this hype over the stuff getting nicked is making most of them even worse — you know, proving how tough they are and trying to look like they don't give a stuff. Most of them are probably shitting themselves, but they daren't let their friends know. Wankers! What I do know is that it's sent the prices rocketing! In some cases the collectors' items have doubled in value.'

'Wow!' Kevin breathed, knowing what some stuff was fetching even before the warnings.

'I'd better get back. You just watch those pants, mate. They're getting serious stares.' Bez raised a knowing eyebrow and strolled off to rejoin his group.

'Hell, it's a win-win situation for the thieves, isn't it?' Robbie said. 'The more you nick, the higher the resell value gets. It's the perfect setup.'

'Hey-up! You've hooked a fish at four o'clock.' Kevin had noticed a very well-dressed young guy approaching them, his eyes fixed on Robbie's Hybird X trousers.

'Hi there. I'm Aidan. You're new here, aren't you?'

Robbie lifted his drink in salute. 'Hi. I'm Ryan, and this is Lee. Yeah, I've not lived round here for long, and a friend told me to try this place.'

'Friend?'

'Him.' Robbie nodded towards where Bez was talking to his friends.

'Ah, yes. I know him. Nice kid.' His gaze returned to Robbie. 'Listen, I know someone that's new to the collecting scene, if you get my drift. He's looking for something special by way of a grail.'

Robbie looked back at him blankly.

Aidan laughed. 'Come on! Don't pretend you don't know what I'm talking about. Those.' He pointed to the brightly coloured trousers.

'Oh, sorry, but they're not for sale. I'm kind of attached to them.'

'How much money do you think it'd take to "unattach" you?'

Robbie shrugged. 'Dunno. I've never even thought about it.'

'My friend is willing to pay top dollar. And you know as well as me that those are a Hybird X, done in collaboration with a French fashion designer, so I won't insult you. I'll offer you a thousand pounds in cash tonight.'

Kevin took stock of the guy, this Aidan. He was a bit older than some of the other men there, but probably no older than Robbie. His clothes were fashionable, certainly, but there wasn't a Hybird label on them. If he was a collector, he wasn't advertising the fact.

Robbie played it cool. 'I'm not offended, Aidan, but I'm assuming that's your opening offer? Because you seem to know their pedigree, I'm thinking a grand could be on the lower side of what they're really worth.'

Aidan smiled. 'That's my offer right now, but if you get any better ones, talk to me first. I could quite likely match them, and I'd like first refusal.'

Indifferently, Robbie said, 'Maybe. But as I said, they're really not for sale.'

'Maybe when a couple of the others have made their bids you'll think again.'

'Others?' asked Robbie.

Aidan glanced around the crowded bar. 'They're not in yet, but news travels fast. I'm pretty sure you'll get a visit from at least two serious collectors.'

'Do they have names?' Robbie kept up his bored attitude. 'Just so as I know that I'm dealing with true collectors and not some shites that want to flog them on.'

'One's called Lance, and the other's Dean. They're always on the lookout for grails, and they both have readies in their pocket. But don't forget — talk to me first.'

'Okay.' Robbie raised his glass. '*If* I change my mind.'

Aidan turned to go, then stopped. 'And, Ryan. Watch yourself. Wearing Hybirds like that could be dangerous. You've heard what's happening around here, haven't you?'

Robbie nodded slowly. 'Yeah, but I don't like anyone telling me what I can or can't do.'

Aidan looked unimpressed. 'Just so long as you know, but I'd back off sporting the grails and stick to stuff like what your mate here is wearing. It's good, but he certainly won't get mugged for it.'

Kevin watched Aidan go, wondering if he was on the level. Could he be involved somehow? He really wasn't sure, but was inclined to believe that the guy was just heavily into Hybird streetwear. He just wasn't sure whether Aidan wanted the joggers for someone else, as he had said, or for himself. Whatever, he certainly knew his subject. Neither Kevin nor Rob had known that those dreadful pants were as collectible as they obviously were.

'There's an awful lot of guys with smartphones out,' Rob murmured. 'I've seen a couple take sneaky pictures of you, and I reckon the rest are searching the Hybird sites to check out their value.'

'I'm suddenly starting to feel rather vulnerable.'

'Not without cause, mate. Maybe we've overstepped the mark a bit?' Rob said. 'But who'd have thought you were wearing a fortune wrapped around your shapely butt!'

'Then perhaps we should go sit at a table, rather than stand here at the bar looking like I'm advertising bloody Hybirds.'

'Sensible move.' Kevin spotted a small table towards the back of the club, and they made their way towards it.

They sat down. Kevin surveyed the amount of surreptitious glances they were getting. 'If your idea was to set yourself up for a visit from the Hybird thieves, I reckon you've done a sterling job. And here comes your next prospective buyer, I do believe.'

This man didn't introduce himself. He took the third chair at their table and said, 'Whatever Aidan offered you, I'll give you that and half again.'

'And as I told Aidan, they aren't for sale,' Robbie said.

'Okay, I'll double his offer.'

Kevin swallowed. Two grand for a pair of pants that he wouldn't be seen dead in?

'Look, mate, I like my Hybirds, okay, and I'm not selling any of 'em. I can't seem to get that over to you guys.'

The man raised his hands. 'Have it your way.' He stalked off.

'I liked the hint that you have a wardrobe full of them,' Kevin said.

Robbie smiled.

In the hour and a half they were at the club, Robbie was approached three more times. He was bought several drinks by total strangers, most of which he tipped into a potted plant before realising it was artificial. Several younger men came up and chatted, just in order to get a look at his famous pants. One even asked for a selfie with him.

In a quiet moment, Robbie whispered to Kevin that he recognised several guys that had been at the Ginger Sheep the night before. All of them had admired his jacket, so now they could verify that he had more than one highly sought-after Hybird X grail. As Aidan had said, news travels fast.

At around half past midnight, Robbie decided they'd made their point and it was time to go. Kevin knew that this would probably be the riskiest part of the exercise. Coming out of the crowded club onto a deserted street left them well exposed. 'Just popping to the little boys' room, then I'm ready.'

The gents was empty, so he went into a cubicle and quickly sent a prearranged text to one of the uniformed crews working Fenchester that night. No one would be arriving on blues and twos, but at least his colleagues were aware of their situation. He went back into the bar.

'Ready when you are.'

Robbie nodded, and with a friendly wave to Bez, they made their way to the exit.

A man with a scary haircut and a lot of tattoos that didn't quite go with the smart Lemon Tree uniform smiled at them and said he hoped they'd see them again soon. Kevin hoped he'd never have to step inside this bar again in his whole life. He didn't like the odd, intense atmosphere that seemed to accompany anything to do with Hybirds. Everyone was too fanatical, and it didn't make for good vibes.

The air outside was bitterly cold, and Kevin pulled his jacket tighter around him. He looked up and down the street, and then they moved off towards their parked car.

Robbie appeared relaxed, but Kevin knew there was as much adrenalin rushing through him as he had. They had a three-hundred-metre walk to safety, and the best they could hope for, the thing that would make the whole horrible evening worthwhile, was that they'd be watched from a distance, then discreetly followed back to Robbie's apartment.

Although they had chosen a safe spot for Kevin's car, when they arrived the road had been packed with vehicles, and they'd had to opt for somewhere less suitable. Now he just prayed that he was looking as casual as Robbie was. Inside, he was feeling very unsettled indeed.

Even though he was on high alert, Kevin never saw the hit when it came. And neither did Robbie.

Three figures erupted from a shadowy doorway and took them down in a matter of seconds.

The adrenalin kicked in, and instantly, they both went from victims to officers facing serious assault.

Clearly, the idea was to immobilise him, and then free Robbie from his precious Hybird pants. They knew exactly what they were doing. What they didn't know was that they were dealing with two young, fit police officers.

Kevin took a hefty punch in the abdomen. It almost winded him, but he'd seen it coming and turned aside, lashing out with a well-aimed kick. He caught his assailant square in the side of his knee, dead-legging him. The kid went down, screaming like a footballer looking for a penalty, clutching at his leg and rolling into the gutter.

Kevin sprang up and threw himself at the two guys who were manhandling Robbie into the kind of position they themselves used on violent drunks. Whoever they were, these weren't any opportunist kids, they were well-trained, professional fighters.

He dragged one off, which allowed Robbie to take on the other guy. After a short exchange of blows, a car screamed to a halt a short distance away, and a deep voice yelled at the muggers to abort.

Kevin spat blood, and drew in a rasping breath. Meanwhile, two of the attackers dragged the other to his feet and made off towards the open doors of the vehicle. Robbie was clawing at his pocket for his phone, and then asking for assistance, barking directions at the Fenchester police.

In his weakened state, Kevin knew it was no use trying to chase after them. Maybe the Fenchester crew were close enough to pick them up. He hoped so, because they had clearly just fallen victim to Fagin's street urchins. Taking one whole unit out of action would be a big thing. 'You okay?' he asked, hauling himself to his feet.

'Think so, except for this.'

He took his hand away from his head. It was covered in blood.

'Shit, Rob!' He pulled his phone from his pocket, found it miraculously still intact and called for an ambulance. He rushed to Robbie's side.

'One of them hit my head on the edge of the curb.'

Blood poured from a wide gash on the side of his head, and his words had become slurred.

Kevin tore off his T-shirt, rolled it into a ball and pressed hard on the wound. 'Keep talking to me, Rob. You're sounding a bit sleepy, and I want you to stay awake, alright?'

'Uhhh . . .' Robbie sighed.

'Come on, man! Wake up!'

Robbie's eyes were closing. Shit! Where were those bloody paramedics? 'Talk to me, DC Melton! I want a report, Detective! Now! Understand?'

'Er, yeah, um, three males . . .' His voice was fading, but he was now aware that he had to remain conscious. 'Dark clothing, joggers, hoodies . . .'

'Yes, yes, and?'

'Young . . .'

'More!' If someone didn't help him soon, he was going to lose this battle.

'They . . . they were trained, like martial arts, or maybe, er, military?'

'That's good, Robbie. Anything else?'

'Kevin? Is he okay?'

'I'm right here, Rob. I'm fine.'

Kevin heard sirens in the distance. *Come on! Come on! For fuck's sake hurry up!*

And then he was being moved aside, and green-suited paramedics were kneeling down beside Robbie, talking to him and caring for him.

Kevin didn't normally show his emotions, but when somebody wrapped a foil blanket around his shoulders, he almost broke down in tears.

CHAPTER TWENTY-THREE

As the ambulance sped across the darkened fen towards Greenborough General, on a different stretch of the cold, inhospitable fenland, Vic Blackwell walked alone.

After Marie's outburst, his immediate desire had been to run into the arms of Big Rita and the insatiable Vee. Instead, shaking his head slightly, he pulled on an old wax jacket and drove out to the sea-bank.

Now, battling a freezing night wind off the Wash, he caught a fleeting glimpse of a crescent moon in the blackness, before it was obscured again by fast-moving clouds. The sight brought back a sudden memory, vivid and painful. *Oh, Tania, how wise you were!*

'What are you reading now?' he asked her.

Tania looked up, over the rim of her reading glasses. 'The Rime of the Ancient Mariner.'

'Oh. Not my thing at all.'

'We can't all read the same stuff, can we? I wouldn't enjoy that action hero stuff you like so much. Actually, I think you'd like this, if you could be bothered to give it a go. Listen to this.'

Tania read to him about the horned moon. According to Coleridge, the sailors of old saw the crescent moon with a star within the tips, and considered this to be a bad omen. 'Coleridge can't have studied astronomy, because the moon's light would eclipse any star lying behind it. He created an impossible moon, and people believed it for centuries afterwards! Would you credit that?' Tania laughed. 'How naïve we can be, believing what we're told, or what we think to be true and continuing to believe it ever afterwards, when it's actually a complete fallacy.'

Back in the cold, black night, Blackwell closed his eyes for a moment. Since he'd run from Marie, his emotions had veered between hate for her — and shame. Could he really have been that stupid? Had he spent years being eaten up with hate and anger over a "complete fallacy?" If he had, then there really was no hope for him. But what if Marie was at fault? What if it was she who was keeping a lie alive? If that were so, then he wanted more than just to make her life hell. He wanted rid of her.

He walked to the observation point he'd chosen for keeping a watch on the drug smugglers, and hunkered down out of the biting wind. A narrow culvert led through a sluice and then out into the main river. There were a couple of ledges and some low walling around the sluice gate that provided somewhere to sit and watch without being seen.

He hadn't made the call to this Michael yet, dreading confirmation of what Marie had said. Had Tania really been so unhappy? Had he really been that much of a shit? But he'd loved her. Hadn't he?

His head ached from all the thoughts and questions hammering into his brain.

He took a packet of cigarettes from his inside pocket, and hunted around until he found his lighter. He hadn't smoked for years. He and Tania had given up together, and unexpectedly, it had been easier for him. Nevertheless, he still carried the lighter with him. He ran a finger over the engraving on the flat surface. It read, *Love forever. Your Tania.*

Blackwell lit the cigarette and coughed. After a few drags, he stubbed it out and let it cool before pocketing it, not wanting to leave any traces.

Turning his collar up, he forced himself to go back to the time just before Tania died. Marie had accused him of being the cause of Tania's unhappiness, saying he'd treated her like a possession. Was that true?

He refused to admit it to himself. Only gradually did he come to realise that this reluctance probably meant it was true. He closed his eyes. It had been the pinnacle of his career. He had been decorated for bravery, everyone wanted to be his friend and he'd had some amazing collars. It seemed that nothing could stop him. Vic Blackwell, the golden boy. He remembered the arrests, and proudly presenting his evidence in court. All those late nights in the local, celebrating with his mates after a conviction had been passed. None of these things involved Tania. Vic swallowed hard. Come to think of it, at that heady time in his life Tania hardly featured at all. He had gone home, crowed about his triumphs, eaten the dinner she'd made, drunk too much, and spent half the night fucking her before it all began again.

The scales were slowly tipping, the shame taking over. Maybe Marie had been right. He'd loved Tania, sure, but that love slid into the shadows while he chased his glowing career. He'd taken her for granted and neglected her. Not only that, it had been Tania who had tried to get help to make things right again when it should have been him.

And the night she died? What of that? He *could* remember, maybe he'd blocked it out. The rows came back to him. Around that time, there had been harsh words between them on numerous occasions. What was the tipping point? No, he couldn't face it. He didn't have the strength to face the fact that he had been responsible for his wife's death.

Vic stared up at the clouds skidding across the night sky. What to do now? First, he would have to talk to this

Michael person. Then what? Step away from his vendetta? Or deny it, and continue to blame Marie Evans?

Struck with a force like a freight train, he felt incapable of doing anything. So there was no hope for him. But wait. Maybe there was? Because, from the moment he walked back into that CID room, he'd been rejuvenated. Suddenly, being part of a team again, doing proper police work, had had a remarkable effect on him, and it was totally unexpected.

Vic stood up. If he did choose to go that route, he had a feeling Marie would forgive him, even though she'd have every right to hate his guts. Deep down, he knew she was a good person. He would have to make her believe in his sincerity. Then he would need to convince Ruth Crooke and Jenny Deane, and he knew both women mistrusted and disliked him. Could he do it?

He climbed back up to the path and began his trek back. Or maybe he could just transfer out, and make a new start somewhere else? He increased his stride along the rough track and resolved to stay right here.

Vic paused at the old Cotterill cottage, and looked in. It was in darkness, as it should be, but when he looked closer he saw a faint glimmer of light coming from inside. That stupid woman! Despite all their warnings, even after being taken hostage, she had sneaked back home! She was really asking for trouble. Not only that, there was a good chance she'd mess up their operation — again. He walked on. He wouldn't scare her by banging on the door in the middle of the night, but he'd certainly be back first thing tomorrow for a stiff word. What on earth was the silly cow thinking of? They could have killed her last time, and they wouldn't hesitate if they knew she was back, sticking her nose in yet again.

It came to him that he was thinking like a policeman again. If only he could leave the past left behind! More than anything, he wanted a proper future, not one filled with misplaced revenge.

And yet. A small part of him, the vindictive, hateful part, refused to admit defeat.

* * *

At Greenborough General, Jackman found PC Kevin Stoner sitting beside Robbie's trolley in the A&E department.

'Concussion, sir,' said Kevin, holding an ice-pack against his own swollen cheek. 'They're doing a scan to rule out serious injury, but they are pretty sure he'll be under head-injury observation for forty-eight hours.'

'Should he be sleeping?' Jackman had always been told to keep people suffering from a head injury awake.

'Apparently sleep is good for you. It allows the brain to recover, so long as you've been talking coherently and have no other symptoms like trouble walking or dilated pupils.' Kevin smiled. 'These nurses here are really informative.'

'Does he have any other injuries?' asked Jackman.

'Nothing serious, just bruises and scratches.' He looked up at Jackman. 'But he scared the life out of me, sir. He couldn't talk properly, and then he didn't recognise me. Luckily the paramedics got him here quickly, and he soon rallied.'

'What about you?'

'Oh, I'm fine, sir, just needed a couple of steri-strips on this.' Kevin pointed to his cut cheek.

'Can you run me through what happened?' Jackman pulled up a chair and sat down. This was not how he'd envisaged his night with Laura. He had been looking forward to telling her of his plans.

Kevin described their evening in the Lemon Tree club, and what happened afterwards.

'The main thing is, it was very carefully planned. If we'd been ordinary lads out for a few jars, we'd have been a pushover for those guys. And even we really struggled.

To be honest, I'm not sure which way it would have gone if this other guy hadn't turned up and called his dogs off.'

Another scene from Dickens, thought Jackman. Bill Sykes and his group of ruffians. 'Did you notice anything about the vehicle, Kevin?'

'Not much, sir. It was a dark coloured full-size SUV. The licence plate was covered, and it straddled the road, so I couldn't see the shape of the grill or any manufacturer's logo. My gut feeling tells me it was a Nissan Armada. It had that kind of boxy squared-off back to it.'

'You didn't see who was driving it, I suppose?'

'Sorry, sir, but I couldn't see a great deal from the gutter. He did have a powerful voice though. He sounded much older than the guys that hit us, and I thought that word he used was a bit unusual, you know, "Abort!" Like Robbie said, it sounded almost military.'

Jackman nodded. Most thieves would call something simple like "Run!" or "Scarper, lads!" The use of "abort" indicated that someone with combat training was running the operation.

'I thought I recognised one of the attackers, sir. There was something about him that looked familiar. I've been racking my brains to think who it might be.'

'As in someone you've arrested before? Someone you've given a warning to?'

'No, sir, I don't think so.'

Kevin looked into the distance, sunk in thought, and Jackman turned his attention to Robbie Melton. He hated seeing any of his team hurt, and now he had a second officer down. Charlie Button wouldn't be back to work for a while, and now Robbie was out of action. That just left Marie, Gary and himself. Three of them against the world!

Jackman dragged his mind back to the case in hand. Several things about tonight troubled him. How could this carefully planned hit have happened? For a start, it was pure chance that Robbie and Kevin had decided to visit the Lemon Tree. Second, Robbie'd never worn those ridiculous trousers before. And thirdly, neither officer had ever set foot in that place before tonight. So how could the hit have been planned in advance? It had to be a case of mistaken identity, or someone Robbie, Max or Kevin trusted, who was passing information to Fagin's gang. Or maybe someone was just sitting in the club, watching for something really tasty to turn up, and then ringing the hit squad. Yes, that sounded right. A simple call describing the marks, then another call as they were leaving, and, bang! Job done.

'Got it!'

Kevin's exclamation made him jump. 'You've remembered?'

'I have, but I'm not liking it one bit.' Kevin looked really worried.

'Spit it out, man!'

'The kid who took out Robbie — he's one of Jim Cousins's residents. He lives in the shelter in Bridle Street. His mates called him Rusty, or something like that.'

Jackman was on his feet immediately. The thieves needed a den. What better place than an upmarket, three storey town house in Bridle Street! 'If he went back to the house, and we can get there immediately, we could catch him before he's had chance to clean up and change his clothes.' Kevin stood up. 'No, you stay with Rob. Uniform will see to it. Do you think this kid was hurt in the fight?'

'He had a split lip, Rob made sure of that. I'm sure he'll be as battered as we are, maybe worse.'

'Good, so he could have DNA from either or both of you on him.' Jackman was already halfway out of the door, phone in hand. 'Stay here. I'll contact you later. And try to get some sleep.'

Running back to the car park, he alerted the duty sergeant at Saltern and arranged for them to meet him outside Jim Cousins's shelter. In all the time Jim had had it open, they'd never had cause to attend it. Well, tonight he'd tear it apart if he had to. This could be the turning point in the whole investigation.

* * *

Mossy had no idea what to do.

Not finding Alice had thrown him completely, and old Mrs Steeples had scared the hell out of him. The fact remained, though. After the old girl had seen a tall, heavily built man watching her house, Alice had disappeared. And since Trez hadn't wanted to say anything about Mossy's letter, he had little option but to believe that Trez had abducted her.

The thought made his blood turn to ice. She was such a gentle girl, how would she cope with it? Oh God! She must really hate him now! And all he'd ever wanted was to protect her.

Mrs Steeples had made him a hot drink, and put a shot of whisky in it. 'For your nerves, young'un. It's good for shock.' How kind she was. He now knew why Alice cared so much about the old girl.

Mossy was at a complete loss.

'So, what's your options?' Mrs Steeples had eased her arthritic self back into her chair.

'I can go back to the man who's training me to be a thief — he might have been the guy you saw lurking in the shadows over the road — or I can run.'

'Mmm, I see.' She thought for a moment. 'As I see it, you can't run. If you do, you'll never know what's happened to Alice.' She had a surprisingly penetrating gaze. 'What I think is, you'll have to go back and put on the performance of your life, Mossy. That's the only way you'll have a chance of knowing what's happened to your girl. Keep in this man's confidence, let him believe you're a loyal little crook, and think very hard indeed about how to find your Alice.' She paused. 'And *then* you run! Both of you.'

She was right.

Mossy stood up. 'Thank you for the drink, Mrs Steeples. I have to go now.'

He hadn't been gone that long, and he could still get back and in unnoticed. He knew that if Trez found out about this excursion, he'd be dead meat. Then there'd be no one left to help Alice.

Mossy arrived back unseen. He had a snack and washed the dishes, showered and went to his room. When Trez came back two hours later, Mossy was in bed, pretending to sleep.

He heard footsteps outside his door, then the door opening. He breathed steadily. To his horror, Trez leaned over the bed and stayed watching him for a few moments, before standing up again.

Mossy fought to keep his breathing even, and he must have succeeded, because Trez finally stepped back to the doorway.

Mossy heard him whisper softly, 'At least something went right tonight. Good kid, you did as I asked, even if you did sneak a slug of my whisky while I was out.' He gave a soft laugh. 'Little tyke!' And then he was gone.

Mossy shivered. Trez had smelt Mrs Steeples's whisky on his breath. And Trez's parting comment had sounded almost affectionate!

Mossy turned over and curled up under his duvet. Please God, don't let my luck run out. Just let me find Alice.

* * *

Jackman drove back to Saltern in record time and arrived at Jim Cousins's shelter to find two marked police cars already there.

'The kid hasn't come back tonight, sir. Jim says he's missed the curfew time.' Sergeant Colin Wakehurst beckoned to him from the doorway. 'Jim's pretty upset. He's never had any trouble before, and he's shocked that this particular kid's been involved in something so serious.'

'I'll have a word with Jim myself, Colin. Where is he?' Jackman asked.

'In his office, sir.'

'Are any of the other residents missing tonight?'

'No, sir, all present and accounted for, except for Rusty.'

Damn. The boy would probably be miles away by now.

Jim Cousins looked upset and angry. Jackman wasn't sure if the anger was directed at them, or his runaway resident.

'A police raid isn't exactly the kind of thing that instils confidence into these vulnerable young people, DI Jackman. It's a shame it couldn't have been done quietly, with my prior knowledge.'

Okay, it was them. 'We needed to act fast, Jim. If he'd returned here, and we'd been able to get DNA from his clothes, we'd have been able to place him at the scene. You know that.'

'Don't I just,' Jim grumbled. 'Are you sure it's Rusty you're after? He's a good kid, no trouble at all.'

'What's his real name, Jim?'

'Barry Winters. He was a runaway, but he's settled really well in here. He was almost ready to move on.'

'Why the name Rusty?'

'He's a redhead. What has he actually been accused of doing?'

'He was identified as one of three muggers who attacked and injured what they thought were two punters from the Lemon Tree Club in Fenchester, but who were actually plainclothes police officers.'

'Rusty? You're kidding me!' His surprise seemed genuine. 'Fenchester cops?'

'No, two of ours actually.'

'How badly hurt?' Jim now looked worried.

'One of my detectives has a nasty head injury, and the other lad has cuts and bruises.'

'Can I ask who it was? The other officer?'

Jackman couldn't see a problem in telling him. The undercover operation was now abandoned, so there was nothing to lose. 'PC Kevin Stoner. It was him that recognised Rusty.'

'Kev? Oh, that's rotten! He's a really good bloke.'

Jackman nodded. 'I agree. And he didn't deserve having three little shites trying to kick the hell out of him.' He yawned. It had been a long night. 'Well, I'm sorry about this, but we have to go through the boy's things and check his room thoroughly, so we'll be sealing it up tonight. Someone will be here tomorrow, okay? We'll also need to talk to the residents that were close to him. And if he should show up—'

'I know the drill, Inspector.' He took Jackman's card and pushed it into his pocket. 'But I don't think we'll be seeing our Rusty again, do you?'

'I'm certain we won't.'

He walked back to his car, weary and dispirited. Then he remembered, and a warm feeling flooded through him. Jackman had someone to go home to.

CHAPTER TWENTY-FOUR

Marie heard her phone ringing. Struggling awake, she looked at the clock. Almost five a.m. It had to be Jackman, or the duty sergeant. Something had happened.

'Marie?'

She recognised the voice instantly, and it wasn't Jackman. For a moment she said nothing, just lay there. What now? 'How did you get this number?'

Vic Blackwell gave a slight chuckle. 'I'm a detective, aren't I? But, please, don't hang up.'

She nearly had, but something in his voice made her stay on the line.

'Marie, I've been up all night, thinking about what you said. I . . . I have no idea where to start . . .' His voice tailed off.

She waited. Vic Blackwell was a master of deception. Well, a few well-chosen words wouldn't make it alright again, after all those years of harassment.

She heard him sigh. 'I have no right to ask this . . .' There was a lengthy silence. 'All this time . . . so much hate, so many accusations. I put the blame entirely on you, when I should have faced the truth and looked closer to home.'

Marie didn't know how to respond. Had her outburst really made him reconsider everything? Or was he using a clever tactic? 'Vic, it's early. I'm not even awake yet. I can't take this on board right now. If you really want to talk, meet me at the war memorial at seven thirty, before we start work. That's the best I can do.'

She hung up without waiting for an answer.

Face to face, she might be able to read him, though after so long, she had no idea if she knew Vic Blackwell at all.

Her mind was now racing, and it was too late to try to go back to sleep. She might as well get up, do her exercises, shower and breakfast, then gather herself together for their second meeting in two days. Would this one really be so different to last night's heated confrontation?

If Vic were being honest with her, what then? For a start, she wouldn't have to consider making any major changes to her life, like moving to another division, away from her team, her dear friends. Even if Vic chose to stay in CID, it would no longer be a problem. But there were no guarantees that he *was* being honest. Maybe it was a way of neutralising her outburst, lulling her into a false sense of security. What had he been planning for her, all that time? Why did he jump at returning to the CID section at Saltern?

She had no answers.

Marie longed for the day when she'd put on her motorcycle leathers again and ride into work, instead of driving. She yearned to feel the chill of the morning air in her face, and smell the ozone off the Wash.

She sighed, and her thoughts returned to Vic Blackwell.

She wanted to believe him. They had been a great team once, trusting each other completely. They'd had some pretty scary scrapes in their time, and she'd missed him when they finally went their separate ways.

Marie poured another coffee. She had been pleased for his success, but had always wondered where Tania fitted in. Tania had been so bright and intelligent, she could have done anything, but instead had become the homemaker, the faithful policeman's wife. It must have been tough for her but she never complained, never ran him down. Marie had seen the changes in him as he became increasingly successful, and she hadn't liked them, but she had never expected things to end as they did. And then to be blamed for everything!

She had no idea if she was about to meet a contrite friend, or a lying snake.

'Okay, Evans. All you can do is listen, and then make your mind up.'

She gathered up her things and took a deep breath.

* * *

Tommy got up early for once. Their evening at the Lemon Tree had been cut short due to some fracas outside, and he had finished up going to bed hours earlier than usual. Dean hadn't been himself at all, and had spent most of the evening on his mobile phone. Tommy had made a few attempts to chat to some of the guys at the club, but he too was feeling the pressure of not knowing what was happening with Darke. The only bright spot was the appearance of two new men to the Hybird scene, one of whom was wearing some very rare grail cargo pants. Tommy had had a few words with him, but then let some of the big boys haggle over the pants. Their owner didn't seem to be interested in selling, and had been swatting away the offers like flies all evening.

Tommy prepared himself some breakfast. All he could think about was Mossy — and his smashed face. How could this Trez, who was supposed to be his tutor, have done that to him? It scared Tommy badly. Mossy was a gobby little shite, but there was something about him that Tommy liked. He felt somehow protective towards Mossy, and wasn't happy about what had happened to him. And Dean was tied in with the great ape. Tommy wanted to work with Dean, no doubt about that, but he wanted nothing at all to do with Trez.

His problem was, if Dean decided to go along with Trez in this "business" proposition, then what would he do? He couldn't go to his parents, that was for sure. They'd made it clear they were glad to see the back of him. Okay, he could get a job, but where would he live and how would he survive until he got on his feet? He'd gotten used to better things.

He munched his cereal. He was going to need to find a means to turn Dean away from Action Man, and make him stick with him. Tommy wasn't blind. He knew Dean wanted him, he'd seen the way he watched him. How much did he want a good life? Tommy bit his lip and gazed around the luxurious apartment. He could have all this, but it came at a price. And he didn't know if he was willing to pay that heavily.

* * *

Although she was early, Vic Blackwell was already there, waiting. This irritated her, it seemed to give him the upper hand.

The war memorial was stationed at the end of a tree-lined avenue, quite close to the centre of town. A paved walkway edged with flower beds and wooden benches led up to the big stone cenotaph. This morning, apart from Vic, it was deserted, as Marie had hoped it would be. He had chosen the end bench, well away from the street, and he stood up when she arrived.

He looked so haggard that she hardly recognised him. Evidently, what she'd said the night before had had a profound effect on him. It constituted a small victory for her.

She sat down at the far end of the bench, Vic at the other.

'I said I didn't know where to start, and I still don't,' he began.

'Have you spoken to Michael?'

'Not yet. I didn't think he'd appreciate a call at six in the morning. But I will.' He stared down at the pavement beneath his feet. 'It crossed my mind that he was a mate of yours, and you'd cooked this up between you, as a cover for what had been going on between you and Tania . . .'

Marie felt her anger mount, but he was speaking again.

'Then I realised I was being paranoid again.' He looked at her sadly. 'This is going to take some getting my head around. Are you really telling me that Tania was faithful to me? That she was just trying to find some way to salvage our marriage?'

'That's exactly what I'm saying, Vic, and I've been saying it since she died, if only you'd believed me.'

'A shrink would probably tell me I couldn't face the truth, so I invented this fabrication to protect myself.'

'And he'd probably be right,' murmured Marie. 'What I'll never understand is why you ever imagined such a weird scenario. You know me, Vic Blackwell, better than most. Okay, I don't look like some fluffy oh-so-feminine woman, but if I was gay or bisexual, I would have told you. I certainly wouldn't keep it secret. And surely you know how much I loved my Bill? I still do, as it happens.'

'I do know.' His voice was husky. 'What I don't know is how I let things get this bad. So twisted and horrible.' He looked into her eyes, and Marie had trouble holding the intense gaze. 'I need to know the answer to a question, Marie.'

She drew in a breath. 'Okay, ask.'

'Is it possible to move forward from all this shit?'

'Anything is possible, Vic. Well, it is from my point of view, but I'm not sure where you want to go from here.'

Vic sank forward, his head in his hands. 'I think I need help to decide, Marie. I've done enough damage in recent years, haven't I?'

Marie had an impulse to put her arm around him, but stopped herself. This could still be one hell of a performance, and she didn't want to get sucked in before the curtain even rose. 'I don't think I'm the one to give that help, do you?' She kept her voice level.

'I know you're not, but I'm still asking you.'

'What do *you* want to do? This has to be your decision, Vic, no one else's. Suppose your life could begin again, in, say, an hour's time. Where would you be, and what would you be doing?'

He raised his head. 'I'd be walking into the CID room ready for daily orders, and I'd be thinking only of the investigation and how we could solve the case.'

'Do you mean that?'

'Like I've never meant anything before.'

He stared at her unblinking, and for the first time in many, many years she saw her old crewmate. 'I don't know how long it will take me to trust you again, Vic, maybe never, but I wouldn't stand in the way of that new life.'

Was she giving in? More to the point, had she been taken in by him? Marie didn't know, but she did know that she wanted his vendetta to end, one way or another.

For a moment she thought he was going to cry, then he just reached out, touched her arm and said, 'It's more than I deserve, I know that. But thank you, Marie.'

They both stood up. Enough had been said for now.

'I'll see you at the morning meeting then?' he said.

'You will,' she replied, and turned and walked away. Her heart was pounding. Had they just signed a peace treaty, or had she just signed herself up to even more persecution? She knew what she wanted to believe. Only time would tell.

* * *

It had taken Jackman considerably longer than usual to bring Ruth Crooke up to date on everything that had happened overnight, and then it was time for him to take daily orders. He hadn't even seen Marie to tell her about Robbie and Kevin, let alone have their normal catch-up before the day kicked off.

He walked into the now rather depleted CID room and looked around.

DI Jenny Deane was talking enthusiastically to two of her detectives, but besides the absent Charlie and Robbie, there was no sign of Marie, or Vic Blackwell either. He began to worry. He had so much on his mind right now. He just hoped he hadn't taken his eye off the ball regarding Blackwell.

The door opened, and Marie came in. He stared. Vic Blackwell was holding the door for her, and then they entered the room side by side.

Jenny flashed him an incredulous glance.

He shook his head. There was a lot to cover, and Jenny Deane clearly had something she needed to discuss. To give himself time to make sense of what he'd just witnessed, he suggested that Jenny go first.

'We've had some major developments regarding the steroid smuggling, and I've just heard that a shipment being brought in by plane has been intercepted on its way to the local airfield.' She looked across to Vic Blackwell. 'I'm going to get you straight out there, Sergeant, and you can take Larry with you. It seems the air traffic controller, who called the Border Agency after an unscheduled landing was requested, was suspicious about the incoming flight and managed to delay their move onto the apron until help could get there. Uniform and border force officials are on scene, and I'd like you out there immediately. It'll be a bun fight, as you can imagine. In a perfect world we'd all work beautifully together, but as we all know, it isn't perfect. We have an ongoing investigation, but border force have jurisdiction too. They're going to want their piece of the action. Do your best to keep everyone on side, and make sure the men involved are brought here, not sent to another station.' She paused. 'And make sure you talk to everyone on the ground. Get the whole story, okay?'

'Yes, ma'am,' Vic replied instantly. 'I'm on it.' He straightened up and looked in Marie's direction, with what appeared to Jackman to be an almost excited glance. He hurried from the room.

Curiouser and curiouser.

'So, what about the river and the suspected smugglers on the marsh, ma'am?' asked another of Jenny's team.

'Well, there is certainly something going on out there, especially since Mrs Cotterill was attacked, but it's pretty clear now that the steroids are being brought in by air, not sea.'

'Maybe they're using more than one supplier and another route in?' said another detective.

'Possibly, and due to what we already know regarding irregular activity in the area at very high tides, I'm going to suggest we go ahead with our planned obbo.'

'I'd certainly agree with that, Jenny,' added Jackman. 'As you say, we still need to find out why someone is using a boat to enter the marsh at night.'

'Exactly. Anyway, after we've questioned the people at the airfield, we may know a lot more about how the smugglers are working.' Jenny sat down.

It was Jackman's turn to speak. As always, he was very aware of Marie sitting somewhere towards the back of the room. 'Our news is not so good, I'm afraid.' Marie threw him a worried look. 'First thing I need to tell you, is that Robbie Melton and Kevin Stoner were attacked last night outside a club in Fenchester.' Marie's hand flew to her mouth. She and Robbie were good friends. 'Robbie has a concussion and is at present being kept in Greenborough General for observation. He is, however, alert and responsive, and I'm reliably told that he's creating havoc because they won't let him out yet! Kevin is bruised and has a few cuts, but is otherwise okay. We know that the attackers were a part of this Dickens-type gang stealing Hybird X clothing, and that they're being run by a much older, possibly ex-military man.' He took a breath. 'Kevin identified one of the boys involved, a young man called Barry Winters, who goes by the tag of Rusty. He's a resident at Jim Cousins's shelter on Bridle Street, but he didn't go back there last night. We'll be pursuing this today. However, we have other serious problems to deal with as well. Most of you will know that Marie and I were called to an incident in Cannon Park yesterday, where a young man was found who'd obviously been subjected to severe mental and physical abuse. He is at present being cared for in the hospital's psychiatric unit, but unfortunately a member of the public took some footage on their mobile phone and contacted the press.'

There were groans.

'I know.' Jackman pulled a face. 'Beggars belief, doesn't it? Anyway, there's a rather scathing report in this morning's paper, and we don't come out of it particularly well, but it could help us in the short term.' He paused. 'They assumed he was a drug addict, end of story, so the press have taken it as such. The heading says: *Addict Shame in Children's Playground. Why aren't the police doing more to prevent occurrences like this?* No mention of anything more sinister. The super will have to hold a press briefing at some point, but for the present, no one other than us is aware that the young man had been tortured and held in captivity before somehow escaping.'

'Thank heavens for small mercies,' murmured Gary. 'We could do with a head start before the media get wind of that.'

'Very true, so I need you to act fast on this. I want every CCTV camera in that whole area checked. I want all the statements uniform took from bystanders gone over with a fine tooth comb. We have to find out where that young man came from, who he is, where he was held, and by whom. I very much doubt that he himself will be able to help us for some time, if at all, so it's down to us to use every means to find out, and quickly.' He looked around the room. 'And on top of that, we have a missing teenage girl. She may just be a runaway from an abusive home, but given what else has been happening lately, we can't afford to ignore it. So, folks, if you came in this morning expecting a quiet day, you were sadly mistaken. I need some results. We have to clear this ever-growing list of crimes, and I need it done fast! Go to it, people!'

He beckoned to Marie, who was already hurrying towards him. 'Robbie's going to be fine. I'm so sorry I didn't get to see you first.'

'My fault. I got held up on the way in.' She looked at him urgently. 'Can we talk?'

'Of course.' He turned to Max. 'Grab us two coffees, would you, and bring them to my office? And by the look on Marie's face, make them strong ones.'

'Right away, boss.'

* * *

Marie didn't quite know where to start. 'I'll quickly explain something. It's about Vic Blackwell.' Jackman's heart sank. He knew he should have kept a closer eye on things. 'Then I have a piece of information that could be really important.'

She told him about how Blackwell had confronted her in the car park, then his early morning phone call, and their meeting just before work.

Jackman listened. 'Why on earth didn't you tell me before you went home?'

'I was in shock, I think. I was so angry I could have killed him.' The tension hadn't completely gone away. 'Then I got upset and just wanted away from him.'

'And now?'

She spread her hands, looking bewildered. 'I have no idea. I want to believe him, really I do. But . . .'

'His behaviour so far leaves you no choice but to doubt him?'

'Precisely. Although I am prepared to give him time to prove himself. When I saw him earlier, he looked gaunt, distraught, eaten up with guilt, or . . .' Something. She wasn't sure what.

'He did look different, didn't he? But as you say, with his track record, why should we trust him?' Jackman was frowning.

Marie knew he was worried for her. 'We have too much on our plates to worry about him right now, so I suggest we just suck it and see. The important thing is you know the situation.'

Jackman nodded. 'You're right. Now, what's this important piece of information?'

'I think I know who the boy on the roundabout is, although I'm having a hard time believing it.'

Jackman sat forward. 'Who, Marie?'

'Justin Hart. He went missing around eight months ago. I don't know if you remember the case. It was Fenchester's investigation, and they only ran with it because the father was a very rich businessman and it was thought that Justin had been snatched and held for ransom. Only no demands ever came, and it was assumed he'd simply run away.'

'Yes, I recall that one. He wasn't vulnerable or particularly young, but his father swore he was happy, and had no reason to leave home.' Tapping away on his keyboard, Jackman brought up a photograph. He let out a low whistle. 'What on earth makes you think this handsome young man is our roundabout boy?'

'This.' Marie leant across and pointed to the photograph. 'Look. That belt — well, the buckle, to be precise.'

Jackman looked. The boy in the photograph was wearing an intricate leather belt with a decorative silver buckle in the shape of a wolf's head.

'As the paramedics carried him past me in the corridor, I saw he was wearing that belt.' Marie stared at the image on the screen. 'I just knew I'd seen it before somewhere, so I checked the files. I'm sure it's him, Jackman.'

'Then check it out, Marie. Let Greenborough General know your suspicions, and see if he's calm enough to respond, at least to his name. No way can we contact Justin Hart's parents until the psych unit have had some time with their patient, and we're sure we've got the right boy. I'd hate for his mum or dad to see him in that state. If there's any doubt, talk to his GP and then move on to hospital records. We'll at least have DNA for a match, if it comes to it.' He was still staring at the screen. 'You could be right, you know. Same height, same age, and hair colouring. It's just the weight and distorted facial features that make him look so different.' Jackman's face was pale. 'My God. If it is him, Marie, I dread to think what that poor kid went through to bring about such a dramatic change.'

Marie had already thought about it. She hoped she was wrong about his identity, but she'd never seen another belt buckle like that one, and it was quite distinctive. 'I'll get straight on to it, Jackman. The sooner we know, the better.'

She turned to go. 'Marie?' Jackman said. 'Be wary, won't you? Of Vic Blackwell. I cannot see how years of festering anger can suddenly be nullified, just like that. It just doesn't compute.'

'I know. But I have to give him that one chance, don't I?'

'You owe him nothing, Marie. He owes *you*, and remember that.'

Marie gave him a weak smile and left the office.

CHAPTER TWENTY-FIVE

Still worried sick about Alice, Mossy forced himself to eat his breakfast. He was actually getting to like the weird food Trez dished out to him. He felt much fitter already, and he certainly didn't miss the sick feeling of an empty stomach when food was scarce.

Eating his toast, Trez stared at him thoughtfully. 'I'm guessing from your previous life that one of your talents would be getting into places where you had no right to be?'

Mossy frowned. What was Trez getting at?

'It's alright, it's not a trick question. And I'm hardly going to be phoning the Old Bill, am I?'

Mossy coughed. 'Yeah. I know my way around.'

'And locked doors?'

Mossy finally grinned. 'No such thing.'

'Good. Because I have a little job for you. Finish your breakfast and grab your jacket. We're going visiting.'

Twenty minutes later, they were parked a short distance from an avenue of big old houses, the type with no front gardens, just some old-fashioned iron railings, and steps up to the front door.

Trez locked the car and they went up to a dreary looking building with big sash windows and a weathered front door painted a dark red colour. Trez pushed the front door open. Inside, was a dim hallway with several doors leading off it. 'Okay, Houdini, it's this one here. I'll just check that there's no one inside.' Trez knocked several times, leaned close to the door, and appeared to be sniffing. 'No one answering, and no dead body smell seeping out, so no one's at home and no one is dead and rotting on the carpet. Go to it, Mossy.'

It took just a minute before the door swung open.

'Nice one, lad.' Trez pushed him inside, followed him in and shut the door behind them.

Mossy realised that he was inside Darke's office, the very place that Gordi and Zak had told him never to go. 'Why're we here?' he asked. 'What are you looking for?'

Trez went over to a big old banker's desk. 'Anything that might tell me where he's gone, or what he's up to.'

Mossy was uneasy. The airless room had a musty smell. Supposing Darke came back and found them?

'Damn,' Trez grunted. 'Not a thing out of order. Everything's so bloody tidy!'

'No desk diary?' asked Mossy.

Trez gave a short laugh. 'Darke? Oh no. Everything he does goes in his notebooks, and he keeps those close.' He sighed. 'Oh well, at least this has proved that he's not had a heart attack behind his desk. And he didn't leave in a hurry.'

'So whatever happened,' Mossy said, 'either happened after he left here, like he got hit by a bus, or he's on a trip somewhere.'

'It doesn't make sense.' Trez exhaled loudly. 'We should get out of here. Come on, Mossy.'

He didn't need telling twice.

Outside in the hallway, just as Trez was closing the door, they heard a voice.

'Can I help you?'

Mossy saw a plump little man standing in the doorway of a room across the hall.

Trez smiled at him. 'No, we're fine, thanks.' He took a key from his pocket and waved it at the man. 'Mr Darke asked me to call in and check his messages while he's away.'

'Oh, I see. Then good morning to you.' The man retreated into his own room.

Back in the car, Trez sat, staring at the house they'd just left 'I'd rather we hadn't been seen, but at least he's not suspicious.'

'Let's go, Trez. He might have second thoughts and ring the cops.'

'I don't think that'll happen.' He started the car anyway. 'I'm pretty sure most of the stuff that goes on in that place is illegal.'

Mossy wasn't convinced. If Darke could bug Trez's flat, he could certainly put hidden cameras in his own office. Maybe Trez had just walked into a trap, and now he was implicated.

They drove back in silence. Mossy's thoughts oscillated between Darke, and his fear of him, and how on earth to begin the search for Alice. He knew he had to keep Trez sweet, but it was tearing him apart. So much so, that in the back of his mind, he was even thinking of blowing the whole thing apart and putting an end to his dreams by contacting the police.

* * *

Halfway between the station and the airfield, Vic Blackwell made his decision. Everything became clear, and he knew exactly what he had to do. The first thing was to make some headway with this case. He needed Brownie points, badly.

Blackwell was interested to know why the air traffic controller had been suspicious in the first place. So he did his bit to establish a fragile entente cordiale between the police and the border control officers, and then he tackled the air traffic controller.

'So, Eddie, why did this one bother you?'

Eddie Davies was an older man. Having worked at both Heathrow and Gatwick, he retired to the fens, but soon gravitated back to his lifelong passion for flying and air safety. Over the years, the small airfield had become his baby, so that now the only voice someone requesting permission to land would hear would be Eddie's.

'Three things actually, Sergeant.' He sounded untroubled by the furore going on at his precious airfield. 'One, we had received a notification from you to be on the lookout for irregular activity regarding a possible smuggling operation. Two, the plane in question had been heading to a small unlicensed fenland airfield quite close by, but altered course and requested permission to land here after they experienced a technical problem. And three,' he looked at Blackwell, 'I don't know if you know much about flying, Detective, but all pilots and air traffic controllers have to speak English, no matter what their nationality.'

'No, I didn't know that.'

'It's called Aviation English,' Eddie said, 'and it consists of around three hundred words consisting of professional jargon and plain English. It was implemented after the Tenerife air disaster, when a message was misunderstood due to language, and two passenger planes collided.' He shrugged. 'It's a safety thing. Anyway, our pilot this morning struggled to speak even a few words properly. As its registration prefix was OO, I knew it was a Belgian plane, but it had taken off from the Netherlands, so he should have been able to communicate easily.'

'No wonder you were suspicious, Ed. But why, if he was so close to his destination, didn't he just land there?'

'Unlicensed airstrips don't have the level of emergency and fire cover that we do, and he was worried enough to chance coming down here. And don't forget, it was still dark early this morning. Landing at these small private strips can be a challenge at the best of times but in poor visibility, with a possibly serious technical problem and no fire tender on hand, really not a good idea.'

Blackwell thanked him and went back to where Larry was talking to a couple of uniformed officers.

'These guys are preparing to take the two smugglers back to the custody suite. And well done — the border force officer in charge has agreed to your request that they go to Saltern-le-Fen.'

Blackwell smiled to himself. One up to him.

'Oh, good,' he said casually. 'Any idea of how much stuff has been found?'

A PC grinned at him. 'A pretty decent haul, Sarge. And they clearly weren't expecting trouble because it wasn't even hidden. They'd packed the steroids in big hikers' rucksacks, ready to just sling over their shoulders and make off with.'

'Nice one, even if that technical problem did play a big part in delivering them right into our hands.' Blackwell still had that niggling worry about what was going on at Cassell Hill Marsh. What was coming in up that tidal river, and under the cover of night? In any case, this was going well. He'd tie up the loose ends here, and then he'd turn his attention to the riddle of Cassell Hill.

* * *

'I was right, sir.' Marie didn't look particularly pleased about it.

'It is Justin Hart?' Jackman asked.

'The psych unit have confirmed it. A combination of information from his medical records, and the fact that after being sedated, he was calm enough to give them his name and date of birth.'

'Anything else?'

'Nothing, Jackman. It took them an hour to get his name. Any other questions and he goes back into his shell. He's traumatised beyond belief.'

'Well, it's not much, but we have a couple of CCTV sightings, and we're slowly tracing his journey to the park backwards from there. Officers are canvassing the whole area, trying to find any witnesses who might have seen him on his way to Cannon Park. We have to find out where he escaped from.'

'I can't stop trying to fathom out what happened in the first place,' Marie said. 'Was he snatched, as was originally believed? If so, why hold him for months and not ask for any ransom?'

'Maybe he wasn't taken for money, but for some other reason. There are a lot of twisted people out there. Maybe those rich boy good looks attracted some predator.'

'A *local* predator. Justin couldn't have travelled far in his state.' Marie puffed out her cheeks. 'That means that the person who's been holding him lives right here in Saltern. We have a monster in our back yard.'

Jackman shuddered. 'I've been checking Justin's file and I had a word with the original officer in charge, DI Bill Coutts. He's moved up to Humberside now, but he was very helpful. He said that for two months after his disappearance, there were several possible sightings of him in clubs and bars around the Fenchester area, which was one of the main reasons for scaling down the search. He was sure that at least one of the sightings was kosher, and as he seemed in good health, he honestly felt that Justin had just had enough of Daddy's high expectations and dropped out.'

'Do we believe there were high expectations put on him?'

'Father says no. Everyone else says yes. I'm going with the majority.' Jackman had first-hand experience of that sort of thing. He'd probably still be suffering from it now if he hadn't excelled himself in the Alistair Ashcroft case and the threats to his family. When he realised exactly what his son confronted in his chosen line of work, his father had undergone a Damascene conversion.

'Which could mean he took some time out, bummed around the bars, then met something very nasty indeed.' Marie pushed her hands deep into her pockets and leaned back against the door frame. 'This is all a very long way from Fagin and his street urchins, isn't it?'

Jackman sat back in his chair and looked up at her. 'I'm not totally convinced that it is, even though it seems very unlikely.'

Marie nodded. 'Can you really connect the gangs of thieves with this boy's incarceration?'

Jackman threw up his hands. 'As I said, it's improbable, but I can't rule it out.'

'Boss?' Gary appeared in the doorway beside Marie. 'We've got another CCTV image, this time close to the Baptist church.'

Jackman and Marie hurried out into the CID room and examined the three sightings on the wall map.

'It's a bit of a zigzag, but this is what we have so far.' With his finger, Gary traced a route from Cannon Park through a couple of narrow lanes and then across a main road and into a side road. 'We've pushed our enquiries further in this direction.' He stabbed another point on the map. 'Although it's anyone's guess where he came from. He was running as if the hounds of hell were after him.'

'I wonder why he headed for Cannon Park?' Jackman said.

'Because his family home wasn't far from there,' Marie said sadly. 'I'm guessing he was running back to his childhood, to safer times and happier memories . . .'

'And curled up on the roundabout for solace,' finished off Jackman, seeing again that pathetic figure on the roundabout.

'At least we have him now, sir, and he's safe.' Gary pulled a face. 'Although I'm not sure how you come back from something like that.'

No one responded.

'Keep me informed of any new sightings, Gary. I need to go and ring the hospital again to check on Robbie, and then I have the unenviable task of talking to the super about notifying Justin Hart's parents that their son is alive, although far from well.'

* * *

When Dean opened the front door to Trez, Tommy was surprised to see Mossy standing next to him. How should he react? They weren't supposed to know each other, nor were they supposed to mix. But if Dean was surprised he didn't let on, he merely led the way to the lounge.

'You two met at the medic's house, but just in case you didn't get as far as names, this is Mossy.' Trez pointed. 'And this is Tommy.'

Tommy nodded casually, still not quite sure how to play this.

Mossy followed suit.

An uncomfortable silence ensued, then Trez told them that he and Mossy had broken into Darke's office.

'Jesus, Trez! Have you got a death wish?' exclaimed Dean. 'What if he finds out? You'll be history!'

'Then I'll say I was scared he'd had a heart attack and needed our help, but get real, he's done a runner, hasn't he? And taken our money.'

'No, Trez. He's a cunning fox. I can't see him running out on a going concern. Between us we are bagging him thousands of pounds every week, sometimes every night. I know he owes us, but not enough to warrant doing a midnight runner.' Dean sounded irritable. 'He's only been gone for a day and a bit, for heaven's sake! He's hatching something, so we just have to stick it out.'

'Sorry, but I think he had an agenda here in Saltern, and he wasn't telling us.' Trez looked fierce. 'I reckon that when he set this scam up, there was a time limit attached, he just never told us about it. Now that the police are all over the place, the rich kids'll start to get too scared to wear their crappy clothes, so he's moved on, and then he'll set up again in another town or city and start all over again. And he's got *our* money to give himself a kick-start.'

Dean didn't look totally convinced.

Trez leant forward. 'I have an idea that could benefit us all, but to make it work, we'll need to trust each other. And that could be a problem.'

Dead right it could, thought Tommy, and then he stiffened. This was it, wasn't it? If Dean bought into this amazing idea whatever it was, Tommy would be stuffed, because he didn't trust Trez at all.

He had been walking around the lounge, listening. Now he flopped down on the sofa next to Dean.

Trez looked at Dean. 'I'd be prepared to trust you with a business deal. We have very different talents, but we're both very good at what we do.' His gaze then travelled to Tommy. 'And if you vouched for your friend here, then I'm good with that too.' He nudged Mossy. 'And I like Mossy. I think he's a slippery little eel, but he has all the attributes of a first-class thief.'

'You have a funny way of showing people that you like them.' The words escaped from Tommy's mouth before he could stop them. He felt Dean tense beside him.

It was Mossy, of all people, that came to the rescue.

'Actually, Trez said he did this,' he pointed to his face, 'to try to save a friend of mine. And I believe him.'

Tommy and Dean stared at the kid, not knowing what he meant. Then Mossy began to talk about Alice. He told them everything, the words just tumbled out.

They listened, shocked. When Mossy finished, Dean said, 'So you think Darke took her?'

'Who else?' said Trez with a shrug.

There was a pause, then Mossy said, 'You.'

Trez's jaw dropped. He rounded on Mossy. 'Me?'

'I want to trust you, but I need to know if you took Alice.' He hesitated. 'Maybe to protect her? To hide her from Darke?'

Tommy stared at the kid.

'No! I never!' Trez almost shouted, then he lowered his voice. 'I wouldn't involve a young girl, especially not with Darke around. *And*, she means a lot to you, Mossy. I'm sorry you feel that way, but I can assure you it wasn't me.'

'I believe him,' Dean said abruptly. 'The thing is, if he's telling the truth, then Alice could well be the reason why Darke has gone off the radar.' He turned abruptly to Trez. 'You suspected Darke had a sideline in trafficking boys for the sex trade? What if he decided to diversify into girls?'

'One of his favourite sayings was, "Always profit out of a bad situation," so you could be right.'

'It's all my fault. I have to find her.' Mossy sounded like a frightened child.

Once again, Tommy wanted to protect him. 'We'll help you,' he said, and looked at the other men, 'won't we?'

'I'm not sure how, but I guess so.' As Trez spoke, he looked at Mossy. To Tommy's surprise he seemed truly hurt by Mossy's accusation.

Dean stood up. 'Yeah, okay, but right now, I need a bloody drink and I want to hear Trez's business plan.'

Tommy didn't want either. He didn't like the direction this was heading. So much for no one getting hurt. Right now it looked to him as though *everyone* got hurt. He realised that if he stayed with this battle-weary and mutinous group, his chances of remaining unscathed were slim.

What should he do? The chance to have money in his pocket and be independent of his dissolving family tempted him to join them. But more persuasive than the money was that he couldn't walk out on Mossy.

He looked at Trez, seeing his gruff fondness for Mossy. Maybe he'd misjudged him.

And what about Dean? His feelings about his friend were just too complicated to think about right now.

He took a deep breath. 'Maybe we could all do with that drink, Dean? Then we'll hear what Trez has to say.'

CHAPTER TWENTY-SIX

Back at the station, Vic Blackwell soon became embroiled in interviews, reports, meetings and phone calls. Hours passed, and for the first time in years, he found himself thinking of nothing but the ongoing investigation.

A hand suddenly came to rest on his shoulder, making him jump, and he raised his eyes from his monitor screen to see DI Jenny Deane looking down at him.

'Good work this morning, Sergeant. Very well handled.'

There wasn't a great deal of warmth in her words, but at least she'd given him the credit, and publicly too, right in the middle of their CID area.

'Thank you, ma'am. And I'm delighted to tell you that our pilot, with the aid of an interpreter, is being really helpful with our enquiries. Even border force are chuffed about it.' He frowned 'Not that the pilot or his cohort seem to know much about their "employers," but at least we now know a whole lot more about where the setup is based and how they transport the gear around.'

'Oh yes, what we have established today will help enormously.'

A thought struck him. 'Ma'am? What about the river, and the boats coming in at night?'

The DI nodded. 'Still on. Do you want to take the lead?'

He nodded furiously. 'Absolutely, ma'am.'

'We are looking at a spring tide tomorrow night. That should allow a boat access to those smaller inlets.'

Blackwell knew a lot more about tides than he did about aviation. A spring tide occurred twice a month. It had nothing to do with the season, but meant a place where water welled up from the ground, and it always brought higher than average water. 'Perfect. We'll be waiting for them, ma'am.'

Blackwell finished what he was doing, then remembered Daisy Cotterill. Damn! He had meant to go out to Cassell Hill and give her an official bollocking! He really didn't want her out there when they were planning a raid. He glanced at his watch. There was still time, and he could do with stretching his legs. He looked across to where Larry was typing furiously, and decided that this time he'd go alone. For one thing, it didn't take two detectives to give a nosey old woman a ticking off, but more than that, his partnership with Larry was not one of the best. If he were to stay here, even temporarily, he needed to get a different crewmate. He recalled how well he and Marie Evans had worked together. They had been a bloody good team, reacting in unison to situations that were sometimes very dangerous indeed. That was the sort of sidekick he needed right now, and he couldn't see himself ever getting it with Languid Larry.

He pushed back his chair and stretched. Sea-bank air was just what he needed right now. He left the CID room, marvelling at the things that had suddenly become important to him. Things other than making desperate visits to whores.

As he drove out to check on the Cotterill cottage, Vic Blackwell experienced a rare moment of contentment. He was on track. All it needed was for his master plan to work out, and everything in his world would be absolutely perfect.

* * *

'We have to keep a lid on this, Ruth.' In his mind, Jackman was seeing headlines about monsters in their backyard. 'If the press print the real story of Justin Hart, half of Saltern-le-Fen will be reporting their neighbours, having suddenly noticed that Fred next door spends a lot of time in his potting shed.'

'I had just arrived at that conclusion myself, thank you, Rowan,' she said dryly. 'Thankfully they seem pretty taken up with this drug addict theory, so that will buy us a little time, but . . .' She didn't have to finish the sentence. 'Now, Justin's parents. I've arranged specialist help through the hospital, plus a dedicated victim support officer. Once the euphoria of knowing that their boy is alive has worn off, they're going to need a lot of help coming to terms with what's happened to him.'

'Whatever *that* is,' Jackman added grimly.

'Yes, that doesn't help, either. It'll mean another set of parents begging us to provide answers about their son. I'm still liaising with the Church family, and that's no picnic, I can tell you.'

Ruth's job was far from easy, Jackman knew, but he needed her to keep the media at bay. There were times when their help was invaluable, and there were times when the chaos they caused ruined an entire investigation. Jackman couldn't afford for that to happen here. He had multiple crimes occurring in his patch, and should they turn out to be connected, he was really going to need his wits about him, preferably without the press on his back. 'I'll simply be grateful for anything you can do, Ruth. Now I'd better get back downstairs. Gary, along with a whole army of civilians, is tracking CCTV right across the town trying to follow the route young Justin took.'

'Of course. You get on. Just keep me up to speed, won't you?' Ruth looked at him apologetically. 'And I do try not to say this, because I'm fully aware that you already know it, but I'm coming under heavy fire for results, so speed is of the utmost importance.'

Jackman did know, only too well. 'We'll get on top of this, Ruth, I promise. Just a couple more sightings on CCTV and we'll have a hot spot, then we'll move in and if necessary, check every house, every shop, every lock-up, every habitable building — and come to think of it, every *un*inhabitable building — until we find where he was held captive.'

'Then don't let me hold you up!' She pointed to the door.

* * *

'Max, you don't look your usual chirpy self.' Marie held out a coffee to the young detective.

'Thanks, Sarge.' He took it gratefully. 'Actually I'm pig-bloody-sick! I knew I should have gone with Robbie! And I knew that we should have kept to the same routine as the night before. I'd have been right there when he came out of that bleedin' club. Apart from getting them on camera, I'd have flattened the bastards. Sorry, Sarge, but I'm just so mad at myself!'

'Max! It's not your fault! Kevin *had* radioed the Fenchester lads with an update of their status, but they got held up with a street fight a few blocks away. It was just bad timing all round, that's all.'

'I know, I know! Plus Rob was so sure they'd want to check out his apartment with a view to grabbing a bigger haul that he never dreamed they'd just try to strip him of his strides.'

'He's going to be okay, you know.' Marie tried to sound confident, but in all honesty, she was as worried as Max.

'Yeah. I did talk to Kevin,' Max said, 'and he reckoned that when he was discharged, Rob was raising hell because he wasn't allowed to go too.' He chuckled. 'And Kevin looks like he's gone ten rounds with Tyson Fury! Best bit was they saved those hideous cargo pants!'

'Those *very expensive* hideous cargo pants. Get it right, Max.'

'Who'd have thought it? Worth a fortune apparently.' Max looked at her hopefully. 'Sarge? Can I slip off a bit early and go to Greenborough General and see him?'

Marie nodded. 'Sure. I'll okay it with Jackman, tell him you needed to debrief Rob so you can continue with your enquiry. But phone first, just in case the silly sod has discharged himself.'

Marie smiled at his retreating back. The team cared about each other. She loved the way they rallied round when one of them was in trouble. She knew for a fact that Charlie and Max were in contact several times a day, just to keep up with how the investigation was going. The younger detective was chipping in with some real Charlie Button insights, apparently.

'We've got another sighting!' Gary called out from his desk, and jumped up to put another marker on the wall map. 'By the look of it, Justin was coming from north of the town centre.'

Marie hurried over to join him and they stared at the map together.

'I'm thinking he can't have come from much further, considering the state he was in,' mused Gary.

'Check the sex offender's register, Gary. See if there's anyone known to us in that part of the town.' Marie tried hard to think of any known criminals or persons of interest that might be living in that particular neighbourhood, but she came up empty. It was a nice, residential area, no rough estates or dubious areas.

'Sarge?' Kevin Stoner came into the CID room, waving a memo. 'I've just had a witness say she saw the "drug addict,"' He made air apostrophes, 'running along Broadacre Lane, north to south.'

Marie handed him a marker. 'Can you pinpoint the spot, Kev?'

'Right here, Sarge.' He made a mark. 'Not very far from your last sighting.'

'Sorry, Marie, there's no offenders in that area,' called out Gary. 'And no one within a good few miles of it either.'

'What *is* in that area?' she asked.

'It's almost exclusively residential,' said Kevin. 'Some of it's very upmarket. Apart from that there is an old theatre that's waiting for demolition, a small empty warehouse that has planning permission for conversion into luxury apartments, a church and,' he traced his finger along the map, 'apart from Jim Cousins's shelter on Bridle Street, all the rest are strictly domestic residences.'

A silence fell. 'Jim Cousins?' Marie said at last.

Kevin looked at her, astounded 'You aren't thinking . . ?'

'I'm thinking that's the second time he's flagged up a mention recently. The kid who attacked you and Robbie lived there, and now he seems to be at the epicentre of our search area for the place where Justin was imprisoned.'

'Yes, but Jim? He's one of the most selfless blokes I've ever met! He protects these kids and gives them somewhere safe to get their lives back together. He'd never do a thing like that! I'd stake my life on it.'

'Kevin, just try and be completely impartial for a moment,' Gary said. 'Just think — what a brilliant cover it would make for something illegal.'

'Most of us think Jim's a hero,' Marie said. 'He's helped us out more times than I could count, so we trust him, don't we? The *police* trust him.'

Kevin chewed at his bottom lip.

'History? What's his history?' asked Marie urgently.

'Self-confessed bad boy,' breathed Kevin, speaking more like a policeman now. 'Did a stretch for aggravated burglary, got three years, because no violence was used and he never produced the knife he was carrying. Got out in two. His uncle left him that big house in his will, and Jim went straight. Not only that, he's worked tirelessly ever since, helping the homeless, the runaways and the kids on probation.'

Marie exhaled. She didn't want to believe that Jim could be capable of such a heinous crime, but she'd seen plenty of baby-faced killers in her time. 'I'm sorry, Kevin, but I think we need to take a really good look at Jim's house.' She felt truly sorry for him. Kevin had forged a really good relationship with Jim over the years, and this could potentially ruin the force's good working association with the centre and its owner, but what if . . . ? What if. They couldn't afford to ignore anything. 'I'm going to get the boss.'

'He's just coming back in,' said Gary, pointing to the doorway. 'Been to see the super, I think.'

Jackman listened to what they had to say, looked at the map, and turned to Kevin. 'You probably know him better than anyone, Kevin. Is there *anything*, anything at all, that could substantiate the fact that Jim Cousins is in some way involved in this thing with Justin?'

Kevin shook his head. 'He's one of the good guys, I'm certain of it.'

'Forget what you want to be true, man, and think like a policeman,' Jackman snapped back. 'Think!'

Kevin drew in a breath. He put his hand to his head, looked uncertain. 'I . . . I offered to help out at the centre. In my spare time of course—'

'And?' Marie urged.

'He said that having a police officer there would upset the residents. When I thought about it, I realised he was probably right, but now . . . ?'

'He just didn't want you there,' Gary stated flatly.

'Sorry to interrupt.' A civilian hurried across to Gary. 'We've found another sighting of your man, and we think it's the last. The monitoring centre and the control room have now checked the footage from every camera, apart from private ones, of course. This bit's been isolated and enhanced as best we can, and we think you should take a look at it, sir.' He handed Gary a note with the camera location, and left.

Gary turned to the map, picked up a felt-tip and silently made his mark. The dot marked a crossroads between Drakes Avenue — and Bridle Street.

A few moments later they were all watching a terrified young man stumble and lurch down the road.

'Is that it?' Kevin sounded disappointed,

'Run it through again, Gary,' said Jackman.

'Here, look! Hold it!' Jackman pointed to the screen. 'Justin's holding on to that gatepost to steady himself, and he's looking back over his shoulder.'

Marie stared unblinking, trying to picture that particular street and what was there.

Kevin's voice was heavy with resignation. 'He's looking directly at the entrance to Jim Cousins's place.'

Marie looked at Jackman, knowing where his mind was going.

'Okay,' he looked at his watch, 'Gary, get straight round to Arthur Lander's office, he's the nearest JP who's likely to be available. And take your bible. We need a warrant, fast.' Gary ran from the office. 'Everyone else, get your Kevlar vests on. I'll get onto uniform. We are going to need support on this one.' He looked around. 'Where's Max?'

Marie swore. 'I let him go early to check on Robbie.'

'Then ring him and get him to divert to Bridle Street. He'll never forgive us if we leave him out of this.'

Marie already had her phone out. 'I'm on it, boss.'

'Right. We go as soon as Gary gets back. And be very careful, everyone. You saw the state of Justin Hart.

Someone is going to be very worried indeed that that young man got away.'

'Worried, or angry?' asked Marie.

'Both, I should think. We need to proceed with extreme caution. We have no idea what we might be walking into.'

* * *

Dean, Tommy and their guests talked for hours. As they began to wind down, Dean decided they had probably struck the best bargain possible. The person he had worried about most was Tommy, but oddly, not only did he go along with Trez's proposition, he added some pretty shrewd suggestions of his own. Dean didn't want to get his hopes up, but young Tommy seemed to be quite prepared to collaborate, should Darke really have done a runner.

'I just wish we had some clue about whether Darke has really dumped us, or whether he's lined us up like little ducks on a fence,' Dean grumbled.

'I cannot believe that between the two of you, you know so little about the man you willingly threw your lot in with,' Tommy said. 'He's a complete enigma. He could be anyone, because as sure as eggs is eggs, his real name ain't Darke.'

Trez frowned. 'It never seemed important before. We did the job well, we got paid, we started all over again.' He spoke angrily. Dean guessed the anger was directed at no one but himself. And Dean felt the same. He should have been more cautious and kept his eyes and ears open, instead of being taken in by all Darke's big talk.

'One thing that bothers me is that notebook of his.' Trez said, taking another gulp of the beer Dean had given him. 'Just say, as a real outside chance, that he's been picked up by the police. He has every last bit of info about all of us in that fucking book.'

Dean nodded grimly. He had a picture in his head of Darke carefully writing down names and addresses, as well as all sorts of other information about his "staff."

'If we only knew where he lived,' Mossy added, 'I could easily get inside, and then we'd know for sure if he's still around, or has packed up and scarpered.' He frowned. 'And if that notebook was still there, I could make sure the Old Bill never got their hands on it.'

They sat in silence for a while, Dean continuing to curse himself for being such a gullible idiot.

All at once, Trez exclaimed, 'Shit! Hell and fuck! What a plank I've been!'

They all stared at him.

'When we broke into his office, there was a small pile of unopened letters and bills on his desk! I never took any notice at the time, but thinking about it now, I'm sure the address on them wasn't his office.'

'Why would they be important?' asked Dean.

'Because they could have his home address on them!' Mossy turned to Trez. 'Take me back to his office before that outer door gets locked for the night. I could pick that one too, but it's in full view of the road.'

Trez was already on his feet. 'Come on, kid!' He turned to Dean. 'We'll be back.'

And then they were gone.

For a while, he and Tommy didn't speak. Then Tommy said, 'Something tells me this is the turning point.'

Dean nodded. 'Yeah. But even if we do track him to his home, what are we going to find?'

'Anything has to be better than this terrible not knowing.'

Dean shivered. He had a terrible foreboding about what Darke's home might reveal.

* * *

Finding no one at Cassell Hill, Blackwell decided that maybe he'd been wrong about Daisy Cotterill sneaking back home. Perhaps she'd just popped in to collect a few things. He felt like celebrating his new life, so he made his way towards Big Rita's place. For once, he wasn't hurting, the agonising cravings had gone. He was just looking forward to having some fun with two talented ladies.

As he drove, he was amazed to find himself thinking about the investigation. Things really were changing. And as he neared Skegness, it wasn't Big Rita that was calling to him, it was Daisy Cotterill. Twice, he had seen someone in that cottage, and whoever it was had kept a very low profile. He parked the car and came to a decision. As soon as the games were over he'd go back and, under cover of darkness, make sure Daisy wasn't playing Miss Marple again. At the next high tide, they would discover just what was going on, and he didn't want Daisy sodding it up for them. Blackwell parked the car and, licking his lips, checked his wallet. Daisy would wait a while. He had more pressing things to attend to.

Big Rita opened the door, and Blackwell grinned. 'Hello, beautiful! Have you missed me?'

'Not half as much as you've missed us, big guy.'

She led him inside.

CHAPTER TWENTY-SEVEN

A small crowd had gathered behind the police cordon around the house in Bridle Street, watching the flashing blue lights and staring at the door in anticipation.

Nothing happened.

Jackman listened to the stream of denials and accusations pouring from Jim Cousins's lips.

'It's because of my record, isn't it? Something bad happens — oh, I know, let's hound old Jim, he's an ex-con! You do know that this will destroy every bit of the trust it's taken me years to build up! I just don't believe it!'

His anger seemed real, but Jackman couldn't afford to accept it at face value. 'It has nothing to do with that, and you know it.' He kept his voice even, almost gentle. 'The last sighting of the victim was right here, on your doorstep, Jim. Would you have us ignore that? We *have* to check it out. We have no alternative.'

'But like this? For God's sake!' Jim stared belligerently at the armed response officer standing silently behind Jackman.

'If you had seen the condition of that young man, who'll probably be spending the rest of his life under psychiatric care, you'd have done the same.' Jackman's voice now had an edge to it. 'He'd been tortured, Jim!'

'It has nothing to do with me, or anyone here, I swear it!'

Marie entered, her face set in granite. 'Nothing, sir. The whole place is clear.'

'See? All this for bloody nothing!' Jim was incandescent.

Was it a very good show, or was he truly enraged by their actions?

Jackman beckoned to Marie. They went outside. 'It's a big house, Marie, and an old one. I want you, Gary and Max to do another sweep. Do it on your own, no banging on doors, no shouting. I'll get uniform out, okay? Double-check every inch of the place. Check partition walls, backs of cupboards, any DIY alterations that look suspect. Roof space, any cellars, the whole lot, top to bottom.'

'Uniform were very thorough, boss.' Marie sounded less than convinced that they'd find anything more.

'Do it anyway.'

'Yes, sir.'

Jackman had a few words with the uniformed officer in charge. He returned to Jim Cousins and sat down opposite him. 'Help us, Jim. We have to find where that lad was held, and we have to find out who did this to him and get the monster off the streets. Is there anyone at all that you are worried about, either in your house, or in your circle of helpers or colleagues?'

Jim's rage finally seemed spent. He leaned forward, head in hands. 'No one, no one at all. Everyone I associate with has the same aim — to help those that need it. Look at Artie Ball from the Baptist church, for example. His whole life revolves around those street kids. He feeds them, for God's sake! And Laurie Stephens too — he's dedicated his life to giving kids some interest that'll get them away from drugs and crime. That's my circle, Inspector, that and my own group of "trusties." They all earned that title, by the way. We just want to help these kids, not hurt them.'

Jackman considered the three men — Jim, Artie and Laurie. On the surface, they were all motivated by altruism, doing a massive service to mankind and the unfortunates of Saltern-le-Fen. But each one of them could be the Fagin he was looking for. Think of it. The perfect cover! They all had legitimate access to the vulnerable. Jackman swallowed. The thought sickened him. For a moment, he wasn't sure how to proceed. He was certain this was the answer. Someone was using public-spirited philanthropy as cover for an evil secret.

He regarded Jim Cousins, hunched forward opposite him. Was he looking at an angel or a demon?

* * *

'Got it!' Trez burst through Dean's front door and thrust a sheaf of letters at him. 'Now my little locksmith and I are going visiting.'

'Not alone you're not,' Tommy said. 'We all go. We're a team, right?'

'Look, lad,' Trez looked at him apologetically, 'sorry to say this but you two need to keep whiter than white if our new venture is to work. If something goes wrong, Mossy and I can vanish. You guys don't exactly blend in with the low life, do you?' He looked from the immaculate Tommy to the scruffy, battered Mossy.

'Maybe, but we should still stick together till we know what's up with Darke,' said Tommy stubbornly.

'I agree,' said Dean. 'But we'll keep well in the background, don't worry. We *need* to know, Trez. I want to move on,' he glanced across to Tommy. '*We* want to move on.'

Trez realised it was going to be useless to argue, and it would just waste time. 'Okay, but you two wait in the car.'

'Alright.'

'Then, let's get this done, shall we?'

Fifteen minutes later, they were nearing the address on the envelopes. 'I'll park a road away, then Mossy and I will check the place out before we make our move. Once we know what the score is, we'll be right back.'

He turned a corner and stopped. Further down the street, flashing lights lit up the nice residential area like a fairground. 'Shit! What's going on here?' He pulled into the first avenue he came to, and killed the engine.

'An accident?' asked Dean.

'More like an incident,' murmured Trez. 'I'd better check it out. It looks pretty close to the address we are — or *were* — about to visit.'

'We'll go,' Dean said immediately. 'If it's the police, neither of you two want to be seen, but Tommy and me look like two young guys just passing by.'

He had a point. 'Okay, but just find out what's going down, and don't hang around. Got it? If there's been some major crime, they could be keeping tabs on the onlookers.'

Dean was already halfway out of the car. 'No problem. Come on, Tommy.' They strolled off.

Watching their retreating figures, Trez said to Mossy, 'Something's worrying me, kid.'

Mossy gave him a sidelong glance. 'Yeah?'

'Something Dean and Tom don't know, and I've only just thought of. There's a hostel type place close to where those blue lights are. It's a place Darke uses to house a couple of cells of his takers, young thieves like you.' He frowned into the darkness. 'One of them thieves was Rusty. He was on that job at the Lemon Tree last night, the one that failed. Luckily I was watching, and I managed to get them all away. Now I'm wondering if this lot has something to do with us.'

'Not good,' murmured Mossy.

'Not good at all. I just hope the others find out what it's all about. Well, whatever it is, you won't be going housebreaking tonight, that's for sure.'

'Why not? Ever heard of diversionary tactics? Just think, with all that going on, who's going to be paying attention to something happening further down the same street? I reckon it's a blessing in disguise.'

Trez laughed. 'You're something else, kid, you know that?'

Mossy shrugged. 'Makes sense though, doesn't it?'

'Perfect sense. Let's see what Dean comes up with, and we'll take it from there.'

* * *

Max climbed down the loft ladder and brushed the dust from his jacket. 'How come it's always me that gets to check out the attics?'

'You climb ladders like a monkey,' said Marie. 'Anything of interest up there?'

'Only if you are into obsolete TV aerials and antique Christmas decorations.' Max coughed. 'A bog standard loft. Lots of tatty old lagging between the rafters and a couple of water tanks, and that's it.'

But he seemed distracted. 'Nothing odd, or worrying?' Marie asked.

'Nope.'

Marie was pretty sure something had triggered a tiny niggle, but deciding that she was probably imagining it, didn't push him. 'Okay, let's move on.'

After another forty-five minutes, they'd drawn a blank. If Jim Cousins was their man, he certainly wasn't using this house for his den of thieves.

Marie walked past the dormitory, and a line of accusatory stares, and wished she'd never drawn attention to the place. If Jim was innocent, she and her colleagues had done a huge amount of damage to an already fragile environment. That was not what policing was all about.

With a heavy heart, she went to find Jackman and give him the disappointing news.

* * *

Vic Blackwell drove out of Skegness with a broad smile on his face. It had been magical, nothing but an evening of pleasurable eroticism. Even the two women had seemed to genuinely enjoy themselves. He hadn't felt driven to push barriers, and he hadn't slunk away from Big Rita's house feeling dirty.

He headed towards the sea-bank, singing along with the radio. Now for Daisy Cotterill. He didn't want to scare her, so he decided on a softly, softly approach. For one thing, he wanted to be sure his suspicions were correct.

He parked in a small area that tractors used for turning, and set off up the steep bank to the path that ran along the top. It would take about five minutes, more or less, to get to the Cotterill cottage, and he was glad of the walk. Apart from anything else, he wanted to get a feel for the place at night. Tomorrow he'd be back here with a team, hopefully intercepting smugglers, so he didn't want any surprises. Too many times he'd seen villains get away because they knew the lie of the land better than the good guys chasing them.

He took out his phone and checked the time. It wasn't too late, and as he was still slightly high after his evening's entertainment, he decided to walk the length of the bank, to the point where they had planned to do their observation from. He'd do his recce of Daisy's place on the way back. Success tomorrow night was what mattered. He needed this operation to be a feather in his cap, for winning hearts and minds was a key part of his plan.

He turned up his collar and strode on into the wind.

* * *

Marie, Gary and Max huddled together outside Jim Cousins's house.

'Where's Kev?' asked Max.

Marie made a face. 'Trying to build bridges. But he's got an uphill battle.'

'And we still don't know if the guy is guilty of something, or not,' added Gary anxiously. 'He doesn't want to get in too deep with Jim, just in case.'

'Kev is convinced we've got it wrong, and nothing's going to alter that.' Max stamped his feet and rubbed his hands together. 'Blimey! It's taters tonight.'

'Why don't you get off, Max? Rosie will be worrying.'

'Rosie knows the drill better than me. But maybe I will. There's nothing more we can do tonight. Where's the boss?' He looked around. Looked again. 'That's weird. Look.' He pointed towards the dwindling crowd of onlookers. 'See those two flash-looking guys talking to WPC Stacey Smith? They're on my mugshot board of pictures taken outside the Ginger Sheep. They're Hybird collectors.'

'Maybe I'll wander over and see what they want,' Marie said.

'I reckon they were just being nosey, Sarge,' Stacey Smith said. 'Asking the usual questions about what was going on and who was involved.'

'Not your average rubberneckers though, are they?' Marie watched the two young men walk away.

'Curiosity doesn't have a type, Sarge. Stick up a bit of blue-and-white cordon tape, and the world and his wife want to know what's happening. It's human nature.'

Marie wasn't so sure where those two were concerned. Anything that overlapped with their other cases made alarm bells ring. 'What did you tell them, Stacey?'

'Nothing. It's a police investigation and not their business. Although they were quizzing a lot of people in the crowd, and I saw them trying to earwig on conversations.'

Marie beckoned to Gary. 'Go and get their names, Gary, and find out what they are doing wandering along here at this time of night.'

Gary returned a little later, and read from his notebook. 'Dean Grantham and Thomas Peel. They live in one of those swanky converted warehouse apartments near the town centre. Gay boys, I reckon, and well-off. The older one said they'd had a few too many cocktails and were just walking them off when they saw the lights.' He shrugged. 'If nothing else, they're certainly not street urchins. The one called Dean has a posh voice and was wearing very expensive shoes, and the younger one had a real air about him. And he was far too good-looking for his own good.'

'As a matter of interest, were they wearing Hybird X clothing?' Marie asked.

'I'm not sure I'd recognise some of the stuff, Sarge. They just looked well dressed to me.'

'Check them out when you have a minute, Gary. It might be quite innocent, but you never know.'

Gary sighed. 'I don't know about anything right now.'

They walked back to Max.

'The boss said to call it a day, so I'll see you in the morning.' He waved at them. 'Night, everyone!'

'Back to the station?' asked Gary.

'I'll go get Jackman.'

* * *

Back in Trez's car, Dean and Tommy gave him an abbreviated version of what had happened, leaving out any mention of the police. 'No one knows for sure, but some said it's a drugs bust on the shelter.'

Trez wasn't convinced. He told them that Darke had billeted a couple of his takers there, one of whom had been involved in the botched mugging of the night before. 'It's too much of a coincidence, if you ask me. But anyway, Mossy's made a suggestion, and I think it's a good idea if we listen to him.'

Mossy told Dean and Tommy that he thought they should continue with the break-in, hoping that the incident at the refuge would act as a diversion.

Dean's first reaction was to protest, and Tommy seemed to feel the same. Then he saw the sense behind it. 'Okay, but for fuck's sake, be careful.'

'Yes, Mossy, no chances, you can't afford to fall foul of the law, and breaking and entering's serious stuff. Jail-time stuff,' Tommy added.

Dean fleetingly wondered what the bond was between them.

It wasn't easy, waiting in the car. Dean played with his phone for a while but soon gave up. He sat, staring into the night, wondering if Darke really had gone, taking thousands of pounds of their money with him.

If he had, maybe it would be for the best. It would sting a bit, but he still had money, and he could always sell all the Hybird gear. He might even make enough that way to help Trez and Mossy out, short term. But if Darke was playing with them, then they really were in trouble.

It had been good for a while, fun too. Now it was turning into a nightmare.

Tommy touched his arm. 'In a few minutes we'll know, one way or the other, so hang on in there, Dean.'

Dean   said   nothing.

CHAPTER TWENTY-EIGHT

Marie drove slowly home, going over the search of Jim's property in her mind. Why did she have this persistent feeling about that place, as if there was unfinished business there? Everything had appeared to be exactly as it should, well-ordered, clean, almost institutional. Yet something still rankled.

Jackman had said he was of two minds about Jim. And were Laurie and Artie possible suspects too? They all worked with vulnerable kids and young adults, and Marie had seen all too many cases where youth leaders committed terrible crimes against those they were supposed to be protecting. Both Artie Ball and Laurie Stephens were frequent visitors to the shelter.

It was certainly something to consider, but right now, Marie just wanted a hot bath, a glass of wine and some comfort food.

Her phone rang just as she was approaching her village.

Marie put the phone on speaker, and Vic Blackwell's voice filled her car.

'Marie, I need your help,' he said.

She stiffened. For starters, she certainly hadn't given him her mobile number. And why would he ask *her* of all people, for help? Was this what he'd been working up to?

'Marie? Are you still there?' His voice sounded more urgent.

'Vic, it's late and—'

'Marie, I'm out at Cassell Hill, at the Cotterill place. There's something really odd going on here.'

Marie spotted a layby, swung in and turned off the engine. 'How do you mean, odd?'

'I don't know, but someone's in the cottage and I don't think it's Daisy.'

'What the hell are you doing out there in the pitch dark?'

He explained. 'Can you come, Marie? I need some help.'

'Then get uniform, Vic! Especially if you're expecting trouble.'

'Please, Marie. If I'm wrong, I'm going to look a complete prat, and I don't need that right now. The super's watching me like a hawk. One wrong move and I'm history.' He sounded tense and on edge. 'And you're better than anyone in situations like this. I remember just how sharp you were back in the day, and I'm sure nothing's changed.' He paused. 'I'm certain something's going on here, but I just can't afford to cock up. Help me out, Marie?'

Marie took a deep breath. 'I'll be there in ten. Where are you parked?'

He told her.

'I know the place. Meet me at your car, and we'll decide how to proceed.' Marie hung up. Maybe this was the most absolutely stupid thing she'd ever done. She would have phoned Jackman, but she knew exactly what he'd say. Plus, he was hoping to grab a few hours with Laura, and Marie didn't want to drag him away.

No, this was her call. If something bad really was going down, she'd bring in the cavalry. And if it was just Vic scheming again, she'd make damn sure she didn't come off second best.

Marie started the engine, swung the car round, and headed for the marsh.

* * *

'They're coming!' Tommy nudged Dean.

Trez and Mossy were hurrying towards them. This was it!

Trez flopped down in the driver's seat, slammed the door, and started the car. 'We'll talk at your place.'

'Fuck that, Trez!' Dean shouted. 'Has he gone or not?'

'No, he hasn't.' His voice was heavy. 'Everything's still there. Clothes still in cupboards, food still in the fridge, TV still on standby . . .'

'But no Darke,' added Mossy.

The rest of the journey passed in silence. Back at the flat, the first thing Dean did was bring out the whisky. 'Help yourselves. After *all* that, we know no more than when we fucking well began.' He threw himself into a recliner and stared at the ceiling.

'Okay, so what *do* we know?' asked Tommy.

'That he's still around,' Mossy said. 'Although he must have either gone out before the post arrived, or not been home the night before, as there was some mail still on the doormat. But more important, Alice wasn't there. I searched that dump from top to bottom, but there was no sign of her. We can't forget about her.'

'No one has forgotten Alice, Mossy.' Trez took a drink and put the glass down. 'I'm sorry we didn't get any clues, kid, though I never thought he'd stash her in his own home. But there was a chance, I guess. Other than that, it's as Dean said, we still have no idea where Darke's gone or what he's up to.' Trez looked at each of them. 'More's to the point, what the hell do we do now?'

'I'd say cut and run,' Dean growled, 'and be done with the arsehole, but I can't.' He waved his arm around. 'I can't sell this, it's in my father's name, and he'll cut me off without a penny if I really piss him off.'

'Welcome to the real world,' muttered Mossy. 'I didn't even have a bed to sleep on till I met Trez.'

'If we don't get some money from that creep, none of us will have beds anymore,' Trez said. 'Shit! What a mess!'

Dean felt like screaming. They were still under Darke's control, even though he was pulling the strings from the shadows. Dean was beginning to unravel. Suddenly he saw that his privileged status, the father that always bailed him out of serious trouble, had done him no favours. When the real world forced itself in on him, he was weak and unprepared. All he wanted was to run away, and that was not an option. Trez was right, it was a mess.

* * *

Marie approached the spot where Blackwell had left his car, suddenly aware of how remote and inhospitable this place was, especially at night. She had left herself wide open to danger. For a minute, she contemplated turning round and getting the hell out of there. Instead, she slowed down, looking for the pull-in.

The night was typical of the east coast at that time of year — bitterly cold and windy. There was a bright moon up there somewhere, and the fast-moving clouds caused the landscape to flicker, switching from stark, moonlit panorama to pitch black nothingness.

Vic Blackwell was waiting by his car, and he lifted a hand in greeting.

She coasted in, turned off the engine and got out, closing the door with a click. Sound carried over the flat fenland, especially in the strong wind.

'Thanks, Marie. I really appreciate this.'

'What's the situation?' she said bluntly.

He straightened up. 'When I came by the other night, I was sure I saw a light inside the Cotterill cottage. I didn't want Daisy wrecking tomorrow night's raid, so I came back to take another look and warn her off.' He scratched his head. 'I went round the back of the cottage to check it out, and then I heard something. At first I thought it was a night bird, or one of those weird noises the water makes when it moves into a sluice, but it wasn't. It was a sort of cry, I'm sure of it.'

'Describe it.'

'Kind of snuffling, mewling sound, then almost a howling cry.'

'Sheba?' asked Marie.

'Sorry?'

'Daisy has a dog, a German Shepherd called Sheba. Could it have been her?'

'I don't think so. But that's not all. Before I checked the cottage, I walked along the sea-bank to make sure I'd chosen the right spot for tomorrow's observation point, and there's a boat moored out midstream on the river. It's too big to get anywhere near the inlet, and there was no visible activity going on, like night fishing.'

Marie weighed it all up. There could be a perfectly good reason for a boat to moor up in the river, and the noise he heard could have been anything. The marsh produced very strange noises, some so odd that they gave rise to numerous superstitions and old wives' tales.

'Will you come and take a look at the cottage with me?' he said.

The warning bells rang louder, but she ignored them. 'Well, I'm not here for a pleasant moonlit stroll.'

Blackwell set off immediately.

Daisy's cottage was in darkness, but as soon as she saw it, Marie had the feeling that Blackwell was right. Something was wrong. Using a brief window of opportunity the moon allowed her, she surveyed the scene, and noticed small indications that someone other than

Daisy had been there. Stone garden ornaments were lying on their side. One of Daisy's shrubs that grew close to the door was broken, as if something heavy had either been dragged past or fallen into it. Every curtain was drawn tightly across, not neatly as Daisy would have done, but with the edges overlapping, so that no crack of light could be seen.

'Something's not right, is it? You feel it too?' whispered Blackwell.

Marie found herself back in the past, the days when she and Vic Blackwell had been a team. 'Let's get closer.'

Like two wraiths, they slipped through the shadowy garden and took up positions on either side of the door. They listened, but there was no sound.

Silently, Blackwell pointed to the side of the cottage. Marie nodded, and they circumnavigated the small house, meeting at the back door.

Marie stood next to the kitchen window and listened hard. From inside came a faint noise. She put a finger to her lips, and they both strained their ears.

Blackwell had been right. It was an odd mewling sound, followed by a muffled groaning.

Had an animal got in somehow? There were animals in the area, cats, foxes, squirrels, rats, even badgers. But it wasn't that kind of sound.

Beckoning to Blackwell, Marie crept down the back garden path, through the gate and into the small parking area on the overgrown track outside. There, she hunkered down out of sight and whispered, 'We need to get in there, but we also need backup, just in case.'

'Can't we just check it out before we call for assistance? What if the old girl had a cat or something? Get them out for nothing and Ruth Crooke'll mark my card, Marie. You know that.'

'I also know there's something very wrong here. The place reeks of it.'

'Okay, but let's try to get a handle on what's going on first? Please?'

Marie wavered. 'The second I get twitchy, Vic Blackwell, I'm calling it in. And I'm warning you, I'm pretty twitchy already.' She inhaled. 'Okay. Charlie Button said it's easy to get in the dining-room window without being seen from the kitchen or the lounge. That's how he went in. I know which one it is, so let's try that first.'

Blackwell squeezed her arm. 'Let's do it.'

She still wasn't sure of him, but at least it kept her on high alert. The threat could come from anywhere, including right beside her.

The dining-room window was closed. But Marie found a loose clasp, and was able to slip the blade of her penknife inside and lift it up. She opened it slightly, eased the curtain back and listened. Nothing. Unless — were those low, muffled voices?

Blackwell moved past her, opened the window further and, without a word, pulled himself over.

Marie cursed silently. They were supposed to just open the window and listen, for God's sake! *Ah well*, she mouthed, and followed him in.

Marie pulled the curtains shut, in case someone noticed the open window, and stood beside Blackwell in the doorway.

Now they were inside, she could make out hushed voices. The peculiar noise was now louder and even more disturbing. Marie looked through the doorway and into the kitchen.

Two men sat at the kitchen table, silhouetted in the light of a single candle.

'Sooner we get them out of here the better. That whinging is driving me mad.'

'Chill out, man! Half an hour, and we can get rid of them. The water will be high enough by then for us to get our boat out to meet Darke's.'

She and Blackwell glanced at each other. Marie took her phone from her pocket and pointed to it. She wanted to get uniform out here, and fast. And all they had was thirty minutes before something serious happened.

Blackwell mouthed "wait." He pointed to the sitting room and breathed, 'Whatever's making that noise is in there.'

Marie frowned. It might be possible to slip across the hall unnoticed. The hallway was in darkness, but there was a faint glow coming from Daisy's sitting room. Okay, they'd see what they were dealing with, and then she'd get out and ring it in.

Blackwell went first.

It was difficult not to gasp. They'd found the source of the unearthly noises.

Two lads were seated back to back on hard dining chairs, tied tightly to each other, their heads lolling.

They looked as if they'd been drugged, but not enough to knock them out completely. They were struggling feebly against their restraints, whining pathetically and crying.

Neither boy seemed to be aware of their presence.

She looked at Blackwell, and pointed to the dining room. The last thing they wanted was for the boys to notice them and start yelling their heads off. That would certainly bring their captors into the room.

Back in the dining room, she murmured, 'Time to get help.'

This time Blackwell agreed, but added, 'And in the meantime? What shall we do? There are only two of them, and we have the advantage of surprise. I suggest we rush them and take them down.'

'They're probably armed. Do you have a stab-proof vest on?'

He shook his head.

'Me neither. These are people smugglers, Vic. They may have guns.' Marie was no coward, but she liked the odds to be at least slightly in her favour. Blackwell nodded. 'Get out, Marie, and make that call. I'll stay here and keep listening, in case they say anything we can use later.'

'Then get out as fast as you can.'

Marie pulled herself over the sill and dropped easily into the garden. She'd need to get a short way from the cottage, in case they overheard. Keeping to the shadows, she made her way to the back gate, but just as she reached the far side of the back wall, she heard an engine. It was coming straight up the track towards where she was standing!

Immediately she sprinted back, in full view of the cottage. She had to warn Blackwell to get out immediately.

Before she could get even close to the dining-room window, the beam of a powerful headlight swept across the garden. Marie dove to the ground and lay still.

The engine noise died, and she was up again, running to the relative safety of the side of the old building. How the hell was she going to get to Blackwell? Before she even tried to work that one out, she pulled out her phone and put in an urgent request for assistance. Now, somehow, she had to get to Blackwell.

She heard car doors slam, and the crunch of footsteps up the path.

Chancing a glance around the corner of the cottage, she saw a tall man carrying two heavy suitcases towards the back door. As soon as he went inside, she broke cover and ran to the dining-room window.

Blackwell wasn't there.

Oh, Jesus! Where the hell had he gone? Back to the boys? Or had he heard the car and escaped? In that case, surely she'd have seen him? So he was somewhere inside the cottage, along with three people smugglers and two of their victims.

Against her better judgement, Marie swung herself up and back through the window.

Now the people in the kitchen were talking normally. Marie knew that she only had seconds to get across the hall and find Blackwell. She took a breath, held it, then hurled herself across the darkened hall.

She heard someone sigh. Blackwell had been behind the door, about to attack his would-be assailant.

'Out! Now!' She hissed. 'Unless you fancy a posthumous medal. There's another man turned up. How fast can you run?'

'I'm no sprinter, but lead on.'

When they were halfway across the hall, the lights came on.

'What the fuck?' One of the men, obviously on his way to check on the abductees, stopped in his tracks, his mouth open.

He yelled for his mates.

'Marie! Get out! I'll stall them.'

'No! We both go, now!'

He was right behind her as she threw herself out of the window. They both landed heavily but were up and running in seconds.

There was a furore behind them, and she knew immediately that they were being chased.

'Sea-bank!' Blackwell shouted.

Wise move. The smugglers' vehicle was in the back lane. No access to the bank.

They ran around the cottage and out onto the track that led up to the sea-bank.

The moon disappeared beneath scudding night clouds. At least they weren't so visible to their pursuers, but it slowed them down. The path was rough and uneven, chewed up by tractors and trampled by cattle. Some of the ruts were deep enough to break an ankle.

They ran on, as fast as they could. At the top of the incline she stopped briefly to catch her breath, and Blackwell scrambled up behind her. Just as she was about to take off again, she heard him shout.

She glanced back, from him to the man who was closest. And as the moon broke cover from the clouds, she saw the wicked glint of metal.

Almost immediately, she was on the ground. The fall on the winter hard ground, and the weight of Blackwell's body, drove the air from her lungs.

He didn't move. As she struggled to get out from beneath his inert body, she heard one of them shout to his accomplice to leave them. They needed to get out and reach the boat.

'Vic? Vic?' She eased him onto his back, and the pale moonlight revealed a dark stain in his side. Marie pulled out her phone and screamed out their location, adding that they had an officer down.

She thought he was dead. She cradled him to her, rocking to and fro, tears streaming from her eyes. All the bad stuff had vanished, and she held her old crewmate, the man who had just saved her life.

Then he stirred, coughed and let out a ragged breath.

'Vic! Stay still! Help is on its way.'

'Need to know . . .'

'Ssh, it can wait. Just keep breathing slowly, and try not to speak.'

'No . . . just tell me, Marie . . . Tania *did* love me, didn't she?'

'To the end, Vic.' Marie sniffed. 'It really was just an accident. With her poor night vision, she shouldn't have driven in the dark. But she loved you, no doubt.'

'I'm sorry, Marie.' He coughed again, and she saw blood on his lips. 'So sorry . . .'

Marie laid him down gently, stripped off her own coat and wrapped it around him. 'You hang on in there, Vic Blackwell, we have a lot more talking to do! That's an order!'

Then she put pressure on the wound, and lay down beside him, holding him tightly to keep him warm. 'Come on, Vic. Hold on! Please!' As the cold of the night seeped into her bones, she began to pray for blue lights and sirens.

* * *

A little further along the sea-bank a dark figure stood, one hand resting on the head of the big dog that sat beside her, and the other holding her mobile phone. She was quietly praying that her reputation as a troublemaker hadn't meant that the emergency services had ignored her two calls. If they had taken her suspicions seriously, she would see their lights any moment now.

Daisy stared at the access point to the sea-bank, and saw what she'd been praying for.

She pushed her phone back into her pocket and, with Sheba at her heels, ran to help the injured man and his friend.

CHAPTER TWENTY-NINE

At around four in the morning, Marie saw Jackman coming through the doors to the family waiting room. Marie had waited for hours in the hospital for news about Vic. Now, she had never been so pleased to see anyone in her life, except maybe the paramedics that had run to her aid on the sea-bank.

'I'll give you the full bollocking later.' Jackman tried to look stern, but his concern for her was stronger. He sat down beside her and put his arm around her shoulders. 'Are you okay?'

'I'm fine, but Vic's fighting for his life.'

'We've got the guy who shot him, and the others too.' He shook his head, smiling. 'Mostly thanks to Daisy Cotterill. That woman just can't stay away from Cassell Hill! She'd already seen the boat moored up midstream, then she noticed that someone had been in her cottage, and rang it in. She then phoned again when she saw you and Vic doing your Batman and Robin routine.'

'She came and helped me.' Marie paused. 'But those poor kids! Are they in the same state as Justin Hart?'

'Not at all, they're already recovering from the drugs they were given, and just like the gang members we picked up, they're singing like canaries.' His face clouded. 'They thought they were being taken to safety, would you believe! I could be wrong, but I think they're our two muggers, the ones who killed Denis Church. We have such a lot to try to piece together.'

'Jackman? The man who drove up later, he had suitcases.'

'Packed with a fortune in Hybird X collectors' items. We got it wrong when we thought it was drugs coming into the country, it was stolen Hybird goods going *out*. Plus the occasional special delivery of boys being sold for the sex trade.'

'So it's all connected?'

'I'm sure it is.' Jackman yawned. 'But we have a long way to go yet. This setup is multifaceted, and we've only nabbed one unit. I'm not sure how big the whole thing is.'

'The boat?' Marie tried to think. 'One of the smugglers referred to it as Dark's boat. Is that who owns it? Could he be the Fagin character that runs this group? Have you traced the licensed owner of the boat?'

'Whoa! I've only had a few hours! The boat got away, but it was hired, we know that much. And the name Darke, spelt with an "e," has been thrown at us by everyone we've spoken to. There is no honour amongst thieves where that one is concerned, believe me!'

'So who is he?'

Jackman sighed. 'I haven't the faintest idea and sadly, nor have the people who worked for him. He's the epitome of Mr X.'

'Mr *Hybird* X actually.' She gave him a weak smile, and then jumped up. 'Jackman! Justin Hart — he kept telling us he was frightened! We thought he was saying, "of the dark," but what if he was really saying "frightened of *Darke*?"'

Jackman closed his eyes. 'My brain aches. But I think you're right. If we can prove it, we have another connection, don't we?'

Marie looked out through the half open door of the family room. 'I wonder how Vic is? He saved my life, Jackman. That bullet was heading my way. He took that one for me.'

'Case closed? All debts settled?'

'In full. I just hope he pulls through,' Marie said.

'Have they given a prognosis yet?'

She shook her head. 'Too soon to say, apparently, but I don't think the odds are in his favour.'

'You should go home, Marie, and get some sleep.'

Her look said "you have to be joking."

'Thought as much.' He sat back and held out his hand.

She settled down next to him and leaned against him, her head on his shoulder.

'Then I'll wait with you, but sleep if you can.'

'Fat chance of that.' She closed her eyes and fell asleep.

* * *

Trez and Mossy stayed over at Dean's place that night. They were too drunk to do anything else, Trez crashed out on the sofa, Mossy in a recliner. Tommy, being the only one to stay sober, threw travel rugs over them and left them to sleep it off.

He barely slept at all. The police questioning them outside the shelter had given him the jitters. He lay awake, trying to fathom out a way of salvaging something from the situation. Dean was next to useless. As soon as he heard that Darke hadn't done a runner, he started to fall apart.

He hated to see Dean in that state. Dean was a leader, all confidence and charm. It was unnerving to see him haggard and anxious. Well, to bring Dean down so low, Darke must be a pretty evil bastard.

Tommy turned over again and lay on his back. There must be something he could do. Of course! There was something! And it could benefit not only him but Mossy as well. He would just need to get it absolutely right, and their problems would be solved.

Tommy smiled into the darkness. First thing in the morning, he'd work out how to put his plan into action.

* * *

Tommy wasn't the only one lying awake. Next to his wife, Max was afraid to toss and turn too much for fear of waking her. Rosie wasn't sleeping well, and as her pregnancy progressed into the third trimester, she rarely slept for long. Now, to see her actually asleep was a miracle, and the last thing Max wanted was to spoil it.

But his mind was racing. Jackman had phoned and told him what had gone down that night, and he was going over everything, trying to add up what they now knew.

No wonder the Hybird grails hadn't been advertised on the usual resell sites, they had been swifted out of the country for sale abroad. And there were lots of eager collectors out there willing to pay big money for them. Would the villains give up now that their exit route had been blocked? Or would they find another method of moving them on? Most likely the latter. There was still a lot of mileage left in the Hybird resale market.

Rosie shifted uncomfortably and gave a slight moan. He took her hand. He should be thinking of the baby, but instead he was thinking about smugglers and people trafficking. And the sarge! Shot at! And that slimeball Vic Blackwell had taken the bullet! Amazing. Maybe he should revise his opinion of him, but only when he'd heard the whole story from Marie. Whatever, the guy was in a critical condition, and he was sorry for him. At least they did have the shooter, who'd go down for a very long time for attempting to murder a copper.

His mind wandered off again. From baby names, he found himself going over their raid on Jim Cousins's shelter. He still felt he'd missed something, but he couldn't work out what. They'd been so thorough. He so needed sleep! Two hours and he'd have to be up again. There was no way he could be late when their whole team was so depleted. Jackman had said Marie was going to wait at the hospital until she knew about Vic Blackwell's condition, so that would leave Gary and himself! Great. A dark thought slid into his mind. Wouldn't that be just the right time for Alistair Ashcroft to resurrect himself. He quashed the thought.

At last, he felt his eyes closing. He dreamed about searching Jim Cousins's house, but he didn't know what he was looking for, and he kept hearing sounds that he didn't recognise. In the end, he was lost in a labyrinth of rooms, all packed with camp beds occupied by strange young men with dark, hollow eyes. All around him were the cries of boys begging to be allowed to go home.

* * *

Jackman arrived home at around five a.m. and slipped into bed, trying not to wake Laura. He failed.

'Bad night?' she murmured sleepily.

'One officer down and now critical, and Marie knowing the bullet had been meant for her. So no, not too good.' He drew her to him, and sighed. 'But we had a damned good arrest. Three smugglers safely locked up in the custody suite, plus two possible muggers under close surveillance being treated in the local hospital, and every one of them with verbal diarrhoea.'

'That's unusual.'

'Very, but their elusive boss doesn't seem to have made too many friends along the way. Most Hated Villain 2018, as nominated by his friends!'

'Well, that's a bonus, surely?' Laura snuggled closer to him.

'It would be, but despite the diarrhoea, we know nothing about who he is.'

'Then try to get some rest, and start again tomorrow. When you go over everything they've told you, there'll be something you can use. Someone will know something that will lead you to this man. Someone *always* knows something.'

With that, Laura fell asleep.

He lay there, sizzling with the overload of activity in his head, but at the same time almost peaceful. How wonderful to be embracing this woman in his own bed.

He closed his eyes. What he had right now with Laura was to be savoured and enjoyed, if only for a couple of hours. He stroked her hair gently, and tried to match his breathing to her rhythm. Though sleep was trying to claim him, he fought it. He didn't want to miss a moment.

CHAPTER THIRTY

Looking around at the officers gathered for the morning meeting, Jackman realised that the biggest contingent by far was uniform. In the absence of any close family, even DI Jenny Deane was at the hospital attending a meeting with Vic Blackwell's consultant surgeon.

Jackman had already given a detailed report of the happenings of the night before, and was now emphasising that finding the mysterious Darke was their first priority.

'He seems to be at the heart of everything, and he's a very dangerous and perverted criminal. We *must* uncover his identity, and get him off the streets. I want particular attention paid to three men — Jim Cousins, Artie Ball and Laurie Stephens. Now, as these men could and may well be, exactly what they profess, upstanding pillars of the community, this needs to be done with the utmost diplomacy. We can't be seen to be targeting them without cause, but,' he spread his hands, 'we also can't afford to ignore what history has taught us, that some men who work with youngsters are doing it for their own malign purposes, not for the benefit of those in their care.'

'Dirty perverts,' someone muttered.

'Okay, down to business. One of the men in custody has given us the address of Darke's business premises, a poky office in a big old house let out as offices on a cash basis. All the landlord knew was that the man renting this particular room was called Darke, and that he'd been there for two years. Uniform made a dawn call, but there was no one there, and not a single clue that could lead us further. We will have fingerprints, and hopefully DNA, so all we can do is hope that he's known to us.' He pulled a face. 'Or maybe his prints will tie up with one of our possible suspects.'

'If he's a nonce, then he's most likely on a register, or at least on a watch list somewhere,' said WPC Stacey Smith.

'Let's hope so. We need a name, and we have to hurry. This man could simply close everything down after last night's arrests. He will know his days are numbered, and if we can just link the incarceration of Justin Hart to him — and my gut feeling says Darke *was* the man who abducted and tortured him — then he'll be very worried indeed.' He straightened up. 'Right, I want officers talking to those two teenagers who were rescued last night. Go with them, Gary, and get everything you can from them, especially a description, even a photofit, of the man called Darke. I want the same from the company that hired that boat, everything they have on the person who hired it, how he paid, and all available info on him. And someone, maybe you, Max? Chase up the lab for all the prints taken from those suitcases and their contents. I doubt the people packing up the Hybird X stuff wore gloves. There are a lot of operatives involved in this setup, and we want as many as we can, just in case someone actually knows who Darke really is.'

Max nodded. 'Wilco, boss.'

'Forensics are handling everything from their office, so we can only wait for that. As for me, I'm going to make it my job to lean hard on the man who shot DS Vic

Blackwell. There must be some kind of hierarchy in this gang. If we can get one of the smugglers that we arrested last night to cough up some names, we could have our lead.' He took a breath. 'That's it. Let's find this creature, before he does any more damage to the kids of Saltern-le-Fen!'

When Jackman returned to his office, PC Kevin Stoner was behind him.

'Could I have a word, sir?'

'Come in.'

Inside the office, Kevin said, 'Could I be the one to keep an eye on Jim Cousins, sir? Since they already know me, I might just learn more than a strange face.'

'And because you still think Jim is innocent, you could keep the peace better than another officer?'

'Kind of, I guess, but if he is involved, I'd be the first to slap the cuffs on him, believe you me!'

Jackman laughed. 'I know. You're a good cop, Kevin. Just try to stay neutral. And yes, I agree you should cover the shelter. I'm going to suggest you clear it with your sergeant, but go in plain clothes. It could get the residents to relax more around you. And keep your ears open. We mustn't forget that Justin was first picked up on camera close to the Cousins house. I know the search found nothing, but that place was also home to one of the street kids that attacked you and Robbie, so we can't rule it out.'

'I know that, sir, and thank you. I'll be vigilant, I promise.'

Kevin left, and Jackman's phone rang.

'Rob! I was just thinking about you. How are you?'

'I want to come back, sir. I'm right as rain. They discharged me late last night.'

'They discharged you? Or did you discharge yourself?'

'Let's say it was a compromise, sir. They were glad to see me go.'

'And as much as I need you back, Robbie, you had a serious blow to the head, and I'd never forgive myself if you came back too soon.'

'Sir, I'm good to go, I promise, and if it makes you happier, I'll tie myself to my desk. I just want to be back working the case.'

Jackman hesitated. 'You swear the hospital signed that discharge note, and not you?'

'I swear. So . . . ?'

'Four hours, this afternoon. See how you go. No more than that, understand?'

'I'll be there! And thanks, boss.'

Jackman replaced the phone with a shake of his head. He knew exactly how Robbie felt. It was awful to be left out at such a critical point. At least in the office, they could keep an eye on him. And right now they needed all the help they could get.

* * *

Laura Archer sat in on the psychiatric unit's morning board meeting. Every day, the doctors and nurses, with some of the admin staff, met and reviewed their patients before going onto the wards.

A psychiatrist read out the name, 'Justin Hart.'

Laura listened while Justin's medication and indications were discussed. Apart from assessing the extent of damage to his mind, they needed to keep him calm so as to address the physical problems, the malnutrition and the actual injuries, mainly lacerations and bruising. It was vital to build him up and rehydrate him while adjusting the withdrawal from the drugs they'd given him.

Laura knew this was no easy job.

'It's important to remember that each individual responds differently to abuse. After talking to his parents, it seems that Justin was never one to cope easily with emotional stress, so whatever he was forced to endure may have done irreparable damage.' His consultant, a woman

317

called Hester Travers, shook her long greying ponytail, and looked grim. 'I will be recommending moving him to Saltern Hall Psychiatric Hospital.'

This was no surprise to Laura. Saltern Hall was a top notch facility. But she needed to be able to talk to Justin herself, find out what had caused him to cry out about the dark. Or was it Darke?

Laura put the question to them, adding that it was vital for the police to find whoever had done this to him.

Out of the question, she was told but after some cajoling, she managed to persuade them to let her talk to him briefly. She was to stop immediately if he seemed distressed. The last thing Laura wanted was to undermine the progress they'd made, but she knew how desperate Jackman was to solve this case.

The meeting over, she spoke to Justin's personal nurse. Yes, now would be a suitable time, as he was sedated, but not too sleepy.

'He's not aggressive, that's one blessing,' said the nurse, who was called Sally. 'This morning I asked if I could get him anything and he said ginger beer. It's the first time I've got a response from him.'

Laura accompanied Sally down the corridor. 'I understand a specialist police investigative officer is being assigned to question him. Is that right?'

'Yes, just as soon as Professor Travers, his consultant, allows. And we've stipulated that it has to be a woman. It's lucky Prof Travers is looking after him and not one of the other psychiatrists. Justin won't have a male near him, not even a nurse or an orderly. He just freaks out.'

Laura sighed. 'That says a lot, doesn't it?'

Sally turned to her. 'Sometimes I wonder what people are capable of, then I get a patient like Justin, and I know I can't even get close to knowing the answer to that.'

'Best you don't, I reckon.'

Sally looked through the observation window in his door. 'What are you going to say to him?'

'First, I'll just reassure him that we're here for him, that he's safe now, and when he's ready, I'll listen to whatever he has to say. I think I'm going to have to wing it a bit, depends on how he reacts.'

'I'll help if I can,' Sally offered. 'But he's volatile. I wouldn't hold out too much hope if I were you.'

Laura went in. She smiled warmly at Justin, who lay on the bed. If she were seeing him for the first time, she'd have been horrified, but actually he looked better. She'd never forget what he'd looked like on that roundabout. 'Hi, Justin. I'm Laura. Can I sit with you for a while?'

No answer, no acknowledgement that she was even there. But he didn't object either. She placed her chair a short distance from the bed, so as not to crowd him, and began to speak, saying all the things she'd told Sally she would.

She talked on, and after a while, she noticed him giving her a suspicious glance from under his lowered eyelids. It was a start.

She continued, speaking softly. Then, to her surprise, he suddenly said, 'Don't let him find me!'

'He won't,' she said soothingly. 'He can't get in here, I swear. We have security everywhere.'

'Don't let him find me!' he repeated.

'We won't, I promise. But, Justin?' She took a chance. 'If we are to protect you properly, we have to know his name. Can you tell me his name? If you could say it, just the once, that'll be enough.'

His eyes grew wild, fearful, and he began the strange plucking motion, at his clothes and at his skin while he rocked backwards and forwards.

She saw Sally's warning look.

'It's alright, Justin, you're safe here, really. You're safe.' Laura almost crooned the words.

Then there was silence. Laura cursed herself for pushing too soon. She stood up. 'Thank you for letting me sit with you, Justin. Maybe I'll see you again.'

With a sigh she walked to the door. Then he uttered a single word, the one she wanted to hear.

'Darke.'

She turned and looked at Justin Hart. She nodded her thanks, and that seemed to be enough. He stopped rocking, and in moments he was back to lying unmoving, staring into space.

She closed the door with a small glimmer of hope. Maybe he would somehow get his life back. Not his old life for sure, but one that might pass for an acceptable existence.

Outside, she rang Jackman and gave him the news. She kept the call short and businesslike, and he responded in kind, but she sensed the undercurrent between them. This time around, their relationship was going to work.

* * *

Jackman hung up, elated that Laura had come up trumps with Justin. His desk phone rang. It was the duty sergeant. 'I've got a call about your investigation, but the caller will only speak to the OIC.'

'Put it through.' Most likely a time waster. 'Can I help you?'

'I know someone who knows where the man you're looking for lives.'

Jackman stiffened. The caller sounded young, but well-spoken. He certainly wasn't a street urchin. 'Can you ask him to come in? Or call me?'

There was a short laugh. 'No. So please listen. He needs an incentive. If you offer a reward, a *substantial* reward, for information regarding the real name and address of the man you know as Darke, I will see he comes forward. And he's no criminal. He's just frightened, okay?'

At the mention of Darke's name, Jackman knew this call was for real. And he was pretty sure he was talking to one of Darke's boys.

'That's all. Just do it, Inspector. Put a poster up at the police station, and save yourself a lot of time.' The line went dead.

It would be pointless trying to trace the call. He'd be using a throwaway phone with an unregistered sim. After the call, the phone would be ditched.

One-off rewards were not something they used often, preferring to stick to known informants, but they occasionally paid out to someone who offered solid, actionable information that led to an arrest and a conviction.

Jackman went to the outer office and called to Max. He explained what had just happened, and also that Justin had confirmed that it was Darke that had hurt him.

'Boss, if that's the case, and Darke was shipping boys abroad, do you think he's abducted Alice too? Perhaps she's being held in the same place as Justin.'

'Possibly. Although I can't think how a neglected teenage girl is connected with Darke's operation. He seems always to have taken boys.'

'Maybe the kid saw something or recognised someone and Darke got to know about it. Maybe she was a threat to him, and he swifted her away.' He scratched his head. 'I think the reward is a great idea. Not many people come forward when a reward is offered, so we could get lucky.'

Jackman didn't like being told what to do by money-grabbing little chancers, but time was not on their side. A thought kept nagging at him. What if Justin wasn't the only captive? What if there were more young men somewhere, in the same state as him? It was a sobering thought. He went straight to Ruth Crooke's office to request permission to activate a reward via the Community Action Trust, or whatever they called themselves nowadays.

* * *

Marie got into work at eleven, having had very little sleep. She'd spent a good twenty minutes of her precious rest time talking to Rhiannon, her mother. Just hearing that Welsh lilt, the voice that had seen her through a dozen crises in her life, was enough to ease her tension.

Vic had survived the operation, though he was still unconscious. The bullet had penetrated his transverse colon and his liver, and infection was a major concern, especially with the extensive internal blood loss after the bullet nicked an artery. Now he was being treated with antibiotics and monitored round the clock in ITU. There was nothing Marie could do at the hospital, so she returned to the station.

It was weird. Though last night had been so terrible, it had also been cathartic. Suddenly the dark, heavy shroud she'd been living under had been lifted, and a dreadful period in her life was over. Now she just hoped that Vic Blackwell would recover, so that he could feel it too.

On her way in, she met Jackman in the reception area, asking the duty sergeant if he would put up a poster on the outside noticeboard. She saw that it was offering a reward for information leading to the arrest and conviction of a man known only as Darke. To her surprise, the figure offered was twenty thousand pounds, much more than she'd have expected. Then she thought of the extent of Darke's criminal activities.

On their way up to the CID room, Jackman told her about Laura's success with Justin Hart.

'So that's why the reward is so high!'

'That, and the fact that I think this young guy was on the level. Maybe it's him who knows where Darke lives, but whatever, he's the best hope we've got of finding this man.' He exhaled. 'Marie, I'm afraid that Justin might not be the only abductee.'

'Have forensics come back with anything yet?' she asked.

'Fingerprints, lots of them, from his office. Most aren't known to us, but at least we have them on file now.'

'How about a description of Darke?'

Jackman frowned. 'They're rather conflicting. The two young muggers aren't the most articulate of witnesses. "Fat, ugly and slimy, creepy perv," were the best descriptions Gary could coax out of them.'

'Surely the landlord he rented that room from could do better than that?' said Marie.

'Says he rarely saw him. He doesn't live on the premises, and someone else collects the rent for him. He thought he was middle-aged, overweight and with smarmed down hair.'

'Maybe I'm clutching at straws, but did any of the other people who rented rooms know him? Maybe the one who collects the rent?'

Jackman smiled faintly. 'Yes, I'm afraid you are. No one in that place seems to want to get too chummy with us. The woman who passes on the rent to the landlord said that Darke always put an envelope with the cash in it in her mailbox. She says she doesn't remember actually seeing him at all. From the way they all clammed up, I suspect there's a lot of shady dealings going on under that roof. It's on my wish-list to go over that place with a fine toothcomb when all this is over.'

When she walked into the CID room, Gary ran over and hugged her. 'Glad you're safe, Sarge. But I'm never going to forgive you for going out onto that marsh at night without me.'

'Ditto!' called out Max. 'You'd have skinned us alive if we'd done the same thing ourselves.'

Touched, Marie said, 'I consider myself duly chastised. You're right, Max, I'd have been livid.'

'Right. Having got that out of the way, I've got some news,' Gary said excitedly. 'Our two boys have thrown up their hands to attacking Denis Church and stealing his Hybird trainers. And in order to make things a little easier for themselves, they've also told us how their side of the operation worked.' He looked at Jackman. 'Your theory was pretty well spot on, boss. And we now have another man to try to find. The one running the thieves is called Trez. No surname that they knew of, but we do have a better description of him.'

'Excellent!' Jackman clapped Gary on the back. 'Good work. Get that description circulated. If we can nail him too, I'll be well pleased.'

'Already done, sir.' Gary returned to his desk. 'And I have some juicy dabs on that Hybird gear, sir. One set belongs to a bloke who's already known to us. He's had his collar felt for receiving stolen goods, and he did a short stretch a year or so back. Name of Bradley Shaw. Uniform are tracking him down as we speak.'

'So the net closes in,' murmured Jackman. 'If we can just land Darke . . .'

'How long do you think it'll take for your caller to respond?' asked Marie.

'Not long, I reckon. He sounded pretty intense. He wants Darke found.'

Marie frowned. 'It's a bit odd, isn't it? All these people who work for Darke, and who obviously get paid by him, want him banged up. Why? Why, when just like that, he could get each and every one of them in serious trouble with us?'

'Let's hope we get the opportunity to ask,' Jackman said. 'Right now, I need to talk to the man who shot Vic Blackwell. Sorry, Marie, under the circumstances, you have to sit this one out. I want you to stay in my office and wait for that call, and if he rings, send someone downstairs to get me immediately.' He turned to Max. 'With me, please.'

Marie would have dearly loved to go with Jackman and look their would-be murderer in the eyes, but that wasn't going to happen. She wouldn't be allowed near him, even if it had just been a minor assault. But it didn't stop her wanting to see him.

She made her way to Jackman's office. Things were hotting up. If they could just get an address for the monster who had imprisoned Justin, they'd be flying. And a call to say that Vic Blackwell was out of the woods would be the icing on the cake.

Marie settled down in Jackman's captain's chair to wait.

CHAPTER THIRTY-ONE

Jackman had just returned to his office when the call came. 'He's at the war memorial. Send a police car to pick him up. It's safer for him if it looks like you're taking him in for questioning. He'll put up a bit of a show, then back down. Scrawny kid in black joggers and a black hoodie. Answers to the name of Mossy.'

'Got it. We'll be there,' Jackman said.

There was a pause, and then the voice seemed to falter. 'Thank you, Inspector,' he said softly. Then he was gone.

But there was no time to reflect. 'Marie! Get a marked car and go with the crew. Pick up a kid from the war memorial!' He gave the name and description, and Marie hurried from the office.

The reward would cost the trust a fair amount of money, but it would be worth every penny if it led them to that predator.

Jackman picked up his phone and alerted the custody sergeant, asking him to have an interview room ready and waiting. This could be the beginning of the end for the mysterious Darke.

Mossy certainly did put up a show of resistance. Finally he was sitting next to her in the back of the squad car. She gave him a surreptitious glance.

'I'm DS Marie Evans. Thank you for coming forward.'

Mossy said nothing for a while. Then, 'Where's your boss? I don't want to talk to the monkey, alright? And can we take these off?' He indicated the cuffs around his wrists.

Marie rather admired the kid's bravado. The hard-nut talk didn't quite go with his childlike, if slightly battered, appearance. She wondered what had happened for him to get as bruised as that. 'Don't worry, Mossy, he'll be the one talking to you. His name's DI Jackman by the way. And we'll keep the handcuffs on until we get you inside the station. It's procedure, and it'll make your "arrest" look kosher.'

Mossy snorted, but said nothing more about them. 'What's he like? This Jackman?'

'The fairest copper you'll ever come across.'

'No such thing.'

'You're wrong there, sunshine, as you're about to find out.'

'Bollocks. You're all the same.'

Marie smiled to herself. He was keeping up a good show, but there was something vulnerable about him. She wondered just how involved in Darke's criminal organisation he really was.

They drove into the police station yard. Mossy was silent. Was this all a hoax? Marie glanced at the scruffy kid beside her. No, he knew Darke. Now it was up to them to find out just how much he knew.

Jackman was waiting for them in Interview Room Two, where three coffees stood waiting, along with a heap of sugar sachets. He pushed a cup towards Mossy. 'Your friend said you could help us.'

Mossy emptied three sugars into the coffee. 'Maybe. As long as I get the reward.'

Jackman explained how the system worked, emphasising that the information had to be solid and actionable. Mossy listened in silence.

When Jackman had finished, he said, 'As I see it, I know exactly where Darke lives. You don't. Info like that's worth paying for.' He stared at Jackman over the rim of the beaker. 'Or you can just bumble along as you have been doing, without a clue.'

'Who is Darke?'

'A sleazebag who terrifies kids and does God knows what to them.' His shiver wasn't put on.

'Kids? Just boys?'

Mossy looked down. 'Boys, although . . .' He stopped. 'Do you want this address or don't you?'

Marie watched the boy closely. What had he been about to say? Was it, "although not always?" The name Alice Delaney sprang to mind.

'Yes, we do want that address, and if turns out to be instrumental in finding Darke, you'll receive the reward, every penny of it.' Jackman looked at the lad. 'I know you're on the level, Mossy. And your friend too. We need your help to find this Darke. We believe he has killed at least one young man, sold several others into the sex trade, and destroyed another by incarcerating him somewhere . . .' Jackman noticed Mossy's puzzled expression. 'Sorry, by kidnapping him and keeping him locked up somewhere so that he could torture him.'

'I'll tell you what you want to know, but that's all. I can't tell you about other people involved. Is that a deal?' Mossy said.

'I can't make a deal like that, I'm afraid, son. But I promise that the money's yours if that address leads us to Darke.'

Mossy seemed to need to weigh that up.

'Have you done anything illegal while you were working for Darke, Mossy? This is between us, okay?' Jackman kept his tone reassuring and even. 'No recordings and no strings.'

'No, nothing, not yet. Except . . .' He made a face. 'I did break into Darke's house. That's how I know where he lives. But I didn't take anything. I was just trying to find out where he was.'

Puzzled, Jackman glanced at Marie.

'I've done nothing illegal for Darke, I swear.' Mossy stared hard at Jackman.

'Okay. But can I ask you one thing? Do you know a man called Trez?'

'The address, copper. That's all I have for you. Take it or leave it.'

Jackman stood up, and a look of fear crossed Mossy's bruised face.

'Then I'll sort out the paperwork,' Jackman said.

Mossy seemed to sag. Relief, Marie supposed. She had no idea where this kid fitted in, but having enough money to get out was obviously the most important thing in his life right now.

'Your friend? The one who rang?' She looked at Mossy and smiled. 'He must think a lot of you to set this up.'

'He's awesome.'

'We can help him, if he's mixed up in it. He just needs to come in and talk to us.'

'No, he doesn't. He's no villain.'

'And Trez? Is he a villain?'

Mossy glowered at her. So Mossy did know Trez. 'Okay,' she held up her hands, 'I know! The address, and nothing more.'

After a while, Mossy said, 'All that stuff about Darke killing someone? Was that for real?'

'Sadly, yes.'

'And what did he mean about torture?'

'It's best you don't know. And I can't tell you anyway, it's an ongoing investigation,' Marie said flatly.

'Lady? I *need* to know what Darke does to them people he kidnaps.'

'Why?'

'Because I do!' Mossy's façade was beginning to crack.

'He's taken someone you know, hasn't he?'

'I dunno! I dunno!' Mossy cried out. 'Maybe.'

Marie put two and two together. Mossy was around sixteen, a local kid, and from an abusive background, that much was obvious. Just like Alice Delaney. That was why he'd said, "Boys, although . . ."

She sat back and regarded him. 'If I tell you what I think, just between you and me, then you won't have told me a thing, you won't have grassed up a single person. What do you think?'

He shrugged. She took it as a green light.

'Your friend, Alice. She's missing. We know all about Alice. It's believed she just had enough of her drunken parents and ran away. You think differently, don't you? And now you know what a monster Darke is, you're shitting hot bricks.'

Mossy hung his head.

Bingo! thought Marie. 'Thought so, and I'm really sorry, but we'll take one thing at a time. First let Jackman sort out your claim, then we'll check out the address you gave us, and we'll take it from there, okay?' She gave him an encouraging smile. 'Want another coffee?'

* * *

Jackman stared at the address Mossy had given him and, without a word, passed it to Marie.

He jumped up, and spoke to one of the uniformed officers on duty in the interview rooms. 'Get the boy some food, and keep him here until I get back. He must *not* leave, understood?'

The officer nodded. 'Absolutely, sir.'

He beckoned to Marie. 'Come on. We need to inform the duty sergeant and arrange a firearms team, fast.'

Sergeant Alex Unsworth looked at the address. 'Bridle Street? But that's where—'

'How soon can you sort an armed response vehicle, Sergeant?' asked Jackman briskly.

'Gimme ten.'

'We'll rendezvous in the car park, with as many uniforms as you can spare. We have no idea what we might find, but I'm preparing for the worst.' He turned to Marie. 'Get the team together, everyone in stab-proof vests. And if Robbie's in, ask him to stay in the office to be the liaison between us and whatever help or info that we need. He won't like it, but that's an order, Marie. I need someone I can trust right here.'

The next stop was Ruth Crooke, and as expected she'd immediately contacted a JP to organise a warrant, as well as everything else he was going to need.

'Have we got him, Rowan?'

'I'm pretty sure we have his lair, and that's a start. Whether he's there or not we have no way of knowing, but the kid who came forward didn't make this address up.'

'Then good luck. I'll get things rolling and I'll see you there.'

Jackman hurried back to the rendezvous point, his head full of pictures of what might await them in Bridle Street. Alice Delaney featured heavily. He pushed them away. This was no time for guessing games.

* * *

PC Kevin Stoner had just got into his car when he heard the call. He was to stay put, and keep a careful eye open for anyone entering or leaving the house on Bridle Street. DI Jackman was on his way with armed officers. What was happening? It didn't make sense.

He didn't have long to wait. His colleagues came in swiftly and with no fuss. There were no blues and twos. In minutes, the road was sealed and the four houses along the terrace cordoned off.

Kevin ran up to DI Jackman. 'Sir? I've just been talking to Jim. I swear there's nothing going on in that shelter.'

'It's not the shelter we're interested in. It's the house at the far end of the terrace, and we're going in now.'

Kevin looked stunned. 'But that's Mr Hawkins's home, sir. I was in there the other day, there's nothing there. He's just some miserable sod who's always complaining.'

Jackman stared at him. 'You *know* the owner of this house?'

'Not know, exactly, but I did check it out because he was complaining about the noise coming from Jim's place.'

'What does he look like?'

'Around forty. Slim build, fair hair, really old-fashioned clothes. And he's bloody rude. Sorry, sir, but he called the homeless kids vermin, and I didn't like him.'

'Don't go anywhere, Kevin! I want you right here after we've been inside.'

Jackman ran off to join the armed team, with Kevin staring after him in total confusion.

* * *

Thirty minutes later, Jackman and Marie were standing in Isaac Hawkins's lounge.

'I believed him,' Marie said flatly. 'But there's nothing here. Nothing at all.'

Jackman looked determined. 'I still believe him.'

'Does this look like the lair of a predator?' asked Marie. 'My grannie would feel at home here. It's probably the naffest house I've ever been in.'

Jackman was pacing the floor. 'Very true, but something about this place isn't right.' He stopped pacing. 'We're sure there are no cellars, aren't we?'

'Absolutely. Solid floors and foundations. I had Max check the attic, but apart from boxes of old, unwanted stuff, there's nothing there either.'

Jackman sank down into a chair. 'Justin was seen here, on this very street, but no other cameras picked up any images from before that, so . . .'

'Could he have been dumped here? Our dead Geordie was dumped, wasn't he?' Marie suggested.

'No, he was running away. He'd escaped from somewhere alright.' He couldn't shake off the conviction that this was Darke's house. But he had no clue as to why he felt that way, other than that he believed a feral kid called Mossy. 'Where is Hawkins?'

'Did you get the Marie Celeste feel in the kitchen? Judging by the state of it, a couple of days ago he just walked out. There's half a bottle of milk in the fridge, and bananas still in a fruit bowl. Washing up done, but left in the drainer, half a loaf in the bread bin with a bread knife beside it.' She shook her head. 'Winter coats and jackets still hanging in the hallway, and a row of boots and shoes. I'm beginning to think he just evaporated!'

'There's no sign of a struggle either, and nothing seems to have been disturbed.' He looked around. 'Although I'll wager a pound to a penny, Mossy's fingerprints will be all over the place.'

Before he could say any more, Max and Kevin joined them, both looking anxious.

'We've been talking to the people who rent the rooms in the property next door. None of them are impressed with this Hawkins character,' said Max. 'He's always trying to get them to complain about the noise coming from Jim's place. They reckon sure, it does get a bit rowdy sometimes, but as one said, they all have several kids, and they're probably equally as bad.'

'We asked them what they actually knew about Hawkins, and it's not much.' Kevin shrugged. 'They rarely see him, except when he has one of his rants.' He looked at his pocket book. 'They say they see his lodger more than they do him.'

'Lodger?'

Max nodded. 'Mmm. They say he goes out to work very early, and often comes back quite late, and sometimes he's in and out during the day.'

'Name? Description?' asked Jackman.

'They don't know his name,' Kevin said, 'but they said he was older, fatter and wore dark suits. Oh, and according to one of the women next door, he had a particularly bad comb-over.'

Jackman tried to work that one out. It could be a description of Darke. So where was he? Had he evaporated along with Hawkins?

'They've done a runner, haven't they, boss?' Max said. 'Left everything and legged it. I bet they were on their toes the moment they realised Justin had gone awol. Anyone with half a brain would know we'd be down on it like a ton of bricks.'

Jackman didn't answer. Nothing was slotting into place. 'Okay everyone, just be quiet for a moment, will you?' He closed his eyes and took a long deep breath. He tried to imagine a big whiteboard with him standing in front of it with a marker, writing what they knew to be true, then collating the fresh evidence into some sort of order.

Without opening his eyes, he said, 'No matter how it looks, this is the focal point of our investigation. This house is not right. It feels as if no one actually lives here. It has all the accoutrements of human habitation, but it's like a museum.'

'Even the beauty of the period when it was built has been removed,' added Kevin. 'It's an ugly place, when it should be beautiful. I felt that the first time I walked in here.'

'Good point,' said Marie. 'Even Jim's renovation has ornate ceilings, dado rails and lovely old fireplaces.'

'I want to know as much as possible about Hawkins. Marie, get Robbie to do a search, an in-depth one, right now.'

She relayed his request. 'And what about this lodger? Now we know there are two people living here instead of one, we need to go over the place again, more thoroughly. I want his name and I want to know what he does for a living.'

'Probably abducts boys,' muttered Max.

Kevin raised his hand. 'DI Jackman? I know this sounds a bit like stating the obvious, but Jim told me the other house in this terrace, the one next to him, is waiting for probate to come through, so it's empty at present. Has anyone checked it out?'

Jackman looked around, and was met with blank stares.

'Jim told our officers that there'd been no comings and goings there in months,' Kevin said, 'and no noise or anything suspicious. But maybe we could find a key holder?'

Jackman cursed himself. They should have checked the place long before this. What if Darke was using it as his "prison?" He had a whole string of young housebreakers on his books, access would have been a doddle. And sandwiched between a house full of rowdy misfits and another with a gaggle of children, any unusual noises would be attributed to one of them. Jackman felt slightly sick. Was it that obvious? 'We won't wait for a key holder. I'm categorically stating that I suspect someone's life to be in danger inside that house, so we go in immediately. Marie, alert the OIC of the armed unit, and get an enforcer on the front door.'

CHAPTER THIRTY-TWO

Luckily the power was still on. Max gazed around the unoccupied house in admiration. If Hawkins's home was a creepy museum, this one was a showcase. Tasteful, and decorated in the traditional style, it was like something from *House Beautiful,* despite the dust. But there was no trace of the slightest disturbance anywhere, with the exception of the damage to the front door, and that was down to them.

After the firearms officers' last 'Clear,' Max and Kevin walked from room to room in silence, taking everything in. For once, Max had been excused loft duties. Good. He hated getting messy.

They stopped in one of the top floor bedrooms, and listened.

'Yes, you can hear some of the residents next door,' Kevin remarked, 'and you can hear children too. There's a game going on in the family house, and maybe Ragga's kicking off again in Jim's shelter, but it isn't unacceptable by any measure, is it?'

'The walls are thick and the house well-built, so it's just muffled noises. The house I grew up in was far worse than this.' Max frowned, thinking about it. The only sounds Hawkins could have heard from his end of the terrace were the children, so why keep blaming Jim Cousins? He asked Kevin what he thought.

'Probably because he looked on Jim's residents as vermin, and he didn't like them on his doorstep. He was a nasty piece of work, Max. I can see him trying to shift the blame for anything and everything to Jim's door.'

They walked back down and looked across to the cordon, where Jackman was in earnest conversation with the superintendent. He didn't look happy.

'Poor sod! He's going to have a lot of explaining to do after this, isn't he?' Max said.

'Looks that way, but . . .' Kevin sighed.

'I know, I feel the same, it's as if there's a pot of gold on the other side of a locked door, and we can't find the bleeding key.'

Suddenly all those weird feelings that he'd had when he'd been in these houses, connected with a resounding thud. Max left Kevin standing with his mouth open and sprinted over to Jackman.

'Sir! I've just had an idea and I need to know what you think!' He turned to the superintendent. 'Sorry, ma'am, but this could be vital!'

Ruth Crooke threw up her hands, 'Be my guest, Detective. We need something to dig us out of this bloody great hole.'

'Thanks for the lifeline!' murmured Jackman as they hurried back to the houses. 'So what is it?'

Max punched a fist into his other cupped hand. 'Look, I don't know much about architecture, boss, but when I was a kid, my favourite book was *The Magician's Nephew*, and I'm wondering if this place is like the row of terraced houses in the story, only it's been altered over the years.'

Jackman nodded. He knew the C.S. Lewis book. 'Yes, it's possible, Max, so explain what you're saying!'

'When I went into Jim's attic, the connecting wall between his and the empty house was bricked up, but it was done in different brick to the rest of the house. It had been added at a later date. Hawkins's attic had a completely different kind of partition between him and the family house, more like thick plasterboard, and not brick at all.'

Jackman's eyes lit up. 'So you believe these houses had one long, open connecting loft space. It was often the case with terraced houses of this age, and like in the book, before the partitions were added you could have walked right through.' He rubbed at his temples, thinking hard. 'And the other two loft areas?'

'The empty house's loft hatch was pretty well sealed up. They can't have had any problems with the water tank or anything, the hatch was painted shut and obviously hadn't been accessed for donkey's years. The families in the rented property have no rights to the loft space, and the landlord had put a padlock on it.'

'So we haven't been in either loft space?'

'Exactly, sir! I want to go back into Hawkins's attic, and take a closer look at that partition wall.'

'Damned right!' Jackman clapped him on the shoulder. 'Good man! Let's go!'

* * *

Max was first up the ladder, closely followed by Jackman and Marie. Jackman had suggested that Marie stay down below, because of her leg injury, but the suggestion was met with a stony stare. Wisely, he didn't argue.

The loft was strewn with dusty boxes and old cases. Jackman looked around and saw little of interest. They would find no forgotten treasure here, there'd be no cash in this attic.

Moving cartons and packages to one side, they made their way to the wall that this house shared with the rented one.

Jackman pulled a stack of cardboard boxes away from the wall. 'You were right! Look!'

Cut into the partitioning was a door, the handle smooth and dust-free. It had no lock or padlock.

'He's pretty sure of himself, isn't he? Leaving it unsecured like this,' Marie whispered.

Jackman paused, fingers on the door handle, and the memory of an old case flashed into his mind. Once before they had opened a door like this. And walked straight into hell.

He took a breath. 'Ready?'

'Ready,' echoed Marie and Max.

There was absolutely nothing in the loft space of the rented property, other than a water tank, some piping, and a defunct TV aerial. What they did find was a boarded-up passageway, about a metre wide, leading straight from the door where they stood to another one in the far wall. A well-trodden path. Even from here, the beams of their torches lit up a big reinforced door set into a sturdy, stud-partition wall that seemed to be constructed from steel panels in a metal frame.

That terrible feeling of déjà vu swept over Jackman again. He really didn't want to go in there.

Max walked across the boards and stopped at the door. 'I've seen something like this before.' His voice was low. 'Rich geezer had a panic room installed in his home. It had fortified walls just like this, and it was insulated and sound-proofed.'

They stared at the door, all of them wondering why there was a big key still in the lock.

After a puzzled glance at his friends, Jackman turned the lever handle and pushed. The door was locked. From their side, with the key left in it.

'Max?' Jackman's voice broke the silence. 'Go back down and get two armed officers, and maybe Kevin Stoner too. We're entering this place blind. We have no idea what's behind this door, and no way of knowing what to prepare for.'

'It could be empty,' Marie said, fearfully. 'It could just be some kind of secure store . . . or it could be a prison.'

'Have you got a phone signal, Marie?' Jackman said.

She checked. 'A good one.'

'Phone Robbie. Tell him to find out everything he can about the owners of this empty house, as fast as he can.'

Marie made the call. 'He's on to it, sir, but what about Jim Cousins? He might know, and he's only next door.'

'Call down to the others. Tell them to get him in here, now!'

Marie hurried back across the loft space and into Hawkins's attic. Jackman was left alone with that steel plated door, and his fear of what might be behind it.

For a moment, his courage deserted him. He'd seen terrible things in the past, some still haunted him and always would. Would another one finally tip him over the edge?

He stared at the door. As Marie had said, there might be nothing on the other side. Closer examination told him that it wasn't new, and had been there for many years. What did that mean?

It meant Darke hadn't installed it for his evil purposes, he'd discovered it, and then made use of it. But for what? This could be the perfect storage place for the stolen clothes before they were shipped out. But Darke also smuggled teenage boys, and the same could be said for them. The perfect storage facility. With some relief, he heard Max and the others returning.

Jim Cousins stared incredulously at the door, and at the wall it was set in, and nodded slowly. He turned to Kevin. 'Remember what I told you about my uncle?'

'Sure, Jacob, wasn't it? He owned all these houses years ago.'

'Yes, and apart from being an astute businessman, he was also a very successful criminal.' Jim continued to gaze at the door. 'I was never allowed up here when I was a kid. Now I think I know why.' He looked at Jackman. 'I'd say my uncle constructed this to store stolen goods, and possibly large quantities of cash.'

'But when he sold it, it must have been seen by the surveyors,' Jackman said. 'And what if the new people wanted to store stuff, or access their cold water tank?'

Jim shrugged. 'No idea, but Uncle would have thought about that, I'm certain. Knowing him, he would have turned it into a selling point! He was no fool. And maybe this secured area doesn't occupy the full loft space, and the tank is still accessible? I really don't know.'

Jackman thanked him and asked him to stand back. He could hold off no longer.

'Okay, let's see what we have here.'

He meant to sound calm, in control, and thought he'd pulled it off. Inside, a small boy was struggling to keep up a show of bravado in front of his schoolmates.

Jackman turned the key.

The first thing that hit him was the smell. His stomach heaved.

Jackman was first into the room.

The scene unfolded in slow-motion, in a factual kind of way, as if he were watching clips from a documentary. As far as he could make out, he was looking at three live occupants, and one dead body. The others stood, frozen, behind him, like a tableau in a waxworks museum.

'Help me!' That desperate cry broke the spell.

It galvanised Jackman. 'Paramedics! Max, get ambulances here, code Red! We need three of them! Marie, call the super and organise the specialist victim retrieval team, now! And everybody? Don't touch anyone or anything, okay? This is a crime scene.'

'Help me!' He sounded like a small child.

Jackman's first reaction was to rush in and help the boy. But this situation called for specialists — officers and doctors trained to deal with trauma. A too-hasty approach could cause even more terror. These poor boys.

Jackman spoke to the one boy who seemed able to communicate. 'We're here for you. You're safe now, I promise. We'll get you out just as soon as possible. Can you tell me your name, son?'

'Anthony. Please, please help me.' He was whispering now.

'We will, Anthony. Help is on its way. We'll soon have you out of here.'

Marie was at his shoulder. 'I can't leave him like that, he needs us!'

He put a restraining hand on her arm. 'We don't know what he's suffered or how he'll react, Marie. A team is on its way. We have to wait.'

She let out a shuddering sigh. 'What has happened here?'

Jackman struggled to make sense of what he was seeing. This fortified area of the attic had been divided into four separate compartments. Each had a camp bed in it, bolted to the floor. The nearest thing Jackman could compare them to was his mother's stables — three-sided stalls with a door at the front made of heavy mesh wire. Three were occupied by what he believed to be teenage boys, or young men. It was hard to tell.

One was in a similar state to Justin when they had found him in the children's playground. Another was curled up on his bed, staring at them from huge, frightened eyes. The boy called Anthony was on his feet with his fingers through the mesh at the door, shaking it in frustration. Like the others, his ankles were secured by a link chain, enabling him to shuffle but not take a stride.

'Sorry, Jackman.'

Marie had slipped past him to Anthony's "stall." She crouched down in front of the mesh and started to talk to the boy in a soft, gentle voice that Jackman rarely heard her use. She held out her hand, and when he didn't recoil, she lightly touched his fingers with hers, reassuring him that his ordeal was over.

The boy said, 'He left us. He ran away and left us. I thought we'd starve, I thought we were going to die here.' Tears were now pouring down the boy's face. Jackman guessed that Marie was crying with him.

Did he mean Justin? Ran away and left them? He recalled the turned key in the door, and he understood. Justin had run in a state of blind panic, turned the key on the thing he was running from, keeping it back there, away from him. There had been no room in his mind to consider the other boys.

Much as he didn't want to, Jackman had to face what was in that fourth cubicle. Hesitantly, he approached it.

Then Kevin Stoner was beside him. 'It's Hawkins. I recognise the old-fashioned clothing.'

What on earth happened to him?

Max stood just behind Kevin, and let out a low whistle. 'He's been practically ripped to shreds.'

There was blood, and, from the ankle chain still around his neck, and the distorted purple, livid face and protruding tongue, Jackman guessed he had been strangled before being torn apart by a crazed boy.

'What goes around comes around,' murmured Kevin. 'He got his.'

'So, are we really looking at Darke?' asked Max, 'or should I say what's left of him.'

'There's little doubt about that,' said Jackman flatly. He looked across to where Marie was still crouched down in front of the caged boy. 'And with luck, we'll have a credible witness in Anthony. From his condition, I should think he's not been here very long, not nearly as long as these other two poor souls.'

'And can fill in some of the gaps,' added Max. 'Because I don't think the other two will be up for a natter any time soon.'

It was true. One boy was locked in a nightmare world of his own, and the other, well, he hadn't moved a muscle since they entered, and although his eyes followed them, Jackman didn't think it had registered that they were there to help him.

'I knew I never liked Hawkins, but I never dreamed he could be Darke!' Kevin shook his head. 'If only I'd delved a bit deeper, maybe—'

Jackman stopped him. 'Don't beat yourself up, Kevin. How could you possibly have known?'

'Sir? The team are outside. They want a sit rep before they go in.'

Jackman called his team to him. 'Okay, guys, the professionals can handle this now.'

'I'm staying with Anthony,' said Marie bluntly. 'Just until someone takes over his care. Sorry, but I can't leave him on his own again. I just can't.'

Jackman nodded. 'You stay. I'll go and give the situation report, and then as soon as he has someone with him, you can join us outside.'

She nodded, her eyes never leaving the terrified boy.

In the adjoining loft space, Jackman found six members of the specialist team assembled and ready to begin the lengthy process of evacuating the boys. For a moment he was shocked to see Laura amongst them. He didn't want the woman he loved to have to deal with such horror. Then he brought himself up short. Laura was a skilled professional, and it was just as much her job to be there as it was his.

Amidst the chaos and horror, Jackman allowed himself a brief moment of hope. If they could manage to work as they were now, then there really was a future for their relationship.

'Thank you for getting here so quickly. So this is the situation . . .'

CHAPTER THIRTY-THREE

It took hours to get the boys to safety, and Darke's remains to the morgue.

For once, Rory Wilkinson did not extend his usual compassionate welcome. Rory had left a team of lab technicians and SOCOs working the attic crime scene and had hurried back to start work on his latest visitor.

The first thing Rory told them was that Hawkins/Darke's blood matched that found on Justin's clothes, thus proving an indisputable connection between them.

'He was asphyxiated as a result of mechanical strangulation, ironically with the same ankle cuffs that he used on his victims.' Rory pointed to the dark bruising around his neck, and then to his face. 'There are petechial haemorrhages in the eyes and, as is often the case with these kinds of strangulation, I found some strands of his attacker's hair under his fingernails, no doubt he grabbed at it while fighting for his life.' He looked with distaste at the corpse. 'I'm only sorry that once the airway is blocked and the blood supply to the brain is interrupted, loss of consciousness can follow in a matter of seconds, and death very shortly after, and I mean just seconds later. So, he was spared the pain and horror of what our young man proceeded to do next.' He glared at them angrily. 'A travesty, don't you think? After what he's been doing to all those beautiful young men, he should have felt every agonising second while certain parts of his anatomy were ripped apart. Better if his attacker had omitted the strangling, and just left him to bleed out on his own prison floor.'

Jackman had never heard Rory speak like that about anyone, and although he whole-heartedly agreed, he was shocked at this anger.

'I saw those teenagers, didn't I?' He jabbed a finger towards the dead man on the mortuary table. 'This man was truly evil.'

'We're wondering why Justin's ankle cuffs were taken off, Rory. Any thoughts?'

Rory drew in a long breath. 'I should think Darke removed them in order to abuse or humiliate the boy. All of them were terrified of Darke, so until Justin snapped, they'd probably been totally compliant and submissive.'

Jackman had wondered as much. There seemed no other logical explanation. And hopefully, with the right care and encouragement, Anthony would be able to tell them exactly what happened in that attic room. Jackman just hoped he'd have the stomach to listen.

'On a slightly lighter note, my other team of SOCOs, those working Hawkins's house, have just rung in with some interesting news. They have found a hairpiece, and something that looks like a fat suit in a storage locker under a bed. It wasn't one of those joke things, it was more like the kind they use in filming to either give someone muscles, or extra weight.'

Light dawned. Jackman looked at Marie. 'Our Mr Hawkins never had a lodger.'

She shook her head in amazement. 'So the man the neighbours saw going off to work was Hawkins in disguise.'

'Bang on, old fruit!' Rory seemed finally to be emerging from his uncharacteristically bitter mood. 'And DNA tests will confirm, of course, but my guys assure me that there's only one set of fingerprints on everything in that house, and they all belong to Hawkins.'

Marie stared down at Hawkins's mutilated body. Jackman wondered if she was thinking of the boy called Anthony. Somehow, in the midst of all that horror, she had managed to connect with him. Jackman recalled how her words and gestures had soothed and calmed the traumatised teenager.

'I have this awful picture in my head,' she said. 'It's nothing that we witnessed, it's just this horrible thought, and I can't get rid of it.'

Like a blackbird listening for worms, Rory tilted his head. 'Tell us.'

'I keep imagining him tiptoeing across that loft space, key in hand, like some night creature from a horror story, going right over the heads of little children lying innocently asleep.'

Jackman got the picture. All too vividly. 'Well, he'll never do it again, Marie.'

'But he *did* do it, didn't he? We had a real live monster living here in Saltern-le-Fen, and we never suspected a thing. If it wasn't for that street kid and his phone-in friend, he'd still be doing it.'

'But he isn't, that's what matters,' said Rory. 'It doesn't matter how you get to the end of the story, the important thing is getting there, and that somehow order is restored.'

Jackman wanted to agree, but couldn't. 'We aren't at the end yet, Rory. We believed we would find Alice Delaney, but we didn't. I'm now worried sick that Darke, or Hawkins, had another dark hole where he hid his prey.'

Rory shook his head. 'Then go and do what you do best. You now know who this Darke character really is, you have his home to sift through, and his office. You have some of his minions under lock and key, and from what I hear they can't wait to dump him in the doo-doo. You'll soon know everything there is to know about him, and if he has another place, you'll find it, Detectives. I *know* you will.' He smiled benignly. 'Now, I suggest you get some sleep. You both look positively haggard! And I . . . well, I'll be spending a happy hour taking unbridled delight in slicing and dicing what is left of this bag of shit!'

* * *

Having been assured repeatedly that the reward was his, Mossy was allowed to leave. He couldn't go to Trez's place, and he didn't dare go to the posh pad where Tommy was living. He was bound to be followed, and no way was he going to drop them in it. So, as agreed, he would slip quietly off the radar, and meet Tommy in the twenty-four hour McDonalds on the outskirts of town. Mossy knew a guy who worked the night shift there, and he was sure he'd let him use his phone for a quick text to Tommy.

He wanted to be elated, but he still didn't know where Alice was. It had taken the edge off everything. He bought a coffee and waited for Tommy.

'They never explained it properly, Tommy, but they said the reward was mine. It's complicated, because I ain't got a bank account and I don't even have a home, but they said they'll sort it somehow.' He looked at his friend. 'They've found him, Tom. They've definitely got Darke, and the bastard's dead. I overheard lots of stuff, and you could tell by the mood in the nick, it was electric.'

'Jeez! All that time Dean and Trez were so sure that he was hatching some devious plan to steal their money and screw them over, and he was dead! We've all been tormenting ourselves for nothing!' Tommy shook his head in disbelief, then sighed and said, 'Have you eaten, kid?'

'A sandwich, and some really bad coffee.'

'I'll get us a couple of burgers, and you can tell me everything.'

They ate in silence for a while, then Mossy said, 'They're looking for Trez. I said I'd never heard of him, but I don't think they believed me. I don't want him to get caught, but I do need to talk to him about Alice.'

Tommy looked down at his plate. 'Sorry, kid, but Trez's gone. He heard that one of the couriers had shot a copper. It was a guy who knew all about his part in the racket, and Trez thought he'd shop him, so he took off. It's a while ago now.'

Mossy felt gutted — alone and vulnerable. Trez was a scary guy alright, but he was also the nearest thing to family that Mossy had ever had.

'He said to tell you he was sorry. He said you were the best boy he'd ever trained. And he also said to tell you that he did deliver your letter to Alice, in person. He wished you well, Mossy, and he meant it.' He leaned forward. 'So what now?'

'Well, our new venture is right down the pan, but I was going to tell you I wanted out anyway.' Mossy grinned sheepishly at Tommy. 'I might be Trez's best boy, but I don't want to go down that route. I want to find Alice. That's all I want to do. Then, since I'm going to have some money at last, I'll decide what I really want later.' He sniffed. 'Never thought I'd say this, but a lady came to talk to me while I was in the nick. I suppose she was some kind of social worker, but she was really nice. She's going to give me some help if I want it. I'm thinking about it.'

Tommy nodded. 'Good. I think you should take all the help you can get. You've had a shitty life, and now you deserve a lucky break.'

'About the money,' he looked earnestly at Tommy. 'Half is yours, you know. It was you that made it happen.'

Tommy shook his head. 'No! Keep it, kid. Dean and I'll be alright. We're going to stick together. We're working on a new scam, but it can't be around here. Dean's already spoken to his father. He told him he got mixed up with a bad crowd and wants to start again somewhere new, and his old man is going to sell the apartment for him, and we'll move on. His dad has a lot of clout, and Dean's going to make use of it.' He laughed. 'We've already got a load of cash coming in from selling Darke's Hybird X collection on the resell sites. So the reward money is yours, okay?' He leaned down and picked up a carrier bag from the floor beside him. 'And so is this. Two hundred quid to tide you over, and a little memento from Trez.'

Mossy opened the bag. The money was there, and one of the Hybird X bomber jackets that Darke's boys had used to practise mugging kids with.

'He said you'd earned it. I reckon it's worth a couple of grand at least.'

Mossy looked at it. He'd thought it was sick to own clothes worth that kind of money, and he still did. 'Sell it for me, Tommy? I've got enough mementos, thanks.' He touched his broken nose, and they laughed together.

'Meet me here at midday tomorrow. I'm sure Dean can cough up for this, and we'll sell the jacket later.' He frowned. 'Where are you going to stay tonight?'

'I'm fine, Tom, don't worry. I've got a place to go.'

'As long as you're sure?'

'Honest.' Mossy stood up. 'I'll see you tomorrow then.'

Tommy nodded. 'And then we'll be gone. If they've found Darke, they will have found his notebooks, so rather than get a visit from the police, we're staying with a friend of Dean's. Then it's au revoir Saltern-le-Fen. I can't tell you where we're going, because right now, I have no idea.'

'Just stay safe.'

'You too, kid.'

* * *

It had been a while since Mossy had made his way down the dark avenue to the deserted chapel. So much had happened, it all seemed like some wild dream. He scrambled in through the broken window, careful this time not to tear his clean clothes.

Nothing had changed and no one had been in there, and although it felt safe and familiar, Mossy himself felt very different. He nestled down in the old smelly blankets and knew he would never come back here again.

As he pulled the cover closer around him, he felt something scratch his face. He felt around for the torch he had left there, and saw that it was a note. He unfolded it and stared at it in disbelief.

Mossy, if you find this, I will meet you in the place you said in your letter. I felt so threatened at home that I have found somewhere safe, just until we can talk. I feel bad about Mrs Steeples, but I thought it best that no one knew what I was doing. I miss you. Alice xx

Mossy clasped it to him, then read it again. 'Thank God you're safe,' he murmured. 'Oh, and I miss you too, Alice.'

He closed his eyes and slipped into sleep, grateful that he had never actually committed a crime for Darke, such as mugging some poor kid like the boy who died. He could meet Alice with a clear conscience. Well, kind of. He chuckled. He'd come very close, but he believed she would forgive him, given the circumstances.

Mossy slept, happy in the knowledge that the perverted Darke had never got his filthy hands on her. At last, there were no hidden microphones listening to him, and no dark figures watching him sleep.

CHAPTER THIRTY-FOUR

Three weeks later, Jackman was setting off to the morning meeting. So much had happened in that time that he felt punch-drunk. Those weeks had been a frenzied series of meetings, reports, media conferences, all while tying up a tangle of loose ends. It wasn't over by a long stretch, but things were finally getting slower, enough for him to catch his breath.

Laura had been supportive and incredibly helpful, especially when a thought hit him in the middle of the night, and she was there to talk it through with him. As his mother had said, they had survived a baptism of fire, and come through unscathed. She had high hopes that maybe one day . . . ?

He smiled to himself. He wasn't quite ready for that yet, but he was prepared to admit that, for the first time ever, it wasn't beyond the realms of possibility. Maybe he wasn't the loner he had always believed himself to be.

He walked into the CID room, where the talking and laughter ceased immediately. This was an important daily orders, and there was a lot to cover.

He looked around and saw that the whole team was finally reunited. Only one man was missing — Vic Blackwell.

Somehow he had survived. Marie, who visited him regularly, said that he was hell-bent on making it back to work, and she believed he would.

Jackman walked to the front of the big room and turned to face the officers assembled before him. 'Yesterday I received the assessment reports from the team caring for Isaac Hawkins's victims, along with transcripts of the recorded interviews.' He swallowed audibly. 'It was harrowing stuff. It will be available for you all to read later today.' He glanced at his notes. 'The young man called Anthony Yates had spent less time in the attic than the others, and although he suffered considerable mental trauma, he had only minimal physical abuse inflicted upon him, compared to his fellow victims. He responded quickly to the care and specialist help he was given, and has played an integral part in this investigation. Fortunately he was, and is, willing to speak out about the man he knew as Darke.'

There was a murmur around the room. This was a big thing.

'Another piece of extraordinary luck was that Hawkins was an inveterate writer of notes. He had diaries and notebooks locked in a safe in the attic room, and they have been invaluable in understanding why these atrocities took place.'

'Because he was a perverted, sadistic bastard,' muttered someone.

Jackman let it go. Some of the officers had teenage kids themselves, and feelings had naturally run very high.

'I want you all to read the reports, but in a nutshell, this is the psych team's consensus of opinion, derived from what they found in the diaries, and from Anthony Yates, and from extensive searches Robbie Melton made into Hawkins's family history. It appears that Hawkins came from a well-off, but dysfunctional family, who neglected him, and he formed a rather unusual and obsessive relationship with his sister. This might not have had any serious consequences but, when he was still a youngster he came home one evening and found her dead.' He looked at the report. 'It seems it was a case of asphyxia, brought about by sexual activities. We'll need to get hold of the death certificate and the report from the inquest to confirm.'

'Already done, sir,' Robbie interjected. 'Christine Hawkins suffered cerebral hypoxia, lost consciousness and her tongue blocked her airway. She'd been dead for more than an hour when her brother found her.'

'Thank you, Robbie.' Jackman returned to the report. 'It is worth noting that Hawkins, or Darke as they knew him, only took good-looking boys. The others he sold to the highest bidder in an expanding sex trade market on the continent. Anthony Yates has described a rather creepy ritual that Hawkins liked to perform. He would make his victims sit on their beds and listen while he told them stories about his sister, Christine. The main theme of these stories was how incredibly beautiful she was. He would describe her in minute detail. He was obsessed by her stunning good looks, and with the fact that a man had turned her into something repulsive. He declared that if his sister could no longer be beautiful, then they had no right to be either. He set about destroying them. He kept them high on drugs most of the time, partly to keep them quiet, and partly because drugs helped to ruin them.'

'Like his home,' added Kevin. 'He took away everything that was beautiful.'

'Sir? What would he have done when the probate issue on the empty house was sorted?' Charlie Button asked. 'Surely the new owners would have had a survey done, and they'd probably not be too impressed by how their loft was being used.'

'Hawkins had thought of that. He put in a very generous private offer on the property with the deceased relatives. When probate was finalised, the property would have been his,' said Robbie. 'Jim Cousins would have been really pleased about that!'

Kevin raised a hand. 'Just thought you'd like to know that Jim has received funding to extend his facility in Bridle Street. If things go well, he'll purchase that house himself.'

Jackman felt bad about Jim, but they'd had no choice but to put him under the microscope. At least he had bounced back and was now accepting all the help he could get, as well as building a better relationship between his residents and the police.

'So, now that we know that Alice Delaney had simply run away, something we've learned from our little informer who, I have to add, is a reformed character, the main task now is to gather in all the other villains connected to Darke's organisation. The man referred to as Trez has vanished. And although another man has been hinted at, no one has given us a name. One of Darke's notebooks has a string of names, and they're still being followed up, but it's my suspicion that he's miles away by now. Naturally we won't give up on tracking them, but I'm guessing it won't be easy.'

'One big question remains, doesn't it?' Marie said thoughtfully.

Jackman nodded. 'The boy in the rubbish. Our little Geordie, Darryl Townsend. He doesn't fit in anywhere, does he?'

'No connection at all to Darke's boys. Could it just be a terrible coincidence that someone completely unconnected just dumped him there at the same time as all this other bad stuff was happening?' Marie said.

'Doubtful. There has to be a connection somewhere, we just aren't seeing it.' Jackman drew himself up. 'And that is going to be our priority, as soon as all the paperwork for this case is under control.'

'Good,' Marie said. 'I don't want to be forever haunted by the mystery of that boy's last meal. It still has me foxed. A runaway eating fillet steak? No way!'

'Well, at least the Hybird X thefts have ceased,' said Robbie. 'Much to the relief of a lot of streetwear fanatics, although those grails are still fetching huge sums.'

'Sold your bleedin' awful trousers yet?' asked Max.

'Might have.' Robbie smiled innocently.

'And made a fortune?'

Robbie glanced at Jackman.

'Go on, Detective, don't keep us in suspense.'

'Josh Baker, who gave them to me, would only accept a couple of hundred pounds — what they cost him years ago. He told me to give the remainder to the Church family, for whatever charity they were supporting in memory of Denis.'

'That's a really nice thing to do,' said Gary. 'How much did you make, Rob?'

'Um. Nine and a half thousand pounds.'

There was a gasp of disbelief.

'But they were hideous!' Max exclaimed. 'Hey, Rob? What about the jacket? He gave you one of those too.'

'It wasn't quite as rare, but I sold it too, paid off Josh and put the remainder aside for some other good causes.'

Jackman glanced at his watch. 'Come on then, Rob, I need to close this meeting. Who benefits from some tasteless clothing this time?'

'I've split it in half. I'm giving half, that is three thousand pounds to Artie Ball to help him feed the homeless, and another three thousand goes to Jim Cousins for the shelter. Oh and there's a couple of hundred over, and that,' he turned to Max, 'is for you and Rosie, mate, for the new baby.'

Jackman glanced at Marie. She smiled at him and nodded. His team were fantastic.

* * *

Marie pulled on her coat and glanced at her watch. She just had time to get to the motorcycle showroom on the main road out of town. She'd narrowed her choices to two sports models, and she wanted to actually sit on them before she decided which one to buy.

On her way out, she called into Jackman's office to say goodnight. Just as she stepped inside, his mobile bleeped, telling him he had a message.

'One minute, Marie.' He opened the message.

His expression went from relaxed to one of utter shock.

Without a word, he passed her the phone.

It was a photo of Darryl Townsend.

She stared harder and saw that the photograph had been taken along a footpath which bore a signpost. It read, "Little Fen Walk, five miles." This walk started on the outskirts of town and ran along several waterways and fen lanes, and was popular with ramblers and dog walkers. The teenager was leaning casually against the post, and smiling at whoever took the picture.

She passed the phone back to Jackman. 'Unknown number?'

He shook his head. Then he tried to dial back, but there was no ringtone, just a tinny voice saying that the number he required was not available. 'Why send us this?'

Marie could think of lots of reasons, but before she could speak, her own mobile registered an incoming message.

She was almost afraid to open it.

And not without reason, as it turned out to be a video clip.

She held out the phone so that Jackman could see too, and pressed play.

Darryl was walking along the lane beside the water, his hands plunged deep in his pockets and his jacket collar turned up against the wind. He was still smiling. "Come on!" he called out and beckoned to the photographer. "Selfie!"

Marie held her breath.

The boy called out again, and the person with the camera protested. On the third time of asking, the picture zoomed in on Darryl, then suddenly there were two faces in the frame.

Marie gripped Jackman's arm.

Alistair Ashcroft was smiling broadly at her, then he lifted a hand, as if in greeting, and the clip abruptly ended.

With shaking fingers she scrolled down to the message.

'Hello, Marie, thought you'd appreciate my little addition to your recent investigation. Nasty piece of work that Darke fellow. Makes you wonder what people are capable of, doesn't it? But back to Darryl, I hope you enjoyed the conundrum. I wanted to get your attention and I knew you wouldn't let that anomaly go! It was just the condemned man's last meal, the Last Supper that we shared. Sweet boy, shame really . . . Anyway, places to go, people to see. Catch you soon. AA'

She read it. Read it again, then passed it to Jackman.

Neither spoke.

After a while, she said, 'It's a funny kind of relief actually, to know he's back. It's no longer a hidden threat, hanging over us, it's tangible now, something we can deal with.'

Jackman narrowed his eyes. 'Really? You're not just saying that?'

'No, I'm not.' And she meant it. 'Just think. In a matter of weeks, Vic Blackwell has stopped being a threat. Darke is dead, we have an answer to who killed Darryl, and now Alistair has put himself back in the field of play again. This is police stuff now, it's what we're good at.'

Jackman broke into a slow smile. 'Yes, we are, aren't we?'

Marie felt as if a weight had lifted. Alistair Ashcroft was not going to blight her life. If anything, her determination to put him behind bars would give it fresh energy, rekindle her love for her job. This world had no place for men like Ashcroft, or Darke, and it was their duty as police officers to take them down. Okay, Darke's life had been terminated by a strange quirk of fate, but Ashcroft was not like that. Only clever policing would bring Ashcroft to justice.

Jackman stood up. 'I'd better go and tell Ruth the news. Want to come, or do you want to get away?'

She saw the time. 'Hell! Sorry, but I need to go. I'll see you tomorrow. And don't worry about me! This is a new chapter!' she called back over her shoulder.

She called the motorbike showroom on her way down the stairs.

'Danny? What time do you close?' she said.

'As soon as I've sold you a bike, I should think.'

Marie laughed. She knew Danny well. Aside from their shared love of fast motorbikes, she had bought four expensive bikes from him in as many years!

'You're after one of those nippy little sports roadster jobs this time, aren't you?'

'Ah, actually there's been a change of plan.' Marie unlocked her car. 'Nippy and little just aren't me. I want the biggest, most powerful bloody bike that you think I can handle.'

Danny gave a hoot of laughter. 'Then the showroom is yours to choose from! And welcome home. It's good to have the old Marie Evans back!'

Yes, thought Marie. Isn't it just?

THE END

Thank you for reading this book. If you enjoyed it please leave feedback on Amazon or Goodreads, and if there is anything we missed or you have a question about then please get in touch. The author and publishing team appreciate your feedback and time reading this book.

Our email is office@joffebooks.com

www.joffebooks.com

The Prince in Waiting

JOHN CHRISTOPHER

The Prince
in Waiting

COLLIER BOOKS
Macmillan Publishing Company
New York

TO ROSEMARY,
In Lieu of H. or M.

Collier Books
Macmillan Publishing Company
866 Third Avenue, New York, NY 10022
Collier Macmillan Canada, Inc.
First Collier Books edition 1974
Second Collier Books edition 1989
Printed in the United States of America

10   9   8   7   6   5   4   3   2   1

Library of Congress Cataloging-in-Publication Data
Christopher, John.
The prince in waiting/John Christopher. — 2nd Collier Books
ed.   p.   cm.
Summary: Thirteen-year-old Luke has no reason to suspect that anything
will ever change in the primitive society of the future in which he lives,
until he is chosen by the Spirits and his life is irrevocably altered.
ISBN 0-02-042573-2
[1. Science fiction.]   I. Title.   [PZ7.C457Pr 1989]
[Fic] — dc20   89-32902   CIP   AC

Contents

1

Four Swords
in Candlelight

The Armorer's forge was east of the river, in that part of the city called Chesil. It was a large, cavernous building, its floor of ancient stone cracked in places but all of a piece, dark except where the great central fire sent sparks springing up toward the square hole in the timbered roof. In the dimness the dwarfs moved here and there to the clang of metal on metal. They did not look up from their work when I came in. I stood for a moment by the door, watching and accustoming my eyes to the light. The Armorer Dwarf was on the far side of the fire, stooped over the big anvil. I went to stand beside him.

"Health, Rudi," I said.

He did not answer at once. He took a sword off the anvil and held it between himself and the fire, lifting it up and down slightly to judge its trueness by the shifting gleam of light. He nodded and gave it to the dwarf who stood beside him, balancing the blade on his palm and offering the hilt. Then he turned to me.

"Health, Master Luke. How is the world outside? Freezing yet? Your cheeks look as though frost has stroked them."

"It's cold enough. A north wind still."

"A pot of mulled ale, would you say?" He called an order to a dwarf apprentice who went off roll-gaited into the shadows. "Come and sit with me, Master Luke, and tell me how life goes in the city."

My eyes followed the sword which had been taken to the whetstone. The dwarf there treadled with his foot and the wheel went round. He brought the steel edge to it and bright sparks flew.

"Is that . . .?"

"For the Contest? No, those are already made and burnished. Would you see them?"

He lit a candle, thrusting the wick into the fire's heat in a way that would have scorched my flesh, and took it to the wall where swords hung waiting collection. The four made for the Contest rested apart from the others. They were also smaller, no more than two and a half feet from hilt to tip. Rudi took one down and handed it to me. The hilt fitted my grasp. I swung it lightly in the air.

Rudi watched me. He was big for a dwarf, close on five feet in height, and he did not have their squatness of figure to so marked an extent as was usual. His arms were brawny, muscled from his work, but the lower part of his body might almost have been human. His face was broad, brown and wrinkled, his hair and beard white. He said:

"Being chosen for the Contest is not everything, Master Luke."

I did not answer but swung the sword once more and gave it back. He hung it carefully on its hook.

They were not, of course, the swords that would actually be used in the Contest. Those were of wood, unpointed, capable of prodding or sweeping an opponent off his horse but not of penetrating the stiff leather jerkins they wore. But at the Contest's end each of the Young Captains would be given his real sword, one of these four. That nearest me had a red stone in its crosspiece that winked in the candlelight. It would go to the winner of the Contest, the conqueror.

Pots of ale were brought to us. Rudi offered me his own seat, its high back carved with the figures of past Armorers, but I refused it. I sat

on a stool and sipped from the pewter pot.
The ale was hot and sweet, flavored with
spices. It warmed my throat and belly but did
not lift the black depression from my
shoulders.

Rudi said: "You would have been young for
it."

"No younger than Matthew is."

"But his father is cousin to the Prince."

"Yes."

He drank deeply and gave his pot to a dwarf
for refilling. He wiped the back of his hand
across his mouth. "You take things hard, Master
Luke. It is a failing, if I may presume to
say so."

I would not have taken such a criticism
from any other dwarf, but no other would
have made it. In the past I had often taken
troubles to Rudi and had good counsel from
him. This counsel, too, might be good, but I
got no comfort from it.

The Contest was part of the Fair which, in
mid-March, was meant to mark the end of
winter's grip, the coming of spring. (Though
year by year, it seemed, the cold stayed
longer, the trees were slower in budding.) In
it four sons of Captains led their troops
against one another in a series of skirmishes
on the Contest Field. To be chosen one must

be between thirteen and fourteen years of age. My thirteenth birthday had fallen two months ago.

This year three of the four contenders were obvious choices. There was Edmund, the Prince's second son. There was Henry, whose father, Captain Blaine, stood high in the Prince's war council. There was also Gregory, son of Captain Harding, and the Hardings ranked with the Blaines in distinction. And not only rank was in their favor. They were older than I—Henry would be fourteen a week after the Fair—and known to be good fighters. Matthew, on the other hand, was three weeks my junior and I could beat him any day at swordplay or jousting. But his father, as Rudi had said, was a cousin to the Prince while mine had been a Sergeant ennobled on the field of battle, a commoner born. My hopes of taking the fourth place had always been slim, but they had been hopes. And dashed three days ago when the herald cried the news at the palace gate. Matthew was to be the fourth Young Captain, and wear the sword afterword.

Rudi said: "It is not much help to tell anyone that he must bear his disappointments, but it is a truth that has to be learned. Some find it more difficult than others." His pot was returned brimming and he drank. "So they must school themselves harder."

"You can say that," I said, "as Master Armorer."

He nodded. "Master Armorer. And dwarf."

"But . . ."

I stopped. His words had startled me. If he had been a polymuf I might have understood. They, after all, were the lowest of the low, servants to men, landless, holding no property except at a master's whim. These things, as much as their deformities, set them apart, and while many fawned, some glowered. Disgusting to men, their condition must be hateful to themselves.

But dwarfs had pride, not just in their crafts but as a race. For the most part they bred true and could trace their families back for generations, often further than proper men. They had houses, small-holdings, polymuf servants. They could amass wealth and loved to dress their dumpy womenfolk in silks and decorate them with bright jewelry and heavy gold chains. They could not bear arms and so could not be ennobled, but they were, and knew themselves to be, essential to the life of the city as workers in metal and leather, weavers, brewers, grooms to the stables—all kind of necessary crafts. They could rise to positions of high status. Rudi himself had a seat at state banquets: below the second salt but at the Prince's table.

He said: "Even though you do not lead a troop at the Contest, next year you will be squired. In time you will be a Captain like your father."

"Rudi," I said, "would you have wished to be a warrior?"

I still could not believe it. I had heard dwarfs talk, and never known such a thing even hinted. They saw their kind as the builders and producers of the city's wealth, war as a sickness that afflicted proper men, laying waste to the land's prosperity. I had heard one say once that if there were only dwarfs all cities would be at peace and grow rich.

Rudi finished his second pot and laughed.

"A warrior, Master Luke? When I am Master Armorer? And will die at last in my bed, with no scars on my body except the small scars of my trade. But you would find it hard, I think, to make swords for other men to use. There are disappointments in all men's lives, even those who have achieved their ambition, and there are compensations. You are young and strong, and gaining skill in arms. You will go far in the Prince's service, and prosper. Not to be chosen for the Contest is a small thing to bear."

It was true, I supposed, but it did not help.

I looked past him at the four swords on the wall, only dimly visible among the shadows that moved as the fire rose and fell with the blowing of the bellows. I had worn one of them in imagination all winter, sometimes the one with the red stone winking in its crosspiece. I had rejected that particular part of the daydream as futile, but the other had seemed possible. Having to abandon it was bitter.

Rudi threw his pot to the assistant dwarf and stood up.

"There is work still to do," he said. "Come, and I will show you how to put an edge on steel, in case a fairy touches you in the night and your legs shorten."

When I left the forge I crossed the river. There was confusion on the bridge, with carts jammed together and men shouting angrily, smoking the chill air with their curses. An overloaded cart had overturned and the way was blocked. The river, pouring violently from the millstream, ran free and turbulent at its center but the verges were rimmed with ice and downstream, between the grazing meadows, the ice spread right across from side to side. Farther down still it was thick enough for skating; or had been yesterday, and there

could be no thaw with this sharp wind. I meant
to go there in the afternoon but the morning
had worn away and my chief thought was of
dinner.

My home lay higher up in the city, among
the houses that surrounded the Prince's palace.
I did not go that way, though, but turned right
along the street that ran parallel with the
river for a while, and was called the River
Road. The house into which I went was small
but well kept, shutters and door painted bright
blue, window sills and flagstones underneath
them scoured and whitened. Bedding hung
from the open windows at the top and would
do so until mid-afternoon, when mattresses,
sheets, blankets and eiderdowns were taken in
for the beds to be made up and heated with
the wrapped bricks that now lay at the back of
the hearth. Everything was spick and span and
in good order. This was my Aunt Mary's
house.

She was not truly my aunt, but my father's
first wife. They had known each other as children and he had married her when he was a
young warrior. They had a son, my half
brother Peter, whom I called cousin. Riding
to war with the Prince (the old Prince, our
present Prince's father) my father had seen a
farmer's daughter, my mother, whose beauty

had amazed and confounded him. It was in that campaign that he was made Captain and so could divorce his wife, on petition to the Prince, and take another. He divorced my Aunt Mary and brought his young bride back to the city, and the next year I was born.

He had made provision for his first wife and child. He would have done so even if the law had not required it because he was a just man. Moreover, although he no longer loved her, he respected my Aunt Mary and came to her house often, not just to see his son but to talk to her and listen to her advice. And I, from my earliest days of roaming abroad, treated her house as my second home.

In some ways, even, I preferred it to my own. It was smaller, pokier, but clean and sweet smelling. My aunt had only two poly-muf servants, my mother eight or nine, but the two were closely watched and supervised, the eight or nine for the most part slack and grumbling. From time to time my mother, in despair, would have my father dismiss one or more and get others, hiding in her room while this was done, and would make resolutions that in the future everything would be different. It never was. I heard my father say one day in exasperation that no one could have imagined such a thing—a farmer's daughter

who knew less of running a house than a lady
of five generations' idleness. She wept, and he
forgot his annoyance in comforting her.

She was beautiful. At thirty she had the skin,
the face and figure of a girl. Her likeness hung
on the walls of half a dozen great houses,
including the palace itself: Margry, the
Prince's painter, had had her sit for him a
score of times. And yet she aroused no spite
or jealousy among the ladies of the court.
Everyone recognized she was without malice
and therefore she provoked none. I had seen
her petulant sometimes but never angry. For
the most part she was happy, talkative, eager
to please and to be pleased. She liked sunshine
and pet animals and glancing at her own
beauty in the glass.

My Aunt Mary was very different. She was
gray-haired and had a long harsh face scored
with years of work and brooding. She was
deep-natured. She did not make a show of
her feelings—she spoke little and smiled less—
but their strength was shown in small things:
a brief condemnation of that person, a rare
word of praise for this. Of all men she most
respected my father and continued to treat
him as master of the house which he had left
when he divorced her. Toward others, with a
single exception, she was reserved. That one

was her son, my cousin Peter. Him she loved
with the depth and fierceness of a river forced
to run between narrow banks. Even this she
strove to hide, but it could not be hidden.

She would have accepted me because of my
father—it was his house and his son, though by
another wife, must be made welcome in it—
but I fancied she liked me a little apart from
that. She was strict, as she was in everything,
and I would never have dared to go to her
table with unwashed hands as I had sometimes
done at home. But she showed me some kind-
ness, and somehow my black moods sat on me
less heavily in her house. It was not that she
indulged me in them, if anything the reverse,
but that my misery seemed less important in
the presence of her watchful austerity.

This morning she greeted me with a nod
and told me that dinner was almost ready. I
had scented it, a stew whose rich smell made
my appetite clamorous. At home the polymuf
cook used the best of meats and vegetables but
the stews were thin and tasteless. I went to the
kitchen to wash and saw one of the polymufs
scouring a pan. (My aunt did her own cooking
but kept her servants busy with cleaning and
polishing.) This was Gerda; she had short
arms and the mark of an extra eye on her forehead, though it had never opened. She bobbed

her head to me without ceasing her work. My aunt allowed her servants fair periods of rest but required good labor the rest of the time.

I was at the table and eating when Peter came in. I heard him tethering his horse outside and he pulled off his big leather coat as he entered. Gerda brought a bowl of hot water, soap and a towel, and he washed in the hall as befitted a grown man. He was eighteen, a Sergeant under my father's command, soon to be made Mister, as the Junior Captains were called. When he had finished he took the seat at the head of the table, which was his except when my father dined here. He said to me cheerfully:

"Have you heard the news, Luke?"

"What news?"

"Matthew Grant went skating this morning and broke a leg."

I looked up quickly and saw him laughing. I flushed and turned back to my dinner, for which, suddenly, my appetite had gone. Aunt Mary said:

"Do not tease him."

Peter said: "You are not brooding over this, Luke, are you? You would have had no chance of lasting beyond the first round. You would have been cut down in a few minutes and earned nothing but jeers."

He had seen that the jest had hurt me and was doing his best to put things right. I knew he would not wound me except by accident. He was slow-moving and amiable, a smiling contrast to his mother's dourness. Not slow in thought; his mind was sharp enough. Except where people were concerned. There he did not look below the surface, accepting them as they were or as they seemed to be.

In appearance he was tall, broad-shouldered, fair, resembling my father much more than I did. I was of no more than average height, stockier, swarthy in my looks. I suppose I was more like my aunt, who was no blood kin to me, than either of my parents. Peter, like my mother, had no enemies, and for much the same reason. But unlike her he was warm in his affections. He went on talking, saying too much was made of the Contest. He had not been chosen and what difference had it made? Digby, who won the jewel in that year, was giving up soldiering to marry a merchant's daughter and turn shopkeeper.

What he did not understand was that I was different from both him and Digby. It had not mattered that he had not got a place because he had not minded, but I did. It only made it the more bitter that someone like Digby, willing now to give up being a warrior, should

have had the chance to win the jeweled sword.
If Peter did not resent it, he ought to.

But he soothed me enough for the smell of
Aunt Mary's stew to tempt me back into hunger and I ate my dinner. There was apple pie
to follow, made from apples picked in the
autumn, then peeled and ringed and hung to
dry on long lines in the attic. Afterward we sat
in front of the fire in the living room until the
clock on the mantel struck two. At that Peter
yawned and stretched and stood up, his fair
head almost touching the low whitewashed
ceiling.

"Time to be back. More formation training.
I think we must be the best formation riders
this side of the Burning Lands. We may not
fight, but we ride very well."

He spoke in jest but there were others who
said much the same and more sourly. The city
had been five years at peace and men were
restless.

In this we had separated ourselves from the
customs of the civilized lands. The summer
campaigns were a part of the pattern of living,
as much as the feasts of spring and autumn and
mid-winter. In the yearly challenge to its enemies a city maintained its pride, and through
pride purpose. This was, moreover, the source
of all honor. The dwarfs might be content

with their crafts and trades, but for a proper man in his youth and strength the only true glory lay in fighting for his city. If he was killed his body was brought back to lie with the other heroes in the Citadel; if he was crippled his Prince cared for him as long as he lived. And if, as was more often the case, he returned unscathed or with minor wounds he had his fame; and stories to tell, boasts to make during the long idleness of winter.

The Prince's father, Egbert, had been a great fighter; it was under him that my own father had been ennobled in a savage battle against the men of Basingstoke. Our new Prince was very different. Each year he found some reason for not taking our army into the field. From the beginning there had been doubts of his valor and the doubts had grown as summer succeeded summer with fresh excuses. He was a big man with a black curling beard but had a strangely empty look, like a vessel that had missed being filled.

There was a tale which had never been forgotten of a wrestling contest when he was a young man. It was that form of wrestling in which the object is not to throw one's opponent to the ground but to lift him off his feet and hold him in the air. Stephen, though even then big for his age, had chosen the smallest of the group to contend against, presumably because he doubted his chances with the others. And after a great struggle this one, though inches shorter and narrow of chest, had lifted him not once but twice, the second time carrying him helpless round the ring.

So his excuses now—an illness of his Lady, the weather being unpropitious or the crops needing special attention, once a warning from the Spirits in a dream (he said) of disaster to the city if the troops went forth—were suspect. Last year he was supposed to have injured his back, so that he could not ride or even walk without pain, and he had kept to his bed for two months. But it had been remarked that he walked well enough when the Autumn Feast came round, and rode to the Hunt afterward.

And all this time the reputation which his father had gained, for himself and for the city, was dissipating. It did not happen at once: our warriors had made themselves feared and respected as far afield as Guildford and Newbury and Ringwood, and our neighbors were glad enough at first to be free of their attentions. But lately it was known that they had begun to mock him and us. Last year the men of Alton had ridden into our lands while Stephen lay on his bed, with blocks of wood tied to his feet to straighten out the kink he was supposed to have in his spine, and carried away more than four score head of cattle. It was important that this year we should go after them and teach them a lesson, but no one really believed that our Prince would move. Year after year he had built the city's walls higher and deepened the ditch beyond them.

Aunt Mary said: "There is no sense in fighting for the sake of fighting. They wound and kill each other and are no better for it."

Peter shook his head. "That is the way a woman thinks."

He smiled and put a hand on her shoulder. She impatiently shook herself free; she would not admit how much she welcomed the signs of his affection.

"It is not a question of men or women," she said. "I am not against fighting—or killing—if it is for something worthwhile. But not for empty glories, paid for with real deaths."

Peter smiled past her at me. What she said meant nothing to him, nor would it have to any warrior. A man fought for the sake of fighting, for his own honor and the honor of his city. Accepting the complicity he offered me, proud of being spoken to as someone who would one day be a warrior and understood the way a warrior thought, I said:

"I wonder how our Prince will get out of it this year. Maybe he will have them take him into Sincross!"

Sincross was the big house in which the old men lived whose wits had failed through age. It was a feeble enough joke at best but as I saw Peter frown I remembered something. Younger people also were taken there when the Spirits had crazed their brains. This had been the case with Aunt Mary's brother many years ago, even before Peter's birth, and he had died in madness when not much more than twenty. And I remembered too that I had heard talk once, among servants who did not realize I was listening, that it had been thought the same might happen to Aunt Mary herself at the time my father divorced her, so strange she had been and so deeply sunk in melancholy.

I was struck into confusion by my thoughtlessness and could not look at Aunt Mary. But she seemed anyway to pay no heed to my remark. She was concerned with Peter, with making sure that he put on his scarf and wound it tight around his body under his leather coat before going out into the cold. As a child, she reminded him, scolding gently, he had had a weakness in his chest and he must take care.

I left with him and watched him unhitch his

horse. Peter's frown had gone. He offered to
ride me up the hill on his saddlebow but I
refused. I might not have been chosen for the
Contest but I felt I was too old for that. Until
I had a horse of my own, I would walk.

Before I could go skating I had to go home
and get my skates and so I made my way up
the High Street rather than along the river
bank. It was a little less cold, or perhaps
seemed so because my stomach was full. In a
few places, missed by the polymuf street
cleaners, snow lay in frozen, dirt-specked
ridges. The last fall had been a week ago. The
sky was hazy with a watery sun peering
through. Winter's grip seemed as firm as ever.
Carts creaked past me, one of them piled high
with fodder. I had heard my father say that
supplies were very low and grain too in short
supply. There would be more cattle slaughtered unless the cold spell broke soon, and
probably some horses.

My name was called from behind. I knew
the voice and involuntarily shivered. I turned
and saw Ezzard striding toward me, his black
cloak wrapped tightly round his tall lean
frame. I waited for him to come up, telling
myself I was no longer a child to be frightened
by the Seer. His Spirits did not venture out of

the Seance Hall, and anyway I had done nothing to offend them.

But he was a man who in himself inspired awe. Taller even than my father, he had a craggy face with a beaked nose and black bushy eyebrows. His eyes were set deep and close together and were cold and blue. His skin was very white, as though he spent all his time in darkness and not just the hours when he was communing with the Spirits. In the summer when the light was stronger he wore spectacles that were darkly tinted; even without these there seemed a strange blankness, an emptiness, in his look.

He said: "Where are you bound, boy?"

I did not care for being addressed as "boy," and even though it was the Seer I answered a little stiffly. But his eyes, staring into mine, made me drop my gaze.

He said: "You respect the Spirits?"

"Yes, sire."

"There are some, of your age, who do not— who mock foolishly."

I said: "I have seen the Spirits and heard them."

He nodded. "Remember that. Remember another thing: that the Spirits take care of those who show them proper reverence. The fools who mock at last are mocked. And they are fools all along."

"Yes, sire."

He raised his hand in the blessing, though as Ezzard gave it it was almost menacing.

"Away to your skating, then. Make the most of it. It will be your last of the winter."

I did not need to seek a meaning to that riddle. The Spirits foretold the weather to him. The thaw was coming and by tomorrow the ice would be too weak to bear. I was flattered that he should have told me this, as though I were one of the Prince's messengers. I nodded and turned to go. As I did his hand grasped my shoulder.

"Perhaps your last indeed."

I shivered again. One skated until one became a man, and one was not a man until fifteen. There were times when the Spirits prophesied a death.

But he was smiling, his face improbably drawn into a grin.

"Go your way, Luke. The Spirits go with you."

I found Martin and we took our skates to the river. In the morning he had been busy with duties; his mother was a widow and too poor to afford even a single polymuf servant. We skated for a couple of hours and by the end of that time one could tell the change that was taking place: the wind had swung from north to west and there was mildness in it. I told him of Ezzard's words as we walked back. He said:

"He is right often enough. But how?"

"Through the Spirits. How else?"

"But how?"

Martin was not even as tall as I, and slim with it. He had a girl's skin, delicate, almost transparent, and his brown eyes were big like a girl's. We had become friends when I rescued him from other boys who were tormenting him. The biggest of them was someone I very much disliked, and it was more through this than through a desire to help Martin that I had taken him on and given him a beating. It was only later that I grew to like Martin. His mind was curious, odd in its way of thinking, restless and speculative. Sometimes absurdly so. I said:

"The Spirits know the future as they know the past. And they tell Ezzard because he is the Seer. There is nothing difficult about it."

He did not answer, and we did not pursue the matter because there was a horseman riding toward us, along Burnt Lane. I recognized horse and rider. My father called:

"Greetings, son! I was told you were down at the river and I came out to meet you."

His lips laughed between the fair beard and curling yellow moustache. He would not have done this for a trivial reason. My heart leaped, but I said as evenly as I could:

"What news, sir?"

"Young Grant is ill. A fever. He will not fight on Thursday. You have his place in the Contest."

I stared at him. He leaned down and swept me onto his saddlebow, and I did not resent it. We rode homeward, Martin running beside us.

And I thought of what Ezzard had said. A Young Captain was called a man, though not fifteen. I would not skate next winter with the boys, but serve the Prince as apprentice warrior. There had been two prophecies after all.

2

The Young
Captains

We had a day to prepare for the Contest and it rained almost continually. It was a cold drizzle to start with, soaking and depressing, and after a couple of hours of slithering and sliding and falling on the practice field Edmund called his team together and rode them off. Henry and Gregory followed suit. To have continued after the Prince's son had stopped would have been to risk being mocked at for too great keenness, and I think in any case they were glad enough to head for home.

I brought my own team off the field but set a slow pace along the road to the city, and by the time we reached the fork at the Elder Pond the others, galloping toward a change of clothes, hot drinks and warm fires, were out of sight. At the pond I called them to take the left fork, away from the city. They halted in confusion. I reined in and rode slowly back.

Laurie, who was the best man I had, said:
"Why left?"

I waited, letting them look at me, for some moments before replying. I said:

"Listen. I am your Captain. We are the weakest team in the Contest. Do you know the odds they are offering in the alehouses against our winning? Fifty to one, and I have heard that some have offered a hundred without finding takers."

They stared at me, drenched and miserable, the flanks of their horses steaming. An unprepossessing lot even without being bedraggled and spotted with mud.

The number of each team in the Contest was fixed at four, apart from the Junior Captain. It would have been fairer if selection had been by lot but the test was as much as anything for leadership and a leader chooses his men. Or is chosen by them. Of those who, being of the age and yet not of noble family, could take part, most naturally would have preferred to follow the Prince's son. Not for the honor only, of course: he was favored to win and the winning team, to match their Captain's jeweled sword, drew gold coins as a reward. The teams coming second and third obtained silver and bronze, while that which was first eliminated got nothing but the mob's derision for its pains.

Because of this I had been left with, for the most part, those already rejected by the other leaders. Martin, of course, had volunteered at once. He was not a good horseman and was a poorer swordsman but at least I knew he would fight hard for me. And there was some consolation, too, as far as the rest were concerned, in thinking that they were willing to take part with so little prospect of victory or reward. Even if lacking in skill they were eager for the fight.

I said: "They believe we are certain to lose. But nothing is certain, neither victory nor defeat. Skill counts for much, but so does preparation and hard work. The others have gone home. Soon they will be stabling their horses and taking things easy. We may be weaker in some respects but we can be stronger in endurance. We are not going back to the city but to a quiet place where we can train undisturbed and unobserved. You are wet and tired. So am I. We cannot get wetter and if we get more tired we shall sleep the better tonight and be more refreshed for tomorrow. Lauriel"

"Yes, Captain."

That was good. He was supposed to give me the title but I had thought I might have to demand it. I said, still harshly:

"You asked: 'Why left?' From now on, in training first and then in the fight, none puts such a question to me. Is that clear?" My eyes went from one to the other, forcing them to nod assent. "I give commands. You obey. If this is done well enough, I shall wear the jeweled sword tomorrow, and you will have gold." I turned my horse from them and from the road to the city. "Follow."

What I had been telling them was, I was sure, nonsense, at any rate insofar as any hopes of our winning the Contest were concerned. What I really wanted was to avoid coming last. As I have said, the team first eliminated always drew jeers from the crowd and I could not bear the thought of it. If we could survive into the second round, I would be happy enough. I had two reasons for pitching things high to my men. One was to shatter the pessimism they must feel over our chances; the second to give them heart for the grueling task ahead, because I meant to keep them at it till both we and our horses were ready to drop from exhaustion. I would risk them going tired into the fight. I was determined we should go in more ready for the tricks our opponents might play, more skilled in evading or countering them.

My father had the lordship of a farm a few miles from the eastern gate. I had the farmer get his polymufs to drive cattle from a field and we went at it there. In the Contest, as in

all fighting on horseback, understanding and
control of one's horse comes first. The horses
we had were drawn from the army stables and
their ways needed learning. To get mounts for
their troop the Young Captains drew lots and
chose in turn. The others had gone, as was
usual, for the bigger horses. I had let them do
so; the ground would be heavy after rain.
From one of the grooms, a dwarf I knew well,
I sought advice as to which of the smaller
beasts were best for stamina, speed, sure-foot-
edness, and I picked them. I had already found
that he had given me good guidance. The
horses were sound; now it was up to me and
my men to learn to handle them. I split the
men in two pairs, myself taking first one side
then the other, and we rode at each other in
mock battle.

The aim of each team must be to unsaddle
the opposing Captains, because once the Captain is dismounted that team retires. There
are scores, hundreds, of different tactics which
can be employed, but nearly all revolve
around a situation in which the Captain has
two defending outriders and two attacking
ones. This, I had decided, must be abandoned
for a start. I could not afford to hide behind
defenders, even if the defense were reliable.
My only hope lay in deliberately taking
chances.

In close fighting there were countless forms
of assault and parry. The wooden swords were
our offensive weapons, and we carried small
leather shields as a means of defense, but by
getting in close enough one could buffet or
drag a man from his horse, or pluck, swooping,
at his stirrup and upend him. I had studied
tricks of Captains in previous years, and there
were one or two of my own that I added. I
rehearsed my men (and myself) in these over
and over again. Beyond that we practiced riding in various patterns and directions in
response to signals of command. It was a slow
business and more often than not ended in confusion and disorder.

After another couple of hours, I ordered a
break. The farmer had prepared food and
drink for us and they were more than ready
for it, but first I saw to it that the ponies were
fed and watered and rubbed down and blan-
keted. We ate heartily and I let the men rest a
while afterward. Then I called them back to
work. They groaned but made no protest. The
rain was still soaking down, as steadily though
perhaps less chilly. We slogged on as the afternoon drew slowly toward dusk. The sky's gray
was tinged with black when at last I gave the
order to break off. We rode back slowly, dog-
tired, to the city.

I swore them to secrecy before we parted; if

anyone asked, we had spent the day in the
farmhouse, penned in by the rain, gambling
with dice. Of the dwarf groom, Murri, I asked
the same confidence. Seeing to the ponies with
me, he said:

"You could have lamed them, Master."

"But did not." I gave him money. "A good
bran mash tonight, with strong ale in it, and
tomorrow the best oats you can find. They will
be all right for the afternoon?"

"They will be all right." He looked up at
me, grinning. "I will cheer for you, Master
Luke."

"Will you back me?"

"No." He wagged his broad head. "We
dwarfs are men of heart, as is well known, but
we do not let our hearts rule our minds. And
we are no believers in miracles."

I nodded. I think I was too tired to smile.

It was my intention to slip quietly into my
home and get the servants to fill me a bath.
But as I crossed the courtyard my father called
from his window and I had to go to him. He
said:

"Where have you been, Luke? The others
were back by mid-morning."

"We went out to the farm, sir. Cooper gave
us food."

"You stayed the whole day there?"

"It was raining. There seemed small point in coming back."

"Doing what?"

"Dicing. And talking. Idling, I suppose."

He looked at me through the open window. "Was that the best way you could find of passing the time on the day before the Contest?"

"I am sorry, sir."

"You are a strange lad. You keep your own counsel, even from me." I waited. The lamp was behind him but I saw him smile. "You cannot see yourself, can you? Or smell yourself. If you roll in muck long enough your nose grows accustomed to it. You are covered not just in mud but cow-dung. Did you dice out in the fields, in the wet? And has idling bowed your shoulders?"

"Sir . . ."

He cut across my words. "I will not keep you in the rain. But listen to one thing. It is proper to be ambitious but do not overreach yourself. Yesterday you had been passed over for the Contest. Today you are one of the four Young Captains and tomorrow you will ride out with your men to the Field. I only ask that you acquit yourself well. Do not hope for too much and risk the bitterness of disappointment. You know how it takes you."

"I will do as you say, sir."

The smile had gone. He stared at me a while longer, then said:

"Get yourself washed and changed. We will meet at supper."

He closed the window and turned away.

I awoke in the small hours of the night, the sweat chilling on my exposed flesh where, in my dream, I had pushed the covers back. The dream was with me still, and vivid. I was alone on a vast field, far greater than the Contest Field, and my enemies were chasing me. I had no help, no hope and no courage to do the one thing I knew I must do: turn and face them. They overhauled but did not quite take me and I knew that this was because they did not wish to yet, because they were playing with me, cats with a terrified mouse. All round and it seemed from the sky above came the mocking roar of the crowd, urging on my enemies, laughing me to scorn.

I lay there, sweating and trembling, and then got up. I fumbled in the dark for my pitcher of water, and drank. Then I went to the windows and pulled them open. The rain had stopped and the night was very still, black except for the glow behind the western hills that marked the Burning Lands. A dog barked far off, once and no more.

It had been a nightmare, a vexation, as Ezzard would have told me, of the unguarded mind by those Spirits who ruled the domain of sleep. I had eaten too richly the night before —in my hunger I had devoured half a loaf of bread and a huge chunk of cheese. Apart from that I could pay a penny to the Acolyte, to ask the Spirits who protected men to give me special care. And now I must dismiss it from my mind, go back to bed, sleep and be refreshed for tomorrow.

I returned to my bed but I did not sleep. Thoughts ran jumbled through my head, not about the dream but the reality. I imagined the fight, looked at it from every point of view, and from every point of view was driven to the same conclusion: we had no chance at all. It was a standard operation for the three stronger teams to concentrate first on eliminating the weakest. I had worked out plans to counter this but here in the still center of the night I recognized their futility. They would only, as I saw, expose us to greater mockery when they failed.

I thought of my father's warning and acknowledged the truth of it. Pride and ambition ran too strongly in me. It would be better to settle for what I had, to be contented with my lot. It was, after all, a good one. I had been born true man, not dwarf nor, God forbid, polymuf. I had been born in this city of a noble father—of no lineage, but noble. I had my health and strength, the use of my wits. Now, by the fortune of another's falling sick, I was chosen a Junior Captain and, whatever happened in the Contest, would wear a sword tomorrow night at the feast. Even if we were ignominiously defeated, I myself unhorsed in the first charge, the defeat and the derision that went with it, the hissing and the laughter, were a small price to pay for what I gained.

That was the sensible way to look at it. But as I thought of the mob and its ridicule the sweat was cold again on my back and down my legs. I turned violently in my bed, striking the pillow with my fist, willing my mind to blankness, willing sleep to come. I must rest, to be strong for the day ahead. But the more I demanded, the further sleep drew from me. At last I turned to pleading. I called on the Spirits of my Ancestors to aid me. That, too, did not help. The window's square had begun to pale before exhaustion succeeded where demands and pleas had failed, and I slept.

Then the maid, Janet, was shaking my shoulder gently. It was broad day. I looked at her through eyes that would scarcely open, my mind fogged and stupid.

"Time to rise, Master Luke."

I asked: "What day is this?"

She smiled at me. She had no visible deformities but she wore her dresses high up at the neck. A good-looking woman but she was past thirty and had not married; though most polymufs did. The destructive Spirits, one guessed, had done their work cruelly on her.

"Contest Day, Master Luke," she said. "Your day."

It rained all morning but the rain was warm now. Blowing direct from the Burning Lands, it left a coating of gray behind it. I could imagine my Aunt Mary's lips tightening as she watched the white sills and flags outside her house besmirched. The polymufs would be hard at work as soon as the rain ceased.

And it did cease around midday. In the early afternoon the Young Captains rode their troops out of the city with leather jackets dry and silver epaulets gleaming in a watery sunlight. We rode in procession across the bridge and through the East Gate. The Prince and his Captains led the way, followed by their ladies. Next came Ezzard and the Acolytes; then the Young Captains in order of lineage. Edmund first, of course, as son of the Prince, followed by Gregory and Henry. I came last. After us the senior burgesses, the Sergeants, farmers in for the day. Then the common people, then the dwarfs. Last of all the polymufs. There was chattering and laughter, and strollers playing instruments and singing songs.

The city would be almost emptied of people, the walls which Prince Stephen had built so high stood unmanned. It was true that this was the time of the Spring Fair when no war was made throughout the civilized lands. The Spirits forbade it. But if someone broke the truce, I wondered, did that mean the Spirits would defend the city lying at the attacker's mercy? Their ways, as even the Seers admitted, were capricious; neither punishment nor reward was certain. I remembered my own desperate pleas for sleep and how they had gone unanswered. Contests like this one were held in the other cities, too. Romsey, for instance, no more than ten miles to the southwest . . . a handful of men, riding swiftly, could take and hold it.

I dismissed the speculations as futile. It was the custom to keep peace until after the Spring Fair. Even to think of anything different was to offend the Spirits. They had not helped me in the night but they might still help me in the fight to come. And I needed help, all the help I could get.

We came to the Contest Field and Ezzard blessed the contestants in the name of the Spirits. Tents had been erected at one end for the nobles. I saw my father and mother there, and Peter. Not Aunt Mary. A woman who married a nobleman became a lady but the wife he had put aside had no rank. I trotted my horse past the throngs of commoners and found her, wedged in at the front. I dismounted and bowed to her.

"Greetings, Aunt Mary. Wish me well."

She nodded fiercely. "I do that, Luke."

A man nearby made a jest about my chances and others laughed. She turned on them and they fell silent. I mounted and rode to where my parents sat. My mother said:

"Don't get hurt."

She spoke in a little frightened voice. She had clapped her hands with delight on hearing that I had been picked to be a Young Captain. She lived in the moment. Nothing was real to her before it happened, or mattered much after.

My father said: "I know you will fight hard, so I have nothing to tell you. The Spirits go with you."

The first gong boomed and it was time to bow our heads before the Prince. On the second gong the Contest started.

Each Captain took a corner of the field. I had the western one, nearest to the city but

farthest from the Prince's tent. I waited with
my men and spoke to them quietly:

"Remember, keep silence."

It was usual for the teams to go into the
fight noisily, yelling threats and imprecations.
To cause fear, I suppose. It seemed to me that
if mine were not already frightened by the
odds against them a few shouts would not
make them so. Our keeping silence would set
us apart from the others but perhaps not to
our disadvantage. It would also, I felt, help us
to concentrate more, and help my men more
easily listen to my commands.

The second gong boomed.

The four teams advanced warily from their
corners. There were a number of ways in
which a Contest might begin. Sometimes the
teams circled the field for a period, keeping
their distances, until one broke into an assault
on another. Sometimes they met right away
in a furious all-in melee toward the center.
There was another possibility which I had
dreaded, and my heart sank as I realized that
this was what was happening. The other three
teams were converging on ours; they were
combining to eliminate the weakest before
settling down to a Contest of three.

I had made my plan and I was committed
to it. If it did not come off it must make me

look a fool or a coward, more probably both. The distances narrowed and I waited for the moment and watched for the opening. It must be left till the very last instant but the last instant could be too late. They had started hurling threats and catcalls at us. I said to Laurie on my left:

"Stand when I break. After that, it's up to you."

They were not hurrying. Edmund's troop were a little ahead of the rest and I saw him rein in to let the other two come up. They were out to crush us completely and were taking no chances. They were within twenty feet, fifteen. The best gap was between Henry's troop and the fence. Sharply I dug in spurs and set my pony's head toward it.

The roar from the crowd momentarily drowned the yells of our attackers. As I have said, a team was eliminated as soon as its Captain was unhorsed. To bolt away from the protection of one's men was unheard of. My team, I knew, were standing fast behind me. Out of the corner of my eye I saw the other teams confusedly trying to change direction. My sudden move had taken them by surprise but they were rallying to follow the obvious quarry. They must think me mad or panic-stricken. Whichever it was their aim remained the same and its fulfillment now was easier. They were certain of riding me down.

One of Henry's men swiped at me but did not reach me as I got through the gap. I eased off, not to put too great a distance between me and my pursuers, and rode not for the corner diagonally opposite but for the nearer north corner. The field was a big one, of more than a hundred acres, but it seemed small to me now. Fortunately they did not have the sense to fan out but came after me in a bunch. Fifteen yards from the corner I wheeled and made my second dash, past their left flank.

I did not clear it fully this time. Two got glancing blows in on me and ahead I saw an outrider. I had to go between him and his nearest companion and they moved as I did, to sandwich me. They almost succeeded. My horse squealed as the shoulder of a big bay slammed against her rump, and a chopping blow from a sword made my head ring and rocked me in the saddle. But they could not hold me. I was through again and this time heard the cry I had been waiting for, Laurie's exultant shout:

"Three down! Against Gregory!"

This had been my plan. I had gambled that, in hot expectant pursuit of me, they would ignore my team. These, under Laurie's command, had ridden in chase of the chasers, with the aim of picking off men in that team which was straggler to the others. And the ruse had succeeded: they had got three of Gregory's men before anyone realized what was happening. Now as I wheeled once more they rode back to me in triumph while the rest, confused again and uncertain, rallied to their own Captains.

The uncertainty did not last long. We were no longer the weakest, to be harried and destroyed. Three of Gregory's men were limping from the field, their horses running free. Gregory, with his last remaining follower, backed toward the north corner. He knew what must follow.

The three teams came in on him for the kill, but here again our intention was not what it seemed. We left the unhorsing of Gregory to the others, going ourselves for Henry. Laurie and I pulled down one of his men while the other three got a second. Then I rode for Henry himself. My sword crashed against his shield. In riposte he got through my defense and struck me in the ribs, jerking me backward. I was struggling to keep my foot in the stirrups when the gong boomed to a new tumult from the crowd. The first Captain was down, bringing the first interval. Henry and I drew away from each other and I saw Gregory walking disconsolately toward the Captains' tent.

The tactics of the second round were simpler. Edmund and I needed no conference to establish the advantages that lay for both of us in cooperation. Our teams were intact while Henry was reduced to a single man on either side. We must join forces to crush him.

But although the aim was simple it proved far from easy. Henry fought tigerishly and with intelligence, again and again forcing a way clear of us and gaining a breathing space. I lost Martin before either of Henry's two men were down. If I lost another we would be as weak as he was—weaker because he had better men—and things could turn against us. I shouted to Laurie and he and I picked out Henry's left flanker and attacked him together. He parried my blow but Laurie's, coming in from the other side, toppled him from the saddle.

Even then it was not over. When Henry was at last alone he fought on for what seemed an age, earning the crowd's acclaim. But we got him in the end, dragging him down almost, as hounds would a stag. The gong sounded and wearily we drew apart. Only then did I realize that two more men had gone, one from Edmund's team and the other, a lad called Carey, from my own.

We were all battered by this time and
Laurie was streaming blood from a gash just
below his ear. My head rang from the blows I
had received, despite my leather helmet, and
my shield arm was so stiff and painful that
even raising the shield was an agony. (Two of
the dismounted, we learned, had broken arms,
a third a dislocated shoulder.) But we had survived two rounds, against odds. We had good
reason to be proud. We could rest on the
laurels we had already won. It would not
matter if Edmund overwhelmed us at the end.

As, plainly, he must do. He had four men
against three and the four were stronger and
better fighters. There was no more room for
tricks of playing one against another. Our
horses were tired, too, their early nimbleness
worn down by the pounding of the fight and
the sticky churned-up mud of the field. We had
done better than anyone could have guessed
and though Edmund took the jeweled sword
he would not take all the credit.

But although before the Contest I would
have settled gladly for the present situation,
now, fiercely, my ambition demanded more.
In a battle of attrition we had no chance but if
. . . I spoke to my two remaining followers.
Laurie shook his head.

"It cannot succeed."

"Perhaps not. But neither can anything else."

The gong sounded again and we came out of our corners. Edmund and his men rode slowly, bunched together. On my command, though, my two swung left while I myself bore right. I saw Edmund halt his team, considering.

He was alert for tricks but he could not see one here. We, the weaker side, had split our forces and I, their Captain, was heading away from my men. His response did not need much working out. He detached two of his men toward my two, to hold them if they could not overcome them. He and his chief lieutenant, a huge brawny lad called Tom, headed for me.

They split as they drew near, to take me one on either side. I had expected that, too. Ten yards, five. I freed my feet from the stirrups. They came at me, swords raised to slash. As they did so, as Edmund's horse came alongside mine, I threw myself out of my saddle and onto him.

He could have withstood me if he had kept his head, but he flinched. I got him by the neck, dragging him down. Tom tried to get round to help him but could not do so for my horse. Edmund and I crashed to the ground together.

The rule had it that if the last two Captains

were dismounted simultaneously they must
remount and meet for a decision, but this time
unassisted. I watched him ride toward me
from his corner. I had thought my shield arm
hurt before but now it felt as though a thousand devils were sitting on it, driving in claws
of fire. He was stronger than I was and had
beaten me often enough in swordplay. Under
normal conditions I was no match for him in
single combat.

But conditions were not normal. Twice that
afternoon I had surprised him. In addition, I
was Captain of a team the others had con-
temptuously decided to eliminate at the start
and we had won through. And he had flinched
when I fell on him, and he knew I knew it.

I had kept silence throughout the Contest.
But as we closed I yelled deep in my throat, a
yell of hate and triumph. I watched his eyes
and saw them wince. Then there was no time
for anything but fighting as our swords
smacked heavily together. He held his ground
for a few minutes and we traded blows. His
horse was heavy enough to have forced mine
back but he lacked the will for it. Instead it
was he who gave way. I prodded his horse's
flank with my sword. It reared and he fell,
almost willingly.

Not looking back I rode my horse toward
the Prince's tent.

3

The Seance
of the Crowns

Two days after the end of the Spring
Fair, the earth quaked. It happened in mid-
morning and I was in the grazing meadows
riding the horse my father had given me for
my victory in the Contest. It was a roan geld-
ing of fourteen hands and he knew of the
quake before it happened, as was often the
case with animals: he halted and whinnied
with fear, and stood there shivering. As my
foot touched the ground, dismounting, it
seemed to move away from me, in a heavy
rolling which made me stagger and almost
fall.

I do not know how long the earth's shivering
lasted—minutes, I thought, but probably I was
deceived. To be without that firmness and
solidity underfoot, which one takes for
granted, even for ten seconds can seem an
eternity. I stayed holding the reins after the

rolling stopped, the horse and I both quivering
as though the quake were dying away in our
nerve ends. But nothing more happened. Dogs
which had been barking in the distance fell
silent. The air was calm. I remounted my
horse and rode into the city to see what damage there had been.

Not a great deal, as it happened. Three
houses had collapsed; there were two dead
and five or six injured. By the standards of
those who remembered the old days it was
very little. But because the earth had been
quiet for so long—I could not recall such a
thing though my father told me there had
been several during the first few years of my
life—there was fear that the evil times were
returning. In the city I found people talking of
sleeping out in the open that night, abandon-
ing the city as they had done in the past, and
some were already loading their goods on
carts. A long line had formed outside the tent-
seller's shop in the High Street and it was said
he was asking twenty pounds for his smallest
tents and finding eager buyers. The bakers had
sold out of bread; all the food shops were
besieged.

As the day wore by, though, with no more
shocks, the panic died away. There were some
who continued to move out of the city, but not
many, and I saw others mocking them as

cowards. Even if more quakes came the risk of
staying was worth taking, provided they were
no more severe than this. Our houses, after all,
were built to withstand the smaller shiftings
of the earth. (Our ancestors had built in stone
and metal, their houses hundreds of feet high,
and had died under the rubble of their tumbled pride.) Our houses were of wood and the
beams so laid that they yielded one against
another under pressure, but the structure itself
remained intact.

In the afternoon a rumor spread which
caused more alarm: that the Prince and his
family were among those who were fleeing to
open ground. Others were minded to follow
suit and the streets began to be crowded again.
Then my father and the other Captains rode
out with troops of horsemen and branded the
rumor as a lie: the Prince was in his palace
and would remain there. The people should
stay in their houses. Through Ezzard, the
Spirits had advised this.

Before supper I was called to my father's
room by Ben, the polymuf who waited on him.
He was hunch-backed and had only two thick-
ened fingers on his right hand, one of them
showing two separate bones beneath the skin. I
found my cousin Peter there already. They
both looked grave.

My father said: "You are old enough now,

Luke, to listen to warrior's business. But you know that, without my permission, you do not talk of things I have told you outside these walls." I nodded. "There is trouble in the city."

I waited. Peter said: "This may also be a rumor, Father."

My father shook his head. "They were seen. And the Prince's rooms in the palace are empty. It is no rumor."

I asked: "Edmund, too?"

"Yes," my father said. "But it is no disgrace to him. He obeys his father in this, as is proper. But for Stephen to run like a scared child . . ."

"He may find the going easier than the coming back," Peter said.

"That is what I want to talk to you about. As Peter knows and you too may have heard, Luke, there have been grumblings before about this Prince of ours, who has kept us five summers behind walls. If the Captains could have agreed on a successor he would have been deposed a year ago. This has brought them to the sparking point. They are agreed—all but his near kin and even some of those—that an end must be made."

Peter said doubtfully: "How? We have sworn loyalty to him, all of us. We asked the

Spirits to take vengeance on us if we break our vows."

"Who crowned him?"

"Ezzard."

My father nodded. "In the name of the Spirits. And our oaths were made to him whom the Spirits, through Ezzard, named as Prince. What can be named can be unnamed."

"Has Ezzard done that?"

"The Captains have spoken to him and he has called a Seance for tomorrow noon."

"And will the Spirits unname him then?"

"You know Ezzard. He makes no promises. Nor can he. But the Spirits guard the city. Providing there is someone to take his place, I do not think Stephen will rule tomorrow night."

"Who have given way," Peter asked, "the Blaines or the Hardings?"

They were both great families, the Hardings with the longer lineage but the Blaines with, in recent years, more wealth and power. When my father had spoken about the difficulty of the Captains in agreeing on a successor to the Prince we had, I had guessed he was referring to the rival claims of these two factions.

My father said: "Neither as yet."

"But if they don't . . ."

"Neither will accept the other in authority over him. But they talk of the possibility of both accepting a third choice."

"Who is that?"

My father did not answer right away. I thought from his silence that it must be someone of whom he disapproved. He said slowly:

"This is why I called you to talk with me. There are risks, a dozen ways in which it could lead to disaster; and the disaster would fall on a man's sons as well as on himself."

I understood then. I did not say anything. I could not mistake my father's meaning but it was still incredible. He had been known as a great warrior in the time when the city's army went out to fight its enemies and I knew he was well liked among the Captains. But he had been born common, ennobled within the lifetime of his elder son. They could not think of making him Prince in place of Stephen.

Peter said: "The honor is well deserved, sir. But . . ."

My father said: "I have put the questions to myself. Shall I tell you the answers I found in my mind?"

We waited for him to go on. He did not hurry. He was a man who thought slowly, except when he had a sword in his hand, and watched his words. He said:

"I found two answers. The first is that if the

Blaines will not see the Hardings set above them, and the Hardings will not accept the Blaines, neither would wish to bow a knee to such as the Greenes or the Farrars." These were both important families in the city. "They would rather have a Prince whose father's adz marks can still be seen on the beams of their houses, which he helped build as a carpenter. It stings less."

I was not sure I agreed but I held my tongue. I thought of Henry and Gregory whom I had beaten in the Contest along with Edmund. With them, I felt, it would sting more, not less, if my father became Prince.

"The other answer stems from the first. A Prince of poor lineage will be Prince, they may think, whom they can rule. He has the title but the Blaines and the Hardings will have the power. Until such a time as one or the other feels strong enough to act. And then such a Prince is someone that can be discarded, having fulfilled his purpose."

"The Spirits . . ."

"If the Spirits unmake one Prince they can unmake another. I do them honor, but Seers have acted under duress before, and the earth did not open up. I do not know that Ezzard would have called the Seance for tomorrow without a little prodding."

Peter said: "You can refuse, if you wish. No

one can say it is from lack of courage. You could think it too high an honor."

"Do you say I should refuse?" my father asked him.

Peter said: "There are arguments on both sides. We accept your decision whatever it may be."

"And I will make it on my own judgment. But tell me what you think."

"You have said it: they plan to use you. It might be wiser to say no."

My father turned to me. "Luke?"

"Take it, sir!"

"You speak fiercely."

"He is very young." Peter smiled at me, though it was with affection. "And after winning his jeweled sword he lusts for action."

"Yes," my father said. "A good fault, but a fault. Your advice is better, Peter. You are beginning to acquire wisdom. All the same, I shall do as Luke urges. I am to be a weapon against the Prince, discarded when the crisis is past. But they may not find it so easy. I knew a Captain once, many years ago in the fighting against Alton, who was proud of a sword that was longer and sharper, he claimed, than any man's in the army. It slid off another's shield and hit his foot. It did not take it off, quite, but the surgeon did later. Weapons can turn in the hand.

"And there is another thing. Our forefathers were only common men but they lived in this city and fought for it. The Captains are right to turn against this Prince. The die has been cast and there must be bloodshed. For the city's welfare, for the common good, we must have a swift end to the struggle, not a long-drawn brawl that leaves us weakened."

Peter said: "We follow you, sir."

He bent his knee in the ceremonial bow that is made by a subject to his Prince. My father stared at him for a moment and then, smiling, clapped a hand on his shoulder.

"I am well defended! I had already decided what to say to Ezzard, but I shall do it with a lighter heart for that."

"To Ezzard? Not to the Captains?"

"To Ezzard first." He laughed. "We must give the Spirits time enough to prepare."

I met Martin next morning by the Ruins. There were other ruined buildings in the city, where people had not thought it worthwhile to clear the ground and build again, but these were by far the greatest and, it could be seen, of one vast building. Once, out of curiosity, I had measured the length of the mound of stone and it was more than two hundred paces. It staggered the mind to think of what it must have been like before the Disaster. Of course our Ancestors, as we knew, had used powers of magic for which the Spirits at last had punished them: how else could so monstrous a thing have been erected? They had buried their dead in its shade—there were worn stones bearing names and dates set in the ground—and it was said the Christians had used it as a place of worship. That, too, was hard to believe when one thought of the Christians in the city, a handful of wretches living mostly in the hovels by the North Gate, so warped and degraded that they accepted polymufs as members of their sect and as equals. (They would have accepted dwarfs, too, but got no chance: dwarfs had their pride.)

Although no one now would be so foolish as to build in stone it was used in foundations, and from time to time men took loads from the Ruins for this purpose. In doing so paths had been made in toward the center, and one led to a place where there was a hole in the ground and stairs leading to a vast cavernous place underneath. Boys would occasionally dare one another to venture down and the dares were taken; but no one went far in or stayed long.

Nor would I have done so, on my own, but Martin wanted to and I was determined not to show fear in front of him. We had explored it

together, finding strange things—figures of
men and women, carved life-size in stone, mil-
dewed robes and banners, a pile of small
pieces of colored glass. We also found a door,
almost hidden by a heap of collapsed masonry,
leading to a small room, and on Martin's urging we made a den there, furnishing it with a
couple of wooden chairs we found in the outer
part and taking in a stock of candles to give us
light. It was cool in summer, warm in winter.
We had sat and gossiped there through many a
blank, wet day, private and secure from inter-
ruption. Martin, I knew, went down on his
own as well, but I did not. And this morning I
demurred at going down at all. It was not actually raining though the sky was a threatening
gray. We stood and threw small stones at
marks among the rubble. I was on edge, thinking of the Seance at noon and what might
happen. I had not said anything to Martin, but
he himself spoke of it.

I said, astonished: "How do you know that?
It is supposed to be secret to the Captains."

He smiled. "The news is running through
the city like wildfire. That the Prince is to be
deposed and your father made Prince in his
place."

Awkwardly, I said: "I'm sorry. I could not
say anything. I was sworn to secrecy."

He nodded. "I thought so."

In his place, I knew, I would have been jealous and resentful because in the past we had kept no secrets from each other. But his mind was easier than mine, less given to brooding. I said:

"It may not happen like that, my father becoming Prince. So far it is only something suggested."

"It will happen. Everyone is sure of it. I suppose I shall see less of you from now on."

"I don't see why."

"As son of the Prince."

"What difference does that make?"

"And the Prince in Waiting."

This was the title given to the Prince's heir, who normally would expect to be Prince after him. Edmund had not had it but his elder brother, Charles. I said:

"But even if my father is Prince, that will be Peter, not I."

"Your mother will be Prince's Lady, not his."

"It is nothing to do with mothers. Peter is my father's eldest son, therefore he will be Prince in Waiting. He must be."

Martin shrugged. "That is not what people say. They say it was an omen, your winning the jeweled sword in the Contest."

"Then they say nonsense!"

I spoke angrily but I was not sure what it was that made me angry. My mind was confused. A magpie flew down into the Ruins and I threw a stone at it but missed by yards. I turned away and walked toward the High Street. Martin followed me. We walked together but in silence.

It was always dark inside the Seance Hall, there being only a few small windows to give light from outside, but since the Spirits did not manifest themselves by day the curtains had not been drawn and one could see without the aid of lamps. Only the first few rows were occupied, since the summoning had been merely of Captains and their sons. Ezzard stood in front of us and above us, on the platform that was carpeted in black, surrounded on three sides by and canopied in black velvet. He wore his Seer's robe of black silk, trimmed with white at cuffs and neck, and his white face stared down at us, sharp and deathlike.

He said: "The Spirits be with you."

We muttered back: "And with you, Seer."

"The Captains of this city," Ezzard said, "have called for guidance to the Spirits, as their forefathers did before them, begging the Spirits to help and advise them in a time of need, in the distress of the city. As Seer I have consulted with the Spirits and they have made answer: he who was Prince . . ."

There was a noise in the doorway. Ezzard halted his speech. We all looked and saw Prince Stephen standing there, Charles and Edmund behind him. After a pause, Ezzard went on:

"He who was Prince shall be Prince no longer. Forsaking the city in fear he loses right to the city's fealty . . ."

Prince Stephen interrupted him. He shouted:

"Ezzard, I left the city on your advice!" Ezzard watched him in silence. "On the warning of the Spirits, given through you."

"No."

"By the Great, it is true!" I heard his voice crack. "You told me . . ."

"I told you that the Spirits saw danger, to you and to your house. Anything more came from your own fears. And the Spirits spoke truly through me: the danger is here and now but your peril is of your own making, not due to the shivering of the earth."

"You let me think . . ."

"The Seer counsels the Prince; he is not required to teach him self-control. Even if the danger had been of earthquakes, would not a true Prince have looked after his people instead of fleeing from the city in panic?"

It was a charge that could not be answered. Prince Stephen tried, floundering:

"You said the Captains would see to it . . ."

"And they have." Ezzard looked away from him, to the Captains. "He who was Prince shall be Prince no longer. In his place the Spirits offer Captain Robert Perry for the approval of his peers. Does any man say no?"

There was silence. Ezzard said:

"Who acclaims?"

We all shouted together, in a roar which echoed. Ezzard said:

"Therefore, as Seer . . ."

Prince Stephen broke in again:

"I am Prince and this is treachery. I challenge the traitor to prove himself with his sword."

My father had no need to respond. He had been acclaimed by the Captains and so was Prince already. But we watched as he rose to his feet. He said:

"Not here, in the House of Spirits. We will see to this outside."

Ezzard said: "You are a dead man, Stephen. No man can fight when the Spirits forsake him."

There was an open yard between the

Seance Hall and Ezzard's house, which stood
behind it, with a high fence on either side. We
watched them fight there. By the standards
that judges use in tournaments Stephen was a
better swordsman than my father, who had
learned his skill in battle, not from a fencing
master. But under any circumstances my
father's strength was much the greater. His
sword smashed aside the thrusts and parries of
the other, carelessly it seemed. And as Ezzard
had said, what man could fight when the
Spirits had forsaken him? Stephen's last throw
had been hopeless when he made it, a desperate alternative to the miserable wandering
exile which otherwise was the best future he
could expect. He retreated a few times round
the ring and then rushed on my father, offering no guard. My father's sword took him just
beneath the ribs. He gasped and fell forward
on it and blood gushed from his lips.

I was in my aunt's house the next day when
my father came, his first visit to her since he
had been made Prince. She called him Sire
and bent her knee, but he shook his head,
laughing.

"Leave that to the courtiers, Mary! It suits
them better. I come here for peace and quiet."

She ordered Gerda to fetch ale and herself

knelt and undid his boots. He said, looking round the small room, smoky from a fire that would not draw on a day of blustering wind:

"But we must find you a better place than this."

"It is good enough for me, Bob," she told him.

"But things have changed. You must learn to live like a Lady."

She said: "No, I am no Lady."

"That is soon remedied. The Prince makes whom he will noble."

"Not I."

"I say yes!"

"Please. Let me stay here as I am."

He looked at her. "Is there nothing you want?"

She put slippers on his feet. "For myself, nothing. I have it all."

That night Ezzard presided over a true Seance. We sat in darkness while the Spirits manifested themselves in strange sounds and sights: weird music, fluting high up in the rafters, tinkling bells, lights that moved across the blackness overhead, faces suddenly appearing as the Spirits put on again the flesh they had long outgrown. Voices.

A woman asked for help, her husband being

sick, and was answered by the Spirit of her mother, ten years dead. She was told of herbs to pick, at a certain time and place, and of a broth to be made of them which would cure the sickness. There was a little dim light now, from the lamps of the Acolytes who stood on either side of the Hall, and I could see her, a small thin woman, nodding her understanding and thanks.

Others followed with questions. One of them, a farmer, said:

"I lost six lambs last year. I paid gold to the Seer for an audience and was told all would be well. This year I have lost eight. What of the promise?"

He spoke almost truculently. The Spirit who answered was that of his grandfather's father. He said:

"Thomas, you farm the land I farmed. Do you do your duty?"

"I do."

"Do you keep the laws?"

"I keep the laws."

"Then you would have prospered. Unless . . ."

"Unless what?"

"Unless you have kept polybeasts that should have been killed at birth, and raised them for meat." There was a pause, but the farmer made no reply. "You lied, Thomas, when you said you kept the laws. That is why your flocks have sickened a second time. No gold will save him who defies the Spirits."

He went out, shuffling. There were others, some rebuked, some advised, some comforted. Then when the questions were over the little lamps were turned down again and the darkness returned. And in front of us a face grew, like a stern majestic man's but larger. A voice cried, deep and resonant:

"I speak, Stephen, Prince of this city in years gone by, ancestor of one who dishonored my name and lately died for it. The Spirits who guard this city have given you a new Prince. He will rule you well and lead your warriors to battle against your enemies—to battle and to victory."

There was a deep hush, not even a chair squeaking. The voice said:

"The Spirits crown your Prince."

It floated down from above, gently, gently, in the shape of a crown but having no substance, a faintly glowing crown of light. It came down to where my father sat, and hovered just above his head.

This, though a wonder, was expected. What followed was not. The voice spoke again:

"A great Prince and the father of one yet greater. His son shall be Prince of Princes!"

A second crown appeared out of the darkness. Peter stood on my father's right hand and I watched for it to move toward him, to rest over his head as the first one rested over my father's. And then my heart pounded, the blood dinned in my ears and I put my hand to the chair behind me so that I should not fall from dizziness. And my eyes were dazzled with the light shining down onto my upturned face.

4

The Prince
of Winchester

The summer of that year—a year that ended wretchedly—was the happiest time of my life. This was not because the Spirits had named me heir to my father, a future Prince of the city. At least that did not seem to be the reason, though I suppose it must have been a part of it. There was excitement in the air and the city buzzed with activity and expectation. The resentments which had gathered over the years against Prince Stephen's policy of skulking behind walls turned into a feeling of release. It lifted my father to a height of popularity which I do not think the other Captains, when they acclaimed him, could have anticipated. Wherever he went in the city people crowded round him, touching him when they could, blessing him in the name of the Spirits. When he rode out at the head of his army they cheered themselves silly: I saw a fat middle-aged man, having been pushed or having stumbled to a fall, lying in the gutter but still yelling for the Prince. He was drunk, of course, from ale, but the whole city was drunk on the subtler brew of pride.

I had begged to be allowed to go with him on the campaign but had been refused. He smiled at me.

"In a couple of years you will have all the fighting you want. But even with a jeweled sword you are no match yet for the men of Alton. And though the Spirits having promised you a crown greater than your father's no doubt will protect you, they require a man to look to his own safety as well. The Spirits like to be respected but they are inclined to grow impatient with anyone who trusts to their help beyond common sense. This year you stay in the city."

Peter said: "There's a price to pay for everything, Luke, including being heir to the Princedom."

They smiled at each other and grinned at me. I had been uneasy with Peter after the Seance of the Crowns, thinking he must resent my being preferred over him, even though the preference was that of the Spirits. Even when he had congratulated me I had been wary, looking for signs hidden in his face and bear-

ing. But I came to realize that there was nothing to find. His feelings for me were as warm
and friendly as they had always been: he rejoiced in our father's rise to power and also in
my being chosen heir.

We were in the palace. The room was quite
small, merely an antechamber to the great
Room of Mirrors which Stephen had most
used for retirement. My father said it was too
big: he did not like to hear his own voice
echoing back at him. Nor did he care to see his
own face whichever way he looked. So he had
furnished the antechamber with simple things,
including his wooden armchair from our old
house, and he escaped there when court life
bored him beyond bearing—which was not
infrequently.

He said now to Peter: "A price for everything, you are right, and a duty, but the duties
lie heavier on some than on others. I have
never been a nay-sayer and I have already
ordered the dwarfs to brew an ale to celebrate
a victory at the Autumn Fair, but accidents
can happen. I may fall off my horse and be
trampled."

We smiled at that. He was a superb horseman, his horse, a big chestnut called Guinea,
the surest-footed in the city's stables. He
smiled as well, but went on:

"Or die of eating Alton's ailing cattle. If any such thing should happen, Peter, I leave you a duty, to look after Luke."

"I can look after myself," I said.

"I don't doubt it, but a wise man takes help where he can. As you know, there are some among those who have acclaimed me who do not wish me well. It did not please them when the Spirits crowned Luke. They are quiet just now because they have no choice. But if I were killed in battle . . ."

Peter nodded. "I follow that."

I said: "Watch whom you ride with, Father. The men of Alton may not be the only danger."

"Good advice, but I am already watching. That is part of being a Prince: one's eyes do not get much rest. And the more so in a case like mine, a man born common and chosen Prince because others with better claims could not resolve their quarrel." He looked at Peter. "You will see to this?"

"I will see to it," Peter said.

The person who was bitterly aggrieved by what had happened at the Seance, and showed it, was my Aunt Mary. When I went to her house, although she did not say anything and I sat down to dinner at her table as I had always done, I could tell her disapproval. It was not that she was sharper with me or smiled on me less—her tongue had always had a roughish edge and her face did not seem to have been made for smiling—but I sensed resentment, anger, in small looks she gave me. I was not surprised by this. Peter meant everything to her, and had since my father divorced her. Peter was my father's eldest son, born in wedlock, and his natural heir. What the Spirits said meant nothing to her; she would have defied all the Spirits in the universe for Peter's sake.

I thought that her disappointment and bitterness would lessen with time and for a week or two carried on with my visits as though nothing had happened. Then one day I went to her house following heavy rain. I cleaned my muddy boots on the scraper outside her door but did not do it well enough, and there were dirty footprints on the polished boards of her little hall.

She saw them and tongue-lashed me. It was a thing she had done before, but again I found a difference in the scolding, a note of hatred almost. And she said:

"Even if you are to be Prince of Princes, you can still wipe your boots before you enter this house. Or do you already think we should all be servants, to do your bidding?"

The jibe stung and I felt myself flushing. She finished:

"Take your boots off, wash your hands, and come to the table."

Gerda the polymuf had heard her, and I was the Prince's son and heir. I looked at her, my own anger sharp:

"No, thank you. I will eat at the palace."

And I turned, saying no more, and left her house. I have wondered since whether things might not have fallen out differently if I had contained my rage, accepted the rebuke, and eaten my dinner with her that day. Or if I had done as I intended next morning and gone to make amends. But I thought that when I went she would scold me further and my pride would not bear it. Two days later I saw her in the street. We approached from opposite directions, saw each other but did not show it, and I was torn between the desire to go to her and the fear that she would treat my overture with scorn. We were near the Buttercross and there were boys I knew sitting on the steps there: they would see and probably hear all that happened. So I passed her in silence with the smallest of nods to which she made no acknowledgment.

After that it was, of course, even more difficult to put things right, and with the passage of time, impossible. I missed her, but there

were so many things to do that I forgot about
her most of the time. For her, though, there
were no such distractions. She had never had
much to do with her neighbors. When I
stopped going to her house—and a little later
my father and Peter rode away on the campaign against Alton—she must have been
lonely there with no company except the two
polymuf maids and her cat. I did not think of
that then, though I did later.

If my father's triumph had turned sour for
Aunt Mary, my mother reveled in the change.
She had always been a sunny person but was
happier than ever in being the Prince's Lady.
She had new dresses made, a dozen at least, in
bright silks and satins and brocades, and a
polymuf woman whose entire concern was to
arrange her hair each day. There were no
housewifely duties anymore—a butler saw to
everything—and all she need do was look
beautiful. She had always had beauty, but as a
precious stone is made ten times more splendid by its setting, so hers was enhanced by the
things my father lavished on her. She adorned
herself to delight him, and he showed his joy
in her. He said once when she told him (not
seriously, I fancy) that he spent too much on
her that it was for this reason only that he had
become Prince.

Although there were things to do in which

he could not accompany me I still spent a lot
of time with Martin. With him I could forget
about being the son of the Prince and there
were times when, however much I enjoyed my
new life, I was glad of this. We rode together
—I found a pony for him in the palace stables
—and fished for trout and explored the
country for miles beyond the city boundaries.
Once, deep in a wood, we found a dozen cherry
trees laden with fruit. The fruits were so big
and juicy, for all the long neglect of the trees,
that we thought they might be polymuf
cherries, but we ate them no less heartily for
that and with no worse result than an ordinary
griping that evening from having gorged
ourselves.

We had one falling out. It happened in our
den under the Ruins. We had arranged to
meet there and I was late. I found him reading a book by candlelight. He looked up and
greeted me. I asked him:

"What's that you've got?"

Books were rare things—few of the common
people could read and not all the nobles—and
this one looked strange. Its covers were not
stiff but limp, and the shape was odd: higher
and wider than usual, but thin. There had
been a picture on the front which damp had
turned into a meaningless mess of colors,
but I could read words across the top: POPU-

LAR MECHANIX. "Popular" I knew, but "Mechanix" meant nothing to me.

Martin said: "I was digging in the rubble at the back of Clegg's." That was the baker's shop in the High Street. "I saw the corner of an old cupboard—I suppose the quake moved whatever was on top of it—and I thought I'd see if there was anything inside. There were only books. Most of them were rotten but this one wasn't too bad."

There was a strangeness in his manner— part excitement, part something else. I went round behind him to have a look. There was a picture on the page where he had the book open. Because it had faded I could not tell what it was at first. Then I saw and knew what the something else was. It was guilt. The book was a relic from olden days: the picture was a picture of a machine.

I could not tell what kind of machine it was and did not want to. I put my hand over his shoulder, sweeping the book from his grasp. It fell closed on the floor and I put my foot on it.

He said, sharply for Martin: "Don't do that!"

"A forbidden thing . . ."

"I was only looking at it."

"That makes no difference. You know it doesn't. Seeing is thinking and thinking is as bad as doing. Have you forgotten old Palmer?"

He had lived in a cottage outside the city walls, a long way from the road. A peddler, desperate to sell his goods, had called there one day and later reported what he had seen: this man, neither farrier nor armorer nor metalworker, was brazing metal and building something from it. The soldiers rode out of the Prince's command and took him. He was tried and found guilty and hanged. For a week his body hung on the gibbet outside the North Gate.

Martin said: "He was *making* a machine. And in his cottage, where anyone might find out. We are the only ones who know this place. I have not shown the book to anyone else and will not. I will hide it; not even in here. Under rubble, outside."

"But it is a forbidden thing! Whether you are discovered or not, that is true."

"But why forbidden?"

"You do not need to ask that. Because our ancestors made machines and the machines destroyed the earth, causing earthquakes and volcanoes that killed men by the hundreds of thousands. That is why the Spirits decreed that the making of machines was an abomination."

"I suppose there were bad machines. But there may have been others as well. This one —I cannot follow the details properly—but it is about something that cuts grass. How could that cause earthquakes and volcanoes?"

"I tell you the Spirits condemn machines. All machines."

"The Spirits, or the Seers?"

"The Seers are the servants of the Spirits."

"Or their masters."

"You must be mad! No man can rule the Spirits, who are eternal."

"If they exist."

"You have seen and heard them."

"I have seen strange things, in the dark."

"That is blasphemy!"

I spoke in anger. I almost hit him, moving a step forward and doubling my fist. We stared at each other in the flickering candle's light; then I stooped and picked up the book. Martin made no protest as I shredded the pages: they were not parchment but made of some flimsier material. There were more pictures of machines and I averted my eyes so as not to see them. He watched me as I crumpled the pages on the floor and put the candle flame to a corner of one. They burned slowly because there was no draft down here, and smokily. When the heap was charred and black I put my heel on it and ground it into fine ash.

I said: "I'm going up now. There might be news of the fighting. Are you coming?"

He nodded. "All right."

I wanted to tell him why I had been angry.
Not because of the blasphemy in itself but
because of the risks that it involved. It was
true that he had only said these things to me
and in a place where we were quite alone, but
even that was dangerous. What point was
there in giving word to thoughts like that?
One took risks, in battle for instance, but only
for a worthwhile end. There was none here.

But I said nothing because, my anger cooling, I thought it best to let it all drop, to forget this unprofitable and perilous subject. We
did not talk about it again except one night,
weeks later, when we stood together on the
northern wall and watched the red glow of the
Burning Lands beyond the hills. As we
looked a spot brightened, sign of a new erup-
tion. Martin said:

"How could they have caused it?"

"What?"

"The machines. How could any machine
make the earth produce burning mountains? I
have listened to a man who has seen them
quite close. Thousands of feet high, he said.
How could any machine do that?"

I said: "It doesn't matter how. And it is not
worth talking about. It happened, and that's
enough."

I was not angry now but anxious for him.

For myself, too. I could hear voices from an alehouse behind and beneath us, spilling out through the night air. But Martin said no more.

I had the chance of making many new friends at that time. Boys, of my own age and older, paid me a lot of attention, seeking my company and flattering me when they had it. I suppose something of the sort might have happened simply because of my victory in the Contest, but of course there was more to it than that. From being nobody, the second son of an obscure Captain, I had become the Prince's heir.

This flattery did not please me as at one time I would have thought it would. On the contrary the few fits of depression I endured during that splendid summer were directly caused by it; because it all seemed meaningless when it was lavished on me and worse than meaningless: destructive. The victory had been a true one, and hard-earned; my father's acclamation and the honor paid me by the Spirits were both great things. To hear them mouthed by sycophants was to have them cheapened, and I was forced to turn away before they were made entirely worthless. Two or three times I went back to my room in the palace, not wanting even to see Martin, and lay on my bed, my thoughts black with despair. What sense was there in striving for anything, when all achievement ended as the prey of mean minds? But the moods were few, and they passed quickly.

I knew what was said of me when I turned away—that my head had been swollen by my success and my father's, that I was too proud to mix with those I deemed lesser mortals. So at times I gritted my teeth and made an effort to put up with them; not because I cared much for their opinions but because these were my father's subjects and would, in due course, be mine. Between a Prince and his people there must be good will or at least its semblance. I do not know how far I succeeded in my wooing of them. Not much, I fancy. My heart was never in it.

The one whom I did take to my heart and who became my second friend, strangely enough, was Edmund. My father had been magnanimous in his dealings with Stephen's family. There had been some who had argued that his sons should be killed and many who had favored exiling them from the city. They had stood with their father in defying the Spirits and removing them meant removing a future danger. But my father would have none of this. They had done their duty as sons in supporting their father and provided they

made due allegiance to the new Prince no
harm should come to them: Charles was per-
mitted to keep his Captaincy.

But their position was a poor one. Poor as
far as money was concerned—their father's
goods were forfeit and they and their mother
went to live in a small house, a hovel almost,
in Salt Street—and poor in reputation. No
one now had a good word to say for the dead
Prince and his sons incurred the same scorn.
The boys who crowded round me spurned
Edmund, whom a few weeks earlier they had
courted.

One day I was with a group of boys at the
Buttercross when Edmund joined us. There
had already been attempts to make an
Ishmael of him by showing that he was unwelcome, but he had stubbornly refused to accept
it. The boys started this again and one of them
said something about a smell of death and
traitors. Others laughed. I saw Edmund go
white. He said:

"My father was no traitor, but killed by
one. A traitor from a gutter in Dog Alley . . .
and now you lick his boots!"

It was true that my father had been born in
that street, one of the meanest in the city. The
eyes of the others watched me greedily to see
what I would do. I did not want to fight him
here, in front of them. I made a jest instead.

"Dog Alley—that runs into Salt Street, doesn't it?"

They laughed in support of me. Edmund said:

"Yes. Times change. Scum comes to the top."

He spat at my boots as he said that. I had no choice but to hit him. They formed a ring around us, and we fought.

His family had been noble as long as could be remembered in the city—since the Disaster, it was said—and he had a look of breeding, being tall with a long face, thin lips, arrogant blue eyes. But he was strong, too, and he fought with the anger pent up since his father's death. He threw me and leaped on me. I rolled clear and got to my feet. We grappled and he threw me again. He knelt on me trying to spread-eagle my arms. Panting, sobbing almost, he whispered: "Scum . . . scum!"

I realized I could be beaten, disgraced before this mob, and the demon inside me rose in a fury to match his. I tore free and as he came for me got a wrist and brought him across my body to land heavily on the cobbles. The blow winded him but he was up as soon as I was. He came at me. I straight-armed him, punching to the body. He winced and tried to hide it.

After that I kept him at a distance. Although he was the taller my arms were longer. My demon served me well as he always did. There are some who fight wildly in the rage of battle, their minds hot and confused, but mine goes cold and thoughts come quicker and more sharply. I concentrated on body blows, on that vulnerable part between and just below the ribs. These sapped his strength. He went on fighting and once succeeded in throwing me a third time but he could not press it home. I was up before he was and punched him as he rose. From that point it was only a question of how long he would last. It seemed an age to me and I was giving the punishment, not receiving it. I had switched my attack to his face which was smeared with blood. At last he dropped and could not even attempt to rise.

Our audience was cheering me and mocking him. I went to the horse trough below the Buttercross, soaked my handkerchief, and returned to bathe his face. It was swelling already and would look terrible in a few hours.

I said: "It was a good fight. The Spirits were on my side."

He stared at me, making no answer. I crumpled the handkerchief in my pocket and put an arm out to him.

"You are filthy, and so am I. Let's leave this lot." I gave my head a small contemptuous jerk in the direction of the watching circle. "Come back with me, and we'll get ourselves cleaned up."

"Back" meant the palace, which had been his home. He still did not speak and I thought he would refuse. But at last he nodded slightly. I helped him up and we went off together. The onlookers parted to give us way and watched us go in puzzled silence.

After that Edmund and I were friends. One day the three of us—he and Martin and I— were strolling down the High Street past the Seance Hall when the Seer came out. He stopped and spoke, addressing himself to me.

"You keep strange company, Luke."

I said: "It is the company I choose, sire, and which chooses me."

The remark must have been aimed at Edmund—he had seen Martin and me to-gether often enough—and I did not like it. It was said that the Seer had been among those who were for killing the sons of Stephen, and I supposed he was angry that Edmund had escaped and angrier that I should befriend him. But he went on:

"It is good to see quarrels mended before

they become feuds." He turned to Edmund. "Your brother is with the Army?"

"Yes, sire."

There was something in his voice which was not quite contempt but a long way from the deference which was reckoned to be the Seer's due. He had not been to a Seance, I knew, since his father's death. He believed in the Spirits, I think, and acknowledged their power, but hated them. His long face was without expression but I saw scorn in the blue eyes under the high forehead.

Ezzard, disregarding this, if indeed he saw it, said:

"He fought well in the battle."

"What battle?" I asked.

"The battle at Bighton, where Alton was defeated."

I stared at him. "We have only just come from the Citadel. There is no news yet. The pigeons have brought none."

Ezzard smiled his thin cold smile. "The Spirits do not have to wait on the wings of pigeons."

"This is from the Spirits?"

"Would I tell you else?"

"And a victory?" Martin asked. "At Bighton?"

"The pigeons are already flying," Ezzard

said. "They will be in their cotes before sunset."

It must be true. I asked:

"And my father . . .?"

"The Prince is safe."

I was too excited to speak further. But Martin said:

"How do they bring the news?" Ezzard looked at him. "The Spirits? If not on wings, how?"

Ezzard said: "A wise man, or boy, does not ask questions concerning the Spirits. They tell him what he needs to know. That is enough."

It was a rebuke, but Martin persisted. "But you know things about the Spirits, sir, since you serve them and talk with them. Is that not true?"

"I know what I am told, boy."

"But more than the rest of us do? How they bring their messages without wings, perhaps?" Ezzard's eye was on him. "I am not asking how, sir—just if you do know."

"I know many things," Ezzard said, "and I keep my knowledge to myself, imparting it only to those who have dedicated their lives to serve the Spirits. Would you do that, Martin? Would you be an Acolyte?"

It was a good reply, and one that must stop his questioning. Even if I had not heard him blaspheming the idea would have been ridiculous. One would have to be crazed to be an Acolyte—shaving one's head, fasting, droning prayers to the Spirits all day and half the night. I expected him to be abashed.

But to my astonishment he said: "I might, sir."

Ezzard stared at him keenly, nodded, and went his way. Edmund and I poked fun at Martin when he had gone. He joined with us. It had been a joke, he said, at the Seer's expense; and the old fool had believed him! I accepted what he said but I was still not sure. I had watched his eyes as well as the Seer's. If the earnestness had been deception it had been marvelously done.

Two days later I stood on the walls by the North Gate and heard the wild cheers of the crowd as our army returned victorious. A big man led them on a big chestnut horse: my father, Prince of Winchester.

5

Fire in Winter

The victory over Alton was overwhelming. Five Captains were taken for ransom, including the Prince's nephew—his probable heir since he had only one son whose poor health prevented his being a warrior. A sixth Captain had been killed and they left more than three score men dead or badly injured on the field. We for our part had one Captain crippled and scarcely more than twenty men dead or seriously wounded.

We had a triumphant Autumn Fair. They had ceded the village of Bighton to us, and altogether over a hundred thousand acres of land. Feasting went on for more than a week and the special ale my father had ordered the alemakers to brew was exhausted in half that time, in toasts to his health and the city's victory. (There was no shortage of milder ale and they strengthened it with raw spirits; men lay drunk in the streets not just at night but at broad noon.) The Hardings and the Blaines were quiet, raising their glasses with the rest but doubtless thinking their own thoughts. These were mixed, I fancy. I have no doubt they rejoiced in our triumph, for which they themselves had fought also, but it could not have pleased them to see so much honor paid to their stopgap Prince. We guessed that behind locked doors they were talking hard, with grim faces.

When the Fair was over and the prisoners exchanged for Alton gold, the Court rode out to hunt. I was one of the party, for the first time. I asked that Martin and Edmund might come also but my father would not agree: to belong to the royal hunting party was a great privilege which must not be awarded lightly. Martin was a commoner and it would be a scandal if Edmund, son of a man condemned by the Spirits, were included. Martin, I knew, was not sorry about this; he was neither fighter nor hunter by nature though he had helped me in the Contest. I had seen him turn pale when we watched a pig's throat being slit at the slaughterhouse. But for Edmund, though he said nothing, it was salt rubbed into unhealed wounds. This would have been his first year for the hunt also.

One of the things that had made the summer

memorable had been the weather. It was not just that it seemed better to me (one sees brighter skies in times of happiness): others, even the old ones, agreed that it was many years since we had been so fortunate. For more than a month, in July and August, no fires were lit in the palace except those in the kitchens. Very often the sun shone clearly, sometimes through the whole day with cloud obscuring it for no more than an hour or two. The harvest was good: all the granaries were filled and corn piled in bins in the mills.

And the sun which had shone on my rambles with Martin and Edmund and on my father's campaign had not yet deserted us. We rode to the hunt on a morning sharp but clear; frost crackling in the grass under our horses' hoofs, but the sky blue all round. I read a book once, the ink in places fading from the parchment, in which it was said that before the Disaster the sun shone almost all the time in summer. I had thought it a fantasy like some of the other things written there—as, for instance, that one of the wonders with which the devils seduced our ancestors before they destroyed them was the power to talk with and even see one another when they were a hundred miles or more apart. But now I could almost believe it. I was sorry for Edmund, left behind in the city, but it was impossible not to take joy in the air's crisp freshness, the horse under me, all the colored beauty of the dying year.

We rode south, following the river, toward the forest of Botley. There had always been boar there and it had long been a royal hunt, but new stories had come back lately from the country people who lived on the outskirts of the forest. Their fields had been attacked by beasts of incredible size and wiliness. Polymufs, they said, and implored the Prince to destroy them.

It was forbidden to keep polymuf cattle or poultry: all deformed creatures must be destroyed and burned or buried. (There were some who would have done the same with polymuf children, but the Spirits decreed that they should live, though separate from proper men and serving them.) Wild polybeasts were killed also, within civilized lands. Elsewhere, in the barbarous places, it was said they lived and flourished, in all sorts of strange and monstrous forms, from rats that built houses, or at least mounds to dwell in, to the terrible Bayemot that destroyed everything in its path. From time to time, polybeasts came down into our lands and when they did it was the Prince's duty to exterminate them. Not that we believed these boar were polymuf: country people are given to exaggeration and alarm. But a boar hunt was justification in itself.

We found nothing on the first day. We came on their spoor—tracks and droppings—but they were not, in the judgment of Bannock, the Master of the Hunt and one with great skill in reading signs, even fresh. Tents were set up that night in the fields by Shidfield village. My father had been offered lodging but declined, on the grounds of not inconveniencing the villagers; but as he said, laughing in private, also because he had never yet encountered a village lodging that was not overrun with fleas, and polymuf giant fleas at that. As it was, they brought meat and ale to us, and bread and cheese and honey cakes. Of no high quality: if it was their best, my father said, they deserved to have their taxes remitted on grounds of poverty, but he had no doubt it was not their best. They too were aware of conclusions that might be drawn and were wary. After being entertained by them three years before, Prince Stephen had increased their tax assessment.

On the second day we drew boar and killed two. They were good specimens but although Bannock examined them long and carefully he found no trace of polymuf. We roasted one that night on a spit turned by two kitchen lads recruited from the village. The flesh was good and sweet. We killed another beast on the morning of the third day, an old tusker who crippled two dogs before Captain Nicoll ran him through. On the fourth day we found the polymuf.

We had ranged farther from our base, to a new part of the forest. The trees for the most part were thin enough for us to ride without difficulty, but there were patches of thicker growth. Spoor was found which impressed Bannock: the hoof marks were very big indeed, and the droppings also. We cast around and the dogs at last gave tongue. They led us to a stretch of dense undergrowth. While the beaters were working round it the beast broke cover and rushed straight for our lines.

It was enormous, five feet from ground to shoulder and large in proportion. And it moved fast, more like a horse than a boar. It got through while two men stabbed futilely at it with their spears. We turned to give chase but as my horse's head came round I saw with astonishment that the beast had also turned, with amazing agility, and was heading back toward us. I did not waste time thinking about this but, realizing that it was coming my way, set my lance and spurred my horse to meet it.

All I saw was a massive blur of motion, gray and hairy, racing through the trees. Perhaps my horse saw more, or more clearly. At any rate he reared in fright. In controlling him I let my lance tip hit the ground. With bucking horse and the shock from the lance I could not keep my seat. I hit the ground, rolling to break my fall. I was cursing my misfortune and the fact that there was now another gap for the boar to break through our lines a second time. I looked for it and saw it. It was not going for the gap. It had changed its course and was bearing down on me. I could see it well enough now, see red-rimmed eyes and the savage white gleam of tusks. I tried to get to my feet and realized, as pain shot down my leg, that I was injured. Voices shouted, but a long way off. The boar smashed a bush aside like straw. The sight of it, almost on me, and its stink dried my throat with fear. Then from my left there were hammering hoofs. I saw a horse and rider and a lance which raked the boar along its ribs, forcing it away with a huge squeal of pain. The horse cleared me as I lay there. The rider was Peter, who had stayed close by me throughout the hunt.

He had not killed the boar but the wound helped the rest to run it down within an hour and dispatch it. It was a fearsome beast, I was told, seven feet in length from snout to tail. The size alone branded it polymuf but apart from that it was double-tusked and its head was bigger in relation to its body than was usual. A polymuf strain was sometimes thought to be an indication of greater intelligence, as with the building rats that tales were told of, and this one seemed to have behaved with more than mere cunning, in doubling back to attack its enemies and in going for me when it saw me unhorsed. I gather it led them a fine dance before they finished it off.

My father said he would have dearly liked its head to hang on the palace wall: Bannock, in more than thirty years of hunting, had never seen anything that could come near matching it for magnificence. But the law held. They built a pyre and left the carcass burning. I did not see anything of this, having been helped back to the camp after Bannock had set my leg, broken in the fall.

I was taken back on a litter strapped between quiet horses. For two more weeks I had to lie on my bed, my leg splinted. After that for long enough I hobbled with a crutch. My friends came to see me to help me pass the time, Martin every day but Edmund less frequently. I knew why: it was still an ordeal for him to come to the palace, and I guessed he had to steel himself afresh on each occasion.

Autumn closed into winter. The good weather had broken even before the hunt was over and we paid for past beneficence with freezing fogs and, in early October, with blizzards that sent snow whirling round the city walls, piling high against houses, blocking the streets and drifting up against the windows of the palace to obscure my view out over the town. In other years I had loved the coming of the first snow, when gangs of boys were formed in snowball fights that raged all day (apart from the break for dinner at midday) through the grazing meadows and even up into the streets of the town until our elders put a stop to it. I was past the age for that, and for skating: my enforced inaction only emphasized my inability to take part, but it emphasized my boredom, too. I played games with Martin—chess and checkers and liars' dice—but he beat me too easily at the first two and I won too easily at the third: he had no guile.

In November my father went to Romsey, to visit the Prince of that city. Prince Stephen's refusal to send his army into the field, his reliance on walls built higher every year, had been part of a more general isolation. There had been no state visits, made or received, for some time. My father's accession, followed by his victory over Alton, had changed that. It was not only Romsey that wished to see the new Prince of Winchester.

My father took his bodyguard with him, of course, and a few of his Captains, but for show rather than protection. Men did not make war in the winter and such a visit as this was in any case safeguarded under the customs of all civ-

ilized peoples. We waved him good-by as he
and his entourage rode out from the South
Gate and then we turned back to our ordinary
occasions. Dull always at this time of the year
—halfway between the Autumn Fair and the
Christmas Feast—I found them duller still
with my father away, and the summer's excite-
ments fading into memory. The days passed
and the evenings lengthened as winter tightened its grip. I wearied of games played by
lamplight, and of the amusements which
delighted my mother and her friends: the
polymuf jugglers and clowns, the guitarists
strumming and singing melancholy love songs.
My leg was still splinted so I could not ride
during the day. I was restless, bored, wanting
something to happen. But when it did happen
it was not during the dragging day or tedious
evening but at night, while the palace slept.

I awoke to a smell that was so strong one
almost tasted it, and sat up coughing, the
smoke in my throat and lungs. It was pitch
black. I hobbled to my window and flung the
shutters open. Cold fresh air streamed in. The
night was dark apart from the glow of the
Burning Lands, and a light nearer at hand,
blossoming from a window beneath me, and
with it the dreaded crackling that told of fire.

I shouted an alarm and, wasting no more
time, headed for the door and the stairs. My

room was to the right of the staircase, my
mother's apartments on the far side of it. But
as I opened the door the crackling was more
like a roar and automatically I shielded my
face from the light and the heat. The staircase
was a torrent of flame, spreading, moving upward. It had passed the landing and was
ravenously eating its way up toward the attics.

If I could leap it, I thought, and get across
to where she was . . . The surgeon had said my
splints could come off in a few days. I got back
to my room and, needing no light from the
brilliance of the fire behind me, found my
knife and slashed the binding cords. My leg
was terribly weak and I winced with the pain
of putting my weight on it, but it would do. I
headed back to the staircase.

It was impossible. In the short time I had
been away, a matter of seconds only, the fire
had spread and strengthened. It was frightening to look at, like a living creature in its rag-
ing hunger and power. I could not get within
feet of it without being scorched.

There was another chance. Wooden gutterings ran along the side of the building, below
the windows. I got to my bedroom and clam-
bered out, holding onto the sill with my hands.
People were gathering in the courtyard, more
than twenty feet below. I heard their voices,
shouting, calling, a woman screaming, and

tried to ignore them. The gutterings were wide and shallow and I had already discovered that one could use them to get from room to room. It was not easy—one had to stand on this narrow ledge and inch one's way along with one's face flat against the wall—but it was possible. I started on my way. I thought only of my progress, closing my mind to everything else: to what I would do if I reached her and also to the terrifying possibility of a misstep.

But what I could not close my mind to was the increasing heat of the boards against which I was pressed. The fire, triumphant inside, was beating out against its confines. In a spot where the timbers were not properly caulked I caught a glimpse of the furnace within. But I was getting past the worst, I thought, the part that lay over the staircase. I risked a look in the direction in which I was edging and saw no sign of flame. I had come at least a dozen feet and probably had no more than that to go before reaching a window. I was cool in mind and increasingly confident. And I remember no more until the point at which I woke up, in bed, in daylight, my head splitting with pain.

One of the pegs that supported the guttering, weakened by the heat perhaps, had given way and I had fallen. A soldier in the crowd below had tried to break my fall. He succeeded in part—my recently knitted leg did not snap again—but my head struck something which knocked me unconscious and, as sometimes happens, took away my recollection of the accident as well.

Wilson told me this, sitting beside my bed with his long face, never much better than melancholy, a solemn mask. He was Sergeant in charge of the palace, an old and well-trusted follower of my father. They had served in the ranks together as young men. My father, on becoming Prince, had wanted to make him a Captain, to ennoble him, but he would not have it. He had had a wife many years before but she had died, broken-hearted, after giving birth to a polymuf child. He had not married again and apart from my father had no real friends.

My mind was confused, my head aching. I sat up and it was worse. Wincing, I said:

"And the fire? What happened . . .?"

"That wing is gutted. The rest was saved."

I think it was his look of misery which recalled what my own purpose had been. I said:

"My mother . . ."

He shook his head very slowly. No more was needed. I could not believe it, though I knew it was true. I had seen her only a few hours before, her eyes half closed, foot tapping, head slightly swaying to a tune she loved. She was fond of music which I was not.

I had slipped away without, I now remembered so sharply, bidding her good night.

I concentrated my wits and asked Wilson questions, which he answered. I think he thought me strange, perhaps callous, to do so at such a time; but it seemed to me that my sorrow was my own, a private thing, and not to be talked over even with one so well known and well trusted as Wilson. Pigeons, he told me, had been sent to Romsey, calling my father back. To my query as to how the fire had started he said it was fairly sure it had been deliberate, a murderous act. This had always seemed likely because, living in wooden houses as we did, we observed strict precautions against accidental fire. A special patrol checked the palace each night. But it was not a matter of supposition only. One of the guard had found a polymuf watching the fire from hiding. He had flint and steel on him, and oil-soaked wadding. Moreover he was known for a crazy loon who loved playing with fire. There had been trouble before and he had been exiled in the end; he was not allowed in the city and lived in a ramshackle hut beneath St. Catharine's Hill, shunned even by the other polymufs.

I asked: "How did he get into the city?"

Wilson shrugged. "It is not difficult."

That was true. The gate guards were supposed to check all who passed through but I had myself slipped past their backs when I did not want to call attention to myself.

"And why the palace?"

Wilson said: "That will bear looking into."

"Has he been questioned?"

"No. We await your father's return. But we have him safe. I set the guards myself. No one will get to him, either to rescue him or to close his mouth."

"No other trouble?"

If this were a plot, laid by the Hardings or the Blaines, maybe both, now would be the moment to rise, before my father could get back. I saw by Wilson's face that he took my meaning.

"No trouble. And we are ready for any that comes."

My father was back before evening. It snowed heavily in the afternoon, obliterating the familiar tracks, but that did not stop him. He rode up through the city streets and into the courtyard in advance of his laboring escort. I heard a distant cry—"The Prince!"—and the clatter of hoofs on stone and ran to the window of the room in which I had been bedded. I saw him dismount, a snow man from a snow horse, and stand there, staring in front of him, while the horse was taken by a groom.

He was looking at the wing in which we had lived. It was a sight I had already seen, with sickness and a sad thumping of the heart. The snow, which had mostly been cleared from the courtyard, lay thick there, in uneven mounds from which a few blackened upright timbers pointed toward the gray sky. It was a whiteness and desolation that chilled the blood, a wilderness made more horrifying by the buildings which still stood all round. I saw him take a step, as though to go toward it and then with a twist of his head turn away. Then I called to him from the window; in a low voice, but he heard me and looked up. Even from that distance and with the light beginning to fade I could see the grief and anger in his face.

I threw clothes on and, ignoring the protests of the nurse who was attending to me, hurried downstairs. I found my father in the Great Hall along with others—Peter, three of his Captains, and a number of commoners, including Wilson. Wilson was talking, telling the story of what had happened, and my father was listening. His face was a cold hard mask now. He said at the end:

"Has the polymuf talked yet?"

"Only in crazed words."

"Have him brought in."

Peter said: "It may be he acted on his own. He is known to be a lunatic."

"Yes," my father said, "well known. And therefore a good weapon to another's hand."

Neither Blaine nor Harding was there, and none closely linked with them. If the polymuf had been set on by someone, I wondered which. Perhaps both. They had made no move but it might have been their plan not to—to wait until my father's return and attack then, while he was shattered by the earlier blow. He looked like a man of iron, waiting for the polymuf to be brought. If they thought a blow could shatter him they were in for a surprise.

The polymuf, his hands chained, was pushed forward by the guards and sprawled at my father's feet. I recognized him as one I had seen wandering alone in the fields beyond the East Gate. The Spirits had marked him with a hare lip, fissured red up to the nostril, and his voice showed that his mouth had no roof. He lay on the floor and talked nonsense, the words themselves scarcely understandable. I heard him babble about fire . . . the Spirits . . . death . . . and fire again.

My father stooped down and took him by the hair. He said:

"Who told you to do this?"

His voice was cold and sharp; only his eyes blazed with anger. The polymuf spoke again, but still in nonsense. My father shook him, with force enough to send his legs skittering across the polished boards but not letting go of his hair. The polymuf howled. My father said:

"I have a gift for you, polymuf. Tell me who put you up to it and you die quickly. It is a good reward. I do not think you care for pain." He shook him a second time, a dog with a rat. "There was another. Was there not?"

"Yes!" the polymuf cried. "Yes, Lord . . ."

"Name him."

"Not a man. It was . . ."

My father dragged him upright and stared into his face. "Do not say it was the Spirits or I will not keep my temper."

"Not the Spirits. It was . . ."

I thought I grasped the words but he spoke so badly I could not be sure. And it made no sense. My father said:

"Say again."

"Your Lady, Lord."

"You fool!" my father shouted. "Are you saying my Lady told you to light the torch that burned her? You get no gift for that. You will . . ."

"Your other Lady, Lord!" My father's hand dropped from him as though it too was scorched with flame. "She who lives on the River Road."

At first my Aunt Mary denied everything, claiming that the story was an invention of the

polymuf to save himself from torture. But
when she was confronted by a farm worker,
who had seen her coming away from the polymuf's hut, she fell silent. Thereafter during
her trial she did not speak, not even when the
sentence of death by burning was pronounced
on her. I was in the court and saw her eyes go
to my father's but I do not think it was in
appeal. It was his gaze that, after a moment,
turned away. Her look followed him while she
was being taken off by the guards.

The execution was fixed for the next day.
That evening I had word that she wished to
see me. It was her polymuf servant, Gerda,
who brought it. She had been weeping, it was
plain, and wept again when I hesitated.

"Master Luke, I beg you! For a few minutes only."

I had never heard my aunt give her anything
but scoldings but her grief might have been
for a mother. That by itself would not have
persuaded me to go. It was my aversion which
did so. I had felt for my aunt, since I heard the
accusation that spilled from the lips of the
crouching polymuf in the Great Hall, both
horror and a kind of fear. I would not give in
to this. I told the maid I would see her.

The Sergeant of the prison guard demurred
at first about admitting me. When he did, he
accompanied me to the cell and himself stood

there while we talked. From time to time he cast my aunt uneasy glances, as though fearing that, although unarmed and helpless, she could by some witch's art strike me dead.

She looked very old in the gray shapeless felon's gown. And feeble, though I knew she had not been put to torture. But her eyes were as sharp and strong as ever; and her mind had not budged from its single concern. She asked me:

"Where is Peter?"

"Under guard."

"What will they do with him?"

I hesitated. In fact, I did not know. There had been no evidence to link him with the crime but to some it was condemnation enough that it had been done for his sake. Others said that even if not treacherous in the past he could not be trusted now, the son of such a mother.

My aunt said: "Speak for him, Luke."

I said: "It was me you wanted dead, Aunt, wasn't it? Not my mother."

She shook her head, as though impatient, almost angry, at an irrelevance. She said:

"Peter knew nothing of it. You must believe that."

"You wanted me dead."

Her eyes met mine, unwavering. "Only because you were named heir. There was no right in it. My son is the elder, born in wedlock."

"The Spirits named me."

"There was no right in it," she repeated.

"You would do it again, if you could."

I did not say that as a question, although in my mind still it was a question. I could not believe that she had tried to kill me. She looked at me.

"Yes."

"And you ask me to speak for Peter?"

"They are burning me tomorrow. Is that not enough? And Peter saved your life in the hunt."

"To your regret."

"No. I would not have him different from what he is."

"But were ready to kill to make him heir."

Weariness for a moment showed through her determination. She said:

"What he is and what I would do for·him are different things. I will pay for my part, in the morning. Speak for him, Luke."

I went to my father from the prison and asked him to release Peter. It was not because of my aunt's plea. (She had only made this to me as a last resort; she had asked to see my father but he had refused.) Except in her reminder that Peter had saved me from the polyboar. By speaking for him now I could cancel that debt and make us quits.

My father listened in silence then, but ordered Peter's release the next day, as soon as the burning was over. I did not go to see it. My father did, and sat, I was told, like stone.

It was not a long one; he had made sure of that. The people cheered, for his safety and the destruction of his enemy. The only trouble came from the Christians. They opposed the taking of life, even in battle or the execution of murderers, and always made a nuisance of themselves on such occasions. The people pelted them with filth and abused them. And one who called the Prince a murderer was taken by the guards. He was tried later but only condemned to the stocks for a day. The Christians, it was well known, were all mad, and no one took them seriously.

6

The Machines
of Petersfield

It was a wretched winter. The palace was a place of gloom, ruled by a man who did not smile but drank greatly in an endeavor to forget what would not be forgotten. The heaviness of the atmosphere, so strong a contrast with the lightness that my mother's presence had engendered, of itself kept her in mind. And the weather was in tune with all this. Day after day the blizzards raged, until it was impossible for the polymufs to clear the streets and snow packed higher and higher against the walls of the houses: people had to cut steps down to their doors. It was impossible to exercise the horses, who grew vicious in their stables. We could not exercise ourselves either, and turned stale and sour from the lack. The Christmas Feast was held as usual and my father took his place at the head of the long table. But there was little enough cheer.

It was said that Christmas had started as a Christian business, celebrating the birth of their god, and this year one could believe it; it was so dreary a time. The polymuf jugglers and clowns, the musicians, had no occupation. My father saw to it that they did not go hungry but they were unhappy, not being able to use their gifts and gain applause. In the new year, when the weather held clear for a week, many of them left the city for more promising courts.

Martin and Edmund and I quarreled often enough during this drab confining time, but we remained friends. I cannot speak for their feelings but I had great need of them, with my father withdrawn into a private misery, and my own thoughts wretched enough. Strangely, the impulse to go to the house in the River Road, an impulse which had disappeared in the summer and autumn, came back now at intervals, quite unexpectedly. Doing some ordinary thing, I would think of going there, hearing my aunt's sharp voice bidding me wipe my feet, sitting down to dinner at the little table in the poky room. Then I would remember that all this was past, and how it had ended, and would feel a pain like the twisting of a knife in my chest. The pain went quicker if the others were by.

And Edmund was more willing to come to

the palace than he had been. It was as though what had happened dissolved his resentments. My father, as anyone could see by looking at him, had paid a heavy penalty for becoming Prince. I don't think Edmund took any joy in this. He had changed from a hatred of him, which could not be hidden even though unexpressed, to a different feeling, almost one of admiration.

He said one day, about Peter:

"Does he ever visit your father, Luke?"

I said truthfully: "My father receives few visitors."

"But Peter?"

"No."

He had not been to the palace since his release. I myself had seen him once or twice in the Citadel, going about his duties as Captain, but we had not spoken. Edmund said:

"He was fortunate."

I had not spoken to them or anyone about my meeting with my aunt and my plea to my father for Peter. I doubted, in any case, whether my words had turned a scale. My father's circle of affection was small and he had lost two from it already; he would not have wished to forfeit a third unless it were forced on him.

I said: "He had no part in it."

"There are some who think differently. He usually slept in the palace, but not that night."

"Because he was on duty in the Citadel. My aunt knew that."

"And I've heard it said he was against questioning the polymuf, insisting he was a madman who had acted on his own."

"I was there," I said. "It was a remark, no more. It meant nothing and there was no insisting."

We were in the east wing of the palace, in a parlor on the first floor. It was a part that had been left empty and unpainted for many years. The walls were dingy and cracked: Strohan, the palace butler, had asked my father if he should set the polymufs to decorating them but had been told no. Edmund and I were playing chess. Martin, who in any case was too good for either of us, was reading a book. He looked up from it, and said:

"The city is full of rumors. Being penned in, people have nothing to do but talk."

"And mostly nonsense," I said.

"Yet it is worth listening to it," Edmund said. "Even if it is nonsense, it is often useful to know what kind of nonsense men believe."

I accepted that, surprised only that he should have said it. But he had changed in the past months, as we all had. He thought more, and more deeply. And although we were friends I knew I did not have all the secrets of his mind, any more than he had mine.

Martin said: "People even say he is turning Christian."

I asked in surprise: "Peter?"

"He has been seen with them."

"If he does," Edmund said, "you are safe, Luke. Christians may not kill, and so he could not take revenge."

"Revenge?" I asked. "For what?"

"For a mother burned in the market square. It is not something one forgets. They say your father is a fool to have spared him. I don't think so. I think he knows his own strength. He is like a dog I once saw come into a pack that were snarling and fighting. The pack made way for him and when he turned his back on them, though together they could have fallen on him and killed him, they dared not even show their teeth. But you may need to take more care."

"I can look after myself."

"Still, if he turns Christian it makes it easier. And he would have to give up his Captaincy."

"That shows what moonshine it is! He would never surrender his sword."

Martin, while we were talking, had left his

book and strolled restlessly about the room. He stopped in front of a picture which hung on the wall. It was very old and showed animals in cages, but like no animals we had ever seen. There was one that was tawny in color, shaped something like a cat but with a mane behind its head; and judging by the size of a man in the picture at least a hundred times bigger than any cat could be. Another, roughly resembling a man, was hideously ugly with receding head and chin, hairy and tailed. And near the cages a second man walked what might have been a horse except that it was covered with black and white stripes.

Martin said: "This must be from before the Disaster. And yet they say that the polymufs, both beasts and men, only came after the Disaster, as a punishment for the wickedness of our Ancestors."

"It may not be from before the Disaster," Edmund said. "We don't know how old it is."

"But there are polymuf beasts in it, full grown, and men with them, so in any case something is wrong."

"They may be only the imaginings of a painter," I suggested.

"They don't look like imaginings."

Edmund said: "Take it to Ezzard and ask him."

"He would destroy it probably. I should think it has only survived because no Seer has noticed it."

"Take care when you speak of the Seer," Edmund said, "or you will never be accepted as an Acolyte."

The joke was long threadbare but we all laughed. We needed something to laugh at.

One day, during the period of easier weather, the time when the clowns and musicians and jugglers were leaving the city, the thought of the house in the River Road came on me again, a joy and a pain together. I was on my own in the lower part of the city, below the Buttercross. I had been meaning to go across the river to the Armory but on the impulse I changed my direction. I walked the familiar street where I had not been for so long. The polymufs had cleared the High Street of snow but here it still lay, packed in the center, at the sides drifted against the houses. I came to her house and stared at it. Steps had been cut before this door as before the rest, and smoke rose from the chimney. I wondered who lived there now, but I did not care. The journey had done me no good; I would have been better staying away.

I turned to go and found him almost on me: the snow had muffled his footsteps. We looked at each other, for the first time really since the fire, and I saw the deeper lines in his face, the marks of grief and long brooding. He said:

"Health, Luke. You have come to see me?"

I said stupidly: "To see you? Here? You live here?"

"Why not? It is my home."

As we both knew, he had left it last summer to join my father in the palace, at the time when Aunt Mary refused the offer of a bigger house. I had assumed that from the palace he had gone to live in the Lines, with the other unmarried Captains.

I said: "You have no woman to tend you."

"I have the maids."

"Polymufs . . ."

He shrugged. "They see to things."

It was unheard of for a man, except sometimes when bereaved and old, to live without human care and companionship, of wife, mother, sister—some womanly relation. It showed how badly he had taken things that he should do so; and made the notion of him turning Christian just a little less incredible. But even apart from the solitariness, how could he bear to go on living with such memories as the house must continually call to mind? I found it bad enough to have to look at the snow-topped ruins of the palace's north wing. To be in the house—listen to the ticking of the clock she wound each night, look at the plants in pots of which she had been so proud —was to seek pain which anyone in his right mind would shun.

While I hesitated, trying to think of something to say, he said:

"Are you coming in?"

"No. I have . . . someone to see."

We looked at each other. I do not know what he thought—that I had come to gloat, perhaps—but I knew there was nothing I could say which would bridge the chasm between us. We called each other cousin, and in fact were half brothers. We had been friends. We could not become strangers. It left only one thing: we must be enemies.

Winter ended at last in a thaw accompanied by rain storms which made the river flood its banks; the waters rose at one point to lap against the block of stone in the High Street which still carried the broken legs of what had been a statue—of a great Prince of ancient times, it was said. But when the rains stopped and the west wind died away there was fitful sunlight and everywhere the trees began to bud, bursting into green as though to make up for time lost.

It was the Spring Fair again, and the Contest. Not a good one: the favorite was Mark

Greene and he won without much difficulty and took the jeweled sword. I sat with the spectators, my own sword hanging from my belt, and heard people talk about how much better the Contest had been last year. They said flattering things and I made awkward replies. Later Edmund, who had sat with me, said:

"One would think you did not like praise, you receive it so awkwardly."

"I like the thought of it," I said, "but the reality makes me uneasy."

He smiled. "You must learn to overcome that. Or at least not to show it."

"Praise is worth having from a few. Those whose judgment one values."

"And if *I* tell you it was a better Contest last year?"

We laughed. I said: "And would have been better still with a different ending?"

"True enough!" He paused. "If I had not underrated you as I did . . . I fought it over in my mind often enough afterward and knew I could have beaten you. I would have liked a second chance."

"There are no second chances."

"Not in the Contest, I agree."

"Not in anything that matters."

He shook his head. "I will not accept that, Luke. I will never accept it."

It was at this time that my father roused himself from the torpor which had held him for so many months. Orders were given and obeyed. The ruins of the north wing were cleared away by polymufs, and after them came builder dwarfs and there was sawing of wood and hammering of nails all day. Others worked on the rest of the palace, mending and cleaning and painting.

Nor was that the end of the city's new activity. The dwarfs were also busy in the Armory and at harness-making. People had said that with the Prince sunk in melancholy there would be no fighting this year. Now they knew differently. He still did not smile but he seemed possessed by a fury that drove him toward action. He was up at daybreak and busy all day making preparations for the campaign. In the middle of April the army rode out to the southwest.

I rode with them. Not, it is true, as a warrior, though I wore my sword, but as assistant to the Sergeant in charge of the camp followers. These were the men who looked after the Prince and the Captains in the field, putting up tents, seeing to equipment, cooking and so on. It was work which in the city would have been done by polymufs but no army took polymufs with it even as menials. These were men unfit for one reason or

another to be warriors but glad enough to go
with the army, for pickings or maybe just
for the excitement. They were a rough lot
and unruly when they were in drink but the
Sergeant, a gray-bearded man called Burke,
with a limp that came from an old sword
wound, ruled them well.

We made up a baggage train, the gear
loaded on carts pulled by mules. We did not
always take the same route as the army—the
mules were sure-footed but the carts themselves could not always go where horses
could. It was particularly true on this campaign, for we were riding against Petersfield
which lay in a fold on the far side of the
Downs. The ground to be traversed was
hilly and often rough. We made our way to
appointed places and worked hard, having a
longer road to travel.

I learned a lot, from the best way of sleeping on hard ground with only a single blanket
to keep out the cold to the techniques of killing and skinning and jointing a bullock: once
we were out of our own territory we lived,
as raiding armies always did, on the land
we were invading. I had thought myself fit
but soon became much fitter. My hands were
first sore then calloused from the labors of
mule-driving, loading and unloading, hauling
on ropes to free carts whose wheels were

stuck in the mud. I wished often enough that I could be with the main body of the army, riding high up across the shoulder of a hill while we struggled along beneath them, but this at any rate was better than being left with the garrison in the city.

Our boundary followed the river as far north as West Meon. It was there the army crossed, taking the broader southerly route through the Downs, and I looked on foreign fields for the first time in my life. They seemed no different from our own, growing wheat and potatoes, very few with cattle. (Dairy farming was for the most part carried on in parts closer to the cities, where the beasts were not so vulnerable to raiders.) We passed through a hamlet less than a mile inside the border. Its single street was empty, the windows tight shuttered on the houses, silent except for a dog barking somewhere out of sight. But we knew that eyes would be watching us, and that the pigeons would be in flight, carrying word of our coming to Petersfield.

The battle took place a week later and I saw it all. We had come up from cultivated land to higher ground cropped by sheep and halted. We had a spring-fed stream with a good head of water and the sheep kept us in fresh meat. My father waited for the Prince of Petersfield to meet him. The scouts brought news of his coming one drab gray morning with a chill east wind driving gusts of rain in our faces. Our camp was in the lee of a rounded hill topped by a clump of trees, like our own St. Catherine's. I told Burke I wanted to go up there to watch.

He said: "If you like, Master. I've seen enough fights in my time but you're young enough to have the appetite."

"You don't need to come with me."

He shook his head. "I'm to see you safe home, if things go wrong. And that's not easy. The rats may lie quiet in their holes while you go through in advance, but they come out with their teeth sharpened for anyone straggling back."

He saw that our haversacks were well supplied with rations and our canteens filled with water. The Spirits, through Ezzard, had prophesied victory for Winchester, a greater one than last year's, but as he said, an old soldier might believe in the Spirits but was not such a fool as to trust his life to them. If our army were scattered the baggage train would be lost and it was difficult enough escaping through hostile territory without going hungry and thirsty as well. We led our horses up the hill and tethered them in the grove of trees. The wind howled through, shaking the branches, but the rain had stopped. Then, our cloaks wrapped tightly round us, we looked down and watched the armies come together.

It was a slow business at first. Our army, more than five hundred men on horseback, stood grouped about the blue and gold standard, near which I picked out the tall figure of my father on Guinea, his helmet topped by the royal spike. The Petersfield men came on slowly from the east, in a wedge formation with their Prince and his standard, all green, deep inside the wedge. From time to time they stopped. The taunts and jeers from both sides came up to us, thin, tiny like the figures. At one time I exclaimed as the enemy appeared to turn tail, but Bruke shook his head. It was part of the ritual, he explained, and no retreat but a show of scorn, meaning they held us in such contempt that they could expose their backs.

"If we attacked now . . ."

"It would be to give them best in that."

"But we might win."

"We might. If you can call it a victory, achieved without honor."

I said: "We face the wind."

"It blows from their city."

"But if we had held the ridge on the right

—they could only have come at us across wind, and uphill also. Or would that be dishonorable, too?"

He laughed. "Not that I have heard. But your father is a strong fighter rather than a canny one. He thinks he needs no such aid."

"But if *they* had taken the ridge . . ."

"It would have made things harder for us. Watch! It begins, I think."

The two forces were riding to a clash with growing momentum. My hands were clenched and I felt the nails score my palms. The wedge advanced toward our ragged line and as it drove in I saw swords flashing even in this dull air. Our line, giving way at the center, curved round to embrace their flanks. Then it was a melee, impossible to sort out except by reference to the swaying standards, confusion to eyes and ears alike. The din, though distant, was awful: shouts and cries of men, screams of horses, rattle and clash of swords.

The fight lasted for three quarters of an hour. Then slowly the sides disentangled as the Petersfield men fell back. The green standard bobbed away on a retreating tide.

"Is it over?" I asked. "Have we won?"

"We have won this fight," Burke said. "I think there will be others. They gave way in too good order to be ready to ask for peace."

"If we have beaten them once we can beat them again."

"True enough. Except that next time they will be closer in to their own city."

"What difference does that make?"

"An army fights harder the nearer it is to home."

But they did not stand in our path again. We took East Meon and moved on, downhill at last to the low ground in which Petersfield itself stood, west of the Rother River. We camped under their walls, out of arrow shot, and waited for them either to sue for peace or come out to fight us. We were among their home farms and had food enough. They must do something or their harvest would be lost.

Pickets were set at night, though an attack was unlikely then. Darkness favors the defenders provided they are prepared; we had stakes and ditches ready. Then one morning, as the sky was beginning to grow light in the east, I awoke to what I thought was the crash of thunder. While I was still struggling to my senses I heard another crash, and shouts of pain. I pulled on my boots and got to my feet to find the camp in confusion. There was a third crash. It was different from thunder and in any case the sky was full of high thin cloud. I looked toward the city and saw, just before the next crash, a red flare of light from the walls.

Gradually some order emerged. The Sergeants rallied the men. I went to my father's tent and found him there with his Captains. One said:

"I have heard of these things. They throw metal a great distance. But they are machines. The Seers forbid them."

Harding said: "They bark more than they bite. Two men wounded, I am told."

"So far," another said. "But if they keep on with this long enough . . ."

Harding said: "We can move the camp back. I don't know what range they have but it must have limits. And we are still in their lands."

"Once we retreat it will give them heart. And if they bring these machines with them . . . if we ride against thunder that belches steel, will the men still follow?"

Harding shrugged. "We have no choice but to retreat. We could leave this campaign and ride against Alton again, or south to Chichester."

Blaine, a red-faced burly man with small sharp eyes, said: "What does the Prince say?"

Neither he nor Harding would be sorry to see the campaign against Petersfield called off. It might not bring my father down but it would besmirch the reputation he had gained last year and help undermine his power. I saw them watching him.

My father said: "They use machines. It is not just the Seers but the Spirits that forbid them."

"They can kill for all that."

"The Spirits promised us victory," my father said. "And these men defy them. So we attack."

Harding said: "How, since they will not come out?"

"We attack the city."

They stared at him in disbelief. One of the reasons Stephen had been laughed at, building his walls higher each year, was that in more than a generation no city in the civilized lands had fallen to the army of another. Taunton had gone down, three years before, but Taunton was a border city and the barbarians from the west had taken it. The armies fought, harder, as Burke had said, the nearer they were to home, and won or lost, and peace was made, ransoms and tributes paid; but the cities stayed safe and untouched. What my father was saying sounded not merely foolhardy but almost heretical.

Blaine said, his tone only just concealing the sneer:

"And take it? All the easier, do you think,

for having the machines against us? They may or may not be able to bring them against us in the field. But, by the Great, we know they are on the battlements. Are we to walk like flies up the walls and into their very mouths?"

"Why not?" my father said. "Since the Spirits are with us."

There was a silence and I saw the Captains look at one another. If one spoke up in opposition the rest might rally to him. But it was my cousin Peter who spoke. He said:

"Why not? When the Prince leads, do his Captains fear to follow?"

It seemed hopeless. They had to advance on foot, with the machines, three of them, blasting down at them from above. Even without these, scaling the walls would have seemed impossible. Because of the risk of earthquakes they were of loose construction but they were steeply sloping and more than thirty feet high, manned by archers who could pick off the crawling attackers with ease. One of the Captains had suggested making the attack at some other point where there might not be machines, but my father refused. We went under the Spirits' protection and would advance against the machines whose use the Spirits forbade.

I watched from the camp with Burke. The machines roared again and again and I saw our men fall as the hot steel slashed their bodies. They were in bow range, too, now and the arrows also took their toll. My father led them. I do not think they would have gone forward against such odds under any other Captain. If he fell, they would scatter and run, and I guessed the enemy's fire would be concentrated on him. Even if, by a miracle, he went on unscathed, I thought they must break as comrades dropped and died at their sides.

Then the greater miracle happened. From the central machine came another roar but louder, more shattering, and the wall around and underneath it exploded outward. Dots darted through the air, of rock, of metal, of the limbs and bodies of men. As the dust and debris settled one could see that the wall was breached. At that point it was no more than a pile of rubble with a gap of ten feet or more at the top, and undefended.

There was a shout from the men of Winchester and they moved forward faster, running and stumbling upward over the rocky slope. Then they were through the gap and inside the city.

7

The High Seers

That year we had strange and distinguished guests at the Autumn Fair: the High Seers came to the city.

They came, three of them, black-cloaked on pure white horses, and the city turned out to greet them at the North Gate. It was not a greeting such as had been given to the army when we returned with the spoils of Petersfield. Then the people had shouted their acclamations for the Prince and his followers, and even I, riding with Bruke at the head of the camp followers, had heard my name echo from the city's walls. The High Seers were received in silence, but a silence that was perhaps more impressive than any noise, having reverence in it.

The crazy Christians on one side, there had been always some who were skeptical concerning the Spirits, and Ezzard's powers as

mediator and interpreter of their will. Many,
possibly a majority, contrived to hold belief
and disbelief in dubious balance. There was
something there, they thought, but they did
not quite know what, or what the extent and
limitations of its authority might be. I think
I was among them. Even though I had been
angry with Martin for expressing blasphemy,
it had been chiefly through anxiety over
men's response to it, not fear of what the
Spirits might do. In part I believed in the
Spirits—after all, they had named my father
Prince and myself his heir, a Prince to be—in
part, I doubted.

But it was hard for any to go on doubting
after the fall of Petersfield. My father, calling on the Spirits for aid, had led his men
in an attack against walls which, strong in
themselves, carried also diabolical machines
capable of throwing death from great distances: the camp, on which steel first fell, had
been almost half a mile away. If there were
no Spirits, or they had no power to help, the
project was ridiculous, scarcely sane. But the
Spirits had shown their presence and their
strength, destroying the machine at the very
moment that it belched out death, and by
that destruction opening a way for our men
to pour through and overcome the shocked
and demoralized defenders.

In thankfulness my father had decreed the building of a new Seance Hall, three times the size of the old one. The High Seers were come to consecrate its foundation, and the city greeted them in awe. Each city had its Seer, with his attendant Acolytes, but the High Seers had always stayed in their Sanctuary beyond Salisbury, the holy place. There, it was said, they communicated with the Spirits not just fitfully, for an hour at a time, as Ezzard did, but continuously, even passing through from our substantial world to that strange invisible plane in which the Spirits had their being. It was wonderful that they should have left the Sanctuary and come so far, thirty-five miles at least, to honor us.

That evening the High Seers sat at the long table in the Great Hall, on my father's right hand. Facing them were other Seers: Ezzard and the Seers of Petersfield and Romsey. It was a great concentration of holiness and the banquet was not, at first at any rate, as banquets usually are, noisy with jests and rowdy laughter. Men ate and drank in a solemn hush; heads turned at the sudden squeaking of a chair, reproving the one who sat there.

The Seers ate and drank sparingly, the High Seers eating least of all. I heard it whispered that the little they took was only for politeness' sake, that usually they supped on the food of the Spirits that could be neither touched nor seen by ordinary people. Whatever their customary food was it plainly nourished them; they themselves were solid enough and one at least, sitting between the other two, was big indeed and amply stomached.

They left the table before the sweets were brought and all, my father included, stood in respect as they walked together from the Hall. When they had gone there was a kind of sigh that rippled down the line of guests, followed by noisy chatter that burst out in relief. The clowns came with the sweets, and serving maids filled the pots with the strong dark brew of ale, itself sweet to the tongue, which was drunk after meat. I took some myself but only sipped it. I had seen enough heads fuddled with ale to be careful in drinking. I could never see what pleasure men got from being made silly and stupid by it. To me it was a hateful thing not to have control of one's mind and body.

My father swallowed down his pot and called for another but he had a good head for liquor: even when drinking heavily he never seemed to be the worse for it. Tonight, after his second pot, he rose. The guests that remained rose also but he bade them sit down and continue with their feast; he was excus-

ing himself because he had things to attend
to. He left, as they toasted him yet again:
Prince of Winchester, conqueror of Petersfield! Not long after a servant came to me
quietly. My father wanted to see me in his
private room.

I found him sitting in the old wooden armchair. His boots were off and he was toasting
his feet at the fire. He nodded as I came in
and bobbed my head to him.

"Sit down, Luke. I hope you don't mind
that I took you from the feast."

I said: "No, sir."

"You are young still but there are things
about which I would like to talk with you.
Partly because they are your concern as well
as mine." He shrugged. "And partly, I suppose, because there is no one else to say them
to."

In the past there had been my mother, who
would smile, half listening, and tell him she
was sure that everything he did was right,
and would succeed because he did it. And my
aunt, who would comment more shrewdly.
And Peter. Peter had spoken up for him
before the walls of Winchester and gained
great glory in the battle that followed, fighting with a reckless courage that everyone
praised. But I knew he could not talk to
Peter any more than I could—could not look

at him without remembering that which he
wished with all his heart to forget. There
was Wilson, but old and trusted colleague as
he was, some things could not be said to him.

I waited. He said:

"I saw your face when I spoke to the Captains before the attack on the walls. Did you
think me mad, son?"

"Why, no, sir . . ."

He shook his head impatiently. "Or reckless, or what you will. At any rate, you
thought we could not succeed. As the others
did. They came with me because I shamed
them into doing so. None of you had faith in
the Spirits."

I began to speak again and again he bore
me down.

"Let us talk about faith," he said. "It is a
strange thing. Before you have faith you
must believe, and before you believe there
must be evidence of some sort to persuade
the mind. Faith is remembering that evidence and holding to it against all that seems
to challenge or contradict it. And some evi-
dences are stronger than others, and more
important. I have faith that my dinner will
be brought to me tomorrow, but not such
faith that I would sit long at an empty table."

He paused. I was not sure if he wanted me

to say something and anyway had nothing to say. He went on slowly:

"You know what my mood was last winter, and you know the reasons for it. I think I went on living because it was too much trouble to seek death. Ezzard tried to give me comfort, telling me that your mother was a Spirit now, with the other Spirits, that she lived still in their world and that one day I would meet her again. He brought me messages that he said came from her. There was no comfort in them. Time after time I sent him away.

"Then at last, as winter ended, he persuaded me to visit him in the Seance Hall. None knew of it and no other was present, not even an Acolyte. Just the Seer and I. And there, in the darkness, I heard her voice. She talked to me, in human speech."

He looked at me and his face lightened into a smile, so rare now.

"I do not ask you to believe this because you did not hear it, and a man can be deceived by his ears. But I *know* I was not deceived. I could never mistake that voice. I heard her speak."

I asked: "What did she say, sir?"

"That she was well, that I must not brood over losing her, that we would meet again.

It was not what she said but that she said it. I knew then that Ezzard had told me the truth: that there was a world of Spirits and she was in it.

"There is still more. Before I led the army against Petersfield, Ezzard told me how things would go. He said they would fight us in the field and then retire behind their walls. He said their Prince was a man who defied the Spirits, who had found old machines of war and would use them. So I was not surprised when thunder broke from their walls that morning. He said if we fought against them we would win."

He looked a long time at Margry's painting of my mother which hung on the wall opposite his chair. It showed her smiling, a shaft of sunlight on her hair and face, puppies in a basket at her feet and flowers behind her head: accompanied by all the things she loved best. He said:

"One thing Ezzard did not promise me: that I myself would come back safe. He did not say I would not, but I thought that was his meaning. He spoke strongly of the need to protect you, my heir. But perhaps it was my own desire that misled me there. Because to die in such a way, fighting on behalf of the Spirits, must mean that I would join her, at once, in the Spirit world."

He hunched back in his chair, letting his shoulders droop, and for the first time I saw him as old, a man with a burden in which there was now no trace of joy.

"All happened as Ezzard foretold. And I returned in triumph, and I do not think either the Blaines or Hardings will trouble us in the future. I do not know how many years I have to live"—he spoke as a man contemplating a long and wearisome journey—"but when I die the people will call for a Perry to succeed a Perry. You will be Prince of this city. It is something else Ezzard has told us, at the bidding of the Spirits, but even without their aid it would be so. And because you are the Prince in Waiting, I have another thing to tell you. Ezzard has spoken to me about Petersfield. It is the wish of the Spirits that we do not exact ransom but annex this city, making it and all its lands part of our realm of Winchester."

Despite what he had already told me, I was astonished. The cities were the cities, individual and sovereign. One might defeat another in war and take tribute, outlying land perhaps, as we had done from Alton, but at the end of each campaign the armies withdrew behind their own walls.

I asked: "Is it possible?"

"The Spirits command it."

"But will the men of Petersfield accept? Or will you keep an army there all winter?"

"If necessary; but it will not be necessary. Their Seer agrees with Ezzard on this. He will proclaim it to them and his power is great since their city was taken through defiance of the Spirits. I shall appoint one of their own Captains as my lieutenant. The Seer of Petersfield has given me good advice on choosing him."

The Seers, it seemed, were taking a larger hand in our affairs: much larger. I was not sure I cared for it. But it was true they spoke for the Spirits and that the Spirits had showed their powers. True also that so far their powers had been exercised to our benefit. It would not be wise to offend them.

I was at Edmund's house on the day the proclamation about Petersfield was made. It was his mother's birthday and I had taken her a present, a set of pink ribbons made up into a shape something like a rose, to pin on a dress. As soon as I gave it to her I realized I had made a mistake. It was the sort of frivolous thing which would have suited my mother but Edmund's mother had been, even as the Prince's Lady, a homely woman not given to fripperies, and now was content to dress dowdily in browns and dark blues. It occurred to me that choosing a rose shape made things worse. Her one great joy when she lived in the palace had been the rose garden. I think it was the only thing of luxury she missed when she went to live on Salt Street. The present might remind her of it; she might even think I had meant it to.

She thanked me warmly but I was embarrassed and uneasy. My mood was not improved by Edmund's sister, who was also there. She was a year older than Edmund, a thin, sharp-tongued girl. I was never, at the best of times, at ease with girls, but those who used sarcasm bothered me even more than the ones who giggled together in corners. She said something now about the gift I had brought, which I did not fully understand but which sounded mocking. Then she spoke about the proclamation. What a great Prince I would be one day. Who knew how many more cities my father might not conquer?

"Who knows?" I said. "Maybe Romsey, too. If so, I will bring you a gift from there. A lily, perhaps."

I saw her thin face flush. She had been betrothed to the son of Romsey's Prince but this had been annulled, of course, following her father's deposition and death. Lilies were what brides carried at their weddings. She said:

"I know one thing you will never bring to any lady: that is courtesy. It requires breeding, and if you become Prince of all the cities in the world you will always lack that."

Her words cut like knives, reducing me to tongue-tied silence. Her mother intervened, saying:

"That will do, Jenny. You have been teasing him."

"Does a gentleman insult a lady, even if he is teased?"

"It has nothing to do with that," her mother said. "Some men are at ease with womenfolk, some not. You know Luke is of the latter, and you should not provoke him."

I said: "I am sorry, ma'am."

She smiled. "I know you are."

Then Edmund came in with Charles, whose arm was still in a sling from a wound he had got at Petersfield. She turned to them, smiling again, but the smile was different. It transformed her plain face into great beauty. I had never seen such a look as that in my mother's face. They grinned back at her, and I knew where Edmund had gained the strength to overcome his disappointments and resentment. I was jealous of him.

It was near dinner time. They asked me to stay and share the meal with them but my awkwardness, the consciousness of having put myself in the wrong, was so great that I refused. I realized, from the quick look of scorn Jenny gave me, that I had made things worse. She thought, and probably so did the others, that I was refusing out of a feeling of superiority.

I knew that was not true but could do nothing to remedy it. I was in a black mood as I walked away down Salt Street. It was not superiority, I insisted to myself, but awkwardness. And jealousy? I did not want to look at that. I went back to dinner at the palace and my father and I sat opposite each other in silence. His thoughts these days were far away except when he was concerned with war or statesmanship. And my gloom continued, no less oppressive for being a condition to which I was well accustomed. I expected it would last all day, and it did.

Before the High Seers left the city I was called to private audience. Ezzard took me to them in a parlor of his house behind the Seance Hall. From the window one could see the workmen, dwarfs and men, busy on the new Hall which was already beginning to rise beside the old one. My eyes, though, were on the High Seers whom I was seeing for the first time at close quarters.

My neck, as I made obeisance to them, prickled with unease. I reminded myself that they would not harm me: I had not, as far as I knew, offended the Spirits and my father had been highly favored by them. I had been summoned in good will. And yet my flesh crawled as the chief High Seer, a small, very wrinkled man, his face spotted brown with age, held out his hand for me to kiss the ring on his little finger. It was a band of gold, set with seven emeralds: Ezzard's ring had only a single green stone in it. These were the great ones, the true familiars and servants of the Spirits. Even though I knew they wished me well, I feared them.

"So you are Luke," he said, "the Prince in Waiting, heir to Winchester and Petersfield."

"Yes, sire."

"You have learned your catechism from Ezzard? Tell me, boy, what are the Spirits?"

"They are of two kinds, sire: the Spirits of Men, and the Eternals."

"Describe them."

"The Spirits of Men are those who have lived on earth. Their duty is to watch over their descendants who are still in the body. They are the lower order. The higher order

is the Eternals, who have always been, will
always be. Both orders serve the Great Spirit
whose name and being are a mystery."

"What is the duty of man?"

"To obey the commands of the Great
Spirit in all things."

"How is a man to know these commands?"

"They are revealed by the Spirits through
the Seers."

He nodded, bobbing his head, and I saw a
little of the bare head under the black cowl,
and skin smooth and taut in contrast to the
wrinkled face.

"Well enough. Are the Spirits good or
evil?"

I hesitated. It was not an easy question and
not among those in the catechism which one
answered by rote. I said:

"Some seem evil to men whom they pun-
ish. But it is men's wickedness that is at
fault. The Spirits only do the Great Spirit's
bidding."

"And is the Great Spirit good or evil?"

The catechism came to my aid again. "He
is beyond good and evil. He is, and all things
serve him."

"And you, Luke, do you obey the Spirits
and worship the Great Spirit?"

"Yes, sire."

"The Spirits are good to those who serve them. Like your father. They have rewarded him well. Is that not so?"

I thought of him as he had been when he was no more than a Captain, remembering his laugh which had seemed to come from deep in the belly, and as I had seen him that morning, silent in his chair staring at the picture on the wall. But it was true he had been given wealth and power, rule over not just one city but two. And he himself made no complaint against the Spirits.

I nodded. The High Seer said:

"Remember this always. All men are serfs to the Spirits, but they choose some to fulfill their will in special ways. Your father is such, and you are another. The Spirits have a mission for you to perform."

I asked, curiosity overcoming my unease: "What is that, sire?"

"It is not time for it to be revealed. But the time will come. And when it does you must obey, unhesitatingly, with all your heart and soul. Do you promise this?"

"Yes, sire."

"You must obey whatever the orders may be. Some will seem strange. Remember that while men are bound by the laws of the Spirits, the Spirits are bound only by the commands of the Great Spirit himself. They can change the laws they have made if that seems good to them."

"I will remember, sire."

"Good. Your destiny is a great one. The Spirits will aid you but much depends on yourself. We are glad to have seen you, and that you promise well. We take good news back to the Sanctuary."

If the Seers knew all things and they were such intimates of the Spirits, I did not see that they could take back any news that was not known already. Perhaps, though, it was not meant literally but just as a vague commendation for my having made the right responses. I kissed his hand again before I left, and the hands of the other High Seers. The big one I had noticed at the feast looked bigger than ever, like an over-prosperous farmer, and I wondered again that he could nourish such a bulk on Spirits' food. To my amazement he smiled at me.

"Are you a swordsman, Luke?"

I said cautiously: "I have learned swordplay, and am still learning."

"You will have a sword to be proud of one day. A sword of the Spirits." I suppose I looked uncertain, and he went on: "No, but a real one—tougher and harder and sharper than anything the dwarfs can make. A sword for a Prince of Princes." He smiled again. "We go back to see to the forging of it."

I was to meet Edmund and Martin afterward. They asked me how it had gone and I told them some of what had passed, but nothing of the talk of great destinies or a sword of the Spirits. Edmund said:

"The usual mumbo jumbo, in fact. It is a pity, since the Spirits have such great powers, that they talk such rubbish."

I did not chide him for blaspheming, as I had once chided Martin. I knew that, half believing in the Spirits, he wholly hated them; that remained even though he was now apparently reconciled to what had happened, to my father's being Prince and me his heir. I was sorry that he took such risks but knew that argument would only make him worse. I expected Martin to say something less positive but indicating a measure of agreement: they infected each other in this. To my surprise, he said:

"I saw a Seer today also. Not a High Seer. Only Ezzard."

I asked: "Why?"

"I am to be an Acolyte."

"You're joking!"

That was Edmund, incredulous. Martin said:

"No, it's true."

"You mean—you believe all this, you want to spend your life praying to the Spirits? Because a machine blew up and Luke's father took Petersfield instead of getting himself killed and his army scattered as should have happened?"

"No," Martin said, "because I want to find out."

"Find out what?"

"The truth about the Spirits. Whatever it is, the Seers must know it."

"And if there's nothing to find out?"

He smiled. "Well, I'll know *that*, won't I?"

"Will you tell us?"

"Perhaps."

I said sharply: "An Acolyte is bound by deep oaths. If he breaks them his life is forfeit, and in torture."

Martin smiled again. "Or perhaps not. It depends."

"You should not talk like that. It is dangerous even to have such thoughts."

They both laughed. Edmund said:

"Poor Luke, you must remember he takes his Spirits very seriously. And why not? Perhaps we would if they looked after us as well

as they do him. Shall I turn Acolyte with
you, Martin? I don't think so. I'd look an
even bigger fool with a shaved head than
you will."

Another thing happened before the Christmas Feast: my cousin Peter married. He
married a girl from the Christians, whom he
had still been seeing. But he did not become
a Christian himself and his marriage caused
no great stir. A woman's beliefs were not
thought to be of much importance, and she
was not one of the fanatical sort but a quiet,
well-behaved girl. Not a beauty, either, but
he seemed content with her.

It did not affect his standing with the other
Captains, rather the reverse. With marriage
his manner changed back to his old amiabil-
ity and he was at his ease again and put them
at theirs. To the reputation as a warrior he
had gained in the summer was added popularity. He was thought a good fellow, no
longer under the cloud of his mother's crime
and execution.

But when my father offered him a house
as a wedding gift he refused it, politely
enough, saying he preferred to go on living
on the River Road. And when he and I met,
although we gave each other greetings, we
did not stop to speak.

8
A Head on the East Gate

In December there was a state visit from Prince Jeremy of Romsey, in return for that of my father's which had been cut short a year before. He brought his eldest son with him, and they stayed for the Christmas Feast.

Prince Jeremy was a fattish, small, ineffectual-seeming man with a gingery mustache and beard, both delicately trimmed. His polymuf barber was one of the party and he spent an hour closeted with him each morning and came out oiled and scented. To my father he was deferential, almost obsequious, continually seeking his opinion and only offering his own when it was requested. In fact, his opinions were often worth having. Although he looked weak and effeminate his mind was shrewd.

The son, James, was a little older than I

but a good deal taller and more adult in appearance; when he sometimes missed being shaved (as I think he did by design rather than accident or slovenliness) his chin was blue-stubbled with whiskers. I was astonished by his attitude to his father, which was one of condescension, almost of contempt, and by the father's acceptance of it.

To me he offered at first the same condescension. I made it clear that I would not stand for it, and his manner changed to a rather oily affability. I found that he followed me around; little as I cared for his company I could not without rudeness be rid of it for long. And it was not possible to be rude: this was a state visit and I had a duty to perform. I cut him short in his criticisms of his father but had to tolerate the rest of his whinings. He was envious of Winchester's wealth and prosperity and under cover of praising it continually bemoaned the poverty of his own city and of his father's palace. They had no painter to compare with Margry, their musicians were inferior, their buildings small and mean against ours—even the dogs no match for our Winchester breed. All this, with its barely concealed jealousy and resentment, was increasingly irritating as the days passed and I grew more and more familiar with his complaints.

But if it was bad enough having to endure his company on my own, it was worse when Martin and Edmund were there. Martin he practically ignored, except for a faint air of surprise that I should associate with a commoner. He gloated over Edmund. It was not done openly—there was no particular thing said to which one could take exception—but there was no mistaking it. He had known Edmund, after all, as the Prince's son, and he was plainly delighted by the reversal in his fortunes and the family's present poverty.

Edmund for a time tolerated it, returning an equal but silent contempt which I think James was too stupid to notice. The break in his composure only came when one day in the street we met Edmund's sister, Jenny. She did not notice James right away and stopped to say something to her brother about a domestic matter: a drain at the house that needed unblocking. It was only after some moments that she saw James and her words faltered. Her face, already pricked to color by the frost in the air, crimsoned further.

James said, his voice cool and it seemed to me with an edge of mockery:

"Greetings, lady. We have met before, I believe."

The meeting, as we all knew, had been

two years earlier and had been the occasion of their betrothal: the daughter of the Prince of Winchester and the heir to Romsey.

She said: "Yes, sir."

He smiled at her. "Should you ever come to Romsey, you must call on us."

The tone of insult was unmistakable. Their eyes met and his, in cruel arrogance, bore her gaze down. I had not thought I could be sorry for her but I was. She mumbled something and turned, walking away quickly over the packed snow. James called after her:

"Present my compliments to your lady mother." Jenny did not reply or look back. "Tell her I regret that I shall not be able to visit her in her new home."

Edmund, stung at last beyond endurance, started moving toward him, his fist doubling for a punch. I caught his arm and Martin did so from the other side. No provocation could be held to justify striking the son of a Prince who was a guest of the city: the offender must be charged and convicted and publicly lashed. James had seen his move and was smiling.

Edmund said: "Let me go. I'll . . ."

"No." I tightened my grip on his arm, making sure I hurt him. "It's not worth it." Our eyes locked. He was angry with me as

well and I could see why. I said: "Go after
Jenny. I'll see to this." He still struggled to
get free. I whispered: "If you hit him, I
must defend him. I have no choice. And then
. . . do you want to have him watching while
they take the lash to your naked back?"

He gave me a single look. I let go and he
walked away. I motioned to Martin to go
with him. James said:

"A pity you did not let him try."

I turned on him fiercely, so fiercely that he
started back. I said:

"I did it for his sake, not yours. But if you
insult a friend of mine in my presence again
it will be I that cracks you, state visit or no
state visit."

I walked away toward the palace. He followed, protesting that it was all an error: he
had meant no insult. I did not answer. He
caught up with me, and said:

"All the same, do you think you are wise to
make a friend of such as him?"

I said sharply: "I do not need advice on
choosing my friends."

He laughed, high and thin. "Of course!
But I worry about you, Luke. You are too
trusting."

I kept silent. I wanted no counsel from
him, of any kind. Nor was it true. I knew
myself well enough to know that with me

trust was never constant but something which ebbed and flowed. I might trust a few in my good humor but when my mind was black clouded I trusted no one. This one, though, I would not trust under any conditions.

That evening, talking alone with my father, I asked how much longer they would stay. He said:

"Do you find that young James tries you?"

I gritted my teeth. "Almost beyond bearing."

He smiled. "I have noticed the effort you made and been proud of you for it. One can see why some lads are unpleasant—this one has ruled his father since he was in the cradle —but one does not dislike them less for the knowledge. But it may prove to have been worth it."

"I do not see how, sir."

"No, but I will tell you. The father is a soft man in some ways but at the same time cunning. He has been impressed by our success the last two summers. He realizes that we have the aid and blessing of the Spirits. He wants an alliance."

"For fear that we might attack him next?"

"In part, but not only through fear. He looks for advantages."

"What advantages?"

"This, like all things said in this room, is not to be spoken of." I nodded. "He proposes that next summer we join together in an attack on Andover."

Andover was due north of Romsey, about fifteen miles distant. The cities were old rivals but in recent years the northerners had been greatly the stronger. Romsey had paid much in tribute and yielded valuable land. I said:

"I can see why he wants our help. But there is not much honor for us in defeating Andover with Romsey's help."

"I felt the same. But there is more to it than honor. Or a shared ransom. Ambitions have grown all round since we took Petersfield. He says he can take Andover, as well."

"How?"

"There is a Sergeant in Andover who will see to it that one of the gates is opened. For a price."

"But that is treachery! There would be no honor . . ."

"Listen," my father said. "There are times when the world changes, when the customs of generations shatter and things are no longer fixed. Ezzard has told me we are in such a time. Because of this a man born a commoner became Prince of Winchester. Andrew of Petersfield used machines against us. We in turn took his city; and on the Spirits' command have kept it. The changes are not yet ended. If Prince of two cities, why not three?"

"But if Jeremy's army fights alongside ours, if it is he who has the key to the gates . . ."

"He is a timid man. He is shrewd enough but lacks courage. He is a little dog who wants a big dog to run with and will therefore let the big dog take what he wants and be content with the scraps. He offered me the city without my asking; he will be content with Stockbridge and the land around it. And with our friendship."

I said: "I can think of others I would sooner have as friends."

"So can I. But a Prince is bound by policy, not by liking. And by the Spirits. Ezzard supports this plan. He has told me: I will be Prince of many cities—you, if you are guided by the Spirits, Prince of all the cites in the land."

I was silent. I thought of asking: did we want such an empire? But I guessed the answer I would get—that our wanting or not wanting was unimportant. The Spirits required it. They had served us well so far but their wrath, if we failed them, could destroy us as quickly as their benevolence had raised us. We had no choice.

Edmund kept away for the remainder of the visit, and for a time after. In the end I sought him out at the house in Salt Street, and persuaded him to come with me to the stables. There were just the two of us. Martin was already under instruction to become an Acolyte and busy that morning.

We walked in silence at first. There was constraint between us, the recollection of our last parting. In the end I said:

"I am sorry for holding you back. I would have liked to see you hit him. I would have liked to hit him myself."

He did not reply at once and I thought he was still resentful. Then he said:

"No, you were right. It would not have been worth it to knock him down. What a toad he is! You would not believe how he fawned on me . . . in the old days."

I said feelingly: "I think I would believe it."

"And Jenny—he paid her such elaborate compliments and told her all the time how unworthy he was of her. It was true enough, but you could see he didn't believe it. She hated him even then but of course had to

obey our father. If there is a consolation in
what happened it is that the city is rid of that
alliance."

I thought of what my father had told me
but was silent. Edmund went on:

"She was saying, after that meeting, that
she had only just realized what an escape she
had in not having to marry him. She can
marry whom she likes now, or not marry if
she so wishes. There are advantages in no
longer being royal. I would have had to
marry for policy, too, and I would have
detested it."

I said: "Does it matter so much? There
are more important things."

"Do you think so?"

"One does not spend all that much time in
the company of women. There is riding and
hunting, battle, gaming—the company of
one's fellow men."

Edmund shook his head. "It would matter
to me." He grinned, at last open and friendly
again. "It is just as well that you do not
mind, since you are going to have to obey
the rules. As a matter of fact, Jenny and I
were speculating the other day as to who was
most likely to be the lady of the Prince of
Princes. We were for Maud of Basingstoke."

She had come to Winchester a few years
ago when her father, Prince Malcolm, paid

a state visit. She was dark and swarthy and very short in stature. People said that she should have been called dwarf but her mother pleaded with the Seer at her birth and he allowed her to pass for human.

I made a mock punch at him which he parried, laughing. It was good to be back on our old terms. On our way to the stables we gathered loose snow into balls and pelted each other like children.

Once again spring was late. Beyond the walls the fields lay white until mid-April and the thaw when it came seemed partial and uncertain. There were gray skies and a harsh east wind. Farmers, coming into the city on market day for the Spring Fair, complained that the ground was still too hard for planting; they had never known it so bad.

I was too concerned about the new campaign to care much. This year I would not be condemned to look after the baggage train. I was not allowed to be a warrior but I would be a scout, and Edmund with me. We rode our horses far out and practiced the arts of observation on the downland sheep.

The arrangement was that the army of Romsey was to come first to us, to be joined with our army under my father's command; the combined force then moving north

against Andover. They arrived late one
afternoon and we saw their tents going up in
the Contest Field and on open ground around
it. That was the place that had been allotted
them for a camp. Prince Jeremy had suggested it himself, saying that even if accommodation for his men could be found in the
city it was wiser for them to remain outside.
Even though our two cities were allies, con-
flicts might arise in living at such close quarters. My father, who had had similar
thoughts, praised this as an example of
Jeremy's common sense. There was more to
him, he repeated, than his fat foppishness
would indicate.

Jeremy, with a handful of his Captains,
came in for conference. James came as well.
He had not improved in the months since I
had last seen him; there was the same mix-
ture of arrogance and sly servility, the same
hungry envy for what he saw as our better
fortune. Our horses were in better condition
than theirs and looked faster, our dwarfs
forged better swords.

"And our leather, I suppose," Edmund said
to me when I had slipped James's company
one day and was telling him all this, "comes
from cows with thicker hides. He disgusts
me. You say he is to scout for them? Not
along with us, I hope?"

"No," I said. "I have made certain of that. The armies part company on the second day. They take a line in advance of us and to the east. The idea is that they draw the Andover army onto them. Then we strike north to the city itself where the south gate will be open."

The plan had been divulged to the Captains so I had felt I could tell it to Edmund; what had been said had been in the Great Hall, not my father's parlor. He now said, brow wrinkled:

"I do not like it. It is not a good way of fighting."

It was what I had said to my father and there were still doubts in my mind. Suppressing them, I said:

"The Spirits approve it."

"Oh, the Spirits . . .!"

There was a noise of someone approaching. We were in the den under the Ruins which bit by bit we had furnished into a sort of comfort, with furniture and rugs taken from unused rooms in the palace and with oil lamps now for lighting. Martin joined us. These days he wore the white of an apprentice Acolyte and his shaved head was covered by a wide-brimmed white hat. I still had not got used to the change in his appearance.

Edmund said: "We can ask the expert for advice. Why is it, Martin, that the Spirits who have in the past told men to fight honorably now urge us to rely on treachery to win our victories?"

Martin said: "No expert. I am not even an Acolyte yet, and will not be for another year."

"All right. But give us an opinion, as one who is planning to spend his life serving these same Spirits. Have they changed their minds? Has the Great Spirit sent out fresh instructions?"

He said it with a smile but Martin did not smile in return. He said, stumbling but in serious fashion:

"Without knowledge one cannot understand things. And knowledge is always limited. What I mean is . . . it is not so much that things change as that they happen in a different way."

Edmund said in astonishment: "I believe they have converted him already."

"I'm not very good at explaining what I mean."

Edmund said: "But you've changed, too, like the Spirits, haven't you? You take it more seriously."

"Do I?" His expression showed reluctance. "In a way, perhaps."

"Then you've been told things?"

"Not much. Nothing, really."

"Tell us. We'll judge."

Martin looked more and more unhappy. I said:

"He is bound by oaths and you know it. He must not tell the secrets of the craft and we must not ask him."

"Let him speak for himself," Edmund said. "Do you say so, Martin?"

Martin said uncomfortably: "I've nothing really to say."

Edmund looked at him curiously. "You believe in the Spirits now—is that it?"

"Yes," he said. But it sounded as though the word was being dragged out of him. "I believe in them."

We left the city the day before we were to march on Andover and camped in the fields on the far side of the road from the Romsey army. The reason for this was that Prince Jeremy had invited our men to join his at supper on the eve of our campaign together. He said that although it had been wise to keep the two forces from mixing inside the city, it was also wise that they should meet and feast moderately together before setting out. In this way they would get to know and have confidence in each other. My father was more dubious about this than he had been about the earlier suggestion but agreed that

it could do no harm. The feasting, he pointed
out, would need to be moderate, particularly
as far as drinking went, since we were to
ride next morning.

When we went over I, of course, found
myself saddled again with James. He took
me down the lines, denigrating even his men,
which I thought unpardonable: they were
less stout than ours, he said, but then they did
not live so well. I ignored that and asked him
about something else which struck me as
odd: they had bowmen with them, at least a
hundred. I could not understand what they
were doing with an army in the field. Bowmen were part of the garrison, a defensive
force. James said:

"An idea of my father's." He shook his
head. "It probably won't work."

"I still don't see . . . Even if they could
come up with a troop of horse, the horsemen
would gallop out of range before they could
do any real damage."

"It's something to do with a scheme for
luring the enemy into an ambush where the
bowmen would shoot them down. As I say, it
will very likely prove useless."

"But meanwhile your own walls at Romsey are undefended."

He gave a high laugh. "The women can

toss slop buckets down on anyone who attacks. Apart from that, they can take their chance. The bowmen are defending the one Romsey skin that is precious. In my father's eyes, at any rate."

I said in annoyance: "I do not think that is true, unless it is your own skin you mean. Your father is concerned for you more than himself; and more, perhaps, than you deserve."

"What does he deserve? Does a weak man deserve anything?"

"A son owes a duty."

"You can say that," he said bitterly, "with a father such as yours." He looked at me with hatred for once showing instead of the usual ingratiating affability. "You can respect your father."

It was not worth responding to the remark. We went on down the lines and he showed me the horses, drawing attention to their weak points. But he came back to the subject just before we parted. He said:

"You will grieve, I suppose, when your father dies?"

"Yes, but I do not expect to do so for a long time to come."

"It could happen in this campaign. He fights in the van, doesn't he, not from behind like the Prince of Romsey?"

"But fights well. It would take a good man to unhorse him."

He laughed, but it was more a titter, mirthless.

"Good warriors have been brought down before now by cunning lesser ones."

I said nothing, but left him.

The feasting was moderate as Jeremy had promised: extremely moderate. The meat was barely enough to go round and the ale, which for some unfathomable reason they called the Strong, was thin and sour compared with what our men were used to. There was some grumbling but our Sergeants controlled it well and got the men back to their own lines fairly early on the promise of a measure of decent ale there. It was not a particularly auspicious start to a joint expedition, but it could have been worse: there had been no fighting or even quarreling.

My father did not come back with the rest of us. Jeremy asked him to stay the night in his tent, an ornate affair four times the size of my father's own and lined with silk: in this respect, at least, James could not bemoan Romsey's poverty. Jeremy said he wanted to have a final private discussion about the campaign. I think my father thought he was nervous and needed reassuring. At any rate, he agreed to stay.

In our camp there was for some time a buzz of noise, part of the excitement which always attends the first few days in the field. Gradually it died away as the night drew on. I myself lay awake for a long time, turning restlessly despite my weariness. It was not the hardness of the ground which caused this —I had grown accustomed to hard living the previous summer—but a fit, for which I could find no cause, of my old melancholy. When I did sleep I had bad dreams: I could not remember what they had been but twice I woke in fear, sweating despite the chill of the night.

After that I slept heavily, exhausted. Edmund had to shake me into consciousness. I blinked up at him, and asked:

"What is it?"

"They've gone . . ."

"Gone? Who? What do you mean—gone?"

I was aware of a hum of talk and shouts outside; it had an anxious disturbed note like that of a hive broached by a clumsy beekeeper.

"The Romsey army. They have left camp in the night."

"My father . . .?"

"I don't know."

I pulled clothes on and ran out, Edmund with me, to find the Captains. They too were agitated and most of them talking at once. They paid me no attention. It was some time before I could piece things together. The Romsey tents were still there, with their baggage train and heavy gear. But there was no sign of men or horses. Except for six men. My father's bodyguards lay outside the Prince of Romsey's tent with their throats slit. Of my father there was no sign.

Blaine said, above the others: "They cannot have got far. We can be up with them before they reach home."

"If they are heading for home."

That was a Captain called Greene, a man who did not say much but usually talked sense.

"Where else?" Blaine asked.

"They have left their tents and gear," Greene said. "Would they do that unless they were sure of exchanging them for something better?" There was a silence in which I heard a rooster crowing distantly through the dawn air. "The plan was to take one of the Andover gates by treachery. There are gates nearer than Andover."

As he spoke we knew it was true. Blaine cursed but quietly, not with his usual bluster. Then Greene called one of the Sergeants to

form a troop. The Captains rode with it
and I also. I was not invited but no one told
me I must not. We rode, in near silence,
along the road to the East Gate, past the
abandoned Romsey camp.

Light was beginning to come into the sky
behind our backs but it was difficult to see
much. We had almost reached the East Gate
before Blaine, with an oath, halted his horse
and pointed upward. The pole above the gate
carried a flag, and its colors were not the
blue and gold of Winchester but the yellow
and black of Romsey. We stared at it. While
we were doing so the air hissed and a man
cried out; his horse reared and dragged him
away, an arrow in his throat. We knew now
why Jeremy had brought his bowmen.

Blaine called a retreat. We went, but not
before I had seen something else, stuck on a
spear over the gate, flapped over by Romsey's flag. It was a man's head. At that distance and in the half light one could not see
the face but there was no doubt whose it was.
It wore the spiked helmet of the Prince of
Winchester.

9

Bold Peter

"When I get him," Blaine said, "I will have him scourged each day for a week and in between he will lie naked in a salt bed. Then I will have his chest opened and his ribs pulled outward, slowly till he looks like a bloody eagle. I will . . ."

"Get him first," Harding said drily. "Then you can show us how inventive you are."

They were talking about the Sergeant in charge of the East Gate who, it was well nigh certain, had let the Romsey army in. He was a man called Gray who, people now remembered, had fought well against Alton and Petersfield. He had been rewarded with gold but had not thought the reward enough. He had hoped to be ennobled, having an ambitious wife. But ennoblements were rare, however good the fighting, and his wife was disliked and despised by the city's Ladies.

"Robert should not have trusted him with command of a gate," Blaine said. "He should have been out in the field with us."

Greene said: "His wife is with child and the last she had was polymuf. She expects to bear within a month. That was why he asked leave to stay behind, and was granted it. It could not be known that he was treacherous."

"A Prince should know these things," Blaine said, "or guard against them."

"If he was at fault," Harding said, "he was the first to pay for it."

We were at our camp, in the conference tent. It was a cold morning and rain had begun to fall, rattling harshly against the canvas. I stood in a corner, unregarded. My skin was clammy with a cold sweat, my mind turned in useless narrow circles, fastening again and again on the sight which, above all, I would have shut out forever from my mind. But it would not be dismissed; the harder I tried the faster and more vividly it winged back.

Greene said: "Being deceived by Jeremy was the greater error. But, by the Great, what a fox he is! Promising Robert that he would give him Andover and using that same trick to take Winchester . . . I would not have thought, with his scents and silks, that he had the guts to try it."

Blaine said bitterly: "That's what comes of making a man like that our Prince. You need breeding to be a judge of character."

"Would you have judged Jeremy better?"

"I never liked him."

"Nor did Robert," Greene said. "A Prince does not have to like his allies. And the Spirits favored the scheme."

"Curse the Spirits!" Blaine burst out. "I would have liked to see Ezzard's head beside his on the gate. They have betrayed us worse than Jeremy."

There was a silence. After a moment, Blaine blustered on:

"There are Spirits and Spirits. Remember what Marinet used to say?" He had been Seer before Ezzard, and better liked, though Ezzard had been more feared. "There are Spirits whose delight is to lead men into mischief, which the Great One permits as a means of testing, and of humbling those who puff themselves up beyond their merits. They start with gifts and promises but they end with destruction. Was it not those Spirits who led our ancestors blindfolded to the Disaster? And have they not done the same with Robert? Can anyone deny it?"

Harding said: "It may be." He was a small, wiry, sharp man, who talked less than Blaine but could usually silence him. "Perhaps we shall have leisure to talk of it during the long winter evenings. But there are more pressing needs. Jeremy has our city. We must decide what we should do."

"He has ours but his own is ill guarded." It was Charles who spoke, the brother of Edmund, son of Prince Stephen. "If we rode hard for Romsey we might take it and have something to bargain with. His bowmen are here."

Greene said: "Not all his bowmen, I'll wager. If he is fox enough to plan this he will have made his defenses sure at home."

"We could try at least."

There was no enthusiasm for the suggestion. An army whose own city was in enemy hands attacking a stronghold . . . it was not a picture to inspire much hope. A Captain called Ripon said:

"Well enough for you. But we have womenfolk at hostage."

"I also," Charles said. "My mother and my sister."

"Mothers and sisters!" Ripon said. "We have wives and daughters."

During Blaine's abuse of my father, the cold shock which had stunned me had been giving way to anger. It was against Blaine in the first place, but I knew he was not worth it. It was Jeremy who had tricked my father and slaughtered him while a guest in his tent.

I said: "Why do we wait?"

Their eyes turned to me. Blaine said, sneering:

"The brat has counsel for us. Speak up, then, you that were to be Prince of Princes. What would you have us do?"

"Not stand here talking!" I saw my father's head again with the Romsey flag slow-flapping over it and the memory maddened me. "We should attack the walls at once and force them! We should have done so right away instead of letting two or three arrows drive us back."

Blaine laughed. "Attack the walls . . . he's a merry youngster! Those walls which Stephen built up year after year till they were the highest and strongest in the land. Go and do it yourself, lad—you need no help from us. The Spirits will give you wings or maybe tumble the walls down for you. If you don't know how to summon them, go to the head that sits on the East Gate and ask him to do it for you."

I went at him blindly. He smiled and cuffed me, knocking me to the ground. He had great strength and all of it was in the blow: his anger drove him, too. Dazed, I heard Harding say:

"We waste our time discussing fantasies. It makes no sense to do anything until we have heard from Jeremy. I do not think he will keep us waiting long."

The herald came an hour later, alone and unarmed, riding a black horse with the white cloth of truce trailing soaked, from its reins. He was brought to the conference tent and stood there, wiping rain from his face with his sleeve.

His name was Grant and he was the best liked of the Captains who had accompanied Jeremy when he came to the Christmas Feast. He had seemed a decent and sensible man, level-eyed and level-headed. He did not look as though he enjoyed his errand. Harding said:

"Greetings, Captain. You will not expect much by way of welcome, seeing what brings you here. Do you have a message from your master?"

"Yes," Grant said, "I have a message. He bids you return in peace to your city and your homes."

Harding had been nominated to speak for the rest. He said: "On what conditions?"

"Sergeants and men will be admitted twenty at a time, and unarmed. They will be imprisoned under guard, but only until the peace settlement has been made. Captains may keep their swords."

"Why? To save our honor?" Grant nodded. "Is there any honor left after treachery such as yours?"

"It is not treachery to forestall treachery. By taking your city our Prince only defended his own."

"Do you say that we are weasels like you —that we planned to attack Romsey, not Andover? If so, every man here knows you lie, and knows therefore what trust to put in any new promises fat Jeremy makes."

"Not this year, maybe, but our Prince is far-sighted. Robert took Petersfield last summer and, against all the customs of war, kept it. He was to rule over Andover as well. Where would this have stopped? Was it not said that his son was to be Prince of Princes, ruler of every city in the land? Would Romsey, lying so close to Winchester, have been allowed to escape? Had you been Captains of Romsey you would have had good cause to fear the future. Can any man here deny it?"

Harding said: "And therefore we are to accept the rule of your Prince instead, and of that whining, sniggering son of his after?"

"No. Our Prince restores the ancient customs. There will be tribute, of course, but you may keep your city, choosing a proper Prince to rule it. Petersfield, too, will be free. The Prince of Romsey does not wish to govern lands outside his own."

Harding did not reply at once. I looked at the faces of the other Captains and found them thoughtful.

Harding asked: "Is that the sum of his demands?"

Grant shrugged. "There will be small things to be discussed. But you get your own city back, and your own Prince. He will promise that."

I said: "As he promised to fight with us against Andover? As he promised my father friendship?"

Grant glanced at me but did not answer. He looked unhappy, as though what I said had brought him back from the safe neutral ground of arguing policy to the closer, harsher truth of hospitality polluted, confidence betrayed. It was Blaine who said:

"Shut up, boy. Keep silence in the presence of your elders and betters. You are here on sufferance, so do not try our patience."

Grant asked. "What answer do you give me to take back to my Prince?"

Harding said: "Tell him we have received his message. We will consider it, and send him word."

Grant bowed. "I will take that news to him. I hope we may soon drink together at the peace feast."

No one answered him. Blaine said something that sounded like a curse, almost under his breath. Grant left the tent in silence, and we heard the jangle of harness as he mounted his horse and rode away.

The Captains wrangled until dinner, finding no common agreement. Some, like Blaine, were for defying Jeremy, but could put up no suggestions of how to do this, or none that carried weight. Others, fewer in number, argued that we must accept his terms, having no choice. I managed to hold my tongue, though with difficulty. It was true what Blaine had said: I was there on sufferance and there was nothing to stop them putting me out. It was more important to know what was happening than to offer opinions which in any case I knew would be treated with contempt.

Dinner was brought to us at the middle of the day. It was hard tack: soup, salt beef, hard biscuit, a small measure of ale. The army had its rations but in no great abundance. We had looked to living off Andover's land. It would not make us popular to raid our own farmers. The rain had set in heavily and ran in rivulets between the tents; the horses stamped miserably at their tethers and the men were full of gloom and grousing. A raw breeze blew chilly from the city whose walls, once our safeguard, now mocked us.

When talk resumed, there was a change in atmosphere. Harding talked more. After the herald left he had listened for the most part, sounding out the others for their views. Now, with patience and skill, he was trying to influence the Captains to his own way of thinking. And that way, it became more and more clear, favored acceptance of Jeremy's offer.

"And if we do," Blaine shouted angrily, "what guarantee do we have with our men disarmed and guarded? He will leave us our swords, will he? And what good are twenty swords against an army? Even that fool of a boy"—his small eyes darted in my direction —"could see that. Jeremy's promises are worth nothing. Nothing! Is he to swear by the Spirits? When he has already defied them?"

"He has defied the Spirits that led Robert Perry astray," Harding said. "So he is favored by other Spirits who are more powerful. Or else Robert was abandoned and it is all a game. You said yourself that there are Spirits and Spirits. But if he swears

by the Great Spirit Himself, I do not think
he will break his oath; or if he does that his
men will follow him."

There was a murmur of agreement: an
oath made on the Great Spirit must be binding. Harding said:

"We must not deceive ourselves: he has us
in the hollow of his hand. He speaks softly
now because he hopes for peace, on his own
terms. But if we defy him I would give nothing for the safety of our womenfolk. And
the men will not be easy with the thought of
a Romsey army walking their streets un-
checked. If we choose to fight I would not be
sure that they would follow us. And how can
we fight? Blaine has said it: the walls
Stephen built are the strongest in the land.
We would only break our bones on them."

He spoke calmly and reasonably, therefore
persuasively. I saw some nod their heads,
among them Greene. Harding went on:

"If we surrender now we do not surrender
for all time. He lets us keep our swords, but
I do not think any of us will forget what happened this morning. There will be a time to
fight again. Not for the sake of a Prince
whose ambition is well ended, but for our
honor."

"He may bind us in a treaty of peace,"
Greene said.

"No doubt he will. And we will keep it as long as they do. But who has ever known a treaty of peace that the other side could say they kept in everything? And if they break it, we are free."

He was winning them, and not to his plan of action only. His aim, I saw, was deeper. The city lacked a Prince and he was advancing his claim. Blaine had shown himself rash and the Captains, smarting from being tricked, wanted a man of guile and caution. They had chosen Harding to speak to Jeremy's herald. If they followed him now they would acclaim him even before the men of Romsey rode away.

He had been cunning, too, after stressing the inevitability of surrender, in raising hopes of revenge. Ripon said:

"They will break it! And by the Great, when they do . . ."

Other voices rose, on the same note of resentment but also with new assurance. Then one said, strongly:

"Wait!"

It was Peter, my cousin. He had not spoken in all the previous talk. Looking at him I had thought him stunned, perhaps even more than I was, by what had happened. But he spoke now with strength and confidence. On that single word they listened to him.

He said: "I can show you how to win back the city and not lose a man."

Blaine began to say something but stopped. Harding said:

"This one has gone mad. We know what blood runs in his veins."

Ignoring him, Peter said to the other Captains:

"Or would you rather bend your knees to Jeremy, pay him gold, watch him drive off Winchester cattle and load his carts with your women's jewels?"

"If you are not mad," Greene said, "tell us how."

"I have conditions first."

"You name conditions!" Blaine said. "A Perry, commoner born, naming conditions to us . . .!"

He stared at Blaine. "Yes, I name conditions."

His voice was level, without anger but with certainty. Greene said:

"If this is a jest, Perry, you may find the laughter cut short. Say it quickly."

"There are two," Peter said. "The first is that a ransom is paid, but not to Romsey. We will pay gold to the Christians so that they can build a church to their god."

There was a confusion of protest, laughter, incredulity. I heard Harding's voice: "Mad, as

I said. Do you want more proof?" Peter let them run on for some moments. Then he said, and they went quiet as he spoke:

"This will be done because it is through the Christians that the city will be regained."

"How else?" cried Blaine. "We had forgotten those warriors of ours. I can see them, driving the Romsey men down the High Street with their crosses!"

Peter ignored him. He said:

"You know that in Winchester men despise them, but do not harm them. It is not so everywhere. In some cities they are harried by Seers who have them tortured or killed for refusing to worship the Spirits. And even where they are safe for the moment they have no confidence that the safety will last. If Ezzard does not persecute them, the next Seer of Winchester might. So they take their precautions."

He paused before going on. He had all their attention, even Blaine's.

"I have considered this all day. As you will guess, I have it from my wife. She was bound to keep the secret, but told me. Her trust in me binds me also. If I break it, as I think I must, then I demanded a tribute for her god, to turn away his wrath. Do I get this from you?"

Harding stared at him with cold, appraising eyes.

Greene said: "If it is worth it, you get it."

"It is worth it. A tunnel that goes under Stephen's great walls. Cramped and dirty, but men can crawl through it. It was the way of escape for the Christians and can be a way in for men who will take the North Gate and open it to our army. I know where it starts. Will you give them gold and the right to build their church?"

"By the Great," Greene said, "I will! And I do not think any will refuse."

I heard voices speak approval and none opposing.

Peter said: "That is one condition."

Blaine asked: "And the other?"

"My father is dead. He died by treachery, murdered by his host. Jeremy dies for this. There will be no ransom for the Prince of Romsey."

They roared assent, and he put a hand up to stop them.

"That is not the condition. I did not think any of you would let him live. My father was a great Prince. His Spirit requires more than just revenge; it needs his own blood to follow him in power, his son in the Great Hall."

I saw them look at me. Blaine said:

"He is a boy, too young to govern himself, let alone a city like ours."

Peter looked at me, too, and smiled. I saw the smile but could not read what lay behind it. He said:

"You mistake me, Blaine. My father had two sons. I was first born. I claim his place."

There was silence again and his unwavering, confident gaze went round their faces. Then Greene broke out:

"Do as you say, Perry, and you have my voice!"

The rest followed. Even Blaine and Harding were forced to an assent. Blaine gave it grudgingly but Harding showed no emotion in his voice.

The rain stopped toward evening. The sky above the city was painted in scarlet and orange. Clouds hung huge over the walls, first red then purple, at last black against a deep-blue sky. Occasionally one saw a head silhouetted above the battlements, one of Romsey's men. It was not until full darkness came that the army marched, quietly and by a circuitous path, to take up its position outside the North Gate.

I watched with Edmund. Peter, with two other Captains, one of them Greene, and a band of picked men, had left for the hut, a broken-down shack thought to be abandoned years before, under whose floor the tunnel started. They would come out into the house of the Priest, as the leader of the Christians was called, near the North Gate and from there it would be easy to fall on the Romsey men defending that gate from behind. Our army waited for the sign, a torch flourished in the gateway, which would tell them the way was open.

Time dragged by—minutes, hours it seemed. We did not speak much. We were each occupied with our own thoughts. Mine were confused and bitter. This morning the thought of seeing Jeremy's head set up in place of my father's would have been a joy to override anything. It was so no longer. The blackness of despair was back in my mind, the sense that all was useless: one could not live without hope, but always hope betrayed.

It was cold even though the rain had stopped. I started to shiver but I think it came more from melancholy than from the night air. I tried to stop it, not wanting Edmund to notice, but could not. He shifted beside me, and said:

"Luke."

"Yes."

"When this is over, what do you plan to do?"

"Don't know."

I answered shortly so that he would not hear my teeth chatter. He said:

"If you thought of leaving the city, going north perhaps, I would go with you."

I did not answer and he did not speak again. I was too bitter and wretched to realize what he was offering: that having weathered his own grief and disappointment he would still go into exile with me as a companion to me in mine. Later I understood. Friendship meant much to him, more than it could ever do to me.

We waited and my limbs shook. I set my jaw until it, my neck, my whole body ached with the strain. Then the light shone ahead, the dull tramp of feet went past us, and soon, following after the army, we heard the distant sounds of the struggle. Not for long. We had the advantage of surprise and our men were fighting in their own streets. Inside half an hour the last of Romsey's warriors had laid down his arms. Inside an hour fat Jeremy's head topped the palace gate.

I went back that night with Edmund to the house in Salt Street, though I did not sleep.

Next morning, after breakfast, I slipped
away without a word and went to the palace.
Because he would have insisted on coming
with me I said nothing to Edmund. Whatever
I faced was mine, mine only, and I would
face it alone.

I stood for a while in the crowd that stared
at Jeremy's head. They were in a festive
mood, many drunk already, and from time to
time they roared for their Prince, Peter, to
come and show himself. I saw Christians
there and men slapping them on the back as
comrades while they looked dazed and disbelieving. A player was singing a song made
up for the occasion:

> *Under the walls bold Peter came—*
> *Took the gate with a torch of flame—*
> *And so made good his father's shame . . .*

A new roar drowned it as Peter came out on
the balcony. I slipped away and in at a side
door. I passed polymuf servants; some of
them bobbed to me but others did not. Two
soldiers stared at me and one laughed behind
my back. I went to my room and waited for
whatever was to happen.

Martin found me there, staring blindly out
of the window at wet roofs under a gray sky.
He said: "Luke," and I turned.

"Ezzard wants you."

"He will find me here."

"The risk is too great."

"Poor Ezzard."

"For you both. You must come."

"No must," I said. "I have had enough of must from Fate itself."

"Remember what the High Seers said: that you have a mission and when the time comes you must obey. You promised it."

"I never told you that."

"But I know."

"And you still believe that nonsense?"

"More than ever."

There was passion in his thin face. The tricks by which Ezzard had won him over must have been good ones. I argued for a while but he had more conviction than I, who was waiting for I knew not what except that it could not be good. I went with him, through the palace and out into the street. Someone jeered after us. He did not lead me toward the Seance Hall but along a side street. We stopped at a house near a tavern and, after a quick look round, he drew me in.

Ezzard was waiting in a room upstairs. He looked more white and gaunt than ever. He said:

"Well done, Martin. Leave us now." As the door closed, he added: "We must get you out of here, Luke, and quickly."

I said: "I came for one thing, sire. To curse the Spirits who led my father to his death, and the Seer who spoke for them."

He showed no anger. In a quiet voice, he said:

"Curse if you will, but do as I say. Your life is not worth a halfpenny here. Even if Peter does not order it, someone will have you killed, thinking to please him. You were named heir and Prince of Princes. Alive, you challenge his power. Things may be different later but these are days of doubt and murder. Leaving Peter out of it, there are enough who would rather see one Perry left than two. Your only hope is in flight."

"I will not flee."

"Listen, boy. You are a fool but not a complete fool or you would not have been chosen. Even though he is dead, would you do your father's will?"

"If I knew it. Are you to tell me? But for you he would be living still."

"Did he fear death?" I hesitated. "You know better. He thirsted for it. If the Spirits guided the assassins' knives he thanked them for it with his last breath. Is this not true?"

I was silent. He said: "Your father lived to do his duty and prepare for your succession."

"My succession!" I laughed. "As Prince of Princes."

"Yes. And the prophecy lives while you do. The Captains know that. So does your father's Spirit. Can you deny it? If you will not ask me what he would have wished, consult your memory of him. It is fresh still."

In my mind I saw him, sitting in his armchair in front of the painting of my mother. His eyes were on me. Was everything a waste, all hope and effort, did everything shatter and fail? I could not think otherwise but he had, and perhaps had died with that belief outweighing the pain and betrayal. I owed him something.

I asked: "Where would you have me go?"

"To the Sanctuary. Where else?"

I nodded. "As you wish, then, sire."

10
The Prince
in Waiting

I left the city of my birth in a shameful fashion. Ezzard found rags for me to wear and fixed a cloth hump on my back so that I looked like a polymuf. He for his part put on women's clothes, a tattered gray cloak and a pointed hat, and walked slowly as though hobbled by old age. But the disguise was good. I saw several people who would have known me but they paid us no attention except one, a son of the kite-maker in West Street, who slashed at me with his stick when I was not quick enough in getting into the gutter to give him room.

We went out by the East Gate because there was more traffic through this than the North. Some of the soldiers on guard were drunk and singing. I looked back when we were outside, half dreading that my father's head would still be spiked above it, but it had been taken down. I did not look back after that.

The baggage train of the Romsey army had already been taken into the city. The Contest Field was empty but scuffed and muddied by their occupation. I thought of my own day of glory there and of that last charge against Edmund which had won me the jeweled sword. It hung in my room in the palace now: I wondered who would get it.

I had asked Ezzard if I could say good-by to Edmund but had not been surprised that he refused. I had not even seen Martin again after he left me with the Seer. Already I might have been missed from the palace and word gone out to find me. I wondered what Edmund would think when it was known, as it must be soon enough, that Ezzard and I were both gone. That, having refused his offer to flee with me, I had run for aid to the Spirits, still hoping they would win me my inheritance? I would have liked to be able to tell him it was not so. But it did not really matter. Nothing mattered. It started to rain again. That didn't matter either.

When we were well clear of the city we halted in the shelter of a clump of trees and I was able to get rid of my hump and both of us to dress ourselves in the more ordinary clothes we had brought in a bundle carried under my arm. We looked like farm workers now, or maybe vagrants. Before resuming our journey we ate there—a hunk of bread and cheese with an onion—and slaked our thirst at a stream nearby.

We had simple food to last us three days. It was five and twenty miles to the Sanctuary on crows' wings, probably half as far again by road and at least twice the distance by the circuitous route which we must follow to give a wide berth to any place where we might be sought. The pigeons, if they were not already flying, would soon be out with orders for us to be arrested; and we could not be sure that this applied only in Winchester's lands. The Princes of both Andover and Salisbury might be asked to trace the fugitives and might think themselves well advised to do so, as a favor to the man who had nailed Jeremy's head on his palace gate.

We tramped steadily westward, using roads or tracks but taking cover when anyone came our way and keeping well away from villages. We went in silence, speaking only on necessary matters. I was not sorry for this. It was not that I was contented with my own thoughts: in fact they followed a treadmill of anger, resentment, jealousy and despair. Certain moments and events came back again and again, and seemed each time to leave me still more numb. My father's head on the spike above the East Gate . . . the Captains giving their voice to Peter while the rain slashed against the walls of the conference tent . . . the crowd in front of the palace roaring for him . . . But I knew no conversation, with Ezzard or anyone else, would drive away those images or my feeling of black hopelessness. I suffered them better in silence.

The road to Stockbridge was over high ground but Stockbridge itself lay in the valley of the Test River. We left the road some miles from the town and went north. In the early evening we could look down and see the distant town and the river running through. I remembered we must cross it and wondered what Ezzard proposed. Even from here, a quarter of a mile away, it looked turbulent, swollen with the waters of the spring thaw. Swim it? And spend the night freezing in soaked clothes? I asked Ezzard.

"You see the high-road that runs this side of it?" I nodded. "Two miles north of here it crosses the river."

We made our way across a field to the high-road. At this point it was not, in fact, very high, only a few feet above the level of the surrounding land. We walked beside it

until it was necessary to go on it to cross the
river. Dusk was heavy by now and we saw
no one. The road was carried over the river
by a metal bridge. Ezzard said suddenly:

"Have you ever wondered, Luke, why our
ancestors built the high-roads?"

There were two near Winchester, forming
an ellipse that enclosed the city. I shook my
head.

"No, sire."

"Your friend Martin has done so."

"He has strange thoughts." I realized that
this could seem a criticism and endanger
him, he being an Acolyte, and added: "I do
not mean impious ones."

Ezzard did not seem to notice it. He went
on:

"Or why they are made as they are? We
call them high-roads because sometimes they
stand high above the fields. But in other
places, as at Shawford, they run in valleys cut
out of the hills. Have you ever thought of
this?"

I said I had not. He stooped and pointed to
where one of the thick timbers, which were
still found in places on the high-roads though
mostly they had been taken for winter fuel,
was raised a little above the dirt.

"Or what these were for?"

Near one end the beam carried a metal

socket that looked as though it in turn had supported something, a rail perhaps, running transversely across it. I said:

"I suppose they were to do with machines."

I felt guilt in even speaking the word in the presence of the Seer, but he had asked strange questions. He said:

"And these machines—were they so much weaker than a horse that they could only travel on level ground; and therefore the high-roads had to be raised up or brought down, not taking the shape of the country through which they passed?"

I said: "I do not know, sire."

I was embarrassed. Such speculations surely were forbidden. It might be different for the Seers, who served the Spirits, but I had no right to think them.

He did not speak again for a time. Then he said:

"You must prepare yourself for strange things at the Sanctuary, Luke."

"Yes, sire."

Of course there must be strange things—I knew that. Like a Seance going on all the time, perhaps: darkness with lights and bells and the sonorous voices of the Spirits. Ezzard said:

"Strange things to learn as well as to see. Your mind may be amazed by some of them." He paused but I said nothing. "You are strong in many ways, but curiosity is not one. I do not suppose it is necessary. But it would have been better if we had had more time to prepare you."

I did not understand what he meant but was not sufficiently interested to want to find out. I was tired and hungry, my feet sore from walking all day. I was glad when we came to one of the broken-down huts which you find here and there on the high-roads and Ezzard called a halt.

We slept the second night in a barn. The straw from last year's threshing made a warm bed—it had been cold in the hut with no blanket—but I slept badly. A rat ran over my arm and lying awake I heard them scuffling. I have a dread and loathing of these beasts from the time when I was a child of two or three and an old cat of ours, a hunter, brought one back and laid it on my pillow; and I awoke and in the dim glow of the night light saw its dead face close to mine. I got up and went outside. The night was almost clear, sharp stars everywhere, and the fires of the Burning Lands brighter than I had ever seen them. We were nearer to them now, of course. I huddled up against the side of the barn, staring at them while I went the same dreary round of memory and anger and melancholy. In the end, despite my cramped position and the cold, I fell asleep. I was wakened by Ezzard's voice calling my name in the thin dawn light. I answered and he came to me. There was relief in his face. He said:

"I thought I had lost you, Luke."

"I could not sleep in there."

I would not speak of the rats, and my fear, to him. He said:

"Tonight you will sleep in a bed."

I nodded. "I will be glad of it, sire."

But I was not glad when, at the end of the afternoon, he pointed and I saw the Stones of the Sanctuary ahead of us. They stood like jagged teeth on the skyline; tiny but, being miles away still, having the promise of enormity. The promise or the threat. I had made this journey as a duty to my father's memory, not thinking of its end. There had been vague thoughts of the High Seers, of Seances, but nothing concrete, nothing, really, that meant anything. Those distant pillars were real, and foreboding. They were surrounded by empty downland, cropped only by rabbits. No man would go near, no shepherd graze his flocks in their shadow. It was the place of the High Seers, dread and holy, and that dread touched me, making me want to turn back toward the world of men. I would rather have taken my chance with Peter and his Captains than go forward. But I had come so far that I must go on to the end. And again I would not show my fear to Ezzard.

It was a long walk toward them. The sun, sinking, had come out from behind clouds and cast shadows from the Stones that stretched tenuous fingers in our direction. I could see them more clearly. They roughly formed a circle, great jagged-hewn wedges many times the height of a man and broad in proportion. They were set apart from each other but some were linked by other immense stones resting on top and between them.

Inside there was nothing but the rabbit-cropped grass. I felt a new and different alarm. Could this emptiness be the Sanctuary? I had expected a huge building, a castle perhaps. Where did the High Seers live? There was only grass and the great time-weathered stones. Did one walk through a doorway in one, into the Spirits' world? Or climb an invisible ladder to a stronghold in the clouds?

We crossed a shallow ditch and the stones loomed over us. We passed between two of them, scored by the wind and rain not of years, it seemed, but centuries. Within the outer ring were other stones, some standing and some fallen. Near the center, beside one of these, was a sort of mushroom, made of stone but whiter and less pitted than the bigger ones. It was only a few feet high. Ezzard went to it and put his hand underneath, feeling for something. I stood beside him, telling my limbs not to tremble. We waited in silence, for half a minute perhaps. And then the stone mushroom spoke:

"Who comes?"

The Seer bent his head toward the mushroom.

"Ezzard, with the Prince in Waiting."

I do not know what I expected to happen: thunder and lighting, perhaps, a chariot of fire appearing out of the sky, a solid rainbow leading to a magic land. Instead there was a creaking sound and the ground on the other side of the mushroom moved, splitting and opening. There was not darkness revealed but light, a whiter, brighter light than I had ever seen, the steps leading down.

Ezzard said: "Come, Luke."

I hesitated. They were ordinary steps but they terrified me. And the light . . . the light of the Spirits? I remembered all the events they had set in motion. Maybe they had helped me to win the jeweled sword and my

father to the Princedom. But after that . . .
my mother slain, my aunt executed for her
murder, my father's head set up above the
East Gate, a thing to be mocked. And I myself driven from the city disguised as a polymuf. The good they had done me was surely
outweighed by the evil.

All this was true. What was also true was
that at last I faced their stronghold. They
could do no more than take my life. It was
little enough worth living as it was; if I
broke and ran it was worth nothing. I went
in front of Ezzard into the hole.

A dozen steps below there was a platform
where the staircase turned on itself before
descending even farther into the bowels of
the earth. Behind me Ezzard stopped and I
stopped also. He touched a button set in the
wall. There was a whirring sound, followed
by the creaking I had heard on the surface,
and I saw the gap closing above us, blotting
out the sky. I realized then that underneath
grass and earth there was metal and this was
rising, a trap door to seal the opening at the
top of the stairs. I was less alarmed than
confused, my mind trying to take in what
could not be denied and yet was impossible.
The light, I saw, came from long tubes of
glass. Ezzard touched another button and

more of them flashed into radiance, lighting the stairs below.

"Ezzard!" I cried. "These lights . . ."

He looked at me. I could scarcely bring myself to say it, but it was not possible to be silent.

"They are not the lights of the Spirits . . . and the trap door, that is not the work of Spirits either. These are machines!"

"Yes," he said. "I told you there would be strange things to learn."

I sat at supper with Ezzard and the High Seers. They wore no cloaks but simple clothes—trousers and shirt—as Ezzard did also; and except for Ezzard their heads were not cropped but carried a normal covering of hair. On the senior of the three, who had come to Winchester, it was sparse and white with age but the big one had a heavy thatch of black. And he did not, I noticed, eat with the sparrowlike delicacy he had shown at my father's banquet but heartily, as a man who enjoys his food. Like the shaved heads and the cloaks, that had been done for show.

It was strange, too, to hear them speak in easy, unmeasured voices—to speak and even laugh. They were ordinary men, and relief and disappointment were at war in me, realizing this. I was silent, putting no questions and answering briefly the questions put to me. There were not many of these: I guessed they were letting me get used to things by degrees, accustom my mind gradually to its shock. I learned their names: the little white-haired man was called Lanark, the big dark one Murphy.

When supper was over each took his own plate to the kitchen where they were stacked in a machine that washed them: one could hear the rush of water behind the closed door. There seemed to be no servants—I supposed because there were no polymufs. One of the men operated another machine that moved across the floor with a whining sound, sucking crumbs and dust into itself. The others led the way into a large room with many chairs and couches. The walls had been painted with scenes of landscape framed by pillars—a forest glade, a garden, a view of rocks and sea, and on the fourth the streets of a city, with men and women, children, a dog scratching itself in the dust. They were reminders to men who lived like moles underground of what the world was like.

We took seats. Lanark said:

"Now, Luke, what would you like to know?"

There were so many things that it was

hard to think of one. I said after a moment:

"The machines—what makes them go?"

"Electricity."

"What is that?"

"A force. It is hard to explain. Something which is invisible but which can be used."

"Invisible? Like the Spirits?"

He smiled. "No."

I said, with daring: "Do the Spirits exist?" I still half expected to be condemned for blasphemy. But Lanark said:

"If they do they have not shown themselves to us."

"The Seances . . . the lights and sounds . . ."

"Are trickery, to keep the power of the Seers over men's minds."

"The prophecies . . ."

"Prophecies often fulfill themselves because expectation brings its own results. Where they fail"—he shrugged—"they can usually be explained away."

I shook my head. My mind was fuzzed with doubts and uncertainty. I said:

"I don't understand."

Lanark said: "I know it isn't easy. Best, perhaps, to take things from the beginning. You know what is said of the Disaster?"

"That our ancestors were given powers by Spirits who led them on and then, in the end, destroyed them, casting down their cities and making the earth itself spew flame."

"It has some truth in it. Our ancestors did have great powers, they built cities in which a thousand Winchesters could be dropped and lost, they had machines in which they could fly through the air—around the world in less than a day—or see things as they happened thousands of miles away. They traveled to the distant moon. Then came the Disaster.

"The strange thing was that many men had expected it, though not in the form in which it happened. Because among the machines were machines of war: by pressing a button a man could destroy from half a world away a city so large that Winchester by comparison is but a hamlet. It was thought that sooner or later these powers of destruction would be unleashed and the world driven back to barbarism if it were not destroyed entirely. Men feared this possibility. Later the anticipation was confused with the reality."

I asked: "What did happen?"

"The earth itself rebelled. Except that that is a wrong way of putting it: the earth is inanimate, without will or mind. But it has life, of a sort. It can change, and change violently. Men knew that in the past, the incred-

ibly distant past before man himself existed,
there had been convulsions of the earth in
which vast lands were crumpled like parchment, mountains thrust into the sky, volcanoes belched fire and molten rock. There
were still a few volcanoes, now and then an
earthquake. Occasionally a town was shattered, a few hundred people killed. These
were freaks of nature, unexpected, soon
forgotten.

"Then the earth's fires, smoldering for a
thousand million years, broke loose again.
We do not know why. Some think it was to
do with the sun, which just before showed
puzzling signs—strange bursts of radiation
accompanied by dark spots across its face. At
any rate, the earth shook and heaved and
everywhere men's cities tumbled and men
died in their ruins. The worst of it did not
last long, days rather than weeks, but it was
enough to destroy the world of cities and
machines. Those who survived roamed the
shattered countryside and fought one another
for what food there was.

"Gradually they came together again.
They built houses to protect them from the
weather—of wood, not stone, and designed as
far as possible to withstand the earthquakes
which still continued, though more and more
rarely. They returned to their old places, at

least to the villages and the small cities. Not
to the large ones which were left as rubble.
They did as they had done in the past—grew
crops, raised cattle, traded and practiced
crafts and fought. But they would have no
truck with machines, identifying them with
their forefathers' ancient pride and the reckoning which had followed. Anyone found
dabbling with machines was killed, for fear
of bringing down fresh destruction.

"They had many religions in the old days.
One was concerned with what were supposed
to be the Spirits of the dead and this now
spread like wildfire. Seance Halls were built
and in them, in the dark, the Spirits were supposed to talk to men, to guide and counsel
them.

"But there were a few men, a handful, who
were not content with this, who knew that
machines were not evil in themselves and in
fact could help us back to civilization. They
dared not defy the legends—those who did
were torn to pieces by the mob—but they
could use them. They became Seers and took
over the Seance Halls. They preached
anathema to machines but preserved the
knowledge of them, all the time looking for
likely recruits."

"Martin . . . ," I said.

"Yes, such as Martin. And at certain places,

called Sanctuaries and so holy that no one
would come near them, they built machines
and worked with them. Here, and elsewhere.
Do you understand now?"

"Partly," I said. "But not why I was
brought here. To work with the machines?"

Lanark smiled. "We would sooner have
brought Martin. For you we have different
plans, very different. Do you remember what
I told you when we met in Winchester?"

"That the Spirits had a mission for me to
perform."

"There are no Spirits, that we know of,
but there is a mission. I said that men recov-
ered from the Disaster but only some men,
in a few favored places. These lands are one
such. Outside there are deserts and desolation, and monstrous beasts. There are also
savages. They multiply fast and hunger
drives them against the civilized lands. The
winters have grown longer and harder because the sun's rays are weakened by dust
thrown into the sky by the volcanoes. The
cities themselves are beginning to feel the
pinch, with farmers growing poorer crops
and raising fewer beasts. Four years ago
Taunton fell. Dorchester was besieged all
last summer and the barbarians are at the
walls again. And when a city falls to those
enemies there are no ransoms—only plun-

der and murder, followed by fire and ruin.

"We have spoken with men in far parts of the world who share our aim of restoring civilization. Not through the pigeons; we have machines that can do this as our ancestors did. At one time there were many voices, but they grew fewer. For a year we have had no answer to our calls.

"Men's loyalties were narrowed by the Disaster. The cities, when they were rebuilt, warred fiercely against one another, each remaining sovereign and separate, violently hostile to the rest. There have been similar times in man's history. But the only hope of resisting the savages is for the cities to join together; individually they have no hope."

I said: "So when Ezzard told my father the Spirits wished him to keep Petersfield, against all custom . . ."

"It was part of the plan. There had to be one city that would dominate and unite the others. Winchester was best for this. It is well placed, at the center of the civilized lands, and rich; and there is a memory in men's minds that once, hundreds of years ago, a great Prince ruled from there.

"But having chosen the city we needed a Prince. Stephen was no good to us, a timid, unambitious man. His son, Edmund, might have served. If there had not been someone better we should have had to use him. But Ezzard found you and when, against great odds, you won the prize at the Contest, our choice was made certain."

"But it was only by accident that I was in the Contest at all! If Matthew had not fallen ill with a fever . . ."

"No accident," Lanark said. "It takes no great art to raise a fever."

I remembered meeting Ezzard in the High Street and how he had told me to make the most of my skating since it might be my last winter for it. I said:

"And everything after that . . . my father becoming Prince, the two crowns of light at the Seance . . . all these were contrived?"

"Your father's election needed skill. The crowns of light were a simple trick."

"But the machine that burst and burst the walls of Petersfield—you could not have known that would happen!"

Lanark smiled. "Could we not? When one understands something of gunpowder it is not too difficult to make a cannon blow up. The Seer of Petersfield saw to it."

Disbelief still lingered; and disappointment. I had thought I accepted the loss of a destiny predicted by the Spirits, but a part of me still balked. I said:

"At the Seance of the Crowns . . . there

was a farmer who complained that he had
paid gold to the Seer to protect his lambs
but lost them all the same. And the Spirit of
his grandfather's father charged him with
breaking the laws by rearing polybeasts. He
could not deny it. So surely it was a Spirit
that spoke, and spoke truth?"

Ezzard answered: "There is not a farmer
in the land who has not been guilty of the
same sin. Who is to tell how many horns a
cow had when it is carcass meat? I was on
safe ground in condemning him."

"And my father—he told me he obeyed
your orders because it was through you he
heard my mother's voice after she was dead.
Was this a trick also?"

"In part, but he heard her voice. Through
another machine of our ancestors. Words are
trapped on something like a ribbon, which
can be cut and put together again so that the
words make a message that one chooses."

A new and terrible thought came to me.
"My mother's death . . ."

Lanark shook his head. "That was not our
doing. We cannot control everything as was
shown by Jeremy's capture of the city. We
made use of it to help bind your father to us.
But it was a blow all the same, a bitter blow.
It turned your half brother against you. Be-

cause of that Ezzard had to flee with you and bring you here."

"Your plan had failed already when Jeremy took the city."

"Not failed. We could have worked on him. He would have let you be Prince in your father's place, thinking you a boy and powerless."

I said angrily: "Do you think I would have taken it from his bloody hands?"

"If Ezzard had shown you a hope of revenge at the end, you would. You are a good hater."

I knew it was true. I said:

"But it was all for nothing. Peter has the city and I am here in exile. So you have failed after all."

Lanark shook his head. "We have lost one battle, but there will be more. While you live you are still the Prince in Waiting."

"An empty promise," I said, "from Spirits that do not exist."

"Not just that," Lanark said. "A hope also, the hope of living men."

In the weeks that followed I learned many things. About polymufs, for instance. The word came from an older one, meaning of many shapes. Such freaks of nature had in-

creased after the Disaster and it was thought
they were caused by strange radiations from
the sun, probably the same which were believed to have reawakened the earth's deep
fires. Some, like the dwarfs, bred true, but
most did not. In civilized lands men had
done their best to extirpate all the freaks
among animals, but mothers would not let
their babies be killed. So they were allowed
to live, the dwarfs as a race apart, the polymufs as servants to normal men. In the savage countries, beyond the Burning Lands,
there was no control and misshapenness ran
riot.

I learned about the Seers. This was not the
only nor the most important Sanctuary.
There was another in the ruins of the great-
city which had been called London. They
told me it had stretched over more than six
hundred square miles and eight million people had lived in it: figures so great that one
could not imagine the reality. The Seers had
found a place, under the rubble, where the
wisdom of the ancients was stored in books,
and they quarried there for knowledge.

I learned something of that knowledge
myself: not much, for my mind was not
equipped to grasp it. My purpose, as they
told me, was different: to help create the
conditions in which knowledge could be

brought from hiding and the cities made safe against the sea of barbarism which lapped all round and otherwise must rise and drown them.

And I saw the machines which could do things more marvelous than anything that had been supposed to be done by the Spirits. Machines for seeing and listening at a distance, machines that could propel a carriage ten times faster than a team of horses could pull it, machines that could detect metal under the earth, that could chill meat and keep its sweetness without salting throughout a summer, that could show strange beasts living inside the smallest drop of water . . . a score and more of wonders.

And one day burly Murphy showed me something called an induction furnace. He explained how it worked, through this power that was called electricity. He said:

"It case-hardens steel. You get a hard surface such as no ordinary forge could produce."

I nodded, partly understanding him. He said:

"You left the jeweled sword you won at the Contest behind you, Luke. But do you remember that one day I promised you a sword of the Spirits? Even though there are no Spirits, you will have the sword: we shall make it here and I promise you no sword made by dwarfs will notch it. It will shatter anything that comes against it, if your right hand is strong enough."

"When?" I asked. "When will you make the sword?"

"When it is time."

"But how long will that be? I am tired of living underground, with no wind, no sunlight, no day or night except what we make ourselves."

"We are all tired of it," Murphy said, "but we must wait. There is a moment for striking: too soon or too late and we fail. And if we fail, all hope is gone. You must learn patience, Luke."

He clapped a hand on my shoulder and I nodded unwilling assent. I itched to be on a horse riding through the meadows beneath St. Catherine's Hill, to see the walls of Winchester looming high before me. But he was right, and impatience was at least more easily borne than despair. The time might be long delayed, but the time would come.